Published by Cryogenica, LLC
www.markokloos.com

GW00492689

Table of Contents

ODDMENTS

A Short Fiction Compendium

Marko Kloos

Introduction

Occasionally, people ask me what I do for a living.

For most, that's an easy question to answer. You say *I'm an accountant*, or *I'm a nurse*, or *I'm a car mechanic*. People can instantly put these replies into a contextual framework because they know what accountants or nurses or mechanics do all day long.

For writers, it's a little different. To regular folks, it's an exotic profession because few people even know anyone who writes for a living. When you reply, "I'm a writer," most people will immediately follow up with "Oh, really? What do you write?" (Sometimes it's the slightly obnoxious "Have I read/do I know anything you've written?" *I don't know, dude, because I am not psychic and can't divinate the contents of your Kindle library. Also, if you need to ask that question, the answer invariably turns out to be "no."*)

So, anytime someone asks me what I do, I tell them that I am a novelist. It hasn't eliminated the follow-up question—it just changed to "What sort of novels do you write?". But *novelist* seems to be sufficiently specific to satisfy most curiosities. And it's accurate enough because writing novels is my bread and butter, after all. I'm a novelist. I spend most of my busy time writing stories of 80,000 to 120,000 words that take a few months to a year to finish. I've always preferred long-form writing because it's a bigger sandbox for my ideas than the short story or novella, and because it's easier for me to sell novels than anything else. The market for short stories is limited and low-paying, and almost nobody buys novellas or novelettes.

That said, I have written a good amount of shorter fiction in the last decade. Writing a short story or novella requires the flexing of different writing muscles, so to speak. Personally, I find it harder to write a good short story than to write a full-length novel because there's so much less space to develop the setting and narrative. But it can be a great deal of fun, and it's a good way to sandbox a new idea and play with it. I like to tackle shorter work in between books because it's a good change of pace, and it doesn't require me to keep my head in the same fictional world for a few months at a time.

I took stock of all the short stories, novelettes, and novellas I've finished, and their combined word count is as high as that of a good-sized novel. The most substantial portion of that pile comes from the novellas I've written for Wild Cards, either as part of our mosaic novels or as stand-alone stories for Tor.com. But there was a lot in my short fiction folders that I wrote either as ancillary material for a novel, as a world-building exercise for future projects, or just for my own amusement.

When I read through the short fiction I've written, it struck me that my favorite stories were invariably the ones that I wrote to have fun, the stuff that nobody was waiting for. Those are also the stories that have seen the most success. *Lucky 13* and *On The Use of Shape-Shifters in Warfare*, for example, were adapted for Netflix's Love Death + Robots animated series of short fiction, where they found themselves in the company of works written by science fiction rock stars like Peter F. Hamilton, Ken Liu, Alastair Reynolds, and John Scalzi. *Ink and Blood* was my first professional short fiction sale, to Scott H. Andrews at *Beneath Ceaseless Skies*.

Until now, all the stories in this book were scattered across various media, and someone who wanted to read my shorter fiction had to track them all down individually and buy them separately, or (in the case of the Wild Cards novellas) as part of the bigger work in which they appeared. They'd have to go to BCS, Tor.com, the Amazon Kindle store, and a physical bookstore, and shell out at least fifty bucks in the process.

I thought it would be a good idea to put everything in one compendium and ask rather less than fifty dollars for the convenience.

The collection you are reading now contains every short story, novelette, and novella of mine that have ever been published. It includes two Wild Cards novellas from their respective mosaic novels (*Stripes* from *Low Chicago*, and *Probationary* from *Three Kings*), a Wild Cards novella and a novelette from Tor.com (*Berlin is Never Berlin* and *How To Move Spheres And Influence People*, respectively), a short story from Beneath Ceaseless Skies (*Ink and Blood*), the two short stories from Love Death + Robots (*On The Use Of Shape-Shifters In Warfare* and *Lucky 13*), the short story *Cake From Mars* (from Unidentified Funny Objects Vol.1), and my Frontlines tie-in novella *Measures of Absolution*.

As a bonus, this compendium also includes three previously unpublished short stories: *Steel and Paper* (another story from the *Ink and Blood* world), *Seeds*, and *Rottertown*.

I have lightly revised most of these stories (no matter how often you read your manuscripts, you'll always find more mistakes and typos), and each has a new introduction that explains the story's origin and supplemental behind-the-scenes commentary.

This year marks the ten-year anniversary of my transition into a full-time writing career. What you have in front of you right now is the sum of everything I've written since 2012 that wasn't a novel. Some of them are among my favorite things I've ever written, and I hope you enjoy these stories as much as I have enjoyed writing them.

Marko Kloos
Enfield, NH, April 2023

Werewolf Soldiers: "On The Use Of Shape-Shifters In Warfare"

"On The Use Of Shape-Shifters In Warfare" combines two of my favorite things: military fiction and werewolves.

I don't remember exactly how the idea for this story popped up in my head. I just let my mind wander one day and think about how useful lycanthropes would be in a military application, and how the militaries of the world would utilize them. In a world where lycanthropy is commonly known, it would probably be severely restricted. Maybe there would even be an international treaty prohibiting their use in battle. What would a special forces unit made up of werewolves do if they weren't allowed to fight the enemy?

Well, they have really good noses, I thought to myself. *They'd probably make fantastic scouts and IED detectors.*

So I sat down and started to write about this werewolf soldier and his buddy, assigned to a regular infantry unit as living bomb detectors and alarm systems, used by the Army like pieces of gear and treated with about as much respect. Back when I wrote the story, we were still heavily involved in Afghanistan, so I used that setting as the stage, and everything just kind of flowed from there.

When the story was finished, I didn't submit it anywhere for publication. I just filed it away, pleased at how well it had turned out, with the idea to maybe turn that fictional world into a whole series of novels later.

A few years ago, I received an email from Tim Miller, the director behind "Deadpool" and "Terminator: Dark Fate." He told me that he had read my Frontlines books and the short story "Lucky 13" (also featured in this compendium), and would I be interested in selling him the rights to use the short story in a new project he was planning for Netflix?

I was, of course, *very* interested. During our conversation, Tim asked if I had finished other short works he could read, and I sent him the other stories I had written up until that point. He liked "Shape-Shifters" as well, and we struck a deal for him to use both stories for his project, now known as LOVE DEATH + ROBOTS, an award-winning series of short fiction adaptations on Netflix.

I'm still working on putting together the world for Decker's continued adventures, and I think it has all the trimmings for a fun military fantasy series. Until then, I'll take the success of this story as a good omen for the odds of the future series.

(A side note for the military veterans who have read the story and watched the Love Death + Robots adaptation of it: yes, I know that the TV characters use the wrong lingo for their branch, and that Marines don't refer to each other as "soldiers." The TV production team and their scriptwriters, however, did not. They changed Decker and Sobieski's branch to the Marine Corps but left the Army language unchanged. But as you can read in the story, I wrote them into the Army. I just wanted to get that off my chest because I keep getting emails to this day about that.)

On the Use of Shape-Shifters in Warfare

"The use of lycanthropes as combatants is prohibited. In case of capture by the enemy, such individuals have no right to be treated as prisoners of war, nor shall they be accorded the rights of such."

—Article 2, Section I, Budapest Accords
(not signed by the United States)

"Lykes."

The word is spoken softly but with bile. It comes from the back of the room, where a group of Airborne troops are hunched over their beef and noodles. We have barely made it to the chow line, but now heads are turning, and the din of conversation in the mess hall is taking on a terse quality. Now we're the center of attention, even though few are brave enough to stare at us openly.

Next to me, Sergeant Sobieski is loading up his tray with plates of food two levels high: beef and pasta, mashed potatoes, salad, bread, four slices of pie. I follow suit, even though I'd just as soon have a cold MRE back in our container than choke down the mess hall food with muttered slurs and bits of food getting flung my way.

"You can't sit here," the burly Master Sergeant says when we put down our trays on the dining table.

"I don't see any 'Reserved' signs, Top," I say. Sergeant Sobieski grabs his fork and starts eating, supremely unconcerned with the dozen hostile pairs of eyes on us.

"I said you can't sit here," the Master Sergeant says again. Sobieski doesn't even look up from his food. Sergeant Sobieski is half a head taller than the biggest regular Army guy in the room, and the arms sticking out of the neatly folded sleeves of his ACU blouse are as big around as my thighs.

On a normal day, I would back down, grab my chow, and find a quiet corner on the base to eat in peace. But we just got off a cramped and noisy chopper, I haven't had any food in six hours, and my rebelling stomach is making me cranky. So I stab a piece of beef with my fork, stick it into my mouth, and start chewing it slowly, all while holding the Master Sergeant's gaze. I almost smile when I see his jaw muscles flex with suppressed anger.

"What is your name and rank, soldier?" he asks, with sharp emphasis on the last word. "You're out of proper uniform."

"I'm Sergeant Decker. This is Sergeant Sobieski. And you know damn well that dress regs don't apply to the 300th in theater."

Our uniforms are sanitized: no name tapes, no rank devices, no unit patches. Even our Western allies get twitchy at the thought of a foreign army's lycanthropes present on their soil. Here in the Middle East, where lycanthropy is a capital offense, the locals would get downright apoplectic at the sight of troopers with the unit patch of the 300th Special Operations Company on their sleeves—the first and only segregated all-lycanthrope unit of the Army.

The Master Sergeant looks at us, his jaw still grinding. Then he shakes his head.

"Fucking dog soldiers," he says. "The Army started turning to shit when they let you people wear the uniform. Unnatural is what you are."

Despite the anger welling up in my chest, I chuckle.

"I'm more natural than you. I can see in the dark, hear the grass grow, follow a scent for twenty miles. All without batteries. Your ass rides around in a stinking Humvee, and you're blind at night without your flashlight and your NVGs. How fucking natural is that?"

Next to me, Sobieski puts down his fork and clears his throat.

"No disrespect, Master Sergeant, but if you ever call us 'dog soldiers' again in our presence, I will rip off your arm and beat you with it. Now shut up and let us eat our food in peace. *Sir.*"

Chair legs squeal on the bare concrete floor as the Master Sergeant and all the other regular Army soldiers at the table stand up, murder in their eyes. The burly master Sergeant balls his hands into fists and starts toward us. Before he has taken two steps, Sobieski lets out a growl. It's a deep, ear-tingling sound, so low and resonant that the silverware on my plate chatters. The entire room falls silent instantly.

Sobieski picks up his soda cup and sucks it empty. The raspy slurping sound of the straw is very loud in the room. He looks at the dozen angry soldiers who have stopped in their tracks in front of us, and there isn't a trace of concern on his face.

The Master Sergeant still has his fists clenched, but the sudden smell of fear coming from his pores tells me that he's glad to be on the other side of the table. He glares at us for another moment, snatches his meal tray off the table, and walks off without another word. One by one, the other soldiers follow. The last one to leave the table hawks up some phlegm and spits it onto the floor near our feet. They walk out of the mess hall without looking back. A few stunned moments later, the conversations in the room resume.

"He'll come back with the base MP in about three minutes," I say.

Sergeant Sobieski shrugs.

"*Please*. Let me sleep in a cell tonight, send someone else to do this patrol. Not that he's going to do shit."

He nods at my plate and the mostly untouched food on it.

"I'd hurry up with that, though. Just in case."

At dawn, I walk point on patrol for a squad of Army regulars. It's the tolerable sliver of morning between the bone-chilling cold of the night and the relentless heat of the day.

We trudge up the main road of the nearby village, to look for

IEDs and flush out local insurgents. The houses are untidy stacks of stone, put together without mortar. A few villagers are out on the street this morning. Some return my greeting, but most pretend I don't exist. For a small mountain village like this, there are too many young men milling around.

High explosives have a particular scent, even through a layer of earth and the rusty metal case of an old artillery shell. Freshly dug earth has a different smell. Together, they make an olfactory marker that's as strong and obvious as a ten-foot neon sign on top of the ambush site. Even from a hundred yards away, I can smell death waiting for us by the side of the road leading out of the village, masterfully camouflaged.

"Heads up," I say into my radio. "One o'clock, seventy yards past the last house on the right. Make it two one-fifty-fives, underneath the rock pile by the culvert."

"Fantastic," the squad's sergeant says. "Let's secure the site and call out the EOD guys."

I smell the new danger right as a rifle cracks in the distance. The bullet hits me in the hip, just below the edge of my protective vest. I do a graceless little half spin and fall on my ass. Behind me, the infantry guys take cover. The squad medic starts toward me, but I wave him off. The wound is already knitting itself closed, and even though it hurts like someone rammed a red-hot fireplace poker through me, I know there won't even be a scar by the time I get back to base.

The sniper fires again. The bullet kicks up dust and gravel chips right in front of my feet. This time, I see the flash from the rifle muzzle.

"Left side of the road, one-fifty. The little goat shack with the collapsed roof. He's in the corner at the bottom left."

The soldier manning the fifty-caliber machine gun on the squad's Humvee opens up with his weapon. The slow, thundering staccato of the big gun drowns out the reports from the rifles behind me as the other soldiers return fire as well.

Every time I am under fire, I feel the almost irresistible urge to rip off all these civilized trappings of warfare and change into my more capable shape. In my other form, I can move faster than a sniper can adjust his aim, and I can smell ambush sites a hundred times better than in my handicapped two-legged form. But I'm on a leash, so I follow orders, and stay human.

Every time it happens, I loathe myself—not for obeying orders, but for accepting the leash willingly.

When it's over, the little goat shack is a pock-marked ruin. When the infantry guys move in, there's nothing there but three empty shell casings and some blood on the dirt.

The squad sergeant watches as I walk around the shack to get the scent of the place.

"Two men," I say. "Shooter and spotter. The shooter's wounded. They hoofed it out the back and into the hills. I got their scent, so I'll be able to ID them if they're locals."

"'course they're locals," the squad sergeant says.

The regulars aren't too keen on charging after the shooters into Indian country with just a squad of troops, and I don't blame them. So we radio our contact report, set up security, and wait for the EOD team to arrive and defuse the artillery shells buried by the road. Two people wounded, lots of ammo turned into noise and dust, and at the end of the day, we're right back where we started, soldiers and insurgents alike. And as our days go, so does the war.

"Three weeks," Sobieski says over dinner. "Bring in the whole 300th, let us off the leash, and we'll own these mountains in three weeks."

"Not going to happen," I say. "You know the regs. No combatant use of lycanthropes."

"We never signed that accord."

"No, we didn't, but that's politics for you. Wouldn't want to piss off the allies."

"Fuck the allies," Sobieski says. "What's the point of having us if you only use us as bomb detectors with legs? Such a waste. It's like using Navy SEALs as lifeguards at the pool."

I chuckle into my chipped beef on toast. Sobieski looks past me and out of the windows of the chow hall. Outside, the sun is setting behind the mountains to our west.

"Just think about it. The whole company, almost two hundred of us, out there digging those bastards out of their caves at night. Leave a bunch of heads for the rest of them to find, just like they do with our guys. Like I said, three weeks."

I can't say I haven't felt the same way before. But then I think about the reception we would get back home with network footage of dismembered bodies preceding us, and the kind of treatment we would provoke if the whole world had their faces rubbed into what can happen when lycanthropes group together in a large pack and go hunting for humans.

But I don't voice those thoughts to Sobieski. Instead, I return his grin with a nod of implied agreement and finish my dinner. Sobieski is not the kind of person who spends a great deal of time thinking about consequences.

The Forward Operating Base has an observation outpost. It sits on a hilltop half a mile away. Every week, a different squad is rotated there. With a pair of lycanthropes at the base now, Command has decided to send one of us up with the next squad. I draw straws with Sobieski for the first week, and he pulls the short one.

"Something's off about this valley," I tell him as I help him pack his gear. "It doesn't smell right. We'll be in the shit before the week is up. Watch your head up there."

"Hell, I have nothing to worry about," Sobieski says and fastens the straps of his body armor. "Things go to shit, I'll dump all my gear and go native."

"Try not to piss off any of the regulars. You have to sleep sometime."

"So do they," Sobieski says. "It's just a squad. They have any smarts at all, they'll be trying hard not to piss me off."

I help him with the rest of his gear and watch as he swaggers off toward the waiting Humvees outside, carrying his hundred-pound backpack like a toiletries bag.

The OP is in sight of the base, but it takes a half hour for a

Humvee to climb the steep, narrow dirt road that winds its way up that mountain. If something goes badly wrong, that OP might as well me in another country, because none of us will get up there in time to help.

The little column drives off, rooster tails of dust in their wake. I am now the only lycanthrope on base, only barely welcome, and only for my sense of smell and the ability to see trouble coming in the dark.

They didn't mention these things in the recruiting brochure, but they didn't have to. I've always known what I would be getting into, but I signed the contract anyway, hoping that things would slowly change with time. But they don't—not out there in the mountains, and not in the heads of our fellow soldiers.

The night is moonless. We set out on patrol just after midnight, a full platoon on foot. My fellow soldiers look barely human in their bulky armor, with the dual lenses of their night vision goggles in front of their faces. I go out light—no rifle because I'm not allowed to fight, and no night vision device because I don't need one. As always, I'm walking point at the head of the column, because I want to get the earliest whiff of trouble if it comes our way, and because I'm much harder to kill than the regular troops.

The insurgents are not out for trouble tonight. All I smell is the suspended life of the village all around us, people sleeping in their houses behind ancient stone walls and crooked doors, and dormant fires in ash-heavy hearths. Still, there's a new scent in the air tonight. I get the vague, unsettling feeling of a threat, but I can't quite identify it. The place smells wilder than before, more dangerous somehow.

We're on the road between the village and the FOB when automatic weapons fire crackles in the distance. We all take covering positions out of habit, but the sound of gunfire isn't coming from any place nearby. It's rolling down from the hilltops to the east, where the observation post is perched on the mountain.

There are some urgent radio conversations behind me. I look over to the OP, which is only visible in the distance because of the muzzle flashes lighting up the hilltop. Something about the gunfire sounds odd. I can hear the clatter from M4 carbines firing their three-round burst staccato, but I don't hear the deeper, more rattling sound of insurgent AK-47s, or the slow, heavy thunder of belt-fed machine guns. It sounds like every trooper on top of that mountain is firing his carbine, but nobody is shooting back.

"The OP's not responding," the lieutenant says. "We're redeploying. Back to the intersection, and up the hill, double-time. And watch the flanks, people."

Sobieski and I have our own radios, separate from the rest of the network. I try to raise him on comms, but he doesn't reply. Whatever is happening up there, he's too busy fighting to worry about answering radio calls.

As we rush back to the intersection, the firefight on the distant hill intensifies. Still, all I hear is our own rifles. Then my radio comes alive with the static-riddled sounds of battle, people shouting and firing bursts. There's a scream, shrill and angry— Sobieski's voice, but in a pitch I've never heard before—and the transmission is cut off.

Then an unmistakably lupine howl rises into the night sky from the hilltop half a mile away. It's silver-bright and savage, triumphant.

"The fuck is your guy doing?" the platoon sergeant yells at me over the radio.

"That wasn't Sobieski," I send back, pressing the transmit button with fingers that suddenly seem to clumsy for the task. "Hold the platoon. Don't go up there."

"We got a squad up there, asshole," the platoon sergeant says. "We're going, and if your pal went feral on them, I'll personally shoot him between the eyes."

The hilltop is quiet now, too much so after the short and violent staccato of automatic gunfire.

"I'll go," I say. "If I change, I can run up that hill in a quarter of the time it'll take all of you."

I've decided to go no matter what the lieutenant says. By the time he sends his reply, I've already stripped off my body armor and unbuckled my thigh holster.

"Fine, Sergeant. Go. But we're going to plug everything that comes off that hill on four legs, do you understand?"

"You should," I reply. "In fact, if I'm not back here in five, call in some close air on that hill and let them bomb it flat."

I dash up the hill on all fours as fast as I can. The night air smells like gunpowder and fear, and the heavy copper smell of fresh blood. The new scent I noticed down in the village is up here as well, much stronger now that I am in my more capable form. It's musky and wild, unsettlingly familiar and wholly alien at the same time. I know what I will find at the top of the hill.

The OP is a slaughterhouse. In the darkness, I can smell the blood all over the walls of the little bunkers made from sandbags and Hesco barriers. The dead are all over the OP—on the floor of the bunker, at the top of the main firing position, splayed out in the dirt between the shelters. There are empty cartridge cases strewn everywhere, still warm and smelling of freshly burnt powder. All around the bodies, the dirt has been churned by the struggle, and there are paw prints the size of frying pans in the dust between the dead soldiers.

I find Sobieski in the bunker underneath the heavy weapons emplacement. He's sitting upright against the wall, chin on his chest, as if he's merely taking a quick nap. There isn't an unbroken piece of gear left in the room. I know that Sobieski can hold his own against any three or four guys even when he's in human form, but whatever fought with him in here was stronger and faster. I don't have to check his pulse to know he's dead. His ballistic armor is halfway undone, and his belt is open. When they got jumped, he tried to shed his clothes and gear so he could meet the enemy on equal footing, but he didn't have the time, and then engaged with his bare hands.

His killer is no longer on the hilltop, but he left a scent trail I could follow in my sleep. I want to tear into the darkness, find him, and rip him to shreds, but there's a platoon waiting at the base of the hill, and I don't want them to stumble into this carnage without a word of warning.

When I walk back down the hill, I do so on two legs, in my naked human form, mindful of the thirty rifles and machine guns aimed at me.

"Eleven KIA," I tell the lieutenant. "Don't bother with medics. And don't go up there unless you don't want to sleep well again for a while."

"Your guy?"

"Sobieski's dead," I say. "It got him first, from the looks of it."

"The fuck is 'it'?" he asks, even though I can tell by the smell of fear coming from him that he already knows the answer.

"Get these soldiers off this hill and back to the barn," I say. "Stay out in the open and plug anything you see that has fur. Call in the rapid reaction force. And leave my clothes right here. I'll need those later."

The lieutenant looks at me for a moment, grinding his jaw. Then he glances into the darkness behind me, and the fear seeping out of his pores gets stronger.

"Where are you going?"

"I'm going to chase that bastard down."

Out in the darkness, well beyond the OP, there's another howl, this one a long and mournful dirge.

The lieutenant grips his carbine tighter and reaches for his radio.

"Go," he says. "And good luck. Just don't get too close to these guys while you're out and about. We see something stirring in the dark, we're shooting it."

"Aim for the head and lead your shots more than you think you need to," I tell him.

I pick up the trail again at the OP. Before I change, I kneel in front of Sobieski, touch my forehead to his, and say my good-byes. Before long, Sobieski will be in a body bag and then a zinc coffin. I will not be there when they put him into the ground back home in Pennsylvania.

The werewolf who killed him tore the chain with the dog tags off his neck when they were fighting. I locate it in the dirt by scent, six feet away. I take the two Army tags and put them on Sobieski's lap, for the casualty detail to find. There's another tag on that chain, the five-sided Registered Lycanthrope brass tag we're all required to wear in the civilian world back home. I take the tag and attach it to the chain around my own neck, where it joins another tag just like it.

I don't have any fitting last words, so I render one final salute to Sergeant Jared Sobieski, 300th Special Operations Company (L), and go outside to change. Then I run off into the darkness to track down his killer.

The trail goes cold fifteen miles away. I follow the other werewolf's scent across the rugged landscape for half an hour before it ends in the cold waters of a mountain stream at the bottom of a craggy wadi. I follow the stream for a little while and check the underbrush on both banks for a new scent trail every few hundred meters, but the scent is gone completely. I search the hillsides and ravines in the area until the first rays of the morning sun paint the eastern horizon blood-red, but there's nobody left out here but me.

By the time I get back to my clothes, it's almost daylight, and there are troops from the Quick Reaction Force all over the mountain. I retrieve my stuff, get dressed, and hitch a ride back to base with a passing Humvee, utterly exhausted, and sick with impotent anger.

I get debriefed by a chain of officers that keeps going up the rank ladder as the day progresses. I repeat the same narrative until we're all thoroughly annoyed with each other. At the end of the day, the other werewolf is still out there, and Sobieski is still dead, riding back to Bagram in a sealed body bag on the floor of a Blackhawk. When I get back to the container we shared, all his personal gear is gone, and the place has the smell of disinfectant.

In the evening, the captain comes into my container.

"We're going down into the village for the weekly bullshit palaver with the tribal elders," he says. "I want you to tag along to stand guard, just in case."

I get off my cot and grab my gear. After a moment, I recall Sobieski, dead at the OP with his vest halfway undone, and I leave my body armor next to the cot.

"I want to sit in on that meeting," I tell the captain.

"No can do," he says. "They figure out I've brought a lycanthrope along, they'll be so offended they'll never even look at us again. I don't care to have the State Department jumping my shit."

"They have a lycanthrope of their own running around out there," I say. "They have to know who it is. Ask them point-blank, and I'll be able to smell if they're lying."

The captain mulls my request for a few moments. Then he purses his lips and nods curtly.

"Fine. But you're wearing shades. And if they bring the bastard along, I want you to shoot first and tell me later. I'm taking no chances after last night."

We're sitting on the dusty floor of the village elder's house. It's hot and uncomfortable, with twenty people in a room barely bigger than my living room back home. I can smell irritation and tension all around me, but I barely register the heated conversation between the Captain and the village elders. Right now, I only have eyes for the old man sitting in a corner of the room, sipping his tea impassively. He can't see my own eyes behind the lenses of my sunglasses, but I know he is aware of my attention, because we both smelled each other's presence the moment I entered the room. The old man in the corner is the lycanthrope from last night, the one who killed a dozen of our men.

I know that he's aware of me, aware of the fact that I know what he is. He must smell my nature as clearly as I can smell his. I also know that his companions are unaware. Their protestations of the captain's accusations are genuine. I can smell no deception or duplicity. They don't know.

I could give him away right now—to my fellow soldiers, who would shoot him on the spot instantly just out of fear, or to his fellow villagers, for a much slower and more unpleasant death. To my own, I'm merely a freak of nature, an unsettling curio, grudgingly afforded person status. To these people, in this part of the world, that old man sipping tea in the corner is an abomination, a walking and breathing blasphemy. I want him dead for what he did, but not in these ways.

I watch the old man over the animated debate in the room between us. He keeps sipping his tea, avoiding my gaze.

Then, at the end of the meeting, the old man looks up, and his eyes meet mine for a moment. They aren't yellow, like those of every other lycanthrope I've ever known. Instead, they are milky as opals.

He nods at me, almost imperceptibly.

I respond with a tiny nod of my own and look away.

We just made an agreement without exchanging words. We will settle this among outcasts, in our own way.

"Any luck?" the Captain asks when we file out of the house into the hot and dusty street again.

"They don't know shit," I reply, and find that I'm not bothered by the duplicity of the omission.

In the evening, I find a quiet spot at the perimeter of the base. Then I take off my clothes and put them in a pile. I take the dog tags off my neck and place them on top of my clothes. Then I change.

Tomorrow, I will wear the leash around my neck again. Tonight, I am no one's dog soldier.

He is waiting for me in the wadi, miles away from the nearest village or outpost.

We fight our battle with teeth and claws, not guns. He is strong and fast despite his age, but all feral instinct. I have trained and fought with my own kind for years, and unlike Sobieski, I am not encumbered. We spill each other's blood in a flurry of clashes, but he's the one who does most of the bleeding. But he does not yield, not even when I have him by the throat and he knows he is broken.

His is an honorable death. Better than falling to bullets, or being pulped by rocks while buried to the shoulders in the rocky Afghan soil. Despite Sobieski, I take no pleasure in this kill.

When it's over, I wash off the blood in the cold water of a nearby stream. Then I go back to the still form of my enemy, change back into my human shape, and touch my forehead to his.

I brought no hand tools, and the soil is too unyielding for bare hands or paws, so I bury the old man under a pile of rocks I gather from the banks of the stream. I don't know if despite his nature he was a believer, but I gauge the proper direction by the stars and point the grave toward Mecca anyway.

When I change back to my feral self for the run back, I take a last look around. The place seems a fitting resting spot for the old lycanthrope. The land is harsh, unforgiving, and austerely beautiful. The sky is cloudless, and the moon is painting silver streaks onto the surface of the stream nearby. Out here, underneath the black dome of the night sky and its millions of stars, it's more beautiful than in any cathedral I've ever seen.

I raise my head and howl a dirge for my fallen brothers. It echoes back from the hard and ancient mountains all around me in a distant requiem.

Back at the base, my clothes are still in the sand where I left them. It's the hour of the night when the darkness has not quite started to lift yet, the morning just a sliver of dark blue above the mountains.

I am about to change back into my human form when the door of a nearby container opens and a soldier steps out into the cool late-night air. He clears his throat and spits into the sand. Then he turns toward the corner of the container and opens his fly to relieve himself, too lazy to walk over to the portable latrines at the end of the container row. Even from fifty yards away, his smell is instantly familiar. It's the Master Sergeant who clashed with us in the mess tent.

I sneak close to the spot where the Master Sergeant is emptying his bladder. When I'm almost behind him, I let out a soft growl from deep down in my chest. The Master Sergeant flinches as if I had hit him with a cattle prod. When he turns around with a hoarse yell, I am already gone, hiding in the shadows between the containers. I smell with satisfaction that the Master Sergeant has pissed all over the front of his own pants.

After breakfast, I go to the Captain and tell him what I've done last night. He prods me for two hours to make me tell him where I've buried the old lycanthrope, but I don't budge. All he needs to know is that the threat to his troops is gone. I don't want them to dig up the body and haul it off to be poked and sliced up.

"That won't help your career at all," the captain finally says when he has had enough of me. "I'm sending you back as soon as the next Blackhawk gets in. Let your own people deal with you. I don't want to see you at this FOB ever again."

By lunchtime, I'm on a helicopter back to Bagram.

We fly high, out of the range of machine guns and rocket-propelled grenades. The doors of the Blackhawk are open. Underneath, the landscape rolls by, tiny villages hugging hillsides and valleys, ancient sediment deposited by the currents of history. I look down at those remote islands of humanity and wonder how many of them have secret protectors like the one I buried last night.

I carry my personal documents in a pouch in my leg pocket. My term of service will be up in another two months, and I've been carrying around the reenlistment form for a while. I take it out of the pouch and look at it. The airflow in the cabin is making the form flutter wildly in my hands, like a living thing straining to free itself from my grasp.

I tear the form in half, fold the pieces, and tear them again and again, until I have nothing but a handful of ragged little paper squares. Then I open my hands and let them go. The turbulence whips them out of the helicopter, where they disperse, dancing the currents of the hot summer wind.

Just For Fun: Cake From Mars

"Cake From Mars" originated in a Twitter bet I entered with my friend Chuck Wendig. We tossed around some nonsense titles for stories, and somehow, I accepted his joke challenge to write a story to match this particular title (which in the original was the rather less PC "Cake Whores From Mars.")

This was one of those stories that pop into existence in the writer's head fully formed. I wrote it in two days, and it was one of the most fun things I've ever written. I ended up selling it to Alex Shvartsman for the first volume in his "Unidentified Funny Objects" SF humor anthology. This story reminds me of the times when I didn't have books for multiple series to juggle, and when I would sometimes write a thing just for my own amusement.

Cake From Mars

"All I want for my goddamn birthday is a cake with a hooker popping out of it. Is that too goddamn much to ask?"

Moses Anderson pinched the bridge of his nose and exhaled slowly.

"Dad, keep it down. This is a Church nursing home. I can't have you get kicked out of another one. You're on number three this year."

"Ain't nothing left but the Church ones," his father said. Amos Anderson was a hundred and forty-nine but could still arm-wrestle a nurse. Moses suspected that all the illegal liquor had had some preserving properties, even though Dad was on his fifth vat-grown liver. "Damn Levitican sons of bitches sucked all the fun out of life ever since they started running the damn planet. Now what about my goddamn cake?"

"Dad," Moses said. "Cake's made with sugar. Sugar's illegal. Even if I don't fill it with a hooker, which is also illegal, and expensive to boot. You want me to buy a hooker in a cake, and do fifty years for smuggling her past the customs patrol?"

"You'll only do time if they catch you, son."

Moses pinched the bridge of his nose again. Inhale, exhale, relax. Suppress urge to smother progenitor with pillow.

"Look, Dad. Even if I could get a cake that big, fly to Mars, hire a hooker, bring her back to Earth, and smuggle her past customs, there's still the money issue. I don't know if you've kept up with Martian contraband prices--"

"Of course I have," Amos said.

"--of course you have," Moses sighed. "Then you know that sugar is at over nine hundred a kilo right now. And you gotta use off-world flour for a cake, 'cause the Earth stuff doesn't bind with sugar anymore ever since they passed that Dessert Precursor law. A cake that big, that's fifty kilos at least. I sell vacuum cleaners, Dad. On commission. I don't have a hundred large to spend right now. And that's before you even factor in the hooker."

"I can't believe you're my son," Amos said. He shook his head in disgust and reached over to his bedside table. He put his thumb on the scanner lock, and a drawer slid out. Moses watched as his Dad rummaged through the drawer.

"Are you keeping booze in there? And--shit, is that a pistol?"

"Yes," Amos said matter-of-factly. "Because nothing says 'Do Not Resuscitate' like a forty-five caliber slug to the...ah, here we go."

He pulled out a credstick and tossed it to Moses.

"Take that to First Celestial and exchange whatever you need. I was saving it for a rainy day but being stuck in a damn nursing home without a hooker cake for my 150th is just about as rainy as they come, son."

Moses looked at the credstick in his hand. It had a platinum-colored band around its middle, and the data port still had the bank wrapper on it.

"Dad, how much money is on this thing?"

"Three-quarter million, give or take a few ten thousand. And another half mil in overdraft credit. Now take it and get me my goddamn hooker cake, will ya? Ain't nothing fun left on this rock to spend it on anyway."

"Gateway Traffic Control, this is November Zero Eight One Five Zulu. Request departure clearance outbound Mars."

"Five Zulu, Gateway Control. Declare cargo and purpose of your trip."

Moses glanced at the dozen new Drek-Sukker 3000 vacuum cleaners he had just picked up from the factory on Luna.

"Gateway, Five Zulu. Cargo is vacuum cleaner units, low-grav optimized, count twelve. I'm making the monthly service run to Olympus City."

Customs didn't often scan departing spacecraft--there wasn't much illicit stuff to smuggle off Earth since the Leviticans got into government--but Moses still had a floating feeling in his stomach as he waited for his clearance. There wasn't anything illegal in the back of the company service van yet, but the customs scanners would pick up the charged credstick of Mars dollars in his pocket. Carrying half a million converted New Shekels to Mars was practically a glowing sign advertising Intent to Smuggle. But it was a high-traffic day, and he counted on his vacuum service spacecraft to slip beneath the attention threshold that would merit a close pass from a customs boat--or worse, a boarding inspection.

"Five Zulu, Gateway," the controller said after a minute. *"You are cleared for departure as filed. You are number seventeen in the transit queue. Go with the Lord."*

"Gateway, Five Zulu. Thank you very much," Moses replied, careful to direct his sigh of relief away from the microphone.

Moses had never hired a Martian hooker, but it turned out that their services were as easy to obtain as the sugar and flour he needed for Dad's cake. He did his service calls quickly, and then went over to the Mall of Mars by Olympus City's spaceport. Flour and sugar: commodities level, sections five through eight. Hookers: service level, sections thirteen to fifty-nine. Sexual Services Unlimited, We-B-Hookers, Intercourse Incorporated, Fast & Easy, Copulation Station—the Mall of Mars had more rent-a-hooker services than any two Levitican megachurches back on Earth had copies of *The Ultimate, Unchanging, Unerring Word of God (Eighth Edition, Revised and Expanded)* on the pews. Moses picked a place without tentacles on the marquee and went inside, clutching his credstick full of Martian dollars.

"I gather you're not looking for some personal amusement, then," the hooker said. Moses found it difficult to apply the term to the woman sitting across the desk from him. She was dressed in a business suit that was formal and classy, and at the same time the sexiest piece of clothing Moses had ever seen on a woman. She wore her long dark hair in a ponytail, and her green eyes were mesmerizing. With her high cheekbones and flawless fair complexion, she was a complete knockout. She wore a little golden name tag that said KENDRA.

"Uh, no," he said. "I'm looking to hire someone for a special job. It's for my dad, really." He laughed nervously. "Why do I feel like you're the one interviewing me?"

"Because I am," she said. "We have full control when it comes to picking customers. This is a selective business, Mr. Anderson. Now, I'm curious why exactly you picked me out of the brochure." She gave him an encouraging smile, flashing a set of perfectly even, perfectly white teeth.

"Well," he said. "You're very petite. I need someone who can fit into this." He took a brochure from his pocket and put it on the table in front of her. She looked at it and raised an eyebrow.

"Tell me about this special job, Mr. Anderson."

He explained the situation to her. When he was finished, Kendra laughed a bright silver laugh that made him feel like he was watching the sun rise on a beautiful warm beach.

"I don't usually do contracts on Earth," she said. "Your government is a bit uptight when it comes to pleasure engineers. There's also the fact that what you're proposing is highly illegal on Earth."

She looked at his brochure again and shook her head with a smile.

"But you know what? It sounds like fun. And my legal insurance will buy me out if we get caught. Pay me my weekly rate plus twenty percent hazard surcharge, and I'm in."

His hands shook with relief and excitement when he fished for the credstick in his pocket.

"Great. I must apologize for all the questions I asked earlier. It's my first time hiring a whore."

He looked up, mortified, when he realized what he had just said.

"Gosh, I'm so sorry."

Kendra merely smiled at him.

"That's only a bad word where you live, Mr. Anderson. We here on Mars make it a point to, uh, *rehabilitate* certain Earth terms. Especially the ones your society sees as sinful. The root of the word 'whore' means 'desire'. On Mars, it's an honorable word. It's neither shameful nor immoral to be desired."

He nodded, relieved, but he knew without looking into a mirror that his face was the rich scarlet of a cardinal's robe. He handed the credstick to Kendra.

"Take out whatever you need," he said.

"November Zero Eight One Five Zulu, this is Gateway Control. Welcome home. Do you have anything to declare?"

Moses checked the hold behind the pilot compartment. The sealed refuse cartridges from the vacuums he had serviced in Olympus City were strapped against the cabin walls in a neat row, hazard tags hanging out.

'Uh, negative, Gateway Control. Just some spent trash elements and a few units that didn't sell."

"Five Zulu, understood." There was a brief pause. *"Stand by for customs inspection. Maintain present heading and speed."*

"Fuck," Moses said before pushing the transmit button again. "Gateway, Five Zulu. Sure thing."

"I'm getting a little uncomfortable back here," a voice said from the row of refuse cartridges behind him. "I hope this isn't airtight."

"Sorry about that," he told Kendra. "Your scrubber element has thirty minutes of air in it. That should be plenty for an inspection."

"Awesome. But if I start getting dizzy, I'm popping this lid, just so you know."

"Fair enough," Moses conceded, and watched as the approaching customs shuttle matched speeds on his service van's port side.

"Cargo manifest and operating license, please," the customs officer said without preamble as soon as he had stepped through the docking collar and raised the visor of his helmet.

"Here you go, officer." Moses handed him the requested items and stood by, trying to look casual despite the audible heartbeats in his ears.

The customs goon walked into the hold and turned his helmet light on to illuminate the trash cartridges lining the walls.

"Garbage, eh?"

"And four of these vacuum units. Only sold eight this time around."

The customs officer took out a hand-held scanner and passed it in front of the garbage cartridges.

"These show biomass inside."

"Yeah. One of my contracts...well, they say they're a hotel, but..." Moses lowered his voice conspiratorially. "I think they're one of those houses of ill repute. I have no idea what they're doing in those rooms, but their trash units break all the time. Once I had to crack open one of those cartridges because the seal went bad, and...you don't want to know what kind of stuff I found in there. Disgusting."

The customs goon backed away from the cartridge. "Yuck. And you do business with those degenerates?"

Moses shrugged. "I gotta go where the boss sends me, you know?"

"What's in that one over there? The scanner says it's shielded. What kind of garbage requires Class III radiation shielding?"

"That's plutonium oxide. From the little reprocessing plant at Sagan U. We have the contract for the disposal. They can't dump it on Mars because of environmental regs, so we haul it off for them. Don't worry--that shielding is solid. Touch it, if you want. The alpha decay warms up the casing. It's kind of neat."

"I'll take your word for it," the customs officer said. He took another look around the hold, tapped the hand-held scanner against his leg, and then turned toward the docking collar.

"Have a good day, Mister. And next time they pick you for an inspection, make sure you warn Customs ahead of time that you have nuclear waste on board. Lord bless."

"Yes, sir. Sorry, sir. Happens once or twice a year tops. I totally forgot."

Moses waited until the external hatch had locked behind the

departing officer, and then extended a discreet middle finger out of view of the porthole.

When the customs shuttle left formation to resume its patrol pattern, he walked back to the hold and opened the latch on the second biomass container. Kendra unfolded herself out of the impossibly tight space like a slightly wilted flower.

"That guy was as dumb as a box of rocks," she said. "I can't believe he swallowed that."

"Yeah, well, they don't pick 'em for smarts," Moses said, and helped her out of the trash capsule. "Good thing you Martian settlers are so...lithe."

"Benefit of adapting to a low-gee world." She straightened out her ponytail and smiled at Moses. "Let's get planetside, shall we? I believe you have a cake to bake."

Moses thought up half a dozen different plans to smuggle the cake past the front desk, and then dismissed them all in favor of naked bribery. When he pulled up to the side entrance on the lower level in the company hydrovan, the nighttime janitor opened the security lock for him as arranged.

"There's nothing illegal in that thing, is there? I don't want to get in trouble."

"No, no," Moses told him as he pushed the equipment cart through the security port. "It's just a birthday gift for my Dad. A few of his old Army things. I had them framed and stuff."

The cake was in a large box that used to hold an industrial-sized liquid waste vacuum. It wasn't a huge cake, just tall enough to hold a crouching Kendra, but it represented eighty thousand New Shekels worth of sugar and flour, and fifty years in one of the Ministry for the Prevention of Vice's megaprisons.

"I see." The janitor glanced at the label on the box as Moses pushed the cart into the corridor beyond the security lock. The smell of sugar and vanilla extract was almost strong enough to burn through the nursing home's olfactory aura of disinfectant and old sweat.

"Hey! Kenmore Drek-Sukker. I love those things. Use 'em all

the time."

"I sell them," Moses said, careful to push the cart with the boxed cake away from the janitor before reaching into his pocket for a card. He handed his business card to the janitor. "Give me a call sometime. I can get you great deals on those."

"Awesome. You have fun with your Dad, now. Betcha he'll be surprised, huh?"

'Oh, I have no doubt," Moses said and pushed the cart toward the elevator.

"That was a lucrative two minutes of work for him," he told the cake box when the elevator doors closed behind him. "If he orders a vacuum from me, he'll be able to pay for it with Dad's cash. You're turning out the most expensive cake in the history of confectionery, my dear."

Kendra's chuckle was muffled from inside three layers of cake and a heavy polyfiber box.

"But oh so worth it. I'm a high-quality dessert."

"Of that I have no doubt either," Moses said and pushed the button for the fifth floor.

"Holy shit. The little bastard came through," Amos said when Moses pushed the equipment cart into his father's room. "Looks like I won't have to disown you after all."

"There's not much left on that credstick for me to inherit," Moses puffed. "Happy birthday, Dad. And just so we're clear--this will be your birthday gift for all the rest of them, too."

Amos eyed the big box on top of the cart. "That better be what I hope it is."

"You'll see."

Moses closed the door behind him, took out the media player Kendra had given him, and placed it on the table next to the door. Then he hugged the vacuum box and lifted it upward.

"That," his Dad said, "is one ugly-ass cake. It looks like a trashcan with a turd on top."

"Dad, I'm a vacuum salesman, not a confectioner. That's the best I could do. Now shut up for a second."

He pressed the Play button on the screen of the player, and a Martian pop tune blared from the speakers at impressively high volume. The top of the cake popped off, sending bits of frosting flying, and Kendra unfolded herself out of the center, wearing a radiant smile and very little else. Then she started moving to the music, and Moses found that his overalls were getting very tight in the crotch all of a sudden.

"I take it back," Amos shouted against the music after a few stunned moments. "That is the most gorgeous cake I've ever seen in my life."

He stuck two fingers into his mouth and let out a long, piercing wolf whistle that made Moses clap his hands over his ears.

"Dad, keep it down!"

Behind him, the door opened, and a night nurse walked in. She took one look at the giant cake and the naked woman sensuously gyrating in the middle of it, gasped, and fled the room. Kendra kept on dancing, unperturbed. Moses looked around the corner and saw the nurse hurrying toward the watch station at the end of the floor.

"Great." He reached over and turned off the music.

"She's calling the cops right now, Dad. There's a Vice Police station just around the corner. We'll have the law on our heads in five minutes, tops."

"Well, then," Amos said, finally diverting his gaze from Kendra's lithe form. She stepped out of the cake and gathered her hair into a ponytail again.

"We are completely going to prison," Moses said. "There's no way we can eat all the evidence before they get here."

"Why don't you step outside and keep watch, Junior?" Amos said. "Time's a-wastin', and I want to have a little chat with this lovely young lady here. Just stall those holy rollers for a bit."

"Dad, I really don't--"

"Get out, ya daft bugger. Unless you want to record this for posterity. You know, as a memento."

Moses left the room without further argument.

The Vice Police came up in the elevator just a few minutes

later. Moses rushed ahead to meet them, but backed off when he saw that both officers had their stun-sticks drawn.

"What seems to be the problem, off--"

"Shut. *Up*," the lead officer said. He had the humorless expression that seemed to be standard issue along with those stun-sticks. "There's illegal drugs in that room over there. And *sinful debauchery in progress*. You are under arrest, friend. Mortal Sinning, and Fourth Degree Immorality."

They shoved him up against the wall, and Moses felt a set of restraints locking around his wrists. Then they pulled him along toward his Dad's room, where the loud music had started again.

The lead officer didn't bother with the formality of trying the door handle first. He raised a hobnailed boot, and kicked the door open. Then he went in, stun-stick raised.

"Freeze, sinner!"

There was an ear-splitting boom, and the cop froze in place, the remnants of his stun-stick raining onto the dingy floor.

"Freeze yourself, ya jackass," Amos shouted back. "Hit it, lady! We're busting out of this joint."

There was a sound like a vacuum cleaner engine straining at a clogged intake hose, and then Amos' bed came shooting into the hallway, knocking the lead cop down on the way out. The second officer looked dumbfounded--the expression seemed to come naturally to him--at the sight of an anti-grav bed with an armed centumquinquagenarian and a barely-clothed Martian hooker on it. The pistol in Amos' hand looked much more impressive than the stun-stick the second cop was holding. The bed took a sharp left turn and shot down the hallway, the music from Kendra's media player blaring, Amos whooping and hollering all the way. Moses heard Kendra's silver-bright laugh just before the bed crashed through the window at the end of the hallway and dipped out of sight.

There was a moment of absolute, stunned silence in the hallway.

"You have got to be shitting me," Moses said.

The first cop picked himself up off the floor. The remnants of the stun-stick were still dangling from his wrist on a lanyard. He snatched up his hat, put it back on his head, and went back into Amos' room. The second cop followed him, dragging Moses along.

The cake was still on the floor, an extremely obvious violation of Celestial Dietary Law. The night stand's drawer stood opened and empty. On top of the night stand, there was a large toolkit in a worn nylon pouch, a glass that still had amber-colored liquid in it, and a half-eaten piece of cake. The lead cop walked over to the nightstand, took a whiff of the glass, and made a face.

"Alcohol," he said. "Firearms. Hookers. *Cake*. Someone's going to do a lot of time for this. Fifty to life, and eternal damnation."

They walked down the length of the corridor to the broken window. Moses peered outside, expecting to see a mangled mess of retiree, hooker, and anti-grav bed. Instead, there was nothing below but the smooth concrete of the parking lot. He thought he heard faint Martian pop music fading into the distance.

Moses suppressed the urge to pinch the bridge of his nose. He fished the credstick out of the back pocket of his overalls with shackled hands and held it out to the lead officer.

"Take out whatever you need," he said. "And I'm sure you'll want to secure the evidence in the room, too. Would be a shame if someone made off with fifty pounds of Martian sugar cake. That stuff must be worth tens of thousands."

The cop looked at him with an unreadable expression. Then he snatched the credstick and looked at it. He took out his PDA, put the stick into the transfer receptacle, and checked the balance. Then he took off his hat with his free hand and scratched his scalp.

"Unlock those shackles, Sam. This gentleman here is obviously just an innocent bystander. Sorry for the inconvenience, sir."

"November Zero Eight One Five Zulu, Gateway Control. Declare cargo and purpose of your trip."

Moses turned around to face his passengers and put his finger in front of his headset's microphone.

"Gateway, Five Zulu. Cargo is vacuum cleaner spare parts. I'm making a service run to Olympus City."

It was a Saturday, and clearance came quickly. The controller sounded exceedingly bored.

"Five Zulu, Gateway Control. You are cleared for departure as filed. You are number three in the transit queue. Go with the Lord."

"Thank you, Gateway." Moses turned off the audio feed and punched his departure code into the Alcubierre drive's navigation panel. Then he sat back with a sigh.

"I hope you're aware that I'm only compounding my troubles," he said over his shoulder. "Transporting a fugitive from celestial justice and an illegal sex worker from Mars through the customs blockade."

"Pleasure engineer," Kendra corrected him.

"I don't know why you're still all tense, son," Amos said. "Everything turned out fine in the end, didn't it?"

"Dad, I had to spend the rest of your credstick buying off that cop. There's nothing left on it. You're broke. How are you going to live on Mars?"

"Oh, no worries. Kendra here is going to put me up for a little while, until my residence papers come through."

"Don't tell me you're both madly in love, and that you're getting married. Because that would be too much for my delicate digestive system right now."

Kendra laughed. Moses had decided a little while ago that he could listen to her laugh all day long.

"No, we're not. I don't make it a habit to date customers, let alone marry them. And your Dad's a bit too old for me. No offense," she said to Amos.

"None taken," he said. "Kendra is going to be my sponsor for my asylum application. Once that comes through, I'll get a Mars living stipend."

Moses raised an eyebrow. "Asylum? On what grounds?"

"Religious persecution."

"What?" Moses laughed. "You're an atheist, Dad. Which denomination are you claiming?"

"Hedonism," Amos said. "I've been a life-long practitioner."

The transit light turned green, and Moses pushed the "Engage" button on the Alcubierre panel.

"Lord knows that's the truth," he said as they shot off toward Mars.

Mutant Abroad: Berlin Is Never Berlin

The Wild Cards world, for those who aren't yet familiar with it, is a shared universe of superhero stories. The basic premise is that an alien virus was released over New York City in 1946 that killed most people who were exposed to it but turned some into mutated new forms of humanity. A small percentage of the afflicted, known as "aces", developed various superpowers. (If they have these powers while otherwise looking like a "nat", a normal human, they're aces, that is. If they have superhuman powers and visible mutations, they're "joker-aces". The ones with trivial powers or mere deformities are "jokers".)

When I was offered to join the group of amazing writers that make up the Wild Cards consortium, I had the opportunity to create my own superheroes from scratch and integrate them into the canonical world. My first and favorite of the bunch was Khan, Samir Khanna, a bodyguard and mob enforcer whose left body half is that of an anthropomorphic Bengal tiger. (He's the cover star of the Wild Cards mosaic novel LOW CHICAGO, if you want to look up a good illustration of what that sort of mutation would look like. His novella from LOW CHICAGO is featured in this compendium as well.)

Most of the Khan stories I've written were novellas to fit into themed Wild Cards mosaic novels. "Berlin Is Never Berlin" is a stand-alone novella that I wrote just because the story popped into my head one day. There was no big, overarching theme or storyline to fit it into, so I had total liberty, and Khan is always a fun character to write. I imagined a seemingly low-stakes bodyguard job that goes badly sideways for my semi-tiger. And because the story wasn't tied to a specific location, I set it in present-day Berlin, the capital of my birth country.

(The title comes from a saying about the city that references its seemingly ever-changing nature: "Paris is always Paris, but Berlin is never Berlin.")

Berlin Is Never Berlin

A Wild Cards Novella

The plane was only three hours into its flight when Khan began to entertain the thought of a massacre for the first time.

The surroundings were posh, and it was easily the most comfortable air travel he had ever enjoyed. Sal Scuderi's private jet had the full executive luxury package, and the club seating in the Lear was so roomy that even Khan, all six foot three and three hundred pounds, could stretch his legs a little. There was a bar stocked with premium liquor, and he didn't even have to pour his own drinks because they had a flight attendant on staff. The surroundings were more than fine. It was the company that triggered homicidal thoughts in Khan before they had even made it out over the Atlantic Ocean.

Natalie Scuderi, Sal's daughter and Khan's protectee for the week, traveled with an entourage. There were only four of them, but Khan suspected that she had picked her friends after a long and thorough vetting process to find the vapidest rich kids in the country. They had started with the champagne right before takeoff. Five minutes after wheels-up, they had commandeered the impressively loud luxury entertainment system in the cabin and started listening to Top 40 shit at high volume. It was a seven-hour flight to Iceland and then another three-hour hop to Berlin from there, and Natalie's entourage seemed determined to party all the way through the trip.

A simple job, Khan thought as he watched the scene from the front of the plane, where he had a spot to himself next to the bar. *Babysitting a bunch of spoiled kids. Easy money.*

The center of the cabin had a four-seat club arrangement and a leather couch, and Natalie's friends were all piled on the couch, glasses in their hands, talking loudly over the music and giving

Khan a headache. Natalie herself was sitting in the back of the plane, in the single seat next to the bathroom. She was wearing headphones the size of canned hams on her head, and she was typing away on the computer she had propped on the little tray table in front of her.

Sal Scuderi was a high-risk insurance salesman and one of the main money-laundering outlets for the Chicago mob. His daughter dabbled in acting and singing, but as far as Khan could tell, she was mostly famous for being famous. They were on the way to Berlin, where Natalie was booked for introducing a new fashion line and opening a nightclub. Having a joker-ace as a bodyguard conveyed a certain image, and plenty of entertainment industry celebrities were willing to shell out money just to rent that image for a night or a long weekend out on the club circuit. Khan didn't mind those jobs—they were easy money, just hanging out in clubs and looking mean for the cameras. But even milk run jobs had their hazards, and one of them was a migraine headache. He spent some time extending and retracting the claws of his tiger hand a few times while looking pointedly at the big-screen TV on the bulkhead above the couch, and someone turned down the volume a little. Just to make sure it stuck, he got out of his seat and walked to the bathroom at the back of the cabin. When he was between the couch and the giant TV, he took the remote and clicked the volume down a few more notches for good measure.

When he got out of the bathroom, Natalie Scuderi had taken off her headphones and closed the lid on her laptop.

"How do you like the ride?"

Khan closed the door behind him and shrugged. "Beats the hell out of flying coach," he replied.

"I've never flown coach." The way she said it wasn't boastful, just a statement of fact.

"Count yourself blessed," he said.

Khan noticed that Natalie's gaze flicked from one side of his face to the other, and he knew that she was looking at the tiger half without being too obvious about it. Khan's left body half was that of a Bengal tiger, and the demarcation line between man and cat went right down the centerline of his body. For a mob bodyguard, the tiger half paid many dividends. It gave him the strength, reflexes, senses, teeth, and claws of a tiger, and it made him look dangerous and imposing. Not even the roughest or most drunken blockheads wanted to test their mettle against a guy who was half apex predator. Claws and teeth had a way of triggering people's primal fears.

Travis, Eli, and Melissa—Natalie's friends—had been sufficiently in awe of Khan that none of them had even tried to make small talk with him. Now that he was standing next to Natalie and talking to her, someone had decided that he wasn't going to tear off any heads on the spot. Melissa got up from the couch and sauntered over, champagne glass in hand.

"Hey, can I ask you something?"

"Sure," Khan said.

She gestured at the line that bisected his face, fur on one side and skin on the other. He had grown out a beard to match the fur fringe on the tiger half of his jaw, to keep his looks symmetrical.

"Does that go, like, all the way down your body? Right down the middle?"

She tried to make it sound light and casual, but he knew what she was trying to ask because he had gotten the same question hundreds of times. Under normal circumstances, he would have given her a clever or flirty reply, like *You'll have to buy me drinks first to find out.* But she wasn't a paying client, and her gaggle of friends had been annoying Khan too much for him to tolerate a personal question like that.

"That's none of your business," he said. "Buzz off."

The girl beat a hasty retreat to the lounge area. Next to Khan, Natalie chuckled and opened her laptop again.

"You told Melissa to buzz off. Now she won't talk to you again for the rest of the trip."

"That is fine with me," Khan replied. "She doesn't have to talk to me. She just needs to listen when I tell her to do stuff."

Back on the couch, Natalie's chastened friend Melissa shot

Khan a nonplussed glare. Then she picked up the TV remote and turned the volume up again.

This is going to be a long fucking week, Khan thought.

There was always some security bullshit involved when a joker-ace like Khan traveled by air, but it was magnified when international borders were involved. Scuderi's private plane meant that Khan hadn't had to suffer the enhanced screening before their departure in Chicago, but the Germans weren't going to let him skip a damned thing. He'd had to file his plans in advance, and when the Lear stopped at the private terminal at Berlin's shiny new Brandenburg Airport, there was a welcoming committee waiting for him at customs and immigration.

"What is the purpose of your visit?" the customs officer asked when he checked Khan's passport.

"Business," Khan said. "I'm a bodyguard. My client is going through your no-hassle line over there right now."

"Are you bringing any weapons into the country at this time?"

"No weapons," Khan replied. He knew they'd go through his luggage anyway and check thoroughly. He carried a gun back home when he was working—no point disadvantaging yourself in a fight—but when he traveled out of the country, he didn't pack so much as a nail file. Foreign cops got twitchy enough when they saw the teeth and claws, and if they hadn't been firmly attached to him, he was sure they'd have made him leave those at home as well.

"Very well," the officer said. "In accordance with laws and regulations regarding the admission of foreign persons with enhanced abilities, I have to ask you to follow my colleague back to the room for your entry screening. You can choose to decline, but in that case you will be denied entry into the country."

"Lead the way," Khan grumbled. The world had had seventy years to get used to jokers and aces, and they still got civil rights parceled out to them like the nats were giving them treats for good behavior. Khan wasn't the type for political activism, but something in him bristled at having to ask permission to come and go from some pencil-necked bureaucrats when everyone in the room would already be cut into bloody ribbons if he had violence on his mind. The security kabuki existed to make the nats feel safer, and they knew that as well as he did.

The inspection was Teutonically thorough. They made him strip down to his underwear, snapped pictures of him with a sophisticated spatial camera array mounted on the wall of the screening room, and took prints and iris scans.

"You sure you don't want to put a tracking bracelet on me?" he asked when they rolled his tiger hand over the electronic print scanner—once with claws retracted, once with them extended.

"We only use those for certain criminal offenders," the police officer taking his print said, mild pique in his voice. "You are not an offender."

Could have fooled me, Khan thought, but he decided to keep it to himself. Customs and border police everywhere had a low tolerance threshold for humor and sarcasm.

The circus started almost right after Natalie's entourage left the private aviation terminal. They had transportation waiting outside, two big Mercedes limousines. There was a small crowd of fans and photographers by the exit, snapping pictures with cameras and phones and yelling Natalie's artist name excitedly when they spotted her. Natalie went by the mononym "Rikki," which sounded like the annoying call of an exotic bird when it was shouted by dozens of people at high volume.

Khan stepped ahead of Natalie and walked between her and the bulk of the crowd. When they all caught sight of him, there were some audible gasps. He put on his most humorless face and rasped a low growl when the front rank of excited fans came a little too close for comfort. None of them dared to come within an arm's length, and he ushered Natalie to one of the waiting limousines. As she climbed into the backseat, he stood guard and looked around. The situation was innocuous enough, a bunch of teenage kids squealing and taking pictures, but something made the hairs on the back of Khan's neck stand up.

Over in the group of paparazzi standing twenty feet away, there were two guys who Khan thought didn't quite act right. They weren't shouting at him or Natalie's entourage to pose for shots like the rest of them. They weren't even particularly engaged in taking photos, and when they did, they seemed to focus on him rather than the celebrity he was guarding. When they noticed his attention, they shifted their lenses and snapped shots of Natalie through the car window like the rest of them. Khan tried to get their scents, but this place was full of new and unfamiliar smells, and there were ten or fifteen people between him and the two not-quite-right photographers.

Khan held out an arm to keep one of Natalie's friends from getting into the front passenger seat.

"That's my spot," he told him. "You ride in the back or in the other car."

The kid moved off to the second waiting car. Khan closed the rear passenger door and lowered himself into the front seat next to the driver. He made sure to keep eye contact with the two fishy photographers, just so they'd be aware they had been noticed.

I don't know who you are, but I see you, he thought. As they rolled off past the squealing crowd of fans, one of the photographers lowered his camera, pointed a finger, and cocked his thumb like the hammer of a gun.

Pow.

Khan's tiger half didn't sweat. This was something that he hadn't known about canines and felines before his card had turned. Cats and dogs shed excess heat through panting and through the pads on their paws. If he dressed to keep his tiger side cool, his human side was too cold, and if he dressed to keep his human half warm, his tiger half was too insulated. Finding a happy medium was difficult even on temperate days. In the middle of a nightclub, the heat from hundreds of bodies contesting with the building's inadequate air conditioning, it was downright impossible. Half an hour after the start of Natalie's first engagement in Berlin, Khan's button-down was soaked in sweat. He was standing close to his charge, shielding access to the booth where she was holding court with her entourage, while the crowd was mingling and hopping around on the floor to relentless Europop tunes.

The new nightclub was ostentatiously exclusive. All the patrons wore designer clothes and expensive watches, and Khan was sure that the cocaine being done in the bathrooms was high-grade stuff. He wasn't much into pop culture these days, but even he recognized some of the celebrities lounging in the booths that surrounded the dance floor. One of the nearby booths held a group that was even more conspicuous than Natalie and her entourage. In the center of it was a playboy princeling from the one of the oil-rich Gulf states that had been swallowed up by the Caliphate, someone whose face was featured in the tabloids on a regular basis. He was tan and toned, with a thousand-dollar pair of sunglasses on his face and a Swiss watch on his wrist that was worth more than Khan's car. Khan watched him trying to get Natalie's attention for a little while. Finally, the princeling got out of his booth and walked over to Natalie's corner, two bodyguards in dark suits immediately trailing three feet behind and on either side of him.

"Hold up there, sport," Khan said and held out an arm to bar the way into the booth. The princeling looked at him with an irritated expression. He turned toward his bodyguards and said something that made them laugh, and Khan let out a slow breath and flexed his muscles to get ready for a tussle.

"It's okay," Natalie shouted from behind. "You can let him in. Only him, though."

"You heard the lady," Khan said to the princeling, who still regarded him like he was something rotting the dogs had dragged in. The princeling waved his hand curtly over his shoulder without turning around, and his bodyguards took a step back.

The princeling squeezed past Khan and sat down in the booth with Natalie's group. For a while, they talked and drank together. Khan tried to ignore the insipid conversation while the princeling's bodyguards tried to ignore him. Like their boss, they wore their sunglasses inside, which made them look like jackasses.

Khan smelled the trouble flaring up just as it started behind him, that unmistakable whiff of adrenaline and high emotions right before a fight breaks out. He started to turn around, and something liquid splashed the back of his neck and the tiger side of his face. One of the girls had voiced her anger at the princeling and emptied a drink in his direction, and some of the splash had hit Khan instead. From the way the prince's hand recoiled from Natalie's friend Melissa, Khan could guess the reason for the sharp and sudden outrage. And then, almost reflexively, the princeling back-handed Melissa. The strike was hard enough to make her head rock back. Blood came gushing from her nose, and the metallic smell of it permeated the air.

Next to Khan, one of the princeling's bodyguards caught on to the action and tried to wedge himself past Khan and between Melissa and the princeling. Khan yanked him back by the collar of his suit and tossed him away from the booth and onto the dance floor, where he fell on his ass with a yelp and skidded backward a foot or two.

Behind Khan, the second bodyguard let out a curse in his own language and reached underneath his suit coat. Khan seized the hand holding the pistol with his tiger hand and wrapped his fingers firmly around the wrists of the other man. The second bodyguard dropped the gun with a strangled yelp. Khan caught it with his human hand before it could hit the floor.

"No guns," he growled.

The pistol was one of the new lightweight European cop guns, with a frame made of reinforced polymer. He let go of the bodyguard's wrist, transferred the gun to his tiger hand, and crushed it right in front of the man's face. The frame buckled in his fist and then started spilling little metal tabs and springs from its insides. Khan hit the other man in the face with the barrel assembly. He shook the plastic bits of the frame to the floor and flung the broken gun parts aside as the second bodyguard dropped to the floor.

With Khan blocking the exit of the booth, the princeling scrambled over the back of the seating corner to get away. Khan took two long steps and hauled him up by the back of his shirt. The princeling yelped as Khan spun him around and tossed him onto the seat. Then he wrapped his tiger hand around the princeling's neck and extended his claws just a little, enough to let the man know that hasty movements were now unwise. Khan smelled fear coming from him in big olfactory waves, and his heart was racing. It felt like holding a panicked rabbit by the ears. Next to them, Natalie's entourage was in a headless, noisy panic, trying to stay out of Khan's way and tend to Melissa at the same time.

"Touch them again, and I'll rip your head off, you little chickenshit," Khan said to the wild-eyed princeling. He finished the statement with a low, rasping growl and was rewarded with the smell of fresh piss wafting up from below the man's waistline. Natalie's friends were annoying as hell, but they were his charges, and men who hit women ranked lower on Khan's vermin scale than plague-carrying sewer rats.

He lifted the princeling off his feet and threw him toward the first bodyguard, who was still sitting on the floor and dusting off his dignity. The two men collided hard and went down in a tangle of limbs.

Khan closed a hand around Natalie's arm and pulled her to her feet.

"We have to go," he said. "Right now."

He was glad to see that Natalie seemed too shaken to argue, because he didn't want to have to carry her out of the place like a sack of playground sand. Her retinue rushed to follow when they saw that Khan wasn't stopping to wait, and they hurried across the dance floor toward the exit.

They were halfway across the floor when the doors of the nightclub opened and half a dozen angry-looking guys in suits pushed their way into the crowd. All of them were wearing ear pieces and grim expressions. The crowd around the periphery of the dance floor was densely packed, and the newcomers were pushing people aside with force as they came through. Khan turned and looked around for the fire exits. Things were about to get complicated, and Khan didn't want to wait around to see whose side the cops would take.

There was a bouncer stationed at the fire exit. He stepped in front of Khan and his group as they approached the door and held up his hand in the universal "hold it" gesture. Khan wasted no time trying to figure out language commonalities. He grabbed the bouncer by the wrist of his outstretched hand and yanked him aside. The bouncer stumbled and went to one knee with an indignant yelp. Then he got back to his feet and lunged at Khan, who stopped him cold by raising his tiger hand and extending his claws in front of the man's face.

"Don't," Khan snarled.

The bouncer blanched and backed off. Khan pushed the exit open, and the fire alarm started blaring instantly. The noise felt like a physical thing assaulting his ears despite the earbuds that kept the volume to tolerable levels for Khan, and once they were out in the cooler evening air of the street and the decibel level subsided a little, he almost sighed with relief. Behind them, the bouncer appeared in the door and yelled something in angry German, but made no move to follow them.

God, I fucking hate nightclubs, Khan thought.

Outside, Khan led the group away from the nightclub's back entrance, which proved to be a more difficult task than putting the princeling's bodyguards on their asses. Natalie was surprisingly helpful and collected. She was propping up Melissa and holding a wad of tissues underneath the other girl's nose. Melissa and the two boys, however, acted like they had just survived a flaming plane crash. After the tenth high-pitched *"Oh my God!"* in fifty meters, Khan lost his patience.

"Would you shut up," he told them. "She got slapped in the face, not shot in the head. Now move your asses before someone sends those cops after us."

"He broke my fucking nose!" Melissa wailed, her exclamation only slightly muffled by the tissues Natalie was pressing against her face to catch the blood.

"We'll have the front desk at the hotel call an ambulance," Natalie offered. Melissa glared at Khan, but kept pace with the group.

Khan never used valet services. He had parked their rented

luxury SUV in a garage half a block away from the nightclub. He rushed his charges to the garage as fast as he felt they could go without having to carry Melissa, who was still acting like someone had cut off half her face. The club was in a hip part of the city, and the sidewalks were still busy with foot traffic, but most people gave Khan and his group a wide berth.

He led everyone up the staircase onto the rooftop parking deck and had them get into their SUV. When it was Melissa's turn to board, he held her back and turned her to face him.

"Let me see that nose," he said. She grimaced and lowered the tissue wad she had been pressing against her nose for the last five minutes. The tissue had some red splotches on it, but the trickle of blood coming from her nostrils had already stopped. Khan had seen a lot of busted noses over the years, and hers was as straight as it had been on the plane yesterday.

"That's not broken," he told her. "He just gave you a little nosebleed, that's all. Now let's get out of here."

The parking garage had three levels, with a ramp setup that required Khan to make a full circumnavigation of every deck before descending to the one below it. It was all ninety-degree turns, and the traffic lanes were narrower than the ones in American parking garages, so Khan had to take extra care every time he took a turn with the big seven-seat SUV they had rented. Back home, the size of it would have been nothing out of the ordinary, but over here, it felt like he was driving a monster truck.

He was making yet another right-hand turn at the end of a downward ramp when he saw headlights coming at them from the right. The strike was perfectly timed. Even with his reflexes, he had no chance to react and get the SUV out of the way of the other car, which had been shielded from his view by the concrete wall to the right of the ramp. Before he could even yell a warning, the other car plowed into their SUV. It struck the front of the car and caved in the passenger door. Khan felt the SUV lurching to the left with the force of the impact. To their left, the wall of the garage's lower level wasn't far away, and the driver's side of the SUV slammed into it with the dull crunch of metal on concrete. Behind Khan, Natalie and her entourage shrieked in unison.

The look of tense concentration on the face of the other driver told Khan that this was an ambush, not an accident. The SUV was pinned in a sideways vise between the wall and the front of the other car. To his left, the concrete wall kept Khan from opening his door, and to his right, the other car's bumper had dented in the passenger-side door.

"Get down," he shouted at Melissa and her crew. He made a fist with his tiger hand and punched out the spiderwebbed windshield of the SUV. Khan sliced his seatbelt in half with one claw and climbed out onto the hood.

A second car pulled up behind the one that had rammed them into the wall and came to a stop with squealing tires. All the doors seemed to open at once, and several people came rushing around the first car and toward the SUV. Khan leapt over the hood of the car that had rammed them and placed himself in front of the right rear passenger door of the SUV. Someone in the SUV tried to open the door from the inside, and he pushed it shut again.

"Stay there," he shouted through the glass. "Call the cops. Number's one-one-zero."

He figured they'd send their biggest bruiser against him first, and the attackers did not disappoint. The guy who lunged at him was clearly a wild card. He was easily as tall as Khan and looked half again as heavy, with arms that were as wide around as Khan's thighs. His face was dark gray, the skin ashen and rough like the bark on an ancient tree. Khan dodged a massive gnarled fist and raked his claws across the man's side. It felt like taking a swipe at the trunk of a Pacific redwood. Then Tree Guy swung his arm around and caught Khan in a backhand that sent him flying over the hood of the attackers' car. He tumbled across the dirty concrete of the garage deck and crashed into a parked car, taking out a taillight in the process. Khan scrambled back to his feet. His right arm felt like it had been smacked with a railroad tie.

In front of him, Tree Guy hooked one of his huge hands underneath the wheel well of the car Khan had sailed over. Then he lifted the car off its front wheels and pushed it out of his way in a motion that almost looked casual. His companions seemed content with letting Tree Guy do the heavy lifting of the fight. They were all over the rental car now. One of them yanked on the handle of the one door that was undamaged and reachable. When the door didn't open, he flicked open a collapsible steel baton and swung it at the window, which cracked into a spiderweb on the first blow. Tree Guy wedged himself through the gap he had created between the cars and walked toward Khan with heavy, unhurried steps.

Khan extended his tiger arm to one side and let his claws pop out with a flick of his wrist. The flick wasn't a necessity, but it always made him feel like he was getting ready for serious business, like pushing the button on a switchblade. Usually, even the big mob bruisers flinched at the sight of Khan's curved three-inch claws, but Tree Guy's expression didn't change a bit. Khan bellowed a roar, and one of the nearby parked cars started bleating its alarm as if in fearful protest.

So you're strong but slow, Khan thought. *I can work around that.*

His right arm was out of commission, but his legs still worked fine. Khan tensed his muscles and jumped sideways just as Tree Guy was about to reach him. He landed on the hood of the wailing car fifteen feet away, then pushed himself off for another leap toward the rental. The unknown goons had succeeded in smashing the rear passenger door's window. Khan landed on three of his four extremities right behind the two men who were now fumbling to get the door open. He grabbed one of them by the collar of his shirt and yanked him away from the car as hard as he could. The man flew backward with a yelp, arms flailing.

The other man was still holding the baton he had used to smash the window. He barked an obvious obscenity in some Slavic language—Russian, or maybe Ukrainian—and lashed out with the baton. Khan had expected a swing, and the straight jab aimed at his chest took him by surprise. Even with his reflexes, he barely managed to deflect the jab, his claws clicking against the hard steel of the baton. The other man didn't drop the weapon. Instead, he pulled it back and brought it down on Khan's hand. The pain shot all the way from his hand up to his elbow, and Khan roared again. He made a fist and drove it into the other man's face as hard as he could. Baton Guy's head rocked back and smacked into the door frame of the rental car, and he went down hard and dropped to the ground with a muffled thudding sound. His baton dropped from his hand and clattered away on the concrete.

Khan sensed the blow aimed at him from behind and ducked out of the way just in time. Tree Guy's arm barely missed the top of his head, whistling by so close that it ruffled his hair. Then the swing landed against the upper frame of the car door and crunched into it hard enough to rock the vehicle on its suspension and dent the roof in by half a foot.

Tackling Tree Guy was only marginally less futile than swiping at him. Khan went low and put all his bodyweight into the move, three hundred pounds of enhanced feline strength, but he only managed to rock his opponent back on his heels. Tree Guy's right arm came down, and Khan aborted his tackling attempt and rolled out of the way to avoid getting his spine pulverized. The last goon still standing decided to join the fray. He came around the back of the attackers' car and closed in on Khan.

"He is stronger than you. You will not beat him," the goon said in heavily accented English. Khan saw that he was holding a knife.

"Don't have to beat him," Khan snarled. "Just you."

Tree Guy was almost upon him again, so Khan advanced against the last goon, who widened his stance a little and planted his feet. The utter lack of fear or concern from these men was a little unnerving. At home, nine out of ten bush league crooks would turn tail and run at the sight of his claws and teeth, and these guys stood their ground against him in a hand-to-hand melee, armed with nothing but blades and impact weapons so far. They had to be supremely stupid or very sure of themselves.

With the blade in the game, Khan felt free to bring his own cutlery into play. The goon feigned a jab with his left, and Khan obliged the ruse by raising his tiger arm to protect his face. When the man's other hand flashed forward to plant the blade between his ribs, Khan brought his arm back down in a short and swift arc that was perfectly timed. The knife bounced to the ground, along with two or three of the goon's fingers, and the blow forced him to one knee.

Nearby, the sound of distant police sirens reached Khan's ears. He allowed himself a small grin. Another minute, and the German cops would be all over this parking garage.

Two rock-hard, unyielding hands grabbed him by the fabric of his jacket collar and the waistband of his slacks. He flung the elbow of his good arm backward in an arc and smashed it into Tree Guy's head, but to no effect. His feet left the ground as Tree Guy lifted him up. Khan felt like a kitten someone was shaking by the scruff. Tree Guy lifted him over his head seemingly without effort. Then Khan was airborne. He tumbled in midair, trying to roll around to land on his feet, but the boost he had just gotten was so violently forceful and sudden that even his cat reflexes failed him this time. He sailed over a long row of cars and smashed into the side of a minivan, and the impact knocked all the breath out of him.

When he came to a rest on the glass-strewn garage deck, all his body's warning lights seemed to be going off in his brain at once. He rasped a cough and tasted blood. The car alarms and the police sirens were still blaring, but everything sounded distant now, weak and faded, as if he had stuffed his ears with cotton balls. He tried to draw in a deep breath and muster the will to get up again, but the excruciating pain shooting through his chest made him abandon that impulse. People were shouting somewhere nearby, but he couldn't make out the words. Somewhere in the noise, Khan thought he heard Natalie's voice. Then there was the sound of slamming car doors and squealing tires. He tried to will himself to get to his feet, but his body refused to obey. When darkness finally washed over his consciousness, it felt almost comforting.

Khan woke up to the scent of alcohol and the sharp pain of something piercing the skin of his left arm. He tried to jerk the arm away from the source of the pain, but found that he couldn't move it. When he opened his eyes, he saw that he was strapped down on a gurney, and a medic in an orange uniform was trying to insert a needle into his arm. The medic pulled the needle back when he saw Khan move and said something in German.

"Don't speak the language," Khan mumbled. His arm still hurt like hell, but it no longer felt like it had been worked over with a sledgehammer. He hadn't lost consciousness since he had been sick with the effects of the virus when his card turned.

"Don't move," the medic replied in English. "You have broken bones and a head injury. Your spine may be injured too."

Khan flexed his leg muscles against the pressure of the restraining straps. The buckles creaked under the force.

"Nothing wrong with my spine. Arm's gonna be fine in a few hours too. Save your meds."

"But you are badly injured. You may die without treatment."

"I'm not dead," Khan said. "That means I'll be good as new tomorrow morning. Now take that needle away and unbuckle these straps before I tear them to shit and you have to buy new ones."

The medic looked from Khan to someone else nearby and rattled off a few words in rapid-fire German. A moment later, a police officer walked up to them and looked down at Khan.

"You wish to decline treatment? We can not be held responsible if you do."

"I'll be fine. I'm a fast healer."

The policeman exchanged a few words with the medic, who proceeded to unbuckle the gurney straps. Khan sat up and swung his legs over the edge to test them. Everything hurt, but nothing seemed broken below the waist. He put some weight on his feet and stood up with a grunt. The policeman and the medic took an involuntary step back as Khan unfolded himself to his full six foot three. He looked around to see that the parking deck was lousy with cops. There were at least a dozen of them, and several blue-and-silver police cars were clogging up the passageways of the deck and the nearby ramp, blue emergency lights flashing and radios squawking. The rental SUV stood alone and abandoned, its side dented in from the collision. The car that had rammed them was nowhere to be seen. Khan walked over to the SUV with slow and careful steps. It felt like someone had rubbed down his legs with broken glass, but he had gotten hurt in enough fights to know that he was already on the mend. The medic began to gather his supplies, but the police officer followed him, staying three steps behind.

"There were four people in this car. Two women and two men. Where are they?"

"There were two men and a woman in the car when we arrived. They have been taken to the hospital already."

Khan didn't have to ask which member of Natalie's entourage was missing.

"You're looking for a dark blue luxury sedan with front damage," he said. "I didn't see the brand because the front end was already in my passenger door by the time I saw the car. They kidnapped my client. Natalie Scuderi."

"You will have to come with us to explain what happened and answer some questions."

"Am I under arrest?" Khan asked.

"Not yet," the officer said. He looked over to his colleagues, and Khan saw that he was nervously fingering his duty belt in the vicinity of his holstered pistol. "But we must insist."

The last thing Khan wanted to do right now was to play twenty questions. Natalie's trail was getting colder by the minute, and he had no time to waste. But there were lots of German cops in shouting range now, and they all carried guns and wore dour expressions. There was no way to decline the directive without starting to hurt people, and getting arrested for assault on police officers wouldn't do a damn thing to get Natalie back either. He let out an annoyed sigh.

"Lead the way, then," he said.

It wasn't an arrest, but the whole affair wasn't just a cordial exchange of information either. As soon as the German cops brought Khan into their police headquarters, a pair of officers in body armor appeared by his side and escorted him to an interview room, submachine guns held loosely by their sides but obviously ready for use. As they walked through the halls of the police station, passing officers glanced at Khan and gave him a wide berth. When they reached the room, Khan's escort had him sit down on one of the chairs in front of the table inside. Then they took positions on either side of the door. Two people in plainclothes walked in and sat down on the other side of the table. Neither offered to shake his hand when they introduced themselves, and they started asking him a barrage of questions.

Half an hour later, Khan started to reconsider his earlier decision to comply without violence. The two cops across the table—he had forgotten their names almost right away—seemed to have a fetish for hearing the same information reiterated in twenty different ways. He was sure they were taking a page out of the police interview playbook, to see if they could catch him in contradictions and poke holes in his story, but Khan grew increasingly irritated.

"And you did not know these people at all?" one of the cops asked. "You had never seen them before since you got to Germany?"

"No."

"What about the person you said was a"—he consulted the notepad in front of him—"joker-ace? The man who looked like his skin was made up of tree bark?"

"No," Khan said. "Trust me, I would know if I had. Bastard picked me up and threw me fifty feet. Haven't met a lot of joker-aces who can do that. Look, I love chatting with you fellas, but you really ought to be out there looking for the people who kidnapped Miss Scuderi. I think you won't much enjoy the media shitstorm that's about to come down on you."

"The criminal police are already investigating," the other cop said. "We have set up a dragnet to look for the car you have described, and for anyone matching the description of Frau Scuderi. But in the meantime, we have to be certain that you are telling the truth."

"Of course I'm telling the fucking truth. What, you think I helped kidnap my own client?"

The cop shrugged and smiled in an apologetic way that seemed entirely insincere.

"I don't know how such things work where you come from, but over here, that would not be unusual. We have many organized crime groups. Germans, Russians, Italians. Chechens, Serbians, Turks. There is a lot of competition. People cross over sometimes. For money or power."

Khan felt the blood rise in his face.

"I've been in this business for ten years. The people I deal with, they go by reputation. Loyalty is everything to them. You betray their trust, you end up on your knees in a junkyard somewhere while they take your fingers off with a fucking pipe cutter. That's how such things work where I come from."

He extended his claws a little and drummed them on the table in front of him. They made a hard tapping sound that seemed very loud in the small room.

"Arrest me and inform the American embassy so they can send someone over. Or get off my ass and let me get back to my job. I have a missing client, and I don't see you people doing jack shit to find her."

The two cops exchanged a few sentences in German. Khan wondered what he'd do if they took him up on his challenge and locked him up. Finally, one of the cops rapidly clicked his pen a few times and dropped it on the notepad in front of him.

"You are not under arrest, Herr Khanna. But you will need to keep yourself available for further interviews. We have asked for assistance from our colleagues at the federal office for special abilities. They are sending someone from Kassel to talk to you."

"Great. Tell them they can find me at the Hotel Adlon. If I'm not out and about."

The two plainclothes officers got up from their chairs, and Khan rose with them.

"You will find that we here in Germany do not like it when people try to bring justice about on their own. Leave the police work to the police."

"No worries," Khan said and flexed his tiger hand slowly. "I'm just going to do some tourist stuff. Sightseeing. Maybe get myself some souvenirs."

They'd handed him his stuff back when they released him, and his phone never stopped buzzing with incoming messages on the entire half-hour taxi ride back to the hotel. In her Rikki persona, Natalie was a big enough deal in the pop culture scene that her violent kidnapping would make front-page news on both sides of the Atlantic. Back home in Chicago, they were seven hours behind Berlin time, which meant the news clips reporting on the incident would make the evening broadcasts.

When they were almost back at the hotel, his phone chirped again. This time, it wasn't the chime of a message, but an incoming call. Very few people had his mobile number, and those who did were people who wouldn't react well to being ignored. The caller ID was "unknown," but that wasn't unusual. A lot of his clients were allergic to easy identification. He swiped to accept the call.

"Hello," he said.

"The fuck have you been," Sal Scuderi said, in a voice that was just one or two decibels short of a shout. "I've been trying to get a hold of you for hours. What the hell happened?"

"The German cops had my phone," Khan replied. "Event last night went sideways, and we got jumped in the parking garage when we left the venue."

"They said you were the best in the business. That's why I fucking hired you. To keep shit like this from happening."

"It was three nats and a joker-ace," Khan replied. "They knew what they'd be up against. And they brought just the right guy for the job."

"I don't give a flying fuck if they hired Mighty Joe Young for the job. You were supposed to keep her safe. You find my girl and bring her home. If you want to ever get another job in this town, you bring her home and fix what you fucked up."

Khan gritted his teeth. Scuderi was an insurance salesman, not a mob boss, but plenty of people in the Chicago scene relied on his services. Losing the man's daughter on the job would be a fatal black mark on his professional resume. Khan had never lost a client, and he wasn't about to start a habit.

"I'm going to find her," he said. "That was a kidnapping, not a hit. They'll come to someone with a ransom demand. Makes no sense any other way."

"They already did," Scuderi said. "I got a message this morning. They want thirty million. I have forty-eight hours to come up with the cash."

"Did you take it to the Feds?"

"Fuck the Feds. The message said they'll cut her up into small pieces if I involve the cops. Whatever you do, don't fucking tell the Germans anything."

"I may have to," Khan said. "Not sure I can do this by myself. This isn't Chicago. I don't know the local players."

"Then find someone who does," Scuderi said. "You've worked for enough high rollers around here. Gotta be some favors you can call in. Just don't run your mouth. If they kill my little girl, you're going to be in a world of shit."

"I'll get her back. They won't . . . oh, fuck me." The car had slowed down and taken a turn into the driveway of the hotel, and Khan looked up to see a throng of people under the awning of the entrance, most wielding cameras or microphones.

"What is it?"

"I just got to the hotel. Fucking reporters everywhere. I'll call you back as soon as I can."

Khan ended the call, glad for an excuse to exit the conversation. If he wanted to find Natalie and determine who snatched her, he would need a clear head and no distractions.

The throng of reporters streamed around him as soon as he stepped out of the taxi. A dozen different people stuck microphones in his direction and asked him questions in both German and English. He tried to ignore them and quickly make his way to the entrance, but he found his way blocked by people and camera lenses. His frustration manifested itself in an unhappy growl deep in his throat, and the path ahead magically cleared enough for him to pick up his stride. The crowd of newspeople moved with him, but nobody tried to block his way again, and they all kept at least an arm's length away.

Natalie's talent agency had rented a huge three-bedroom suite on the top floor of the hotel. Khan half-expected to find the place tossed and ransacked, either by the cops or the people who had taken Natalie, but when he walked in, it looked just the way it had when they left it. He went into his own bedroom and changed out of his suit, which was now in tatters and smelled of medical disinfectant. When he peeled his sweaty and torn-upclothes off his body, he looked at himself in the mirror. The fight with Tree Guy had left its mark in the shape of a dozen bruises of various sizes and colors, from light red to angry purple. Khan's wild card had given him the gift of rapid regeneration and recovery from injuries, but for some reason the quick healing factor didn't extend to bruises, which took just as long to disappear as before. He stepped into the bathroom and turned on the shower, cranking the temperature adjustment as hot as it would go, then ran the water until the room was filled with steam. The scalding hot water hurt his bruises as if someone was punching him all over again, but the sensation wasn't unwelcome. It kept his anger simmering, which was where he wanted it so he could bring it to a boil quickly.

It felt good to be in a clean suit and smell like himself again. Khan went through his luggage and took stock of the gear he had brought. There were no weapons in his bag, but even if he had brought any, he doubted that anything in his gun safe back home would make a dent in Tree Guy, who had shrugged off slashes from Khan's claws that could have gutted a steer. He remembered the blows the other joker-ace had dished out, and the feeling of getting tossed over several rows of parked cars like a half-eaten bag of chips. This was not a fight he'd be able to win with his claws or teeth, but his brain wasn't serving up any solutions to the problem, and the bag in front of him held no answers either.

Out in the suite, Khan heard the soft click of the main door lock and the voices of Natalie's friends. They stopped their chatter when they saw him emerge from the bedroom. It took him a few seconds to recall the names of the two boys: Travis and Eli. Travis was wearing a large adhesive bandage above his eyebrow.

"You guys all right?" he asked.

"We're okay, man," Eli answered. "They didn't do anything to us. Travis just got cut by some glass from the window. But they took Natalie."

"No shit," Khan said. "Tell me what you saw after they smashed in your window."

Between the three of them, Khan was able to assemble a sketchy picture of what had gone on while he was busy getting the tar whomped out of him by Tree Guy. The attackers had bashed in the rear passenger window, dragged Natalie and her three friends out of the car, and made off only with Natalie, who had struggled against her abductors while they had stuffed her into the back of a second car that had pulled up while Khan was tied up fighting.

"Did they say anything?"

"Not to us," Melissa said. "They were just talking to each other. Just a few words."

"Any idea what language?" Khan asked.

Melissa and the boys shook their heads. He sighed and sat down on the couch next to them. Everything about this shouted mob hit to Khan. But why would the foreign mob here in Berlin have any interest in a socialite rich girl from Chicago? Kidnappings were usually high-risk, low-reward schemes thought up by desperate bush league amateurs, not pulled off by professional enforcers.

"I need to find out where they took Natalie," Khan said. "If any of you have any ideas or remember anything else, tell me now. I want to know all the details. Even if you think it's not important."

"Have you tried her phone?" Melissa said.

Khan shook his head.

"That's the first thing they would have taken from her. Unless they're dumber than dirt. Everyone knows you can track a cell phone's location."

"Well, let's see anyway." Melissa pulled out her phone and tapped away at the screen. "We use that friend tracker thing. So we can find each other when we're out together."

Khan watched her mess around with her phone for a few

moments. There was virtually no chance the kidnappers would have forgotten to strip Natalie of her phone, but he was fresh out of ideas at the moment, so he decided to humor Melissa. As expected, she let out a disappointed little huff and showed Khan the screen of her phone. It showed a map, and the last location of Natalie's phone was marked with a gray dot. Khan took the phone and zoomed in on the map to see that the spot where her phone had last connected to the data network was the parking garage where they had gotten jumped.

"They turned it off. Or probably smashed it right there," Khan said.

"Hey, I wonder if they got her watch too," Eli said.

"What watch?"

"She bought one of those watches that connect to your phone. So she can track her workouts. You know what I'm talking about."

"I really don't," Khan said. "But go on."

"It's like a computer on your wrist. You can even make calls with it."

"Does it need the phone nearby to work?"

Eli shook his head. "Not the kind she's got."

"Can you track that thing?" Khan asked Melissa. She looked at her phone's screen again and shook her head.

"It's not on here."

"You gotta be the owner," Eli contributed. "It's set that way so you can track down your stuff if you lose it."

"Well, she's indisposed," Khan said.

"But her laptop's here," Melissa said. She got up and walked over to the bedroom the girls shared. A moment later, she came back with the laptop Khan had seen Natalie use on the plane. She handed it to Khan, who opened it and put it on the coffee table in front of him. The excitement that had been welling up inside of him died down again when he saw the login screen.

"Fuck. It's locked."

"I know her password," Eli offered. "I set up all her tech stuff for her. Unless she changed it recently."

"Give it a shot," Khan said. He turned the laptop around and slid it in front of Eli, who hunched over the keyboard and started typing away.

"Got it," he said.

"Holy shit." Khan grinned at him. "So you do have some useful skills. Now I'm glad I didn't chuck you out of the plane on the way here."

The tracking map on the laptop looked like a bigger version of the one on Melissa's phone. Eli logged in, toggled a few settings, and turned the laptop so Khan could see the screen.

"There's her phone," he said. "Same place. And there's her watch. It's gray too. If it was turned on right now, it'd be blue."

The dot that marked the position of Natalie's watch was right in front of a large square building labeled as Flakturm.

"What the fuck is a *Flakturm*," Khan asked. Eli took the question as a directive and did a search, then scrolled through the results.

"Whoa. It's a thing left over from the war. Big concrete tower, for air defense."

"You mean like a bunker?"

"Look." Eli brought up an image. The structure looked square and brutal. The concrete was stained and dirty from decades of weather exposure. There were no windows or other external reference points, but judging by the height of the trees lining the pathways around the building, he guessed the concrete monstrosity was at least six floors high.

"Does it say what's in that thing?"

Eli closed the picture and scrolled through a few more pages.

"It says there's a museum inside now. Some artist commune. And a nightclub. Looks pretty cool, actually."

Something tickled Khan's tiger instincts, and he felt the hair on his neck bristle. Over by one of the windows, there was a soft scraping noise. Khan looked up and saw a hint of movement in the corner of the window, like a fluttering drape. Then it was gone. He heard another sound, the faintest ticking of something hard on metal, this one from above. Their suite was on the top floor, and there was nothing above them but the roof.

Khan got up and walked over to the window. The windows in their suite stretched from floor to ceiling and opened onto a narrow balcony that ran the width of the suite. He made a shushing gesture at Melissa and the boys. Then he opened one of the windows and stepped out onto the balcony. The night air was pleasantly cool and carried thousands of city smells with it. In front of the hotel, on the other side of Pariser Platz, the columns of the Brandenburg Gate glowed in the darkness, illuminated by dozens of spotlight fixtures.

Khan turned to look up at the edge of the roof and sniffed the air again. There was a presence up there, something bigger than an enterprising raccoon. Something was up there in the darkness, quietly breathing.

The part of the roof above the top floor was a sloping face of green-tinged copper sheeting, topped by a rail. The rail was just at the limit of Khan's vertical leaping range. He flexed his leg muscles a few times and extended his claws. The copper roof slope was almost too smooth for him to get traction, but he managed to get a hand on the rail at the top. He hauled himself up and dropped onto the roof.

The rooftop was flat and lined with rubberized material. Every few dozen feet, Khan saw the dome-shaped bubbles of transparent skylights. There were two small sheds in the middle of the roof that looked like maintenance shacks, and a large tripod antenna was anchored between them. In the darkness above the sheds, Khan saw a shape crouched on an antenna crossbar, twenty feet high.

"Don't make me jump up there and pluck you off that thing," he growled.

"Good evening, Herr Khanna," the shape said, in a dry and reedy voice that put the hairs on the back of Khan's neck on edge again.

"So you know who I am. Not too hard to figure out, I guess."

"We know who you are. We have been keeping an eye on you ever since you entered the country."

"Who's *we*?"

He walked closer to the base of the antenna to decrease the

range between himself and the stranger, to improve his chances at making good on his threat and snatching him out of the air if needed. The rooftop visitor shrugged. A pair of leathery wings unfolded and blotted out the stars of the night sky behind him. He stepped off his perch and landed in front of Khan silently, with just a single flap of those enormous wings.

Close up, he made Khan's hairs stand up even more. He was clearly a joker-ace. His body was squat and short, and covered with coarse black hair except for his wings, which looked like leather sails. Even his eyes were uniformly black, and when he opened his mouth to speak again, Khan saw that his teeth were pointed and very white, the only part of his body that wasn't the color of spilled ink at midnight.

"I have several colleagues in the area, and they would not like it if you tried to hurt me," the stranger said.

"I won't pick a fight if you don't," Khan replied. "Again—who the fuck is we?"

"We are with BDBF," the visitor said. "*Bundesamt für Besondere Fähigkeiten*. The federal office for special abilities. What you at home call S.C.A.R.E."

"I just flew in from Kassel, and boy, are my arms tired," Khan said with a chuckle. The man in front of him either didn't get the joke or wasn't in a jovial mood, because he merely cocked his head quizzically.

"My name is Fledermaus," he said. "And five thousand meters above us, my colleague Überschall is keeping an eye on things from above. Rest assured that he can be here very quickly."

"Fledermaus," Khan repeated. "And Überschall. Sounds like the title for a sitcom."

"I am not familiar with that word."

"Never mind. They said you'd come. Are you here to ask me questions about my client's kidnapping, too?"

"You claim there was an enhanced individual involved. So far, the only such person confirmed to be involved was you. That is why the Berlin police asked us to assist."

"There was someone else," Khan said. "Three nats—regular

people. And one wild card. Big, strong guy, looked like a tree. Bark for skin and everything. He held me off while the nats grabbed my client."

"Looked like a tree," Fledermaus repeated.

"Yes, a tree. Rock-hard skin. And strong as shit. He threw me over a whole row of parked cars. Couldn't make a scratch in him, not even with these."

He held out his tiger hand and extended his claws, three inches of curved black keratin knives glistening in the moonlight, then retracted them again so Fledermaus wouldn't feel threatened.

"If that is true, it would be very interesting," Fledermaus said.

"So you know the guy?"

"I have heard of him, yes. That is our main task at BDBF. To keep our eyes on people such as him. And you. But the man you speak of, he is not known to be in Germany."

"Well, unless I got beaten up by his twin brother, I'd say you're wrong. Who is he?"

"We do not know where he comes from. Some sources say he is from Ukraine. We know he works as hired muscle for many groups. Sometimes for the Chechens or the Serbians, but mostly for the Georgian mafia. They call him Mukha. The Georgian word for 'oak.'"

"Georgian mob. Super," Khan said. Back home in Chicago, the Georgians were not to be fucked with. They were not as numerous as the Russians or the long-established Polish mafia, but they had a reputation for stomach-churning violence.

"You think the Georgians took your client?"

"I'm not sure. They were Eastern European, though. I've been around that kind long enough."

"I do not think I have to warn you about these people, then," Fledermaus said. "They have no respect for the local authorities, and they are very violent. If you go after them, the police may not be able to protect you."

"The police sure weren't any help in that parking garage," Khan said. He hesitated, then decided to throw caution to the wind. Time was running short, and he couldn't shop around for allies. "Do you know anything about a local place called the Flakturm? Big, ugly concrete tower in the Tiergarten park."

Fledermaus cocked his head a little. His ears were large and pointy, with tufts of coarse black hair sprouting from the tips.

"I know of it, yes. A relic of the war. They had three of them in the city. I think this one is the only one left. Apparently it was too large to blow up. The walls are very thick."

"They say there's a museum in this one now. And a nightclub. Know anything about that?"

Fledermaus shook his head.

"I'm afraid not. I am not from Berlin, and I do not frequent nightclubs. The noise, you see." He flashed an awkward-looking smile. "But I do know that the criminal element often uses legal places such as this to cleanse the money from their other activities. The Italians use restaurants. The Arab clans have their tobacco lounges. And the Russians and Georgians—"

"Bars and clubs and gambling," Khan finished. "Same as back home."

"BDBF can only intervene in law enforcement matters if we are asked to do so by the local authorities," Fledermaus said. "I cannot help you with whatever it is you are planning to do. You are in our area of responsibility. If you commit any offenses, we will not need a request from the police to deal with you."

"That guy who looks like a tree. Mukha. You must have a file on him. Any idea if he has any weaknesses? Unofficially speaking, I mean. Since you know for sure he's not even in the country right now."

Fledermaus considered Khan's question for a moment. "Officially, I cannot help you, as I said." He smiled again in his awkward way. His teeth were very bright in the darkness. "Unofficially, I can point out that he is very much like a tree. You cannot take down a tree with claws and fists. But there are other ways."

Fledermaus shuffled to the edge of the roof and put a hand on the railing. In the light coming from the square and the Brandenburg Gate beyond, Khan saw that he was wearing some sort of high-tech ballistic armor, cut out low on the sides to make space for his enormous wings. He swung himself over the rail and looked back at Khan. "Just ask yourself, Herr Khan. If you were a tree, what would be your worst fear in life?"

Fledermaus nodded a curt goodbye and jumped off the roof. Khan walked over to the railing to watch the German joker-ace glide over Pariser Platz and soar through the space between the central columns of the Brandenburg Gate before disappearing in the darkness of the park beyond.

"Squirrel shit," Khan said into the silence.

The Flakturm was a foreign presence in the tranquility of the Tiergarten. Somehow, even the peaceful trees and meadows that surrounded it didn't mellow its massiveness or the complete lack of aesthetic concern evident in its architecture. As Khan walked toward it, he felt something like existential dread at the sight of the thing. Near the top of the tower, four round gun platforms jutted out at the corners like the leaves of a giant concrete clover leaf. It was a structure built for war, and it looked out of place here in this park in the middle of a modern, cosmopolitan city. Khan walked around it twice at a distance to get an idea of the layout, and it struck him that nobody had ever tried to pretty up that ugly block of concrete, as if they knew all these years that no coat of paint or architectural surgery could make it look inviting.

Whenever he wanted to get into a place without an invitation, Khan would scale the fire escapes and get in from the roof, or pop open a window on the way. But this place had no windows, no fire escapes, and the roof was more than a hundred feet above ground, atop sheer concrete sides without handholds or other features. There were thin concrete beams jutting out of the walls near the gun platforms, but even those were much too high for him to reach. The Flakturm truly was a fortress by design, with only one obvious way in and out. Khan watched from a distance as late-night revelers arrived and walked into the entrance vestibule, and others left and noisily made their way to the distant parking lot at the edge of the Tiergarten. Every time the front door opened, he heard a smattering of thumping electronic music. He spent half an hour looking for alternative entry points before deciding to throw plan B out the window. On the eastern horizon, the colors of the sky had started to shift from black to dark blue and purple. The best time to bust into a place was this exact time of the night, when everyone was tired and winding down, and reflexes and reaction times were at their worst.

I hope you're really in there, kid, Khan thought as he cut across the lawn and briskly walked toward the entrance vestibule.

The entrance was a set of double doors, one each on the inner and outer edges of the exterior wall. He pushed open the outer door and walked inside, past a group of club-goers on the way out. The wall of the Flakturm was at least ten feet thick, and when he walked through the second set of doors and into the foyer, the temperature dropped a dozen degrees. He pulled out his phone to confirm a hunch and saw that he had no reception. No radio signal would make it through that much concrete, which was why Natalie's watch had dropped off the map as soon as they had brought her inside.

As Eli had learned online, it was a multiuse building now. The interior looked far more welcoming than the outside. The foyer was two floors high and looked like a boutique computer store, all white wood and tasteful accent lighting. There was a broad staircase leading up to what looked like an art installation, and down to a pair of glass doors that had two broad-shouldered guys standing in front of it. Beyond the glass doors, Khan saw the reflections of flashing strobes and neon lights. On the right side of the foyer, there was a bar that had throngs of people standing in it, chatting and swilling drinks. A few of the patrons looked over at him, and some nudged their friends to draw their attention to him, but the stares were curious, not concerned. Berliners seemed used to seeing weird and unusual things.

He walked down the steps to the club. The two bouncers looked like they were unsure how to deal with him. One of them fidgeted with his lapels while the other put a hand under the jacket of his dark suit and tried to look casual about it.

"You can try to draw whatever the fuck that is," Khan said when he had reached the door. "Or you can let me in there without losing a hand."

The second bouncer removed his hand from his waistline and held it up in a placating gesture. Khan saw that he had been reaching for a pepper spray dispenser on his belt. The first bouncer opened the door for him.

"Just looking for someone," Khan said. "I won't be long."

Even at this hour, the club was packed. Dozens of people were gyrating to thumping electronic music, and dozens more were watching from the edge of the floor or hanging out in the seating groups tucked into alcoves along the periphery of the room. The air smelled like weed, spilled booze, and sweat, and the room was radiating warmth, the collective body heat of all the late-night revelers dancing and drinking and groping each other in the corners. It was everything he hated about nightclubs, turned up to maximum intensity. As Khan skirted the edge of the dance floor and walked deeper into the bowels of the club, a smoke machine hissed and spewed a stream of thick fog onto the dance floor. The cloud temporarily displaced all the awful smells of the place, and it cut visibility in the vicinity of the dance floor to three feet or less. He went to the left until he found the row of seating alcoves on that side of the room, and started to map out the periphery of the place. There had to be other exits.

It took him five minutes to find all the doors in the room. Most of them were fire exits that led to dirty concrete stairwells where people were making out or smoking joints. One was behind the bar, and Khan could see people going in and out every few seconds, carrying armfuls of glasses and empty bottles. There was only one door that was locked, secured with a keypad. He concluded that if they were hiding anything in this place, it was behind that door.

Khan looked around to see if anyone was paying attention but saw nothing except for club patrons lost in their own worlds. If the bouncers had called for backup, it hadn't found him yet. He waited until the fog machine blasted another thick cloud of water vapor onto the dance floor. Then he turned toward the door and wrapped his tiger hand around the knob.

The door was reinforced with steel liners, but Khan could max out the weight plates on the gym machines with just his feline arm, and he strained only for a moment before he wrenched the lock out of the frame with a dull crack. The doorknob came off in his hand, and he dropped it onto the ground and kicked it aside. Beyond the door, there was a long, dimly lit hallway that had more doors leading off to the left and right. He counted them: four left, four right. Then he stepped into the hallway on light feet and closed the access door behind him.

The first door to the right was a janitorial closet, shelves of cleaning materials and a bunch of mops and buckets. The first door to the left was an office, a desk with a computer screen and a filthy-looking keyboard, an ashtray overflowing with cigarette butts, and shelves with stuffed binders and untidy stacks of papers. Khan moved on to the second set of doors. Natalie wore a particular perfume, something that smelled like waving a freshly cut lilac over a warm blueberry pie, and he hoped that the whiffs of it he caught in the stale air of the hallway were not just his wishful imagination. He reached for the handle of the second door to the right and yanked it open.

Inside, three men sat around a table littered with ashtrays and bottles. There was a TV set in a corner of the room that was showing a news report. The air was thick with the smell of old cigarette smoke and body odor. One of the men turned around to see who was standing in the door, and his eyes widened. Then he muttered a curse, which got the attention of the other two.

"Shit," Khan said.

For just a moment, the space between them practically hummed with the anticipation of the impending violence. It was that split second before a fight Khan knew all too well, the moment that felt like everyone was holding their breath before committing to action. There was no way to talk these men down, and if he hesitated, he'd give them an edge. He flicked out his claws just as the first guy grabbed a bottle off the table and threw it at him. Khan jerked his head to the side, and the bottle sailed past him and smashed against the wall of the hallway behind him.

There was no grace to the fight. The room was only ten feet square and had a table and a bunch of chairs in it, and there was no way for anyone to execute any fancy maneuvers. It was like an attempted assassination in a phone booth. Two of the men pulled knives and the third swung his fist at Khan, and only his reflexes kept him from getting shanked on the spot. He recoiled from one knife and slashed at the hand holding it, then drove his fist into the face of the second knife's wielder. The bare-handed one of the group was the only one to connect with Khan. His fist cracked into Khan's eyebrow on the human side of his face, and Khan saw a burst of stars exploding in his field of view. He roared, and in the confines of the room, the sound was so loud that it made the ashtrays on the table bounce and clatter.

One of the knives was on the floor now, but the other was still in play, its owner lashing out with quick and practiced moves. Khan jerked away from the edge of the blade and bodychecked the bare-handed fighter into the TV shelf in the process, and the man went down along with the screen as the shelving collapsed. The knife made another arc and stabbed into Khan's shoulder blade, then skidded off the bone to carve open a few inches of his tiger fur. Khan slashed all five claws across the remaining knife wielder's face and neck. He stumbled backwards through the open door and collapsed in the hallway with a wet gurgling sound. The smell of blood was suddenly thick in the air.

The guy who had held the other knife was doubled over and shouting incoherently. Khan saw that his swipe at the knife hand had taken the hand off at the wrist. He picked the man up and hurled him against the concrete wall, then did it again. After the second impact against the rough concrete, his opponent crumpled to the floor and stopped his pained shouting. Maybe ten seconds had passed since Khan had turned the door handle, but he was panting for breath, and his heart was pounding like he had just run a hundred-yard dash. Blood was running down from a gash in his right eyebrow and clouding his vision, and he used the sleeve of his sport coat to wipe it out of his eye.

The man in the hallway was a mess. Khan had opened him up along the whole length of his collarbone. The puddle of blood spreading out from him was already pooling from one side of the hallway to the other. Khan wondered about the depth of the shit he was likely to find himself in over killing someone on foreign soil, even in self-defense. But he'd have to be around for them to charge him, and that was a shaky proposition right now. All it took was another room of mobsters, but ones who were packing guns instead of blades. He had come here to find Natalie, though, so Khan steeled himself and went back to opening doors.

Two of the remaining rooms were stockrooms, haphazardly loaded from floor to ceiling with boxes and crates of supplies, and thankfully devoid of armed men. Khan went to the end of the hallway, where the last two locked rooms waited. He hadn't smelled the scent of Natalie's perfume again, and for a moment, a sort of deep, dark fear gripped his mind as he convinced himself that he'd find nothing, and he would be stamping license plates in a German prison for absolutely nothing in the end.

Then his heart skipped two beats when he saw that the last door on the right had a security keypad next to the handle, just like the entry door had.

He grabbed the door handle, wrenched it down, and threw himself against the door with all the force he could muster. It popped out of the frame, spraying bits of the lock, and swung inward with the grinding sound of steel against concrete as the bottom edge of the door, now crooked in its hinges, dragged across the floor and left a chalky white scrape mark.

Natalie was sitting on a field cot on the far side of the room. There was a little table and a folding chair, and a chemical toilet in one corner. She didn't wear a gag like a kidnapping victim in a movie. They had tied her wrists and ankles to the frame of the cot with several loops of commercial plastic ties. She had her back to him but turned her head at the sound of the door busting open. He could tell that she couldn't turn far enough to make out who had just entered the room.

"Motherfuckers," Khan growled. He peeked into the hallway to make sure he wasn't about to get jumped by reinforcements. Then he rushed over to Natalie's cot.

"Are you okay, kid?"

He saw recognition in her eyes, and she murmured something, but it was slurred gibberish. Her eyes were glazed over, and she looked like she had a hard time focusing. He cursed again. They hadn't bothered with a gag because they had sedated the shit out of her to keep her quiet.

"Let's get you out of this place."

He used one of his claws to snip through the plastic ties, carefully stripping them off her wrists and tossing them to the ground one by one. When he was finished, he put his tiger arm behind her shoulders and helped her up.

"Soft," she mumbled. "'S like you're a cat."

"Half right," he said. "Can you walk?"

She swung her legs over the edge of the cot and tried to get to her feet, then stumbled sideways almost immediately. Khan caught her before she could fall, then raised her and draped his arm across her shoulder again.

"This is going to be a mess," he said. "We have to go, kiddo. Can't call the cops from in here. Gotta get outside. Come on."

He practically carried her up the hallway back to the entrance to the main part of the nightclub. She was holding on to him, but clearly out of it, and the toes of her white linen shoes touched the ground maybe three times in the entire awkward twenty-meter shuffle to the door.

Almost there, Khan told himself. *Across the dance floor, out the main doors, call the cops once we're outside.*

In the nightclub, the thumping music was still churning up the crowd. The flashing lights of the dance floor illumination painted the fog from the machine in bright streaks of red, green, and blue. He went for the most direct route to the exit, straight across the dance floor, bumping people out of the way left and right.

In the space between the dance floor and the exit door, a

familiar shape was making its way through the fog toward him: thick arms and legs, short hair on a square-looking head, beady eyes in a face that looked like it was hewn out of a petrified tree trunk. Mukha moved without hurry, but Khan knew that he would not be able to get past the bastard and through those doors, not with Natalie to safeguard.

He lowered Natalie until she was standing on her own very unsteady feet. Then he drew a deep breath and roared at Tree Guy, the loudest roar he had ever squeezed from his lungs and vocal cords. In the confines of the Flakturm, it sounded like a slowly imploding building.

That got the attention of the crowd. They retreated from his vicinity like the tide pulling away from a shoreline at the onset of ebb. Mukha didn't seem impressed, however. He kept up his infuriatingly unhurried gait, advancing without any hint of hesitation: *stomp, stomp, stomp.*

When Mukha was ten feet away, Khan reached into his sport coat and brought out the bottle he had prepared in the hotel room's bathroom before he had set out for the Flakturm. It held a mixture of gasoline, procured by Eli at a nearby service station, and high-proof alcohol, all mixed in with hand soap and a few scoops of laundry detergent. In his youth, back when Khan was still scrawny Samir Khanna, he had experimented with many flammable and explosive substances with his friends, and he hoped that he had remembered the ratios for this cocktail correctly. He granted himself the luxury of an extra second to aim. Then he hurled the bottle straight at Mukha.

The cocktail hit the other joker-ace right in the middle of his chest. The bottle shattered, and the flammable liquid inside sprayed globs and droplets on the floor in a wide arc in front of Mukha. Most of it, Khan was happy to see, remained on Mukha's body, soaking the clothes he had draped over his bulky frame. Khan reached into his pocket and pulled out one of the road flares he had brought along. He ignited it with a quick swipe on the leg of his pants. Mukha hesitated, then stopped and looked down at the sticky goop that was covering the front of his torso.

"Step aside," Khan shouted in Polish, the only Slavic language he knew. He had no idea whether Georgian had any similarities to his mother's native tongue, but he guessed that Mukha spoke Russian, and maybe he knew some other language that was similar enough to Polish to get the gist. Mukha raised his head again and looked at Khan with an unreadable expression.

"Step aside," Khan repeated, and waved the road flare for emphasis. "Or I swear I will burn you down along with this shithole. I bet you'll stay on fire for days."

Mukha's face showed no indication that he comprehended the threat, but Khan guessed the smell of gasoline and the lit flare in his hand conveyed the message clearly enough even if the guy didn't understand a fucking word of Polish after all, because a few heartbeats later, he raised his hands slowly to chest height and walked back half a dozen steps. Khan loaded up Natalie again and headed toward the exit, road flare extended toward Mukha.

We may make it out of here alive after all, he thought. But the brief glimmer of triumph he felt was extinguished a moment later, when the front door opened and four broad-shouldered guys with pissed-off expressions hurried through. They spotted Khan and Natalie, and one of them shouted something at his companions. Then he pulled out a handgun and held it low as he was advancing.

"Shit," Khan said.

He tossed the road flare in Mukha's general direction, not aiming to hit the guy but not particularly concerned whether he did. Then he scooped up Natalie and carried her over to the nearest emergency exit he had spotted earlier. He kicked the door open at a run and catapulted two of the stoners behind it into the staircase. A few people were hanging out on the stairs, and Khan barged through them, ignoring their yelled protests as he knocked them aside. He took four and five steps at once, up onto the next landing, and then up the next staircase. Below him, the door banged open again. He peered over the railing to see the four broad-shouldered goons taking up pursuit and huffing up the first set of stairs. Behind them, Mukha filled out the doorframe and followed the goons with heavy steps that kicked up cigarette butts and concrete dust. One of the armed goons looked up and spotted Khan. He raised his gun and cranked off a shot. Khan flinched back and heard the bullet smack into the concrete somewhere above his head. For the first time since he had walked through the front doors of the Flakturm, the thought came to him that he could die in here. Too many bad guys, a joker-ace who couldn't be beaten in a stand-up fight, no weapons, no allies, and now nowhere to go.

Make it up to the roof, he told himself. *Take it from there. At least the phone will work again up top.*

He raced up the stairs and the landings. Natalie's weight wouldn't have slowed him down much even under normal circumstances, and with adrenaline flooding his system, it was like she was barely there. By the time he got to the top landing on the sixth floor, their pursuers were only halfway up the stairwell.

A steel door with large rust stains marked the end of the escape path. Khan put down Natalie and threw himself against it. It took several attempts to dislodge the rusty piece of shit from the frame, but on the fourth body blow, it popped open with a sharp metallic squeal.

Outside, the night air was warm and humid. The stairwell door opened onto one of the circular gun platforms Khan had seen jutting from the top corners of the tower. The guns were gone, of course, and nothing but rust-stained concrete remained where the gun pits used to be. Khan could tell that there used to be concrete catwalks connecting the gun platforms, but someone had demolished large chunks of them, and there was nothing left to get them safely across to the next platform. He had run into a dead end, and the only way out was a hundred-foot drop they wouldn't survive. The gun platform had a waist-high concrete balustrade, and he lowered Natalie in front of it so she wouldn't fall off the roof, and away from the door so gunfire wouldn't hit her by accident.

Behind him, the pursuers were almost at the top of the staircase. If he wanted to hold them off, he'd have to fight them while they were trying to make it through the door, not when they had space to spread out and hit him from several directions.

"Call the cops," Khan told Natalie. He hoped that she was awake enough to understand what he was saying. "One-one-zero."

He handed her his phone and turned toward the door. Then he took off his sport coat to free up his range of movement, unsheathed the claws on his tiger hand, and roared a challenge at the unseen pursuers who were just now making their way onto the top staircase landing.

They didn't do him the favor of coming through the door single file and letting him pick them off one by one. Instead, the goon with the pistol stuck his head around the corner of the staircase and aimed his gun at the doorway. Khan leapt sideways as the shot rang out, losing sight of the top landing.

"Come out and let's settle this shit," he yelled through the doorway. The reply came in Georgian, and it didn't sound like they agreed with his proposal. He glanced back at Natalie, who was still looking like she had just woken up from a deep sleep.

For the next minute or two, they were at an impasse. It was a true Mexican standoff. Every time Khan stuck his head around the corner, the mobster with the gun would fire a round in his direction. He couldn't rush them without catching a bullet or two, and they couldn't come out to finish him off without getting cut to ribbons. But time was working against Khan, because he knew that with every passing moment, Mukha made his way farther up the stairs. And there was nothing he could do about it, because he had gotten them stuck in a dead-end kill trap like a fucking amateur.

Khan could smell and hear Mukha as he lumbered up onto the top landing and toward the door. He reeked of gasoline-and-soap mix, and his footsteps echoed in the staircase. Khan bared his teeth and growled. Then he backed up to the low balustrade where Natalie was still hunched and took a running start toward the door just as Mukha filled out the doorframe with his bulk. Khan put all his weight and force into a flying leap, three hundred pounds of pissed-off ballistic feline, thousands of foot-pounds of energy, and slammed his feet right into the middle of Mukha's chest.

It felt like trying to dropkick the front of a speeding truck. The shock of the impact traveled from Khan's feet to the top of his skull. He bounced off Mukha's chest and careened into the doorframe, then back out onto the gun platform, where he landed flat on his back. He turned his head to see that Mukha was on his back as well, lying in a cloud of dust a few feet inside the staircase landing.

Mukha sat up, slowly shook his head once, and started to get to his feet.

"Come on," Khan groaned. "What does it fucking take."

He fished for another road flare, but his hands couldn't find a pocket, and he remembered that he had just discarded his coat. It was on the ground by the edge of the platform, fifteen feet away. Khan stood on aching legs and staggered over to the coat, but it was too late. Mukha was already at the door again, and behind him, three mobsters brought up the rear. They followed Mukha onto the platform and fanned out behind him. One of them aimed his gun at Khan in an infuriatingly casual manner.

He flexed his leg muscles for another jump, even though he knew that he'd never take down all three men in time, not even if they didn't have fucking Mukha as a shield.

Sorry, kiddo, he thought. *I fucked this one up for both of us.*

In the cloudless early morning sky above the Flakturm, a thunderclap boomed. It seemed to come from everywhere at once, and it was so loud that it made Khan's teeth rattle. He felt the impact of something heavy landing on the gun platform behind him. Khan turned his head to see a man in a military-type flight suit straighten himself out as if he had just landed a mildly challenging acrobatic routine. The newcomer was wearing a helmet with a gold-tinted visor that made him look a bit like a robot. The helmet was white, and it bore a call sign: ÜBERSCHALL.

For a heartbeat, time seemed to be frozen.

Then the mobster with the gun raised his arm and moved the muzzle of his weapon from Khan over to the newcomer.

The guy in the flight suit clapped his hands and pushed them outward in a shoving motion. There was another thunderclap, this one so unbearably loud it made Khan roar in pain. When he looked up again, all three mobsters were on the ground, and Mukha was on his back again, twenty feet inside the staircase hallway beyond the door. This time, he didn't try to get up again.

Khan heard the soft rustling of very large wings behind him. He turned around to see Fledermaus come to a soft and gentle landing on the gun platform right near Natalie, who recoiled at the sight of the white-fanged German joker-ace.

"He's all right," Khan assured her. "He's with the good guys."

The man in the flight suit took off his helmet and ran a gloved hand through his hair, which was ash-blond and cut short in the military fashion. He looked like a runway model, blue eyes over chiseled cheekbones. When he spoke, his diction was perfect, even if his accent was so German that it made him sound like a war movie villain.

"Is everyone all right?"

"Yeah, we're okay," Khan replied. "They pumped Miss Scuderi full of sedatives. She'll need to get to a hospital, and soon."

"This is my colleague," Fledermaus said. "Major Florian Lambert, also called Überschall. Also with BDBF."

"I figured. Very nice of you to drop by," Khan said. "Could have shown up a bit sooner."

"Like I said, we were keeping an eye on things from above. Pardon my late entrance, but my colleague here is a bit faster in the air than I am."

"So you knew where we were all along?"

"We were tracking you since you left the hotel. But we are not allowed to intervene unless we have positive verification of a special abilities target."

"This oaf over there," Khan said, and nodded at the hallway where Mukha was lying. "I told you he was around."

"Unfortunately, our rules of engagement make no allowance for hearsay," Überschall said. He walked over to the goons he had knocked senseless and began to tie up their wrists with plastic restraints he fished from a pocket on his flight suit. The pistol was on the ground next to one of the mobsters. Überschall picked it up, ejected the magazine, racked the slide to clear the chamber, and fieldstripped the weapon with quick and practiced motions. Then he tossed the parts of the gun into the concrete dust. Khan watched him walk into the staircase vestibule to the spot where Mukha was laid out, still motionless.

"Not that I'm holding a grudge," Khan shouted after him. "But if that fucker moves, stick a match up his ass and let him burn until Christmas."

When the adrenaline subsided, Khan felt utterly drained. He sat down next to Natalie while Überschall played field medic and checked her overall condition. Now that the fight was over, the top of the Flakturm was an oddly peaceful place. The sun had started to rise above the eastern horizon, painting the sky in shades of deep purple and orange. Down below, life continued as if nothing had happened. Khan heard the laughter and chatter from nightclub patrons as they left and made their way through the park, and all around them, the city was starting to stir from its brief slumber.

"What's going to happen to Mister Woody over there?" Khan asked Fledermaus and nodded in the direction of the unconscious Mukha.

"He did not register with the authorities when he entered the country," Fledermaus said. "That is a violation of our law. I imagine we will have strong words with the authorities in his home country. As for him, we have a facility in Butzbach for people with special abilities. I think he will spend a bit of time there as our guest."

"That's a lot of risk they took. Six guys, two cars. And a joker-ace smuggled in. A lot of effort, and no guarantee of a payout. Why would they do that?"

"They told me," Natalie mumbled behind them. Khan and Fledermaus turned around in surprise. She was sitting up with her arms wrapped around her knees, and she merely sounded drunk instead of incoherent.

"They told you what?" Khan asked and sat down next to her.

"They said my father owed them money. Lots of money. Said they weren't letting me go until he paid up." She shuddered a little and hugged her knees tighter. "Told me they'd start cutting off fingers if he didn't. Send 'em back to him in a box, one by one."

Khan looked over at the still unconscious mobsters and suppressed his sudden desire to grab them by the neck and throw them off the gun platform. He didn't much care for her music or her social circle, but Natalie was just a kid, barely out of her teens, and no threat to anyone. He had killed mobsters and other dirtbags in cold blood before, but he'd never lay a hand on an innocent, especially not one so close in age and appearance to his little sister Naya. Suddenly he didn't have any more scruples about the mook he had slashed to shreds down in the nightclub's back hallway.

In the distance, sirens cut through the tranquility of the park. Khan looked over the balustrade and saw blue lights flashing. At least a dozen police cars were rushing up the access road from the nearby parking lot. The German police sirens had a two-tone pattern that was somehow even more annoying than the shrill ululating wail of the cop sirens back home: BEE-DO, BEE-DO. The blue lights cut through the semi-darkness of the early morning and drew erratic light patterns on the concrete walls of the Flakturm.

"Some things are the same everywhere," Khan said.

"What is that?" Fledermaus asked.

"The cavalry always shows up five minutes too late."

Forty-eight hours and an interminable amount of police interviews later, Khan and Natalie's entourage were in the air again. He had fully expected to join Mukha, the Tree Guy, in whatever high-security facility BDBF had set up for wayward wild cards in Butzbach. But the BDBF guys seemed to have a great deal of pull with Germany's federal police. He'd had to sign a legal paper obliging him to return for a court appearance if the prosecutor decided to file charges, and then they released him on his word and returned his passport, much to Khan's astonishment.

There was no Top 40 music blaring in the cabin of the Learjet on the way to Keflavik. Natalie and her friends were huddled on the lounge seating and talking while sipping drinks. Khan knew the shell-shocked look in their eyes all too well. He spent most of the flight to Iceland thinking about the kidnapping and of all the ways he screwed up. He knew that he couldn't have done much better, but he also knew that the open wound on his professional ego would take a much longer time to heal than the bruises on his body.

Half an hour before their descent into Keflavik, he called Sal Scuderi from the onboard phone. "We're on our way back," he said when Sal answered. "Two-hour layover, then four more hours. She'll be home by dinner."

"How's my girl?"

"She's doing all right," Khan said. "Still shaken. It'll take a while."

"I can't even tell you what kinda state I've been in the last few days. You dropped the fucking ball, my friend. I mean, I'm happy you got her back. But you let them take her to begin with."

Khan sighed heavily

NB. "How much do you owe them?"

"The fuck are you talking about?"

"The Georgians. They told Natalie that you owe them a shitload of money. Said they'd send her back in little pieces if you didn't pay up."

"You know that's bullshit tough guy talk. You don't damage the valuable goods."

"Sal," Khan said. "Cut the crap. How much?"

There was silence on the line for a few moments. Then Sal Scuderi let out a shaky breath. It sounded like the remaining air escaping from a flaccid old balloon.

"Twenty mil."

"You borrowed *twenty mil* from the Georgian mob? Are you out of your fucking mind?"

"They were about to get it back," Sal said. "It would have been okay. If only . . ."

"If only what?"

It took a few seconds for Khan to understand, and when he did, he felt his anger welling up again. "You took a policy out on her. A high-risk one."

"Geez, Khan. The kid has had a policy on her since the day she was born. It's what I do. I got a policy on the wife too. And the fucking dog. What kind of asshole do you take me for?"

Khan looked over at Natalie, who was curled up in her seat, looking like someone who needed about two weeks of uninterrupted sleep.

"The kind of asshole who'd try and pay off his debt with his kid's life insurance policy," he said. "I knew you were shit, Sal. I just didn't know you had no fucking soul left."

"You're one to talk. How many people have you killed for guys like me?"

"Too many," Khan conceded.

There was another long pause. Then Sal cleared his throat.

"You have a rep. You get paid well because you do what you're told. You want to see any of your fee, you keep your mouth shut about this. In front of Nat, or the media, or the cops. You fuck me over, and I'll make sure you never get another job in this town again."

"Don't ever fucking threaten me," Khan said. He could have growled into the phone for emphasis, but right now he was too tired for theatrics. Instead, he just ended the call and turned off his phone.

Across the cabin, Natalie was watching him with concern on her face. He smiled in what he hoped was a reassuring manner, and she returned it.

He got up from his seat in the back of the plane and moved past the entourage to the Learjet's bar. He uncorked the Scotch decanter and poured two fingers' worth of whisky into a glass, then repeated the process. Then he walked over to Natalie and held out one of the glasses.

"Got a minute to talk?"

She looked at him in surprise. Then she nodded and got to her feet.

"Sure. Let's go in the back."

He let her walk ahead. Before he followed, he picked up the remote from the lounge table and turned on the TV.

"Turn it up as loud as you want," he told Melissa and the boys.

On the way to the back, he glanced out of the window. Outside, a steel-blue sky flecked with clouds was meeting a restless ocean, sunshine glittering on waves.

Fuck the fee, he thought, and went to talk to Natalie.

A Girl And Her Drop Ship: Lucky Thirteen

When I wrote the second novel in the Frontlines series, LINES OF DEPARTURE, I built in a four-year time jump from the end of the previous novel. I had to change the occupational specialty of the protagonist, Andrew Grayson, to a more exciting job than the spaceship console jockey position he had in the first book because it's much harder to make things exciting from that perspective. That necessitated a punch of the fast-forward button because the poor guy already spent half the first book in training, and I didn't want to repeat that for the sequel. I set the action four years ahead, when Andrew is fully trained and well-experienced in his new job, and the problem was solved.

The writer brain goes where it wants to go, though, and when the time came to think about stories that could take place in that four-year gap between the first two noels, it wasn't Andrew who came to mind but his girlfriend (and future wife) Halley. She joined the service at the same time—they're in boot camp together in the first book—but she inarguably had the more exciting job for the first year or two of their careers. While Andrew was flying a console and then retraining to be a special operations podhead, Halley was out in the fleet as a junior officer, piloting drop ships into battle and dodging enemy fire.

I didn't have a plot in mind yet when I started writing Halley's tale. I just started with her arriving at her first combat assignment as a green drop ship pilot, and the idea that as the FNG, she'd invariably get the shittiest hardware on the flight deck, the one that the other pilots don't want to fly because it's too old, or because it has a bad history (pilots are a superstitious bunch, after all). Everything else unfolded in my mind as I wrote those first few paragraphs, and I finished the entire story in just a few days.

Lucky Thirteen was lucky for me as well. It was the story that caught Tim Miller's eye for the LOVE DEATH + ROBOTS project, and it led to two of my short fiction pieces making it onto the TV screen as adaptations.

(The LD+R version, "Lucky 13", had to have the Frontlines serial numbers filed off so any future TV or movie development rights for the series would not be affected, which is why the main character is called Lt. Cutter instead of Lt. Halley.)

Fun little piece of trivia: the Netflix adaptation is the thirteenth episode of the first season, and the episode is exactly 13 minutes long.

Lucky Thirteen

A Frontlines Story

The Fleet has a tradition: the rookie drop ship commander in the unit always gets the ship nobody else wants.

My hand-me-down was Lucky Thirteen. There was nothing wrong with her, technically speaking. She was an older model Wasp, not one of the new Dragonflies, but most of our assault wings were still on Wasps back then. But pilots are a superstitious bunch, and it had been decided that Lucky Thirteen was an unlucky ship. Before they gave her to me, she had lost two crews with all hands, one of them with the entire troop compartment loaded to the last seat. Both times, they recovered the ship, hosed her out, and patched her up again. A ship surviving an all-hands loss without being destroyed is very unusual. Surviving two of them is so rare that I've never heard of such a thing before or since.

Her hull number wasn't actually 13. She wore a dark red 5 on her olive drab flanks. But one of the grease monkeys had found her assembly number plate while swapping out some fried parts one day, and the news made the rounds that the unlucky ship's serial number was 13-02313. Not only did it have a leading and trailing 13 in it, but all the digits of her serial number also added up to 13. Thusly branded, she was named "Lucky Thirteen", and put in storage as a cold spare until they needed an airframe for the new First Lieutenant. Then they dusted her off, updated the computers, and handed me the keys.

She came with a new crew chief, too—Staff Sergeant Fisher. I met him for the first time when I went down to the storage hangar to check out my new ride. He was already busy with her, plugging all kinds of diagnostics hardware into the data ports in her bowels. When I walked around Lucky Thirteen for the first time, I noticed that he had already painted my name onto the armor belt underneath the right cockpit window: 1LT HALLEY "COMET".

"I took the liberty," Sergeant Fisher said when I ran my fingers across the stenciled letters of my call sign. "Hope you don't mind, ma'am."

"Not at all," I told him. "She's really yours, anyway. I just get to take her out occasionally."

He smiled, obviously pleased to be assigned to a pilot who knew the proper chain of ownership in a drop ship wing.

"Don't let the talk bother you. About her being unlucky, I mean. She's a good ship. I checked her top to bottom, and she's in better shape than some of the new crates."

"Talk don't bother me, Sarge," I told him. "I'm not the superstitious kind. It's just a machine."

"No, ma'am," Sergeant Fisher replied, and the smile on his face morphed into a bit of a smirk.

"She ain't just a machine. They all have personalities, same as you and I."

Lucky Thirteen did have a personality, all right. Fortunately, it meshed well with mine.

I've flown dozens of Wasp drop ships, from the barebones A1 models they mostly use as trainers now, to the newest Whiskey Wasps that are so crammed full of upgrades that they might as well give them their own class name. None of them had the same responsive controls as Lucky Thirteen. The Wasps have always been twitchy in any version—you have to fly them with your fingertips, because they're so sensitive to control input. No Wasp likes a heavy hand on the stick. Lucky Thirteen was even more twitchy than the average Wasp, but once you had her figured out, you could pull off maneuvers that most new pilots would consider physically impossible. Something about Lucky Thirteen was just right. Maybe it was the harmonics of the frame, maybe the way all her parts had worked themselves into synchronicity with each other—but flying her felt like you were an integral part of the ship, not just her driver.

Thirteen and I had five weeks to get used to each other before we had our first combat drop together. We were the tail end of a four-ship flight, tasked to ferry a Spaceborne Infantry company down to Procyon Bc's solitary moon. We had beaten the local Chinese garrison into submission from orbit, and now the 940th SI Regiment was going to drop into the path of the retreating Chinese troops to finish them off before they could rally and reform.

Intel never figured out what went wrong that day. I don't know if the Chinese managed to hack into our secure battle network, or if it was just a case of shitty luck. What I do know is that our drop ship flight went skids down to let the troops disembark near a ridge line, and that all hell broke loose as soon as we hit the ground. The landing zone was lined with those new autonomous anti-aircraft gun pods the Chinese put in service—thirty-six barrels in six rows of six, each stacked from front to back with superposed loads. The whole thing is hooked up to a passive IFF module and a short-range radar and parked out of sight, like a mine. We didn't get a whiff of them on our threat scanners until they opened fire. Each of those things shoots a quarter million rounds per minute, and while each individual shell won't do a great deal of damage to an armored drop ship, the cumulative effect is like aiming a high-pressure water hose at an anthill.

We had landed in diamond formation, with Lucky Thirteen at the tail end of the diamond, farthest from the row of gun pods waiting for us. That's what saved our bacon that day. My crew chief had just released the tail ramp when I saw hundreds of muzzle flashes lighting up the night in front of us. I yelled at the Sarge to pull the ramp back up and goosed the engines to get us off the ground again. In front of us, the lead drop ship had already started disgorging its platoon, and half their troops were already out of the ship and in the line of fire. For a moment, I fully intended to drop my bird between the exposed troops and the guns, but then the lead Wasp just blew up right in front of me. One moment, it was squatting on the ground, SI troopers seeking cover all around it, and the next moment it was just a cloud of parts getting flung in every direction.

I got us back in the air at that point. I flew Thirteen about three hundred meters backwards on her tail, to keep the belly armor between us and those guns. Then I flipped the ship around, did the lowest wing-over I've ever done, and high-tailed it out of the landing zone at a hundred and thirty percent emergency power.

Lucky Thirteen was the only surviving drop ship of the flight that day. Banshee 72, the ship that blew up in front of me, was dispersed over a quarter square kilometer, along with her two pilots, her crew chief, and thirty-eight SI troopers in full kit. Banshee 73 and 74 got so chewed up that they never got off the moon, either, and the Fleet had to send in a flight of Shrikes to destroy the airframes in place where they did their emergency landings. Lucky Thirteen didn't even have a scratch in her new paint.

After I had the ship back in the docking clamp, I started quaking like a leaf in high wind, and I didn't stop for two hours. Mentally, the shakes lasted a lot longer. I still blame myself for not diving back into that LZ right away, and putting some suppressive fire onto those gun pods, even though I did exactly what you're supposed to do when the bus is full of mudlegs—get out of danger and keep the troops safe.

Nobody from Banshee 72 survived. Thirty-one troopers and one pilot died on Banshee 73, and fourteen troopers and the crew chief bought it on Banshee 74. Yeah, I still blame myself for not going back to help them, even though I played it precisely by the book.

But the first time some jackass Second Lieutenant from SI told me off for not staying in the hot LZ on Procyon Bc, I punched him in the nose, and hit him with his own meal tray for good measure. It was an almost cathartic experience, and well worth the forty-eight hours in the brig.

I flew nineteen more combat missions in Lucky Thirteen after that. I ferried troops into battle, dropped off supplies, made ground attack runs, and picked up recon teams from hostile worlds. In all that time, I didn't have a single casualty on my ship. Three times out of nineteen, my Lucky Thirteen was the only airworthy unit in the entire flight at the end of the mission. She brought us home safely every time, even when the ground fire was so thick that you could have stepped out of the cockpit and walked down to the deck on shrapnel shards. After the tenth mission in a row had passed with my shop remaining unscratched, the other pilots started to mean it when they called her "Lucky Thirteen."

Then came the day we got a pair of fresh-off-the-floor Whiskey Wasps, so new that their pilot seats were still covered in plastic wrap. Normally, a pair of brand-new ships in the wing triggers a complex series of trickle-down upgrades as the senior pilots claim the new birds and pass their old ones down the roster to the junior jocks. This time, Lieutenant Colonel Connolly came to me and offered me the shiny new Whiskey Wasp he was slated to receive, if I let him have Lucky Thirteen in exchange.

It was a singular pleasure to decline his offer.

The Fleet has another tradition: once you find something that works for you, and you get attached to it, you end up losing it.

Lucky Thirteen died on a cold and sunny day out on some desolate rock around Fomalhaut. She didn't get blown out of the sky or stomped flat by a Lanky. I killed her myself, willingly.

I went down to the planet to pick up a recon team that had been compromised. When we got to the rendezvous point, our four Recon guys were engaged with what looked like an entire company of Russians. I've done hot pickups before, but never one where I had to pry our snake eaters from the embrace of half the planetary garrison. The Russian troops were not very keen on having their prize snatched away by a solitary drop ship. As soon as I came swooping into the pickup zone, all kinds of shit came flying our way. Judging by the number of hand-held missiles launched from the ground, every other trooper in that company must have taken an anti-aircraft tube along for the chase. My threat scanner lit up like a Pachinko parlor, and for a few minutes, I was busy dodging missiles and pumping out countermeasures. All the while, the guys on the ground were screaming for us to come back and pluck them out of the mess. Finally, the ground fire slacked off a bit, and I rolled back into the target area with my thumb on the launch button.

The Russians had our team pinned down, and their lead squad was so close to our guys that you couldn't have driven a utility truck through the space between them without rolling over somebody's feet. I made a close pass with the cannons, and the Russians ran for cover. By then, I had the attention of the whole company, and everyone aimed their rifles and belt-fed guns skyward and let fly. The small arms fire pinging off Lucky Thirteen's armor was so dense that it sounded like hail in an ice storm. On my next pass, I emptied most of the rocket pods on my external ordnance pylons, gave my left-seater instructions to use our chin turret on everything that wasn't wearing NAC camo, and then put our ship down right between the Russians and our chewed-up recon team.

Staff Sergeant Fisher was the ballsiest crew chief I've ever had. He had that ramp down the second our bird hit the dirt, and he was out to help the injured Recon guys into our ship, even though the incoming fire was churning up little dust fountains all over the place. Only one of the Recon guys was still able to walk onto the ramp on his own feet. Sergeant Fisher went out three times to get the other guys, dashing across fifty yards of live-firing shooting range every time, and hauling back two hundred pounds of armor-clad Recon trooper on each trip. Finally, he had everyone back in the hold, and I redlined the torque gauge getting our bird off the ground and out of there.

We didn't get too far. The Russians had called in their own gunship for support, and it managed to sneak up on us right above the deck without pegging the threat scanner. I was focused on keeping us going at low level and high speed when I heard a sharp warbling sound from the radar warning sensor. He must have been almost on top of us when he launched, because I didn't even have time to thumb my countermeasures button. The Russian missile went right into our starboard engine, which was running at a hundred and twenty percent, and blew it all to hell. For a second or two, we were headed for the dirt at seven hundred knots, but then I caught her, and brought the ship out of the spin we had been knocked into. I pointed her up at the blue sky and firewalled her last remaining engine.

The Russian had been so close behind us that he ended up overshooting us, which was a stroke of luck, because I still had all four of my Copperhead air-to-air missiles on the wingtips. I launched two of them cold, waited until the Russian pilot kicked out his countermeasures, and then launched the remaining pair right up his ass with a solid lock. One nailed his port engine, and the other one chopped off the last third of his ship's tail, along with the tail rudder and the vertical stabilizers. We were only a thousand feet or so off the deck, and the Russian pilot barely had time to eject his crew before his ship cartwheeled into the rocks and went up in a lovely fireball.

Our ship was only in slightly better shape. I stabilized our attitude, and let the computer figure out how badly we were hurt. The Russian missile had taken out our engine, and some of the secondary shrapnel had severed the main data bus along with three out of the four hydraulic lines, We were still airworthy, but only barely, and spaceflight was out of the question. With the hurt Recon guys in the back, we couldn't do like the Russians and eject, so I backed off the throttle and looked for a good place to put down my wounded bird.

Fomalhaut's moon is a rocky, dusty piece of shit, like most of the places we fight over with the SRA. It looked like the desert out in Utah where I went to Basic, only without even the little bit of vegetation we had out there. With my remaining engine starting to cough up its inner workings, I couldn't be too picky, so I chose the first patch of ground that looked reasonably even and rock-free and directed whatever juice I had left in the battered ship to cushion our descent. We hit the dirt lightly enough for me to put down the skids and do a proper three-point touchdown. The way the landing site was laid out meant that I had to make my final approach facing the way we had come. Those turned out our lucky breaks in the end. The skid landing meant that the chin turret could still rotate, and the approach had the ship come to rest pointing at the plateau where we had just picked up our recon team.

As soon as we were down in the dirt, I turned off the engine to keep it from tearing itself to shreds. At that point, Thirteen was still salvageable—missing an engine, and chewed up by shrapnel, but they had brought her back from near-scrap condition twice before. Our electrical system still worked, and I sent out a distress call while Sergeant Fisher lowered the tail ramp and started hauling people out of the hull. But when my left-seater reached for the Master Power switch to turn off the ship completely, I waved him off.

"Just leave her on until the batteries run dry," I said to him.

We were within line of sight of the plateau where half a company of pissed-off Russian marines had watched our descent, and not two minutes after our landing, the threat warning receiver started chirping again. I glanced at it to see that we were being targeted by millimeter-wave short range radar bursts, probably the Russian version of our MARS assault rocket launchers. One of those could blow up what was left of Lucky Thirteen, but we were at the limit of their effective range, and my ship still had her countermeasures suite. I switched the system to AUTONOMOUS and got out of my seat.

"Sergeant Fisher and Second Lieutenant Denton, get those grunts out of here and to cover somewhere."

"Copy that, ma'am," Lieutenant Denton said. "What's the plan?"

"You wait for the evac birds and stay low. I'll hop into the gunner's seat and warm up the cannon. Now move. Doubletime."

"No need for heroics, ma'am," Sergeant Fisher said from the outside of the ship. "We'll all head for cover, bring some rifles from the armory."

"I'm not planning on getting shot today, Sarge. I'll bail just as soon as that cannon is empty. Now move it, and stay way the fuck away from the ship. Rescue birds don't get here before the Russkies, I'll pull the boom handle on my way out."

I waved Lieutenant Denton out of the cockpit and climbed into the gunner's seat to take control of the ship's chin turret. I wasn't even strapped in all the way when the threat warning warbled again, and the dust on the plateau a mile away stirred up with the launch of a pair of rockets.

You can kill a Wasp with an assault rocket, but it has to be a lucky shot. Those rockets are designed for use against ground fortifications and big biological targets like Lankies, not against fast-moving drop ships with sophisticated electronic warfare kit. Even stationary in the dirt, a Wasp is not an easy kill for a rocket gunner. The jamming suite zapped the warhead seekers of the incoming rockets, and they went wild and exploded in the rocks before they had crossed the distance halfway. The Russians tried again, this time with a brace of three rockets, but being stationary just made my ship's jamming suite more effective, and those went wild almost as soon as they were out of the launchers.

Line of sight works both ways, of course. I plugged my helmet into the gunner's console, cranked the magnification of the gun sight to maximum, and popped the safety cap of the fire control with my thumb. Then I returned the favor, liberally.

The chin turret of a Wasp is fitted with a three-barreled autocannon that fires caseless shells at something like twelve hundred rounds per minute. From a mile away, the chain of impact explosions from the dual-purpose rounds looked like a chain of tiny volcanoes had just erupted in sequence on the ridge line. I held the trigger down for about five seconds and raked the ridge from left to right. There were no follow-up rocket shots from the Russians.

My cannon fire bought us about five minutes. I took the time to wipe the data off the memory banks of my ship, rendering her as dumb as she had been in the storage hangar. The self-destruct mechanism would blow the entire ship into fine shrapnel, but sometimes it doesn't trigger properly, and we were all instructed to lobotomize our birds if we ditched on enemy soil. By the time I was done, the Russians had worked up enough courage again to shoot at us again, this time with small arms fire. I took up my spot in the gunner's seat again and popped off bursts at likely hiding spots. My crew had gotten clear of the ship and taken up position a few hundred meters behind the bird, out of the line of fire for now. The Russians were out for blood now, and if they managed to get around the zone covered by my gun turret, they would have us all in the bag anyway.

For the next ten minutes, it was a gun duel—my autocannon against their rifles and belt-fed guns. Every time I saw movement on the rocky plain in front of me, I put a short burst into the general vicinity. I don't know how many of them I actually got, but I didn't kill enough to discourage the rest, because they kept coming, and their fire kept getting more accurate. The Wasp shrugged off the rifle fire, but some of the belt-fed guns were loaded with harder stuff, and the armored cockpit glass started falling apart under the cumulative hits. One of the Russians had a heavy-caliber anti-materiel rifle, and the first round from that beast came clean through the middle of my center cockpit panel and center-punched the pilot seat I had been sitting in until we crash-landed. I hunkered down behind the front instrument panel and kept shooting back, pumping out explosive rounds and watching the ammo counter work its way down to triple, and then double digits.

The first time one of their rounds hit me, I didn't even realize I had been shot. I just felt something wet run down my right arm and drip off my fingertips, and when I tore myself away from the gun sight to investigate, I saw that something had zipped through the sleeve of my flight suit. As I was peeling the wet sleeve off my skin, another burst of fire finally shattered the front panel completely, and I took a round in the same arm, almost down by the elbow. That one hurt like hell right away.

I guess they knew they had tagged me when I didn't return fire right away, because that's when the incoming fire really picked up. I think every Russian left alive between those rocks started hosing down the front of Lucky Thirteen. I was just about out of ammo anyway, so I slipped out of the gunner's seat and dropped to the floor while the flechettes and tungsten darts from the Russian guns tore up the cockpit just above my head. I crawled through the open hatch and pulled it shut behind me with my good hand. The rounds pinging off the laminated armor sounded like hail hitting a windowpane.

I got up, stepped into the ship's armory to grab a rifle and a bag of magazines, and then went over to the bulkhead that held the trigger for the Wasp's built-in demolition charge.

Removing the safety and pulling that lever felt like putting a gun to the head of a puppy and pulling the trigger. But I knew she'd never fly again, and I didn't want her to end up as a war trophy, parked in front of some Russian company building. Thirteen would have a fast and thorough death, with nothing left behind to rust away in a scrapyard somewhere.

I pulled the lever. Then I gathered my rifle and dashed out of the troop compartment, down the lowered tail hatch, and into the open.

The Russians didn't see me at first because the bulk of Lucky Thirteen was between me and them, and by the time their flanking elements had spotted me, I was already fifty yards away and headed for cover. They still shot at me, of course. It's amazing how fast you can run when enemy rifle rounds are kicking up the dust next to you. The self-destruct mechanism on a Wasp has a fifteen-second fuse before it sprays all the remaining fuel into the ship's interior to make a huge fuel-air bomb. My shipmates were all hunkered down behind a rock ledge maybe eighty yards away, and I cleared the ledge with two seconds to spare.

Nothing happened.

I waited another ten, twenty, then thirty seconds with my face in the dirt and my hands over my ears, waiting for Lucky Thirteen to rend herself apart like a giant grenade, but all I heard was the staccato of the Russian rifles. After a minute or two had passed, I chanced a peek over the rock ledge, and saw Lucky Thirteen still sitting in the same spot, smoke trailing from her destroyed engine, and Russian marines advancing on her in the open. With our wounded, there was no way we could outrun the Russians once they figured out we had all flown the coop. There was only one thing left to do—sell ourselves as dearly as possible. I lowered my head again, checked the loading status of my rifle, and signaled the others to get ready to engage.

The sky overhead was a lovely cobalt blue, the stars bright even in the planetary afternoon. I wondered if our own sun was among them. I briefly marveled at the thought that since the moment those photons left our own sun, I had been born, raised, educated, inducted into the Commonwealth Defense Corps, and trained to fly a drop ship, and that I had still beaten the light to Fomalhaut by a few days.

Then I flicked the safety of my rifle to salvo fire and got up to fight.

We were seven against fifty, and most of us were wounded. When we engaged, the Russians were caught by surprise, and our first bursts of fire took out half a dozen of them. After that, we were screwed. They knew where we were, they had the numbers on us, and they had Lucky Thirteen for cover. We got two or three more, and then the return fire had us ducking back behind cover.

"I got Fleet on comms," Staff Sergeant Fisher told me over the din of the gunfire. "Air support is on the way. ETA ten minutes."

"That's super," I replied. "You speak any Russian? Tell those guys to take a piss break until then, and we're good."

It's not easy to stick your head up above cover to aim your weapon when you're convinced that you'll take a round in the face the second you do. The next time I popped up to fire back, I glanced at Lucky Thirteen, and saw that the Russians were all over her, using her armored hull as cover.

I'll never be able to tell for sure how I knew what was about to happen. There was something in the air—a whiff of burnt ozone smell, and a strange sound, like a piezo switch. It felt as if the air itself was electrically charged. All I remember is that I ducked back behind the rock ledge, and yelled at the others to *get down, get down, get the fuck down.*

Lucky Thirteen blew up with the loudest bang I've ever heard in my life. The shock of the explosion traveled through the rock and knocked us all flat on our asses. From one moment to the next, the air was so thick with dust that I couldn't see my own hands in front of me. My hearing was completely gone—all I could hear was a high-pitched whistling sound.

I have no idea how long we were huddled down behind the rock ledge, blind and deaf, with debris and dust raining down on us. The Russians could have finished us off easily at that point, if there had been any left. When the dust finally settled and we gathered ourselves up, the little plateau where Lucky Thirteen had crash-landed was swept clean. In the spot where the ship had been, there was a shallow depression in the rock, and streaks of black burn marks fanning out in every direction. All around, there were burning and smoldering drop ship parts, none of them bigger than a mess table.

Lucky Thirteen had done me a last favor. The fuse for the self-destruct charge had delayed until the ship had Russians crawling all over and inside her—until the explosion would do the most good.

I'm not one of the superstitious pilots. My rational side knows it was a technical fluke, a delay in the trigger mechanism, a circuit that didn't close in time, a fortunate defect. But part of me wants to believe that the ship saved my life that day—that this collection of parts bolted together thirty years ago in a factory back on Earth, a Wasp-C like a thousand others and yet like no other ship I've ever flown, knew our peril and immolated itself at just the right moment, in a final act of service to its pilot.

The cavalry arrived ten minutes too late, as it often does. The Shrikes made a few passes overhead, but if there were any Russians left alive, they wisely stayed under cover. Twenty minutes after that, a pair of SAR drop ships swooped in, and scooped us up.

While we were waiting for the drop ships, Sergeant Fisher picked up something in the dirt, looked it over briefly, and tucked it into his pocket. Later, when we were strapped into our jump seats and on the way back to the ship in orbit, he fished the item out and handed it to me without a word.

It was a chunk of Lucky Thirteen's assembly number plate, twisted and charred on both ends. The manufacturer's name was missing, but I could clearly read her serial number on the mangled little strip of steel: 13-02313.

I bit my lip and slipped the number plate into my own pocket, also without a word.

They patched us up and gave us medals. I put Sergeant Fisher in for a Silver Star and he got it. The captain in charge of the recon team we picked up recommended me for an award as well. The division brass looked over the records and decided that I should get a Distinguished Flying Cross for killing Lucky Thirteen on Fomalhaut. Two months later, they called me down to the hangar deck, and the regiment's CO pinned the DFC onto my baggy flight suit.

I didn't turn it down, even though I didn't want it. You don't turn down awards just because you think you don't deserve them. If the drop ship jocks started doing that, the only people wearing ribbons would be the desk jockeys, the officers who collect medals after milk run missions that may have involved shots fired within half a parsec. Promotions ride on points, and those ribbons count for a lot of those points. I took the medal, saluted, and smiled like a good Second Lieutenant who wants to make Captain someday.

But back in my berth, I took that DFC out of its silk-lined case and put it into the chest pocket of my Class A uniform, the one I wear maybe once a year. Then I got out Lucky Thirteen's number plate fragment and tucked it into the medal case instead. It seemed a more appropriate tenant for that nice little silk-lined case.

They gave me a new ship, of course. I got a brand-new Whiskey Wasp after all. It's a fine ship, the newest and most advanced version of the Wasp drop ship, twice as powerful and four times as capable as my old crate.

Still, I'd trade it off in a hot second to get back Lucky Thirteen just for a day or two.

Flash Fiction: Seeds

This is a short little piece I wrote in a single afternoon. Flash fiction doesn't sell very well in the short fiction market, so I didn't even bother to submit it anywhere. I just filed it away and mostly forgot about it until Tim Miller asked me for more short fiction that could serve as material for "Love Death + Robots". This story was in the batch I sent him, and he liked it enough to purchase the adaptation right to it.

Alas, it didn't make the final cut for the show, but that's still not a bad showing for something I thought up and wrote in a day.

The seed for the idea, so to speak, originated from one rather grim weekend when I had to cull a bunch of red squirrels that had made themselves at home in our covered porch area, where the power lines from the main electric panel run into the house. Squirrels are very cute but very destructive once they get into human housing, and as much as I hate to kill any living thing, they don't respond to eviction notices *at all*.

Seeds

I killed that damn squirrel for the first time right after breakfast.

I knew it was a killing shot the moment I pulled the trigger. I've shot a thousand of the little bastards, and when you shoot one in the head with a .22, it's usually dead on the spot.

I say "usually", because this one was a statistical aberration. I saw him fall off the bird feeder in that uncoordinated head-over-tail manner of a squirrel that's already dead before it hits the ground. I put the rifle back into its corner by the kitchen window, got on my working gloves, and went out to retrieve the carcass for a trash can burial. But when I got out to the bird feeder, the squirrel was gone. All I found in the snow was a tiny spot of blood and a little crater where the body had landed.

Sometimes I miss a shot, even though it's only twenty yards from the kitchen window to the bird feeder, and Dad's old .22 has a scope that lets you spot wildlife in the next area code. I was pretty sure I had hit that little seed thief's head right below his tufted ear, but I chalked it up to a bad shot. I had probably just nicked his skull and stunned him briefly. I shrugged and walked back to the warm house.

An hour later, he was back.

I had no doubt that it was the same squirrel. He had a bullet wound below his left ear, and the fur on the side of his head was black with dried blood. He stood at the bottom of the bird feeder again, swaying like a punch-drunk boxer, and started eating the seeds the birds had dropped.

I felt bad for winging him and leaving the poor guy in that state for an hour. I aimed for the center of his body to give myself the biggest margin for a miss and resolved to get the scope's zero checked as soon as possible. Then I pulled the trigger.

This one was a clean hit without question. The bullet bowled him over in a flurry of bushy fur and spilled bird seed. He twitched once and lay still beside the feeder. Pop, smack, good night.

Except when I walked out to get the carcass, he was gone. Again.

This time, the blood spot in the snow was larger. As before, the squirrel was gone. All I found was a small tuft of fur with some clotted blood on it.

"Son of a bitch," I said and looked up. The squirrel was dead, no doubt, so I guessed that some opportunistic raven or owl had claimed a quick free meal. But there were no birds flying away, with or without dead squirrels in their grip.

I walked back to the house and put the rifle away again, vaguely feeling like the victim of a prank.

I got a lot of squirrels every winter. Once a clan of them had found the feeders, they wouldn't rest until all the seed was gone. I had to cull two or three every week for as long as the feeders were up. When I saw another bushy-tailed silhouette under the feeder shortly after lunch, I got out the .22 and opened the kitchen window, ready to increase the day's tail count to two. Then I looked through the scope.

Head wound with dried blood: check. Bullet hole in the midsection: check, sort of. I couldn't see his belly because he had his back turned, but there was no missing the exit wound on his back, or the grey intestines bulging out of the hole in his dirty, blood-matted fur.

I was so freaked out that I missed my shot. The bullet kicked up the snow beside him, but the little bastard didn't run. Instead, he turned his head, still chewing, and looked at me with an eye that had the milky opaqueness of a piece of quartz.

I worked the bolt, put a new round into the chamber with shaking fingers, and aimed again.

Crack.

This one hit him in the neck. He did the same thing as before: fell over, flopped around for a second, and then lay still. I reloaded and put another bullet into his body, for insurance. This time, I kept watching his furry little carcass through the scope.

He was properly dead for about thirty seconds: limp, motionless, and very much carcass-like. Then he twitched again, got to all fours like a drunk picking himself up out of a gutter after a three-night bender, and staggered off toward the nearby tree line.

"What in the fucking fuck?" I asked nobody in particular.

It was dark outside when I sat down at the kitchen table with my dinner. There was something moving out by the bird feeder, so I turned on the exterior lights.

The dead-but-not-dead squirrel was back underneath the feeder. He didn't look so good. In fact, he looked a lot like a stuffed toy mauled by an energetic Rottweiler. His fur was clumped with blood and sticking out at untidy angles, and it looked like he was wearing most of his intestines draped around his legs and lower body.

At that point, I was wishing I had kept Dad's shotgun instead of the scoped .22.

I opened the window and took aim. He stopped chewing his seeds and looked at me with milky eyes that were as dead as a pair of deep-sea pearls. Then he let out a shriek, and I dropped the rifle.

It wasn't the high-pitched *chik-chik-chik* I've heard from squirrels a thousand times before. It was a shrill, piercing, tortured shriek that was anger, hatred, and exasperation all rolled into one. *Stop that shit, or there will be trouble,* the shriek said.

I closed the window and put the rifle away. Then I went to the liquor cabinet and had half a highball glass of single malt.

Later that evening, I called my brother.

"You still want Dad's old .22?" I asked him. "The one with the big scope?"

"Yeah, I do," he said. "Why, are you getting rid of it?"

"I need to clear out some stuff. I'm thinking about moving."

"Oh, yeah? Where to?"

"Some place without trees. I've had it with the damn squirrels."

Supporting Character, Center Stage: Measures of Absolution

"Measures of Absolution" is told from the perspective of Corporal Jackson, one of the supporting characters in "Terms of Enlistment", the first Frontlines novel. It takes place concurrently with the second half of the novel.

This novella had its genesis in a reader review. I don't recall where I read it—probably on Amazon, back when I still read every single review. (That's a rookie thing to do, by the way. I don't read the reviews anymore because they're not for me, they're for other readers. And reading reviews is a no-win activity for a writer. The good reviews make your head swell needlessly, the bad reviews ruin the rest of your day, and the incisive three-star reviews make you want to give up writing and take up salmon fishing or carpentry instead.)

The review said that the novel read like two different books, and they liked the first one much better than the second. The split, I suspect, is the moment Andrew leaves the TA and joins the Navy, finally getting his wish of making it off the planet and into space. I had him switch branches because I didn't want to keep him stuck on Earth for the rest of his career. But the review got me thinking, and I realized that the PRCs, the Public Residence Clusters, were a much too interesting setting to only serve as background for half a novel. I started to think about what happened in Andrew's unit after he left, and the impact of the Battle of Detroit on the rest of his squad in his absence. The result was "Measures of Absolution", Corporal Jackson's attempt to find redemption and closure after the welfare riots, and the genesis of the Lazarus Brigade, the veteran-run volunteer militia that tries to restore a sense of order to the PRCs.

Measures of Absolution

A Frontlines Novella

Chapter One: Detroit

For the first time in her military career, Corporal Jackson thinks that she may not make it through to the end of her service after all.

The mobs on the streets of Detroit have done what none of the world's third-rate militaries and insurgents have been able to do-- kill or injure almost everyone in her squad. Without air cover or armor, it's just a running gun battle. They're slugging it out with ill-equipped locals, but there are many more of them than there are TA troopers on the ground tonight.

And the locals are about to win.

The bullets clang against her armor so frequently now that she has stopped counting the impacts. The rioters are using mostly old cartridge weapons, and few of those fire anything powerful enough to pierce the ultra-tough laminate of military battle armor, but there's more modern stuff in the mix as well. Jackson lets the computer pick her targets, but she needs to shoot with one hand because she's carrying the crew chief of the downed drop ship they rescued a little while ago. She needs to shoot burst fire to make up for the imprecise one-handed aiming, and that wastes ammo she can't afford to burn.

In front of her, Grayson and Priest set up a covering position on a street corner. Their rifles start chattering the moment they get sight of the intersection beyond. Corporal Jackson sees a hundred hostile icons popping up, but they start blinking out of existence rapidly as Grayson and Priest are thinning out the rioters' numbers with ruthlessly efficient rapid fire. Dozens fall. Then the others break and run, and the intersection is clear.

"Go, go, go!" Priest shouts and waves her along. Jackson renews her grip on the unconscious crew chief and drags him across the street into the next inadequate cover.

Just as she lowers the crew chief to the dirty concrete of the crumbling sidewalk, there's the familiar chatter of an M-66 salvo coming from the corner of a nearby intersection. Behind her, she hears Grayson groan. When she turns around, he's on the ground next to Sergeant Fallon. Corporal Jackson brings up her rifle and looks for the source of that rifle fire. There's a small group of rioters over by that street corner. Two are armed with old cartridge guns, but the third has a military-issue M-66. Grayson is trying to pick up his rifle, but he's moving slowly, as if in a trance. Jackson puts the target reticle of her gunsight on the shooter and snaps off a three-round burst. The rioter takes all three rounds to the chest. He stumbles backwards and lands on his ass, dropping his rifle in front of him. She moves the reticle up a hair and fires another burst. This one hits him in the face. He drops backwards and doesn't move again. His buddies do an about-face and retreat into the darkness of the unlit street behind them.

"Grayson, you okay?" Jackson calls out over the squad channel. She gets a gasping groan in reply.

"Priest, go check on Grayson," she orders. The intersection is clear again, but she needs to make sure. She runs over to where the man she just shot is sprawled on the ground.

When she is next to his prone figure, she can see that it's not a *he* at all. The rifle next to the body is a standard TA issue M-66 flechette rifle. She can see the armory marks on the polymer shell, rack and slot numbers written down in waterproof red marker. She picks the rifle up and ejects the magazine. It's still mostly full, and she sticks it into one of the empty pouches on her armor. There's a round still in the chamber, and she aims the rifle down the road and pulls the trigger. It spits out a high-velocity flechette with a sharp little bark. All TA rifles have DNA locks coded to the individual soldier and his fellow squad members. She shouldn't have been able to fire that gun, but fire it did.

The dead woman's last expression looks mildly surprised, maybe even annoyed. The flechettes from Jackson's three-round burst all hit within ten centimeters of each other, right in the triangle formed by her eyes and the chin. There's a familiar-looking ball chain around her neck. Corporal Jackson reaches into the collar of the dusty sweatshirt he's wearing and pulls out the chain. She finds two military dog tags at the end of it.

Up ahead in the darkness, there's movement again. Her low-light augmentation shows another group of armed rioters, a hundred meters away, dashing from cover to cover and closing in on the intersection. Jackson seizes the dog tags and yanks the chain off the dead woman's neck. Then she stuffs the tags into one of her empty magazine pouches. She aims her rifle at the approaching rioters and fires a quick series of single shots that send them ducking for cover. Then she gets up and dashes back to where her squad--what's left of it--is hunkered down.

"More incoming," she shouts to the others. "Where's that goddamn drop ship?"

"We'll never make the civic center," Priest says.

"Sit tight. Make every shot count," Jackson replies. "We defend the wounded until we can't."

"Copy that," Priest replies grimly.

The incoming fire picks up again, a discordant cacophony of reports from dozens of different weapons. Priest and Baker move in front of the wounded, and Jackson joins them to form a final defensive line.

Jackson aims at muzzle flashes, sends out flechettes in bursts of three and five. More rioters fall, but others pick up their weapons and take up the fight. She empties her magazine and ejects it from her rifle. When she searches for a new one, the only ammunition she has left is the partial magazine she took from the dead woman with the military dog tags. She loads the magazine into her weapon and chambers a fresh round. Her visor display updates her ammo count: 121.

"I have half a mag left," she shouts to the others.

"I'm just about dry," Baker replies. Priest is too busy shooting people to reply, but from the way he picks his targets off with careful single shots, she can tell that he doesn't have much left either.

She eyes the oncoming crowd and glances at the combat knife she wears on her harness.

They're not wearing armor, she thinks. *I bet I can get a dozen before they take me down.*

Someone up the street opens up with an automatic weapon. The fusillade kicks up dust and concrete chips next to Jackson. Baker cries out in pain and anger.

"I'm hit," he shouts.

They're everywhere now, shooting from alleys, rooftops, windows. Dozens, maybe hundreds of them, all armed and out for blood. Jackson dishes out what's left in her rifle, but they're not dropping fast enough, and there seem to be two more joining the fight for every one she kills. She has never seen such determination and tenacity from the welfare rats.

She shoots down another rioter, then another. Her rifle's bolt locks back on an empty feedway again. Now there's only Priest's rifle returning fire. As if they can smell the weakness of their adversaries, the rioters increase their fire, emboldened.

That's it, then, Jackson thinks.

She tosses the empty rifle aside and pulls her combat knife from its sheath.

The first indication of their salvation is a burst of autocannon fire high above their heads, the long and ripping thunder of a multi-barreled drop ship turret. The high explosive shells pepper the street in front of the squad, where the attackers have advanced almost to rock-throwing distance. Jackson sees bodies disintegrate under the hammer blows of the cannon shells. Overhead, the drop ship descends out of the dirty night sky and settles in a hover right above the intersection.

The rioters are smart enough to see that they've lost. They retreat like a wave pulling away from the shore at ebb. Some brave souls shoot at the drop ship, but they don't have any heavy machine guns nearby now, and the small arms fire pings off the hull like rain off a tin roof. The drop ship's gunner responds in kind. In just a few moments, all the rioters Jackson still sees on the street are either dead on the ground or running away.

Jackson puts her knife away. The profound relief and gratitude she feels make her knees shake.

At Thermopylae, the Three Hundred held back a hundred thousand Persians. Everyone learns about Leonidas and his Spartans in boot camp. One of the epic last stands in history.

Tonight, Corporal Jackson doesn't believe the Spartans went down as heroically as the historians claim. She's pretty sure some of them pissed themselves before the end. Unless they were insane, or inhuman.

Epic last stand stories are such bullshit.

Chapter Two: After

The drop ship doesn't go back to Shughart. Great Lakes is closer, and Grayson and the Sarge are in bad shape. Jackson keeps looking over to where the crew chief and the combat medic are stabilizing Grayson, who looks as ashen as the gunmetal paint on the bulkhead. Sergeant Fallon lies next to him, conscious but doped to the gills with painkiller, what's left of her leg tied off with a tourniquet. Then there's the rescued drop ship crew, and Priest and Baker. There are more wounded than able-bodied in the cargo hold.

Jackson feels helpless. She can't help the medics do their job, and there's nothing around to kill up here at ten thousand feet. She has to fight the urge to unbuckle and go up to the drop ship's armory to refill her magazine pouches and grab a bunch of weapons to replace the ones she left behind on the street in Detroit.

Three years of combat drops all over the country and across the world, and the squad has never received a mauling like this, not even close.

What the fuck went wrong? Jackson wonders. She looks at the leaking bodies of her squadmates and the dozens of impact marks on the outer shell of her armor.

Everything, she concludes. *Ain't a damn thing that went right tonight.*

She reaches into her magazine pouch and fishes out the set of dog tags she plucked off the dead rioter just a little while ago. The services all have their own formats for dog tags, and these are rectangular, with rounded edges and a horizontal perforation right across the middle. Jackson isn't sure, but she thinks they're old Navy tags, a kind they haven't issued in a while.

Military weapons. Squad tactics. Run-of-the-mill welfare rioters don't chew up a hardened infantry squad. They don't blot heavily armored drop ships from the sky. You need a certain kind of training and mindset to pull that off.

Jackson puts the dog tags back into the magazine pouch before anyone can see what she's looking at.

Right then she resolves to find out who's responsible for this ambush—for half her squad laid out bleeding or dead on the deck in front of her. Find the bastards, and kill them.

When the drop ship lands at Great Lakes, the medics swarm the cargo hold before the tail ramp is fully on the ground. They haul off Grayson and Sergeant Fallon, then the dead bodies of Stratton and Paterson. They come to check her out as she unbuckles herself.

"I'm fine," she tells them. "No holes in the armor."

"Let's get you inside anyway," one of the medics replies. "Just to make sure."

They take the combat knife off her harness. She has to suppress the impulse to break the fingers of the medic who unfastens her blade and removes it.

Let them have it, she thinks as they lead her outside toward a row of waiting stretchers. *Like I wouldn't know how to kill someone without that. Dumb fucks.*

She just has a few minor scratches, so they clean her up and put her on a shuttle back to Shughart. They won't let her see the rest of the squad. The flight back to base all by herself is the loneliest trip she has ever taken in the military.

Back in the squad bay at Shughart, the ghouls have already cleaned up. Two of the bunks in the room are stripped down to the bare mattress pads, and two lockers stand open and empty. Jackson walks over to what used to be Stratton's locker and looks inside. The gear is all gone, and someone wiped down the whole locker with an antiseptic cleaner that left behind a faint lemon smell. They even peeled off the adhesive name tag that used to be on the locker door.

She runs her fingers across the optical sensor of the locker's latch, the flaky DNA reader that would refuse to read Stratton's thumbprint sometimes, usually when they were running late for something. Her fingertips glide through a thin layer of cleaner residue. There's nothing left of Stratton in this room, not even his fingerprints. Twelve hours ago, they geared up for a mission in this room together, and now it's like he never even existed.

Battalion doesn't seem to know what to do with her. They put her on light duty, but they don't actually give her anything to do, so she cleans her gear and stows it, then takes it out and cleans it again. She doesn't want to do maintenance. She doesn't want to patch things up, she wants to break them. She wants to go out and kill people. It seems strange to be angry at being the only member of your squad to escape an ambush without injury, but Corporal Jackson is. In fact, she's fucking furious.

She doesn't feel like eating at all, but her stomach reminds her that she hasn't had any food since before last night's combat drop, so Jackson walks over to the chow hall for lunch. For the first time, nobody from her squad sits down with her at the table. She pokes around in her lunch—spaghetti and meatballs—and gets her PDP out of her pocket to read up on the battalion news while she eats. There isn't a word about last night's clusterfuck. The battalion S is probably still trying to figure out how to package the events in terms that don't make it look like the brass screwed the pooch. Like the grunts don't talk.

The dog tags from last night are in her pocket now. Jackson takes them out and puts them on the mess table in front of her, next to her plate of spaghetti. Then she enters the name on those tags into her PDP and runs a MilNet data search.

It takes a lot of digging to find any references to her MCKENNEY A in the archives. Jackson has no access to the personnel files anywhere, so she can't just punch in the military serial number on the tag and pull up a name. Instead, she has to do full-text searches on all the open databases on the MilNet--all the sanitized press releases for public consumption, and the thousands of individual unit news nodes updated by the data entry clerks in every autonomous unit in the Armed Forces.

After thirty minutes of increasingly customized searches on increasingly obscure data repositories, her spaghetti and meatballs are cold, but she finally finds a reference to a Navy sailor named MCKENNEY, ANNA K. It pops up in a reference to an awards ceremony, and she instructs her PDP to ferret out the related file. A few seconds later, her PDP returns an article from a base news bulletin, titled TWO RECEIVE NAVY COMMENDATION MEDAL ON NACS CATALINA. There are pictures of the event attached to the file, and the second one she pulls up makes her sit up straight in her chair with a jolt.

The picture shows two sailors shaking hands with a Fleet officer, presumably their commander. The sailor in the middle is the woman she shot last night in Detroit. In the picture, her long hair is neatly tied into a braid, and she's wearing a Class A Navy smock with petty officer chevrons on her sleeve.

She looks at the picture for a while. She tries to imagine what her voice sounded like, or what her smile looked like.

Petty Officers Third Class Anna McKenney and Pete Willis

accept their Navy Commendation Medals from their Commanding Officer, Lieutenant Commander Alan Carreker, the caption of the picture reads.

Anna McKenney will never age past the way she looks in that picture. All that's left of her is the collection of bytes that make up this picture in some forgotten nook of the MilNet, and the stamped steel tag on the table in front of Jackson.

The article lists Petty Officer McKenney's home town as Liberty Falls, Vermont. A quick cross-reference with MilNet tells Jackson that Liberty Falls is a small city near the state capital Montpelier. Its population is only thirty thousand, which is a shockingly low number to her. There are more residents than that in any five blocks of tenement buildings of any PRC.

When the military lists a soldier's hometown, they always mean the place of enlistment. Corporal Jackson very much doubts that Anna McKenney traveled all the way to that little Vermont town just to visit a recruitment office, and she's willing to bet that some people in Liberty Falls still remember her name.

Chapter Three: Liberty

"Don't make me find you some bullshit job," Master Sergeant Sobieski says when Corporal Jackson walks into his office and renders a salute. The platoon sergeant is a stocky man with a graying buzzcut and a permanent frown on his face.

"Negative, sir. I came to check if I can get a few days of leave. Since I am limited to bullshit jobs right now anyway."

Master Sergeant Sobieski looks at her, his frown increasing in severity as he undoubtedly ponders whether to consider her repetition of his swear word as borderline insubordination. Then he raises an eyebrow.

"Leave? What the hell you going to do with that, Jackson? Got yourself a civvie boyfriend in town?"

"That's a negative, sir. I feel the need for some fresh air all of a sudden."

Sergeant Sobieski studies her face for a moment, his own expression sour as always. Then he shakes his head and sits down behind his desk.

"I sure as shit can't use you for anything before Battalion gets around to your psych eval and lets you near a gun again."

He consults the MilNet terminal on his desk.

"You got five days accrued, Jackson. You want to take 'em?"

"If it's okay with the platoon, sir."

Master Sergeant Sobieski hacks away at the keyboard with two fingers, an activity he clearly finds distasteful. Then he taps a button on his terminal's touchscreen and leans back in his chair.

"I'm the platoon right now, Corporal, and I don't care. God knows you've all earned a few days of drinking and whoring around for that clusterfuck in Detroit. Go over to the company clerk and give him the dates you want for your leave."

"Thank you, sir," she says.

"Now get out and stop bugging me," the Master Sergeant says and waves her out of his office.

The next morning, Jackson puts on her little-used Class A uniform instead of the far more comfortable ICUs. She'd much rather wear the fatigues—the Class A looks a lot more presentable, but feels a lot more stifling—but she obeys the regulations and puts on the dress smock.

After breakfast, she walks across the base to the aviation section. A soldier on leave can hitch a ride on military transports, provided they have a free jump seat in the cargo hold. Some soldiers spend a good chunk of their leave waiting for rides, but

Jackson has no problems getting a seat on an eastbound transport shuttle right away.

She spends the morning hopping across the eastern half of the continent on a succession of shuttles. Finally, after stops at TA bases in Kentucky, the Chicago metroplex, and upstate New York, she finds herself at Burlington, a small TA air base on the shore of Lake Champlain. The base has a public transportation link right in front of the main gate.

As a soldier, Jackson gets certain perks in the civilian world. She can eat at any government facility with a chow room—military bases, public administration centers, transit worker canteens. She can also ride the maglev system for free just by scanning her military ID in place of a regular ticket.

She walks into the terminal building, past the uniformed security guards at the door. Her TA smock gets her respectful nods. She has no doubt that coming up here in her old, ratty civilian clothes would have meant a security inspection and on-the-spot interview instead, to make sure she has a good reason for being up here, and a form of payment sufficient for a maglev ticket. She pulls a ticket with her ID and gets on the regional maglev to Liberty Falls, just ten minutes away.

The town is clean, tidy, middle-class. No high rises anywhere in sight to spoil the view of the Green Mountains which surround the town. It looks like a different world from Dayton, never mind Detroit.

Jackson came to Liberty Falls with only a last name for a lead. The military-issue PDP in the pocket of her uniform trousers only talks to the MilNet, which doesn't interact with any of the civvie data networks. She can check obscure news from backwater TA units, or look up any number of regulations and manuals, but the PDP won't let her so much as bring up a schedule for the hydrobuses berthed outside the transit station. She's almost ready to ask a local to borrow their personal datapad for a moment and rely on the respectability her uniform seems to convey in this middle-class enclave, when she sees a public library up ahead at the corner of the green.

The library has public-access data terminals. She walks in, sit down in front of one, and brings up the public and private Networks directories. There are eight Net nodes in Liberty Falls belonging to people with the last name of MCKENNEY.

She half expects the search for the right McKenneys to require canvassing every address on the list of names she just brought up, but in the end, the resolution is quick and simple. She plugs Anna McKenney's full name into the heuristic search to see what comes back. The data terminal blinks for second, and then spits out four screens of search results. Jackson opens a few to see if they refer to the right person, and the very first hit is her yearbook entry from her school, Miguel Alcubierre Polytechnic Public High School. The girl in the picture is unmistakably a young version of the woman in the image of the military awards ceremony Jackson has saved on her PDP. She never got a long look at Anna McKenney's face back in Detroit, but she has had plenty of time to study her picture since she unearthed it on her PDP back in the chow hall yesterday. There are many more references to her in the public news repositories filed away for posterity, and after a few more minutes of digging, Jackson finds the name of her parents, embedded in a picture of the proud family at Anna's graduation from Alcubierre Polytech back in 2188.

ANNA MCKENNEY, CLASS OF '88, AND HER PARENTS, JENNIFER AND ROBERT MCKENNEY.

She checks the list of addresses she pulled from the public directories and sees the entry for MCKENNEY ROBERT & JENNIFER near the bottom of the list. They are on a private network, Datapoint, but their listing isn't locked, and their Net node number is followed by their street address: 4408 Copley Circle, Liberty Falls, NAC/VT/056593.

It's only when she looks at the address of the parents of the woman she killed when she realizes that part of her wanted to come up empty, to hit a dead end out here in suburban Vermont, and go home to Shughart with an excuse to stop digging. Now, with the address right in front of her, she no longer has the option

to return to the way things were before Detroit, no way to
rationalize keeping herself in the dark.

According to the city map, Copley Circle is a street in a
residential neighborhood two kilometers from the library. Jackson
transcribes the directions to the notepad on her PDP, does a hard
reset of the terminal to clear all the screens, and leaves the library
to go and maybe find a measure of absolution.

Chapter Four: Vermont

Copley Circle is a neat neighborhood. The houses are small,
but there's space between them, and they all have little front yards
with patches of artificial grass. The uniformity of the
neighborhood reminds Jackson of a military base, rows of largely
identical buildings lined up like a TA company at Morning Orders.
There are hydrocars parked in front of many houses--personal
transportation, an almost inconceivable luxury in a PRC.

4408 Copley Circle sits at the end of a long cul-de-sac. Out
here, there are air filtration units in the windows as well, but as
Jackson steps into the walkway that leads from the road to the
front door of number 4408, she notices that their environmental
unit isn't even running. The air is so clean out here.

She presses the button for the doorbell, and once again, she
feels a bit of hope flaring up--hope to have her ring unanswered,
hope that the McKenneys are out to visit friends for the day, or
down in the clean air of Panama for the season, so she can turn
around and get back onto the train to Burlington with a somewhat
intact conscience. Then she hears the sound of footsteps inside.

The door opens, and Jackson finds herself face to face with a
tall man who looks to be in his sixties. He has thinning red hair

that's gray in many spots, and the soft-edged look of a government employee, someone who has regular access to something other than soy patties and recycled sewage. They look at each other for a moment, and he studies her uniform with an expression of mild distaste on his face.

"How can I help you?" he asks, in a tone that makes clear that he rather wouldn't. Jackson takes a deep breath, and then finds that she has no idea what to say to the man whose daughter she killed two days ago.

"My name is Corporal Kameelah Jackson," she says. "Are you Anna McKenney's father?"

He looks past her briefly, as if he expected more people to have come with her. Then his gaze flicks back to Jackson—or rather, her uniform.

"You're not on official business," he says, and it's a statement rather than a question. "They'd never send just a junior NCO all by herself."

"No, sir. I'm here on my own."

"I was hoping I'd never see another one of those fucking uniforms for the rest of my days," he says. The swear word comes out as if he doesn't use it very often. "What do you want?"

"I wanted to talk to you about Anna," she replies.

He looks at her for a long moment, the distaste still etched in his face. Then he purses his lips and opens the door a little wider.

"Well, come inside before you let all the bad air in. And wipe those awful boots."

The table in the dining room has two sets of used dishes on it. Mr. McKenney pulls out a chair and motions for her to sit down before picking off the dirty plates and carrying them off. She takes the seat and looks around in the dining room. There are framed prints on the walls, black-and-white photographs of untouched landscapes long gone. There's a little china cabinet in a corner of the dining room, and a small collection of framed pictures on top of it. Jackson recognizes Anna McKenney in numerous stages of her life--basic school, polytech, proud college grad adorned with the obligatory gown and cap. From the lack of other children in that little picture shrine, she deduces that Anna was an only child, which makes the dread she feels even worse.

"You're not one of Annie's buddies," Mr. McKenney states matter-of-factly when he returns from the kitchen, holding two brown plastic bottles in his hands. As he sits down in the chair across the table from her, he pushes one of the bottles across the polished laminate. She picks it up and sniffs the open mouth of the bottle.

"It's just beer," he says. "You can have one, since you're not on official business."

"Thank you."

She takes a sip and lets the liquid trickle over her tongue. She's never been much of a beer drinker--hard liquor is much more cost-effective for welfare rats, and much easier to make in large batches--but the bitter flavor of the cold beer is pleasing after the long walk in the warm sun.

"How do you know I'm not?" ask him.

He nods at her uniform and points at the green beret with the Infantry badge tucked underneath the left shoulder board of my jacket.

"You're TA. Annie was Navy. Military Police."

Jackson doesn't know how to interpret his use of the past tense, and she doesn't have a way of clarifying his statement without playing her own hand, so she just shrugs.

"So what do you want?" Mr. McKenney says. "If she owes you anything, you've come to the wrong place. She hasn't been home in two years. I haven't even talked to her on vid in a month or two."

"It's nothing like that," she says. She takes refuge in action and pulls the dog tag out of her pocket. She puts the tag in front of Mr. McKenney, and he glances at it for a moment before picking it up. Jackson watches as he turns the worn steel tag between his fingers slowly.

"Where'd you get this?" he says after a few moments. "I didn't even know she still had hers."

She could tell him that she yanked the tag off his daughter's neck after she shot her dead, two days ago and almost two thousand miles away. She has come all the way from Shughart to deliver that battered little piece of sheet steel, and maybe find a measure of absolution in the process. She doesn't feel shame for having killed Anna McKenney--she tried to kill Jackson's squad mate, after all. Jackson is sorry she had to kill her, this man's only child, but she's not ashamed, because she did what she had to do to save Grayson's life. When she came here, she fully intended to come clean and tell her parents what happened to their daughter that night in Detroit, and that she won't ever come home again. Now that she's sitting here, across the table from the man who changed Anna McKenney's diapers when she was little, the man who probably taught her to ride a bike and tie her own shoelaces, she just can't bring up the courage to face his reaction.

"I found it," she tells Mr. McKenney instead. "On the street, in Detroit, a week and a half ago."

He shifts his gaze from the tag in his hand to her, and then back to the tag.

"Is there more to that story, or an I supposed to believe you came all the way out here just to return this thing?"

"No, I didn't," she admits.

"Didn't think so. Where are you stationed, anyway?"

"Shughart, sir. It's just outside of Dayton, Ohio."

"That's a pretty long way from Detroit."

"We were on a call. Didn't you hear about it on the Networks?"

Mr. McKenney raises an eyebrow.

"Hear about what?"

"We were called in to put out a welfare riot," she says. "Broke a bunch of stuff."

"I haven't heard squat about that. There hasn't been a big welfare riot since Miami last year, and they say the Chinks started that one."

"Well," Jackson says, "I can assure you there was one, because we were right in the middle of it."

"Anyone get killed?"

She instantly recalls the dozens of bodies strewn in front of her squad's position after they opened fire on the surging crowd that had seemed determined to kill them with their bare hands. She remembers Stratton and Paterson, cut down in an instant by heavy weapons fire, and crumpling to the pavement like carelessly tossed duffel bags. She thinks of the apartment building Grayson demolished with a MARS rocket. She has no idea how many civvies their TA company killed that night, but if the other squads were only half as busy as theirs, they filled a lot of body bags.

"Yeah," she replies. "A few people got killed. You mean it wasn't in the news at all?"

"They don't usually advertise it when they send you people in to beat up on some welfare rabble," Mr. McKenney says. "Can't blame 'em, really. People might get the impression that the civil authorities can't control the PRCs."

She opens her mouth to tell him that they were the ones who took the beating that night--eight troopers dead, one drop ship lost, and dozens of wounded--but when she reconsiders the equation, it seems like she's about to complain of bruised knuckles after having beaten someone to death. They may have had a rough time on the ground, but the squad dished out much more hurt than they took.

"'You people'," she repeats. "You don't care much for the military, do you?"

"Sure I do," he replies. "The real military. The Marines, up there." He gestures to the ceiling. "The ones that keep the Chicoms and the Russians from kicking us off our colonies. You people," he says again, and nods at Jackson's uniform, "you're not military. You're just cops with bigger guns, nicer uniforms, and less oversight."

"Your daughter was Navy," she points out, and she's briefly satisfied by the hint of pain in his face.

"Yes, she was," he says. "I could have gotten her in with the Commonwealth, a nice shot at a public career. And she has to go off and play sailor. I tried to get Annie to resign, but those contracts you sign, they're one-way tickets. She served out her first enlistment, and she took the money and got the hell out, like anyone with half a brain would."

He puts down his bottle and picks up his daughter's dog tag again. Jackson watches as he slowly turns it between his fingers, rubbing his thumb over the raised letters of his daughter's name and service number. She knows what would be going through her head in his place, and she wants to avoid having to answer the question he's bound to ask sooner or later, so she seizes the initiative again.

"Do you know where I can find her?"

He looks at her and chuckles. It sounds like a stifled cough, entirely without humor.

"Like I'd tell you," he says. "For all I know, you're a lieutenant with Intel, and they just put you in a corporal's uniform to go and sniff around. What do you want from my daughter, anyway?"

"I don't really know," she admits. "Well, for starters, I'm pretty sure she was shooting at me, and I'd like to find out what the hell was going on that night."

"She was, huh?"

"Half the city was. Lots of them had military weapons. They shot down one of our drop ships."

"Are you sure you should be telling me that stuff?" Mr. McKenney says. "I'm not sure I want to know about that. If they don't want to see it on the Networks, you probably shouldn't be talking to me about it, don't you think?"

"I don't think I give much of a shit, sir. No offense," she adds when he looks at her in surprise. "I want to know what the hell was going on that night."

"Now that's interesting," Mr. McKenney says. "A TA soldier who wants to know why they send her out to shoot people."

She's getting tired of his hostility, and for a moment she considers coming clean, just to see the amused smugness on his face disappear. Then she gets a hold of her emotions and pushes the chair away from the table to get up.

"I'm sorry I bothered you," she says. "I guess I ought to be going. Thanks for the beer."

"Oh, sit down and relax," he replies and gets up from his own chair. "You're going to have a thicker skin than that if you want to make it to retirement. The government is full of cranky old jerks like me."

He walks off again, in an unhurried gait. Jackson studies the silk-screened label of her beer bottle while Mr. McKenney rummages around in a drawer in the next room. Then he walks back into the dining room, an old-fashioned paper notebook in his hand.

"I don't have an address for her, just a node number. You can try to get in touch with her yourself. My guess is that she won't be interested in talking to you, but who knows?"

He leafs around in his little notebook for a few moments, and then puts the open book in front of her, his finger pointing to a handwritten Net node address. The rest of the page is filled with notes, written in blue ink, in a neat cursive hand.

"That's the number she gave me last time I talked to her. I'm pretty sure it's someone else's node. Annie's just been sort of drifting from place to place since she got out of the military."

Jackson pulls out her PDP and transcribes the node address into the notepad.

"Thank you."

"You may want to be careful with that," he says. "If there's something going on the government wants to keep a lid on, they'll sic military intel on you if they notice you poking around."

She shrugs noncommittally and slips the PDP back into my pocket.

"I'm just a corporal on leave," she says. "With thirty-four months left to go on my contract. They own me one way or the other, right?"

Mr. McKenney closes his little notebook again and puts it next to his daughter's dog tag on the dining room table.

"Yes, they do. But if you're not careful, you'll get to spend those thirty-odd months in the brig, and you won't get that bank account in the end. Imagine, all that sweating and bleeding and killing for absolutely nothing."

It's a short walk from the front door to the curb of the public road. Mr. McKenney escorts her across his front yard, as if he wants to make sure she's really leaving.

When they reach the curb, Jackson turns around. Mr. McKenney has his hands tucked into the pockets of his trousers. Now that he's standing in front of her in bright daylight, she notices a bit of a belly overlapping his belt.

"Thanks for your time," she says, and now he's the one shrugging noncommittally.

"I'm retired. I have all day to waste."

Last chance, she thinks to herself. Last chance to come clean and confess to this man that you killed his daughter, shot her through the chest with a salvo of flechette rounds, and put another burst right into her face for good measure. Last chance to save this man from getting increasingly worried in the next weeks and months because his only child isn't calling him anymore. Last chance to save yourself from adding just another missed opportunity to the list of regrets that will hang around your neck for the rest of your life.

She wants to extend her hand to say good-bye, but she doesn't want to give him the chance to refuse it. Instead, she just nods and turns to walk away.

"Do me a favor, corporal," he says, and she turns around again.

"If you get to talk to Annie, tell her to give her mother a call when she gets a chance."

"I'll let her know," Jackson says, and the shame of the lie tastes like bile in her mouth.

On her way back to the transit station, she stops at the library and claims a data terminal once more. She takes out her PDP and enters the node number for Anna McKenney into a directory search to do a reverse lookup.

Anna McKenney's last Net node number is not on a private network, and it doesn't resolve to a physical address, just a unified pool of communication nodes. All of them belong to a single party--the Greater Detroit Metropolitan Civil Administration.

Chapter Five: Taps

Jackson hasn't taken a leave in almost two years. She has no family left to visit, and even if she did, they'd be in Atlanta-Macon, and she has no desire to return to that place in this lifetime. So she takes the maglev back to the Burlington base, which has a rec facility on the lakeshore. She spends two days eating, sleeping, and using the entertainment suites. By Day Three of her five-day leave, she is bored out of her mind, so she takes a shuttle back to Shughart. Better to report to duty early, even if it means having to count towels and clean optical sight modules, than to spend another day drinking shitty soy beer in front of a holoscreen.

When she walks back into the squad room, Priest and Baker are there, playing cards at the table.

"You two okay?" she asks.

"Yeah," Priest says. He runs his finger across his forehead, where a thin, pale line marks a fused laceration. "Few dings here and there. Grayson and the Sarge got the worst of it."

"Stratton and Paterson got the worst of it," Jackson says. "What about Hansen?"

"Her shoulder joint is blown," Baker says. "Three weeks rehab."

"We're on light duty," Priest says and gets out of his chair. "Top says we're off the line until the squad gets a debriefing and a psych eval."

Of course, Jackson thinks. They're not going to let us anywhere near a loaded gun until the shrinks and the Intelligence officers have cleared us.

"Top said you were on leave for the week," Baker says.

"I was," she says. "Cut it short. Ain't shit to do out there."

"So what do we do now?"

Jackson opens her locker and takes out her knife and a sharpening stone. Then she walks over to the table and sits down in the chair Priest just vacated.

"We get the edge back on," she says. "Downtime ain't gonna last forever."

She gets her medical clearance the next morning. One of the resident TA MedCorps docs looks Jackson over, checks the medical data from her armor, and pronounces her physically fit for unrestricted duty, as if she couldn't have determined that by herself. The psych eval and Intel debriefing are equally superficial and cursory, standard "how does that make you feel?" psychobabble bullshit, some half-trained shrink checking off boxes on a form. She gives him the answers she knows will let him make his marks in the right spots.

The Intel debriefing doesn't even have any sort of point. Her helmet camera captured everything much more reliably than her memory did.

"Forty-three," the battalion's intel officer tells her at the debriefing.

"Excuse me, sir?"

"Forty-three kills," he says. "Your tally for Detroit. All good kills on armed hostiles. You did well."

Is that supposed to make her feel better, give her pride or a sense of accomplishment? Lighten her conscience, maybe? If anything, it has the opposite effect. Those were not soldiers of a foreign army. They were welfare rats, with no armor and mostly antique weapons. They may have come out on top because it was a thousand of them against four squads, but they paid dearly for their victory if the rest of the company had kill counts anything like Jackson's. Next time the TA goes in, there'll be more of them and they'll be much more determined, because now they know they can win. They almost got a drop ship with a full armory and loaded ordnance racks. Jackson has no doubt they'll try again. She would.

No, there's no way to look at this as anything but a disaster. Going back to that place will never be the same. It might as well be a different country now.

Jackson knows that telling the Intel officer these things wouldn't make a difference. It's like all the staff officers live in a different reality, one with its own language and customs and laws of physics. What the fuck does it matter that she killed forty-three of those shit-eating, savage sewer rats? There are millions more.

Exactly a week after Detroit, the company commander summons Jackson into his office.

"You're the ranking member of your squad at the moment," Captain Lopez says to her when she takes the chair he offers.

"Yes, sir," she replies. "Sergeant Fallon isn't back from Great Lakes yet."

"And she won't be, not for a while. Anyway, I have orders to send people to the funerals. I'm sending Lieutenant Weaving to PFC Paterson's funeral. I'll be attending Private Stratton's. I want you to accompany me as the representative from his squad. Send one of the other privates with the Lieutenant. Your pick."

"Yes, sir," she says. The military has probably already reclaimed all the money in Stratton and Paterson's accounts. Their families won't see a penny of the money they earned while in uniform. If you die before the end of your term, it all goes back to the government. Not that it's ever more than a number in a database somewhere. So why would they even go to the expense of sending funeral delegations? It makes no sense to Jackson. But she's just a corporal and Captain Lopez is the company commander, so she salutes and obeys.

In the old days, they sent dead soldiers home in caskets, big wood-and-metal troughs large enough to hold a body. They'd put flawless uniforms on the corpses, complete with all the ribbons and decorations, even if nobody ever opened the casket before the burial. That sort of waste seems obscene to Jackson—burying a good uniform with a dead soldier. Never mind the idea of burying a body whole, dedicating dozens of square feet of precious unspoiled ground to park a corpse in perpetuity, even after body and coffin are long gone.

These days, the mortuary's incinerators reduce a body to just a few cubic inches of fine ash, and they pack it into a stainless cylinder small enough to fit into a magazine pouch. Stratton's cylinder is engraved with his name, rank, branch of service, and dates of birth and death. Captain Lopez carries the little capsule in white-gloved hands as they board the shuttle together the next morning. Jackson bears the flag they'll be presenting to Stratton's next-of-kin. It's folded into a tight triangle, with the NAC's star, maple leaf, and eagle exactly in the center. She also carries a small padded case with all of Stratton's awards, which aren't many. He had just started his second year of service. The family sent a son to Basic Training a little over a year ago, and now they're getting back a little capsule full of ash and a few pieces of alloy and cloth ribbon worth maybe twenty dollars altogether.

Corporal Jackson doesn't like any of this. The stiff Class A uniform she only wears a few times a year is scratchy and smells of locker dust. The seats of the shuttle are uncomfortable, and she doesn't like the thought of an hour-long flight alone with her company commander. But she figures that she owes Stratton at least this inconvenience. She knows that he would be itching to make fun of her in that Class A monkey suit, but that he feared her just enough to not have dared.

Stratton was from eastern Tennessee, so the shuttle doesn't have to go too far from Dayton. On the flight, the Captain asks her about Stratton. What was he like? Any anecdotes we should share with the family? How did he do on the ground during the drops? Did he get along with his squad mates? Jackson answers the Captain's questions with a growing sense of disgust. She realizes that even though he didn't know Private Stratton at all, he'll use her information to talk to the family about their son's accomplishments as if he has a personal connection to every member of his company. It's all so transparent, she thinks. Trying to pretend that you gave a shit about that boy. If you had, you wouldn't have sent him out into the middle of a riot without proper intel or air support.

The funeral is the most gloomy, depressing event she has witnessed in a very long time. Not just because they're burying a twenty-year-old kid who was her responsibility, but also because of where they lay him to rest. Stratton doesn't even get an outside plot. They stick his capsule into a receptacle on the wall of one of the many underground cemetery vaults of the K-Town Public Cemetery. They lock and seal the compartment, and the little door is barely big enough to hold a palm-sized memorial plaque. They're storing what's left of the kid in a space that's smaller than the valuables compartment of his military locker. Jackson didn't know him very long, but well enough to know that he probably would have chosen to be scattered out of the open tail hatch of a drop ship on the way to another deployment, not locked forever in a little hole in the wall along with ten thousand others.

Stratton's parents are stone-faced during the whole thing. His father, tall and imposing, takes the flag from her without a word of acknowledgment. When Captain Lopez holds out his hand to offer thanks on behalf of a grateful Commonwealth, Mr. Stratton throws the folded flag at him. It smacks into the Captain's chest and falls to the ground, still folded into its tight triangle.

"You can take that and stick it up your ass," he tells Captain Lopez. Then he turns to Jackson and takes the case holding his son's medals out of her hands.

"I will have those," he tells her. "But I have no use for that rag. Or for you. Now get the hell out of here and leave us with our son."

Jackson knows this is deep, desperate grief talking. She knows the man doesn't hate her personally, that his hate is aimed at the uniform she wears. Still, she feels a surge of shame and anger. She liked the kid, served with him for over a year, tutored him, shared meals and played cards with him. She doesn't deserve this loathing directed at her. But there's no point saying any of it to this grieving and angry man who is no longer a father thanks to some overconfident desk pilots at Battalion. The TA didn't kill his son, but they put him in front of the gun that did.

Next to her, Captain Lopez bends over to pick up the NAC flag Mr. Stratton tossed at him. Jackson turns and walks out of the cemetery vault without waiting for her company commander. There is nothing more to say or do here. Maybe someday she can come back here and talk to the Strattons, tell them about the anger she will always feel for failing their son and surviving the battle when he didn't, but today is not it.

On the way back to Shughart, she doesn't speak another word to the Captain, and he doesn't ask her anything else, which is good because she won't have to tell him to go fuck himself. She considers telling him anyway, though. Thirty days in the brig seem like a good start at penance.

Chapter Six: Mazes

When the First Sergeant walks into the squad bay, Jackson is by herself, sorting out her kit and checking for defects.

He waves her off as she snaps to attention.

"As you were. Come over here and have a seat."

She obeys and sits down at the table with the First Sergeant, who is the only person in the battalion that scares her as almost much as Sergeant Fallon.

"I need a squad leader," the First Sergeant says. "After that clusterfuck last week, I'm short a few heads. You up for padding a squad with the rest of your guys?"

"What's the drop?" she asks.

He looks at her and purses his lips.

"Charlie Company is doing a public safety sweep assist in Detroit-22. Fifth-gen PRC."

Jackson feels a unsettling tightening in her chest.

Fifth-gen PRC. Good God.

"I'll take a squad in Charlie," she says. "Just keep my boys off the line for a few more days."

The first-and second-generation PRCs were old school traditional thinking. High rises, none taller than twenty floors, laid out along wide streets, with parks and stuff in between. They meant to give it a regular neighborhood look and feel. All the oldest PRCs are first- or second-gen. They didn't have to tear down the old cities, just clear blocks piecemeal for new high rises. They worked okay, for a while anyway.

The third-and fourth-gen PRCs were much the same, only they tacked ten more floors onto the maximum for the high rises and clustered them all together like small cities. Twenty to a cluster. Most of the worst shitholes are third- or fourth-gen, because they're difficult to manage in a centralized manner. Too many people spread out over too many acres.

The fifth-generation PRCs—now those are something else entirely. The Commonwealth's crowning achievement in efficient people storage. All the latest thinking in crowd control, food distribution, security, and space utilization.

Residence towers a hundred floors high. Built around a hollow core, for convection cooling and to let daylight in. Each tower with its own fusion plant, medic station, security office. A hundred floors, a hundred apartments per floor, average occupancy two. Those are the units. Four towers put together in a square, the spaces between them walled off with thirty-foot concrete dams. That makes a block. The plaza between the four towers is for public services—recreation, food distribution, shops, public safety, transit station. Each block is centrally managed, its own little city. Eighty thousand people put together in a square footprint a thousand feet on each of its sides.

Twelve of those blocks arranged in a much bigger square, four blocks on each side of the square—that's a fifth-gen Public Residence Cluster. Forty-eight towers, split into blocks of four. Close to a million people in a fifth-gen, and that's at designed capacity. Many hold one and a half, two times that number. In the middle of that gigantic square made up of residence blocks are the wastewater and garbage facilities, the main power plant, the food manufacturing and reprocessing stations, administration building, and the main law enforcement and detention center for the PRC. From here, the Public Housing Police can lock down blocks and quarantine them in case of public unrest, and send backup to the public safety stations in the twelve blocks. Three hundred sixty-seven acres, a little over half a square mile, and it's a self-contained, compartmentalized, centrally managed city that houses and feeds over a million people. And the average metroplex has twenty or thirty of them.

In theory, the fifth-gen PRCs are easier to police than the older ones, and that's mostly true. You can shut down a floor, a unit, a block, three blocks, the whole damn place, all remotely from the central law enforcement facility that sits in the middle of the PRC like a spider in the center of a web. For some reason, however, Jackson hates going into the fifth-gens. Maybe it's because she grew up in a third-gen PRC, and she's used to the warrens of high-rises clumped together. In a third-gen, you always have a place to run and hide. It's sprawling and cramped, but everything is interconnected. The fifth-gens are so compartmentalized, you have choke points everywhere. Residence towers have two main entrance halls. Blocks have one entry and exit point, toward the middle of the PRC. It's all too easy to shut down, too easy to trap people, funnel them like animals in a slaughter chute.

They drop into PRC Detroit-22 with a full company. It's a lot of combat power, but Jackson knows that if things go to shit again, it won't be enough, not even close. The four drop ships of Charlie Company circle the towers of the target block at a safe distance. Then the lead ship swoops in and lands on the roof of the ten-story civil administration building, down on the square between the residence towers. Jackson is with Second Platoon, and their drop ship does not follow. Instead, they circle around and settle on the roof of the outermost residence tower, a hundred floors up. Then the tail ramp drops, and Second Platoon's thirty-six troopers rush out to deploy.

From up here, a thousand feet above the PRC, the view is actually almost beautiful, Jackson thinks. The streetlights and shop signs below illuminate the dirty night air in many colors. From up here, she can see clear across this PRC and into the next one, and the one beyond. A hundred thousand apartments, millions of people. Thousands of thefts, hundreds of assaults, dozens of murders committed right this second in her field of view. No guns allowed in public housing, but Jackson knows there are almost as many of them out there as there are people. You'd be foolish not to go armed in a place like this. Without teeth and claws, you're food to everyone out on those streets.

The rooftops of the residence towers are official use only. There's a landing pad for drop ships, and the access doors are controlled by the security office down in the basement of the tower. The entrance vestibule on the rooftop leads into a service area with its own express elevator. A platoon can walk out of their drop ship, onto the elevator, and out into the atrium at ground level in less than two minutes.

From the moment they leave the roof and go down into the service area underneath the roof, Jackson has a strange feeling about this call, a little nagging voice in the back of her head. The place isn't restless enough to justify a company of TA. Something feels all wrong to her. Maybe Detroit has made her shell-shocked, paranoid even, but when she's forced to pick between staff officer judgment and her own instincts, she knows which to pick.

"Hold on," she tells her squad as they wait for their turn to take the elevator down to the atrium. The other three squads of the platoon are already down there, and there's no gunfire, no distress calls, but that nagging voice in the back of Jackson's head screams at her not to let her squad go on that elevator.

"Hunter 2, this is Hunter 22 Actual, do you copy?" she sends over the platoon channel. The Lieutenant doesn't respond. She checks the TacLink, but there's no status update for the first three squads of her platoon, all down in the secure area of the atrium by now. The short-range TacLink signal sometimes doesn't have the pop to go through a hundred floors of reinforced concrete, but she should be getting at least something. Thirty troopers down there, and none of them in a spot to get a good signal?

"Something's fishy," she tells her squad. "We're not taking the elevator. I'm checking in with Company."

She walks to the door leading back to the rooftop. When she pushes the unlock button, the light flashes red. She tries again, gets the same result.

"What's going on, Corporal?" one of her fire team leaders asks.

"It's locked," she says. "They locked it behind us. I can't get on the roof to get better comms. Secure that emergency staircase over there."

One of her troopers tries the door of the escape stairwell.

"It's locked too."

"Those are never locked from the inside," she says. "Break that son of a bitch open."

Two of her troopers take turns trying to kick down the stairwell door, but it's a fireproof hatch with tamper-proof cladding, to prevent the residents from breaking into the maintenance spaces from the outside. They kick it a few times, but for all the good they're doing, they might as well shoot spitballs at it.

"Kelly, Grenade launcher," she says to one of her fire team leaders. "Load buckshot. Aim at the spot where the main lock meets the frame. Everyone else, back to the other door. Cover the elevator door."

"What about the rooftop hatch?" Specialist Kelly asks.

"That's ten centimeters of laminate," Jackson replies. "Can't blow our way through that one without blowing ourselves up with it. Now move it and get that stairwell access open."

"What the fuck is going on?" one of the privates asks.

"Don't know yet," she says. "No comms, and they've locked us in remotely. You want to take that elevator down and find out for sure?"

"Negative," the private says and eyes the elevator door.

Specialist Kelly chambers a buckshot round in her grenade launcher and walks over to the staircase door. The other troopers get out of her way with some haste.

"Fire in the hole," Kelly announces.

Her rifle's launcher barks its deep authoritative thunder. The sound reverberates in the small service area. The buckshot load from the oversized caseless 40mm shell punches into the lock and doorframe like a wrecking hammer. Kelly walks up to the door and gives it a sharp kick, and the heavy steel door pops out of its shattered lock and swings open.

"Where are we going, Corporal?" Kelly asks.

"The fuck away from here," Jackson answers. "Get to the floors below. Reassess the situation. Try to get the rest of Company back on the radio. Now move your asses."

They move down the stairwell to the floor below in tactical formation, rifles at the ready. Jackson can tell that some of the troopers think she's being mental, but she'd rather err on the side of caution than find herself trapped in a steel box with her entire squad. After last week, anything seems possible.

The fire-proof door on the 100th floor only opens from the inside as well, but another buckshot round from Specialist Kelly's grenade launcher takes care of the lock and half the frame. They file into the hallway beyond. There are apartment doors all along both walls of the hallway, but nobody sticks their heads out to see what's going on, not even after the thunder from a low-pressure rifle grenade. The hallway terminates in a little foyer that links the four corridors on this part of the floor and provides a little common area. There are no residents around here either.

Jackson checks her datalink to tap into the local security network. All the apartments have bioscanners and explosives detectors, and any assisting TA squad usually has full access to that information when they do sweeps. You walk up to an apartment door, you can instantly see how many people are present, their security classification, and their arrest history. When Jackson tries the datalink at the next apartment door she passes, nothing comes up. It's like the network for the entire building is out. She knows that can't happen--it's triple-redundant, and she should be able to get at least something from the wireless transmitters. It's either deliberately turned off, or someone is solidly jamming all their data comms.

"Watch the corridor junctions," Jackson cautions. "We'll go to the central core, get line of sight to the atrium."

None of this feels right. The building's security office is supposed to link with them as soon as they are on the ground, keep them up to date, tell them where they're needed. The rest of the platoon is supposed to be online, feeding their sensory data to her and the squad. This total radio silence is the strangest thing she has ever experienced on a drop, and it's unnerving.

At the next corridor intersection, Jackson can see the open space of the building core past the hallway in front of them. Every central corridor on each floor lets out onto a gallery overlooking the big open space in the center of the tower. You can see right down to the atrium on the first floor. There's a chest-high railing and another meter of polyplast barrier above that, to keep people from falling over the edge, or throwing each other. There's a safety net, attached to the gallery of the tenth floor, but without the polyplast, the hood rats would make it a sport to jump into it on purpose. Some still do, barrier or not.

The squad is twenty meters from the gallery when a warning buzzer trills, and the fire door at the end of the corridor comes down and locks into place. Jackson whirls around to see the same event mirrored at the other end of the corridor, back where they had just entered the 100th floor a minute ago. The corridor is pitch dark for a moment. Then the red emergency lighting comes on.

"Visors down," Jackson yells. "Go augmented. Spread out and stay sharp."

She pops her own helmet visor into place and lets the computer adjust the optical input. The section of corridor sealed off by the fire doors is sixty or seventy meters long, but that's not a lot of space for nine troopers to find cover if someone decides to hose them down with automatic fire. The infantry calls narrow indoor passages "death funnels".

Jackson prowls back to the corridor junction and takes a right turn to explore one of the side corridors. It ends at a bare concrete wall thirty meters beyond the intersection. The only ways in and out of this apartment cluster are shuttered with inch-thick armored fireproof doors, and they have nothing in their inventory to break down one of those.

"Hunter 22 Actual, this is OPFOR Actual."

The voice comes over the emergency public address system in the corridor. Jackson stops, dumbfounded. OPFOR Actual? Someone knows military radio protocol.

"I count nine of you in corridor 100-16. Would the NCO in command please approach the public safety terminal at intersection A-16 and patch in?"

Jackson goes to the terminal labeled A-16 and taps into the circuit. This drop has gone so far off the rails that it feels like she's in some sort of alternate reality.

"OPFOR Actual, this is Hunter 22 Actual, Territorial Army. Open those blast doors or I will shoot my way through them."

"That's a negative." The voice on the other end of the connection is clear, businesslike. It would have an unconscious swagger if voices could have those. Jackson has been on military comms for long enough to know that she's talking to a fellow combat trooper.

"You have a squad with rifles. I don't see MARS launchers," the voice continues. "Even if you have HE for your grenade tubes, you'll barely scratch the paint on the blast doors. You can shoot holes in the walls, but I can just seal you in again wherever you pop out."

She looks back at her troopers, who are still hunkered down in the corridor, rifles pointed toward the blast door.

"Who the hell are you?" she asks.

"I'm the commander of the force that just captured three quarters of your platoon without hurting anyone. I'd like to get you to surrender your squad to me so we can keep this blood-free streak going."

"Not an option," Jackson answers flatly. "You think I'll hand over my gun without firing a shot, you're out of your mind."

"You have eight troops. I have a full company in this unit alone. We have the numbers and the home field advantage here. There are two ways for you and your troops to leave this tower: unarmed and in our custody, or feet first in a body bag. Everyone else in your platoon has decided to pick the first option just now. Your lieutenant is unusually wise for a junior officer."

The man's voice is confident, convincing. Whoever he is, he has experience in making people do what he says. Jackson scans her comms and data channels again, but there is nobody in her circuit except for the eight troopers in the hallway with her. Not even the residence towers' electronic jamming systems could turn off her comms and data access so completely. Only her platoon or company commander could cut her out of the loop like that.

"Who the hell are you?" she asks again, this time more to herself than whoever is on the other end of the comms link. Then she cuts the connection.

Ninety-nine floors below them, and a rooftop above that's inaccessible through the half-meter thick ceiling of the maintenance floor. Jackson's squad is trapped at the top of a very large box like rats in a maze, and they have no way to chew themselves out of it. She has no way to tell the drop ships overhead that the platoon is in deep shit. And nine troops, fighting their way down 99 floors in a residence tower with a compromised security office and a hundred hostiles to fight?

Without the schematics of the building on her tactical screen, Jackson tries to reconstruct the floor design of the residence towers from memory. A hundred apartments, in four sections of twenty-five, with four main corridors sectioning the floor into quarters. If they can cut through the apartments to either side of the fire door ahead, they can break into the gallery that overlooks the open space of the building core. If the roof hatch above the core is open, she may be able to get line-of-sight comms to a drop ship overhead.

She'll be able to look down onto the atrium and see just what the hell is happening down there. It's a messy way out and a long shot, but it beats the prospect of hoofing it down ninety-nine flights of stairs while dodging rifle fire from every floor along the way.

"Kelly, Pearson," she says and points when she has the attention of her troopers. "That apartment and that one. Break down the doors. Go soft, just in case there's civvies inside."

Kelly and Pearson do as ordered and kick down the doors Jackson pointed out. Both require multiple kicks and no small amount of cursing. The fifth-gen stuff is built to last, designed for occupation by ten consecutive generations of welfare tenants. Nobody's inside, though. There's furniture and the detritus of daily life scattered about, but nobody challenges their forced entry. Not that it would have been a smart thing to do. Jackson walks into one of the open apartments and checks the layout. Two bedrooms, bathroom, combined kitchen and living room. The far wall of the living room is her demolition candidate—on the other side, there will be the open space of the floor's gallery.

"Launchers," Jackson says. "Buckshot the shit out of that wall right there. Aim for the same spot. We need a hole to crawl out of."

Her troopers ready their launchers. Jackson steps back into the corridor to let them do their thing. The combined bark from three grenade launchers makes the concrete floor under her feet shake. When she sticks her head back into the apartment to observe the results, there's an irregular hole half a meter wide in the far wall of the living room.

"Do another round," she orders. "And hurry up, or every civvie asshole with a rifle is going to be out there waiting for us to pop out."

Her troopers fire another brace of 40mm buckshot into the wall. Whoever lives here just got an upgrade, a nice big window overlooking the 100th floor gallery. Kelly and Pearson extend the hole with their rifle butts until it's big enough for an armored trooper to fit through.

"Let's go," Jackson orders.

She goes through the breach first. There's nobody in the space beyond, which is relieving and worrisome at the same time. Nobody's ambushing them, but the gallery space shouldn't be completely empty. This is the common area for the entire floor, and people are here at all times of the day to socialize, trade, or catch some fresh air and sunlight from above. But there's nobody here, not a soul.

She looks up to where she should be seeing the dirty evening sky above Detroit. The huge retractable rooftop hatch is closed. There will be no line-of-sight comms with the drop ships. If they're even still there, Jackson thinks. Anything seems possible in this new gone-to-shit scenario. Three full squads in the bag without a single shot fired, and the opposing team in full control of the security facilities of a fifth-gen residence tower. Jackson wonders if they control just the tower, or the whole block, or maybe even the entire damn PRC, all twelve blocks and forty-eight residence towers of it. Not that it matters. It's not like she can even take on a company with the few troopers she has.

Jackson knows that this is not going to end well. But she can't just walk over to the nearest security panel and surrender herself and her squad without putting up a fight. There would be no point in ever again suiting up after that.

Overhead, the public address system comes alive again, much louder than before in the narrow corridor.

"I admire your initiative," the voice from before says. "But you have nowhere to go up there. You can't fight your way out of here. If you try, you'll get yourselves killed. Whatever you think they called you in for, I guarantee you that it's not worth that."

There's a pause, and when the voice comes on again, the man sounds almost gentle.

"NCO in charge, contact me on the nearest security panel when you are ready to discuss your surrender. There's no shame in wanting to stay alive, you know."

Jackson looks back at her squad, hunkered down behind concrete benches and planters with rifles at the ready. Most of them look like they're in a death row cell and they can hear the footsteps of the execution delegation. They're all privates, most of them green second- and third-class, and a pair of more seasoned first-classers that have been in the TA and doing combat drops for a little over a year. Jackson wishes she had her regular squad with her. If she is going to bite it on this drop, she'd rather be with Hansen, Baker, Priest, and the others. Her own squad would cause that smooth-talking OPFOR commander a much bigger headache than this squad of green kids. And with Sergeant Fallon here, the other team would be in deep shit.

But she doesn't have her own squad, just these eight scared privates.

"What are we going to do?" Private Kelly asks her. Kelly is a young woman who looks like she just barely made the height and weight minimum for infantry. She's the only other female in the squad.

Jackson ponders her reply for a moment. Of course, there's no real choice, not for her. If Sergeant Fallon were here, she would have potted the comms console with her rifle the second the other guy mentioned surrender.

"We're Territorial Army," Jackson says. "We do our jobs, Private Kelly."

She looks over to the closest elevator bank.

"Kelly, Pearson, cover that. Anyone steps out with a gun, you punch their ticket. No warnings."

Kelly and Pearson look at each other, then obey. They move up to a cluster of planters ahead and train their rifles on the elevator doors.

"Everyone turn off your TacLink," Jackson orders. With their data links compromised, they'll have to go the old-fashioned way, voice and hand signals. Not having that almost omniscient TacLink awareness is a huge disadvantage, but letting the enemy—whoever they are—see through the squad's eyes would be an even bigger one.

Jackson looks around for a way off this floor that doesn't involve a ride in a computer-controlled elevator. There are staircases, but they're at the corners of the floor, reachable only through corridors that can be sealed off piecemeal remotely by the security office. And they can't all rappel down to the atrium ninety-nine floors below. They would have been better off in the staircase back under the roof.

Jackson curses herself for that tactical blunder. She led them in here, and now there's no way out.

Then there's movement to her side. Across the chasm of the central core, on the other side of the gallery, armed civilians are coming out of hallways and quickly taking cover in the gallery. There are two layers of polyplast security barrier between Jackson's squad and these armed civvies, so she can't engage. She signals her squad to take up covering positions and watches the force across the chasm as they take their own cover behind planters and low walls, every bit as efficiently as her own squad. There are a lot of them—three, four squads, and more coming out of the shadows of the hallways beyond, all converging on the gallery. Jackson knows her squad can't take on that many, not in the confines of this rat maze.

"Last chance," the enemy commander's voice comes over the public address system. "Surrender your weapons, or we'll come and take them."

Across the core, a lot of rifles are aimed in Jackson's direction now, and a lot of them look like military hardware.

But they don't have battle armor, Jackson thinks.

None of the civvies have the sealed armor to go with those stolen military rifles, and she wants to bet they're a little short on augmentation too, because nobody over there seems to be wearing a helmet.

"Launchers," she tells her squad in a low voice. "All gas grenades. Lob 'em over the barrier and onto the other side. Give me a volley on my mark."

Her squad obeys. They take buckshot shells out of launchers and replace them with riot gas canisters. Kelly almost fumbles her reload, then readies her grenade launcher and looks at Jackson with wide, fearful eyes.

"Left side shoots left, right shoots right," Jackson orders. "Kelly, shoot straight across with me. On three. Two. One. Fire in the hole!"

Nine launchers thump in a short, stuttering drumroll. Two of the gas grenades clatter against the polyplast barrier on the other side of the chasm and careen off, then fall down into the core spewing smoke. The other seven grenades drop into the gallery space beyond and burst apart. Within a few seconds, the other side of the gallery is blanketed with riot gas.

To a trooper in sealed armor, a gas grenade is just a minor inconvenience. The helmet keeps out the chemicals, and the augmented vision from the sensors cuts through the smoke. To an unprotected civvie, however, it's like getting your face doused with alcohol and set on fire.

Instantly, there are screams of anger and pain coming from the far side. Jackson can see people hunching over or dropping to their knees in the noxious white cloud her squad just conjured with their launchers.

"Flank and flush," Jackson orders. "Southeast corner, doubletime."

She rushes her squad to the corner of the gallery, then turns left to cover the stretch of garbage-strewn concrete that is the south side of the gallery. Then she's at the southeast corner. She looks around the edge of the concrete retaining wall to see the armed civvies retching in the chem cloud. The stuff is pretty persistent, but it won't keep them suppressed for more than a few minutes. Until then, they're blind and in no shape for fighting.

Jackson draws first blood. In the mouth of a hallway ten yards in front of her, two of the armed civvies are still alert and on their feet, at the far edge of the chem cloud. They see her and raise their rifles. She shoots first, letting her computer select the burst length as she sweeps the civvies with her muzzle and holds her trigger down. The M-66 pumps out two three-round bursts, and both civvies fall over. Their rifles clatter to the floor as they die silently.

When Jackson looks to her left again, the remaining civvies have retreated into the vestibules and hallways of the floor beyond the gallery again. She wishes she had some HE or frag grenades to bank off these walls and bounce after them, but the ammo loads for the mission were limited to nonlethal and buckshot for the launchers. Nobody anticipated having to use high explosives for a simple public safety sweep assist. The world seems to have gone nuts since last week.

She has never missed that heavy, unwieldy piece-of-shit MARS launcher more in her life. With armor-piercing rockets or thermobarics, she could crack these walls like eggshells, blast a hole into the exterior wall, radio the drop ship, get out of this mess.

"Back to the hallway," she tells her troops and points at the wide main hallway on the south side. The fire-proof door isn't down yet, and the main hallways lead straight to the main staircases. They rush over to the south side, trying to cover in all directions.

Just as they reach the mouth of the hallway, the elevator bank nearby chimes, and the doors open. Jackson and her squad are maybe fifteen meters away as the elevator disgorges a squad or more of civvies with weapons. They see her group and raise their guns just as Jackson's squad bring up theirs.

She wants to stop time at that moment. She knows what is going to happen, but she's powerless to avoid it. It's that freeze frame of mental acuity when that trigger has been pulled and the striker is racing toward the primer of the cartridge. The civvie in the lead starts to shout something, but Jackson can't understand it, and it doesn't matter in the end anyway.

Oh, shit.

Then everyone opens fire seemingly at once.

Jackson dives out of the way to the left, into the hallway and away from the elevators. She fires her rifle from the hip, into the tightly packed group of civvies coming off the elevators. As fast as she gets out of the way, a burst of flechettes still rakes her arm and right side. Behind her, the squad is out in the open, without the time to get to cover.

At a short range like this, a firefight between two squads with automatic rifles is like a knife fight in a boot camp locker. People scream and fall. Flechettes are piercing armor and flesh, ricocheting off hard surfaces and spraying apart in tiny splinters.

Eighteen, twenty rifles firing in rapid cadence. Jackson has never been in the middle of such a hail, not even back in Detroit.

Her rifle's target reticle disappears from her helmet display. She pays it no mind, just keeps firing her rifle from the hip. Hard to miss at this range. People are on the ground, others are madly scrambling for distance and cover. This isn't holding the line. This isn't a heroic last stand against the odds. It's naked, bloody slaughter.

Jackson's rifle stops firing. She automatically ejects her magazine and reaches for a new one on her harness, reloads, keeps firing.

She catches the movement above out of the corner of her eye. Reflexively, she throws herself backward. Overhead, the heavy steel-and-ceramic fire door of the main hallway entrance comes down quickly and silently. It slams into the concrete floor in front of her with a resounding crash that makes the floor shake. One meter to the right, and she would have been bisected by the hatch that locks into place not five inches from her right boot.

She is alone in the dark. Everyone else, her squad and all their enemies, are on the other side of the fire door.

Jackson screams in rage and frustration. She slams the unyielding laminate of the fire door with her fist. On the other side, the gunfire sounds muffled now, but rifles are still firing on full auto, and people are still shouting and screaming. Her people, her squad. Her responsibility.

"I'm locked in," she shouts into the squad channel. "Covering fire, and retreat to the breech we made."

Nobody replies. She pounds the fire hatch again, and this time there's a sharp pain in her hand that shoots all the way up to her elbow. She examines her hand in the green-tinted augmentation of her helmet's sensors. One of the flechettes from the enemy fire hit her armored glove and shattered. A shard of it must have pierced the armor and gone up her forearm. She can feel the blood running down the inside of the suit even as the armor's computer works on stemming the blood flow with its integrated trauma kit.

There are more holes in her armor, on her right side. Jackson isn't in pain, but her side feels numb, which is bad news. It means she's wounded badly enough for her suit to numb her up. Still, she has her legs, arms, and hands, and everything still works.

There's no way through that hatch except for blowing it up with a MARS rocket, which she doesn't have. Jackson checks her rifle—180 rounds remaining—and her spare magazines. Three left, plus the one in the gun. Maybe enough to fight her way out of here.

The corridor behind her is deserted as well. A whole floor of a welfare high-rise, and it's empty. Jackson wonders how far down they've evacuated. The floor below, five floors, ten? Where did all those people go? And how did these welfare rats become so organized?

On the other side of the fire door, the muffled sounds of automatic rifle fire cease. She tries the squad channel again. No reply.

Jackson replaces the partial magazine in her rifle with a full one and tucks away the partial in one of her magazine pouches. Then she moves down the hallway, away from the heavy fire door that traps her in this section.

The dark hallways of the apartment floor are eerily quiet and empty. Jackson clears the corridor, doorway by doorway, eighty meters of grungy rat warren without any rats inside.

At the end of the next hallway, there's an escape door to a stairwell. The green fire escape sign glows in the dark like a dim beacon. Jackson walks up to the door and pushes the panic bar down to open it. It doesn't budge.

There are two buckshot grenades left on her harness. She stuffs one into her launcher's chamber, steps back, and blows the lock assembly to scrap with a thousand grains of polymer-coated tungsten shot. Then she kicks the door open.

The staircase is dark and empty. It's 99 floors down to the atrium level, and she doesn't really want to go down to where her whole platoon just got bagged by the locals without firing a shot, but there's no other way out of this trap. She could hole up in one of the empty apartments and wait for them to come and find her, but she will not be pried out of a hiding hole like vermin.

The pain in her side is burning through the local anesthetic. The suit's autodoc is keeping her from bleeding out, but she knows that she needs to get to a medical center soon.

She makes it almost ten floors down before she hears fire doors slamming open above and below her. It's a trap, and she has walked into it willingly.

Jackson retreats to a corner of the stairwell and brings up her rifle. The optic on top of her M-66 is shattered, probably taken out by the same burst of flechette fire that tore up her side. The IR aiming laser still works, though. She puts the green dot of the laser on the first silhouette to appear on the staircase above, and pulls the trigger for a burst, then another. The silhouette disappears. The civvies carry high-powered weapon lights on their rifles, and the beams tear through the dark, casting harsh shadows on walls and ceilings.

Then she takes fire from the staircase below. She replies in kind, sending a few bursts downstairs. The ammo counter readout on her helmet screen goes from 250 to 210 in a blink. The civvies above her pop off a few bursts of un-aimed fire, holding their rifles over the railings without sticking their heads out.

Two grenades come flying down the stairs. They clatter on the concrete, bounce off the floor and walls, go in two different directions. Jackson rushes for one, kicks it down the stairs, knows that she doesn't have the time to reach the second one. But she tries anyway.

She kicks the second grenade, and it flies off and hits one of the steel posts for the handrail of the staircase. It deflects at an angle and lands in the space to her right, where she can't reach it without running right in front of the guns of the civvies down the stairs. It never comes to rest before it explodes.

Jackson is thrown backwards against the unyielding concrete of the staircase wall. Then she's on her side down on the dirty concrete of the sub-landing. She gropes for her rifle, but it's gone, blown from her hands. She feels the air leaking out of her, takes another breath, can't get her lungs to respond the way they should. There are footsteps above and below her in the dark. She gives up her search for the M-66 and fumbles for the knife strapped to her harness even as she feels her consciousness slipping away. Then there's just silence and darkness.

Chapter Seven: Lazarus

Jackson wakes up and immediately wishes she hadn't.

There's a bright light above her head that's hurting her eyes, and she is thirsty, thirstier than she has ever been in her life. She turns her head sideways to avoid the painful glare of the light above. She's in a room with unwashed floors and unpainted walls, dirty concrete. The merciless glare from the light fixture on the ceiling makes the place look inhospitable, pointing out every pockmark in the walls and mold spot on the ceiling as it does.

Her right arm is bandaged from fingertips to elbow. There's a dull ache throbbing underneath the antiseptic gauze, but when she tries to flex her fingers, they obey. She uses her left hand to check the right side of her body. More bandages, taped to her skin, worse aching underneath. She feels like absolute shit, like she just woke up with the world's worst hangover.

The room is small, just the overhead light, a toilet, and the bed in it. Her bedroom back home in Atlanta was smaller still, but not by much. Jackson checks the bed and sees that it's bolted to the concrete floor in typical welfare housing fashion. She throws aside the thin blanket covering her and sees that she's in a set of military issue underwear that aren't the ones she put on when she left for this fucked-up drop. Both her ankles are tied together with polyplast restraints, and there's a strand of it connecting her shackles to the bed frame. At the far end of the room, there's a steel door, but Jackson doesn't even have to try to know that her tether is just long enough for her to use the toilet, but too short to let her reach that door.

She sits up, ignoring the pain that shoots up her side, and clears her throat. There's nothing in the room she can use as a weapon, and without a good knife, she can't get rid of the plastic shackles that keep her feet together.

She clears her throat again. Her mouth is so dry that it feels like she's gargling with wood splinters.

"Hey," she shouts toward the door. Then again, louder. "Hey!"

She doesn't have to wait long. On the other side of the steel door, there's shuffling, someone getting out of a chair maybe. Then the door opens, and a surly civvie in combat fatigues looks at her without expression. He doesn't say anything, just studies her for a moment. Then he closes the door again.

Jackson sits and waits.

Two minutes later, the door opens again, and someone else walks in.

The man who steps into the room is tall and lean. His skin is almost as brown as Jackson's. He wears his hair in a military cut, shorn close to the skull on the sides and left just a little longer on top. From his bearing, the economy of his movements, Jackson knows that this man is a combat trooper.

"Good evening, Corporal," he says to her, and it's the same voice she heard over the security feed in the residence tower before things went all to shit. It's silky and sonorous, and it carries the air of authority.

The man carries a plastic cup. He walks up to the bed and hands it to her, along with a handful of pills. She takes them without taking her eyes off his face. He has a closely cropped beard and mustache, shaved so thin it's barely more than a black circle around his mouth.

She takes a sip from the cup. It's water—warm and with a slightly rusty smell to it, but liquid to get the tissues in her mouth and throat back into speaking shape. Jackson downs the contents of the cup briskly.

"Where's my squad?" she asks him.

He regards her with a faint smile.

"No 'where am I', no 'who are you', or 'how long have I been under.' Just concern for your troopers. I appreciate a combat leader with her priorities in the right order."

She doesn't reply, just looks at him without expression. She has already sized him up to see if she can take him down, and concluded that she can't. He has stepped back just enough out of reach that she won't be able to launch a surprise attack, as if he doesn't even want to tempt her into trying. Jackson can tell that this man is as tightly wound as a steel spring underneath his clean fatigues. He radiates a sort of latent, barely restrained energy that reminds her of Sergeant Fallon, who looks like she's always half a second away from unleashing violence.

"Your squad fought well, but they got the short end of the stick in the exchange," her visitor continues. "Five were killed in action. The other three should be back with their unit right now."

"Bullshit," Jackson says flatly.

"We took their guns and gear and let them go," he says. His clinical, calm tone tells her that he doesn't give a shit whether she believes him or not.

"Why would you do that?" she asks. "Let them go when you know they'll be back with new guns soon."

"Because we don't kill people unless we have to, and because I have no interest in going into the prison business. Too many mouths to feed around here as it is."

Five dead, Jackson thinks. Because I told them to fight, and they listened.

"What about the rest of the platoon?"

"A mixed bag," her visitor says. "Most were let go. A few of them accepted our invitation to stay. Nobody was harmed. We had a full company in the atrium, and crew-served weapons. Your platoon commander had the good sense to recognize an unwinnable scenario, unlike you."

He clasps his hands in front of his chest and pauses briefly.

"I do admire your initiative and your fighting skills. After you turned down my offer, you managed to keep an entire platoon busy trying to flush you out. And your squad killed seven of my troops and wounded eight more. But you pissed away the lives of your troopers for nothing at all."

"Not for nothing," she says. "Can't just surrender to everyone who asks. Sets a bad example."

He looks at her with that intense gaze, his face perfectly expressionless.

"I suppose it would," he says.

He takes the chair out of the corner of the room and puts it next to the bed. Then he sits down, just out of her reach, and folds his hands.

"Where did you serve?" she asks him point-blank. He doesn't even raise an eyebrow, just smiles faintly.

"Marines," he says. "2080 to 2106."

If he served four terms, he must be in his early fifties at least. He doesn't look that old, even if his short hair has a lot of silver in it. He looks at least ten years younger than that, which is unusual for a career space ape. That lifestyle wears a body out fast. Could be he's bullshitting her, but somehow Jackson knows he doesn't feel the need to lie to her.

"Officer?" she asks, and he nods.

"I was a Lieutenant Colonel when I left. Never did get to pin on those eagles."

He leans forward and studies her face, his chin perched on his steepled fingers. Then he gestures to the area under his eyes.

"Your facial tattoos. What do they mean? I don't recognize that pattern at all."

Jackson shrugs.

"Saw it in a manga when I was a kid. Thought it looked bad-ass. Thought I needed to look bad-ass back then."

He nods at her explanation.

"You're going to let me go, or kill me?" Jackson asks.

"I'm not going to kill you. I will tell you that the sergeant whose squad you mauled was ready to finish you off on the spot in that staircase. We don't run things like that around here. But I can't let you go just yet either."

"He the one in charge of the people that shot it out with us?"

"Yes, he was."

"Then you should have let him. I get the chance, I'll finish him off."

Her visitor shakes his head, slowly, like he just heard some kid say something outrageously dumb. Then he gets up from his chair and carries it over to the door, out of her reach.

"You were out for a while. You'll be hungry soon. I'll have someone bring you some food. It's not military chow, but I suspect you're no stranger to welfare rations. I'll be back later, when you're fed."

He walks out and closes the door from the outside. The snap of the deadbolts seems loud in her nearly empty room.

A little while later, someone else brings in a meal tray and puts it on the ground without saying a word. Jackson watches him unblinkingly until he is out of the room again. She gets out of bed— slowly and carefully—and retrieves the tray. It's the standard generic soy-and-shit chicken they put into the welfare meals with various flavorings. After she enlisted, Jackson told herself she'd never eat another welfare meal, but she has been famished since she woke up, so she eats everything on the tray and washes it down with the box of bug juice that came with the meal. If she wants to get out of here in one piece, she needs to give her body something to burn.

She makes the bed, pulls the ratty sheet over the mattress and tucks it in tightly, then straightens out the wrinkles. Then she lies down on the bed and closes her eyes for a nap. Fed and rested can fight longer and run faster than hungry and tired.

When the door opens again, she is awake instantly. She swings her legs over the side of the bed and sits on the edge, hands clasped in front of her. At least they didn't shackle her wrists.

The tall, lean, handsome visitor from before walks into the room. He's wearing the same sanitized fatigues—no rank insignia, no name tag, no unit patches. He eyes the empty meal tray on the floor. Then he picks up the chair from the corner of the room again and puts it in the precise spot he had placed it earlier, as close to the bed as possible while still being out of the reach of the shackled Jackson.

"Where am I?" she asks him. "Who are you? How long have I been under?"

He flashes the sparest of smiles. Then he sits down on the chair and straightens out the tunic of his fatigues.

"You are in PRC Detroit-22, in one of the residence towers we control. My name is Lazarus, and I am in charge of the force that captured and disarmed your platoon. You have been under for three days."

"Lazarus," she says, and almost chuckles. "Come back from the dead, did you?"

"In a manner of speaking," Lazarus says. "It's a bit of a long story, and I'm not sure you'd be interested even if I were in the mood to tell you."

"They'll tear this place apart when they come looking for us," Jackson says. Lazarus shakes his head slowly.

"I have no doubt they'll be back soon with more people, but we've long left the block where we ambushed your unit. We never use the same trick twice from the same spot. They'll need to drop a whole battalion just to get control of one block, never mind twelve."

"You control the entire PRC," Jackson says, incredulity creeping into her voice.

"Most of it," Lazarus says. "The wonders of centralized control and command. Now let me ask you a question."

He reaches into one of the chest pockets of his tunic and pulls out a set of dog tags on a chain. Then he dangles them from his fingers for her to see.

"You had these on you when we stripped you of your gear. Would you mind telling me how you got them?"

The dog tags are those of Anna McKenney, of course. She had been carrying them in the water-tight pocket insert where she keeps all her personal stuff. She looks at Lazarus, who is returning her gaze impassively.

"I took them off a woman's neck on the street in one of your shithole PRCs in the center of this shithole of a city."

"Did you kill her?"

Jackson senses that a lot is riding on her answer. She doesn't even consider lying.

"She wounded one of my troopers. Was about to finish him off. I put two bursts into her. Fuckin' right I killed her."

He doesn't say anything to that, just looks at her with this steely, unmoved expression, but she can tell there's a lot swirling behind those eyes right now. Then he lets out a small sigh and looks down at his hands.

"I suspected as much. We never found her body, but we had a lot of missing that night. What a waste."

Jackson agrees, although for different reasons. She doesn't say anything else, though. Lazarus shakes his head and puts the dog tags back into his pocket.

"It's all a waste, you know. Us down here, squabbling about who gets to eat how much of what shitty calories, you up there putting the boot on our throats whenever the pot boils over."

"We keep order," Jackson says. "We hold the line."

Lazarus shakes his head with a sad smile.

"Is that what you think you're doing? Do you see anyone glad for your presence whenever you come down into a PRC? Do you honestly not know how these people see you when you come in with your gunships and your battle armor, and walk the streets like you own the place?"

"Food's shitty," Jackson says. "Life sucks. I know. I was welfare before I joined up. But without the TA keeping you all from burning the place down, there wouldn't be any calories for anyone."

"You ought to know better than that, Corporal Kameelah Jackson," Lazarus says. "You're not there for our benefit. You're there to keep the shit from spilling over into the suburbs and the upper-class gated communities. You're attack dogs, and you don't even know who is holding your leashes. When people see you tromping down the street in the PRC, they don't see law and order. They don't see civilization. They see an occupying army."

Lazarus gets up, puts the chair back into the corner of the room, and looks at the door in front of him, fists clenched. Then he turns around, and for the first time Jackson can see emotion through his disciplined, collected expression.

"Just so you know, Anna McKenney was one of my platoon leaders. She was the kindest person I've ever known. Hell of a fighter, too. She was Navy, you know. Never had a lick of infantry training. We were together. If I had something like a soulmate in this life, she was it."

Jackson feels her face flush, and she's glad her skin color doesn't make it obvious to Lazarus.

"I'm telling you this so you can appreciate how hard it is for me to not just go outside, fetch a rifle, and shoot you right in the forehead."

He turns around and leaves the room. The door falls into its lock in his wake. Jackson doesn't even realize she has been holding her breath for the last few moments until she exhales shakily.

Chapter Eight: Choices

The noise of the door opening shakes Jackson out of her sleep. Two of the uniformed civvies walk in. One stands by the door with a rifle, the other tosses a set of fatigues and a pair of slip-on shoes onto the bed.

"Get dressed," he says. Then he steps up to the foot of the bed and snips her plastic restraints with a tool. "You try any funny shit, Olsen's gonna go full auto on your ass."

She gathers the clothes they gave her and gets out of bed. The pain in her sides is still there, still just this side of tolerable. She wonders if anything got broken permanently.

The uniformed civvies don't look like they have any intention of letting her get dressed in private, so she puts on the clothes while they're watching her. She glances at their gear and the way they're positioned, then concludes that she won't be able to drop the closer one before the rifleman by the door mows her down with the M-66 he's aiming at her.

When she's dressed, they step out of the room and wave her forward.

"We're moving. Go in front of me. Olsen will be behind us. You turn toward him, he'll shoot you. Now move."

She obeys and leaves the room, careful not to give Olsen an excuse to twitch his trigger finger.

Outside, there's a narrow hallway that looks like it's in a basement somewhere. Jackson follows the first civvie as instructed. The hallway leads out into a spacious vestibule. Out here, at least a dozen armed civvies in partial battle rattle are gathered, Lazarus in the middle of the group. He's wearing chest and back plates, a sidearm on a drop holster, and a harness with magazine pouches. When she steps into the vestibule, it seems that every pair of eyes in the room is on her.

"Corporal Jackson," he says. "We are relocating. Please follow along and don't give anyone a reason to shoot you. Trust me when I tell you that most of them would be glad for an excuse. Let's move out, gentlemen."

They rush through a maze of corridors and vestibules, Lazarus' men keeping a wary eye on her every time she strays close to one of them. Jackson's side hurts, and she feels something stabbing into her chest every time she takes a breath, but she knows it would be pointless to ask them to slow down.

Then someone in front throws open a set of doors, and they're outside.

It's nighttime, and Jackson sees that they're in the middle of a residence block. There's a droning noise in the air, and the reason for the sudden rush becomes clear when she sees a Hornet-class drop ship coming out of the night sky and circling around the top of a nearby high rise tower. The dirty nighttime sky is ablaze with the searchlights from more drop ships. Whatever TA unit is making a drop onto this block right now, they're coming in force, maybe an entire battalion dropping at once.

"They're on Tower Thirteen," Lazarus says into the earpiece he's wearing. "Don't engage. Let them have it. Second platoon, fall back to the atrium and take the rabbit warren down to the admin center. We'll meet up with you there."

They're a hundred meters from the admin building in the middle of the square when another Hornet swoops out of the sky and thunders down toward the square. Jackson sees the skids of the drop ship lower out of the belly armor as the Hornet swings around to claim a landing spot. There's rifle fire in the distance between two residence towers, and a moment later, an explosion blooms up in the same spot. The sound of the detonation rolls across the plaza like the rumbling thunder of an approaching storm.

"TA squads on the ground between Thirteen and Fourteen. Also in Blocks Five and Six. They're all over the place, sir," one of the troopers says, listening to the comms in his own headset.

There are civvies on the plaza, most of them without weapons and moving away from the spot where the drop ship is descending. It settles on the landing pad at the top of the admin center, a hundred meters away. Then the tail ramp opens with a low whine, and a platoon of TA come rushing out. They take up positions at the edge of the roof. Behind them, the drop ship guns its engines and lifts off again, raising the ramp in mid-air. It rises into the night sky, position lights flashing in the haze. The TA troopers file into the rooftop staircase one by one, weapons at the ready.

"We have a TA platoon on the ground at the admin center," Lazarus says into his headset. "Second platoon, don't engage them. Pass through and make for the fallback."

Another drop ship weaves its way between two of the residence towers ahead and thunders over the plaza at low altitude before banking and turning to the right. They're so low that Jackson can see the decals on the helmets of the pilots as the ship roars directly overhead.

"Told you they'd come back," she says to Lazarus. He turns around and glares at her.

"They're not coming for you. They're coming for their gear. They're here to send a message, you dumb shit."

There's rifle fire coming from the inside of the admin center now, short staccato bursts of automatic fire. A muffled explosion follows, then another.

"Sir, Second Platoon is engaged in the admin center."

"Goddammit," Lazarus says. He looks over to Jackson, then points at Olsen and the other civvie who escorted her from the room earlier.

"Olsen, Lepitre. Take our guest here over to the warren at Tower Eleven. Head for the spider nest. Don't stop for coffee. The rest of you, with me."

Lazarus leads off to the admin center, and most of the troopers move out with him as ordered, covering corners and sectors like a seasoned TA infantry squad. Olsen points out the way for her with the barrel of his rifle, back toward the tower they just left. She obeys and follows Lepitre.

They're back inside the basement hallway when the overhead illumination switches from white to the dim red emergency light. The change is startling without helmet augmentation to compensate for it.

"What the fuck," Lepitre says ahead of her. On the floor directly above, there's gunfire, the hoarse chattering of flechette rifles interspersed with the lower single booms of cartridge guns.

Two more troopers appear around a bend in front of them. In the dim light, it takes Jackson a second or two to realize that the newcomers aren't civvies in partial battle gear, but TA troopers in full armor, M-66 rifles at the ready.

Everything happens at once.

Lepitre up ahead shouts something at the TA troopers, but whatever he's saying is drowned out by the booming warning coming from the troopers' suit amplifiers.

"DROP YOUR WEAPONS AND GET ON THE GROUND! DROP..."

Lepitre goes for his sidearm, but he's either too slow or too fast for the TA troopers. They both open fire, and Lepitre twitches once and falls to the ground. Behind Jackson, she hears the creaking of the plastic on Olsen's rifle as he brings it to bear.

Jackson stops cold and drops to the ground. Olsen's rifle spits out a full-auto burst, and both TA troopers go down in the hail of flechettes, half a magazine dumped at maximum cadence. Olsen is right behind her, less than half a meter away, and she rolls around and kicks his legs out from underneath him. He goes down, still clutching the rifle, and squeezes the trigger again. The burst hits the wall next to them and peppers Jackson with concrete chips and flechette fragments. She tries to wrestle the rifle away from him, but he's holding on to it with a death grip, and he's stronger. He tries to aim the rifle at her, but she's on top of him, and in those close quarters, there's no space for a sixteen-inch barrel between them.

Jackson drives an elbow into Olsen's face, then his throat, as hard as she can thrust it down. He gurgles and lets go of his gun to clutch his throat. Jackson seizes the M-66 and backpedals, aims the muzzle at Olsen, and squeezes the trigger. The burst takes him in the side of the chest. He stiffens, groans, exhales. Then he stops moving. Jackson has seen enough KIA to know even in the dim light of the emergency illumination that he's dead.

She gets to her knees and checks the condition of the rifle. Without a helmet display, she has to eject the magazine and count the rounds through the witness strip on the side. A quarter of the magazine left, so maybe sixty rounds. Olsen isn't wearing an ammo harness. Dumb fuck ran around without reloads. If he was a vet, he wasn't infantry, she thinks.

The TA troopers are down as well, both drilled with at least fifty rounds from Olsen's full-auto magazine dump. They have magazine pouches, of course. Jackson doesn't have a harness, but the too-big fatigues she's wearing have roomy pockets, and she fills them with magazines as quickly as she can pry them out of the pouches of the dead troopers.

Up ahead in the hallway, a door opens, and another TA trooper appears.

He's less than twenty meters from where Jackson is tugging at the harnesses of two of his dead comrades. She knows instantly that he will not shout a warning, that there won't be time to put-up her hands and explain the situation, tell him that she's Corporal Kameelah Jackson, 365th AIB GODDAMNIT DON'T SHOOT ME

He brings up his rifle, she grabs hers. She shoots from the hip, not wanting to take the time to use the sights. The M-66 in her hands roars and spits out the rest of the magazine at the dumb-ass high rate of fire Olsen dialed in manually earlier.

Her burst almost goes high, but some of the fifty or sixty flechettes find their way into the visor of the TA trooper's helmet. He drops instantly, like someone turned off his power switch. His rifle clatters to the concrete.

Jackson screams a curse. She rushes over to the trooper she just shot, somebody here to rescue her, one of her own. She checks the unit markers on the armor and instantly hates herself for the relief she feels when she sees that his unit isn't the 365th, but the 332nd.

She gets up, changes the magazine in her rifle, drops the empty one on the ground. Then she takes the magazines of the dead 332nd trooper, too.

Her drop two days ago ran into a planned ambush. All of Lazarus' troops, with home field advantage, with control of the security office, using the bottlenecks of the elevator banks. This drop, a whole battalion of TA descending on an unprepared enemy, is a much more even fight. There's gunfire everywhere now—the floors above her, the plaza outside. Jackson finds a staircase and gets out of the basement, up to the atrium of the residence tower. She advances through the hallways, rifle at the ready. There are civvies rushing past her to get out of the way of the shooting, but they pay her no mind. Probably think she's one of them.

When she gets to the gallery, the place is a madhouse. There are groups of TA troopers out in the vast expanse of the tower's public space, exchanging fire with Lazarus' armed civvies shooting down at them from the floors above, and welfare rats scrambling out of the line of fire. If she steps out into this circus, she'll get drilled by the first TA trooper who spots her, oversized fatigues and stolen military rifle. She turns the other way and goes down a hallway that looks it may lead to one of the entrance vestibules, out of this place.

The plaza outside doesn't look much better. There are TA troopers on the roof of the admin center in the middle of the plaza, shooting at targets Jackson can't see. She dashes from cover to cover, sticking to the outside of the building, away from the fighting. Get into the clear, ditch the gun, find a way to a PRC that has a functioning police station.

Jackson is halfway around the perimeter of the plaza when she sees a group of armed and armored civvies, hunkered down behind a low wall, shooting at the TA troopers on the roof of the admin center. Lazarus is in the middle, directing fire teams and talking on his headset.

She brings up Olsen's rifle, drops to one knee. The optic on Olsen's gun works fine. She ranges Lazarus with the rifle's laser. 110 meters, a shot she could take half dead or fully drunk. She puts the targeting reticle on the back of Lazarus' head, switches the fire selector to single shot, puts her finger on the trigger. One round would probably get lost in the automatic weapons chatter that reverberates all around the plaza. They'd think the TA grunts on the roof hit him.

Maybe.

Jackson dials up the scope's magnification all the way, She studies the shape of Lazarus' head, decides where to put the round to cut the brain stem. He moves around a bit, but she has no problem tracking him. One twitch of her index finger, and their outfit loses their leader, maybe falls apart entirely.

She holds her finger on that trigger for what seems like a day and a half. Then she flicks her fire selector switch back to "SAFE" and lowers the weapon. With all the red she has on her ledger, she has never shot someone from behind who couldn't shoot back at her. That's not the way she does business.

The access ramp to the block is only eighty or ninety meters to her right. Beyond it, there's open space—parks, plazas, recreation areas for the welfare rats. Easy to hide there, make her way out of the PRC, back to the urban wasteland in between, the shitty seams between the PRCs where the truly unlucky live, the ones that can't even get welfare housing. Go to a different PRC, one where the public safety offices haven't been infiltrated. Hitch a ride back to Shughart, report back to duty.

Maybe.

Jackson takes one last look at Lazarus through her scope. He may even pull this one out of the fire, if he's lucky. Maybe he even deserves it. She has a feeling that she will see him again someday soon.

She steps back into the shadows between the residence towers and makes for the access ramp. Her side still hurts like a bastard, TA troopers will shoot her on sight in that outfit, but she has clean fatigues and a rifle, and she's in charge of her own fate again.

Call in the TA, turn these people in. Serve Lazarus to her own people on a silver platter. Get a bunch of ribbons and a promotion, then go dig around in the shit again, and again, until her luck runs out.

Or do something else entirely. At least stick around a bit and see if these people are what Lazarus says they are. Someone needs to pay for her squad, pay for Stratton and Paterson and Grayson, but maybe it's not these people after all. But that's not a call Jackson is prepared to make in just one chaotic night.

So I stick around for a bit, she tells herself.

She has filed the image of Lazarus' face firmly in her memory, and as Jackson disappears in the dark no-man's land between the PRC and the rest of the city, she smiles to herself as she recalls his features.

Maybe.

Magic and Fountain Pens: Ink and Blood

When I think back on the stories of mine that turned out best, they usually have a few things in common: they were written longhand first, I wrote them for fun and not because anyone was waiting for them, they pretty much popped into my head fully formed, and I wrote them fairly quickly.

Of all the short stories I've ever written, Ink and Blood is my favorite. It was one of those stories where everything just comes together—the idea, the motivation, the execution, and the end result. Everything just clicked in my writer brain when I wrote this one, and if I could have that experience all the time, I'd get out a hundred stories every year.

If you're a regular reader of my blog (and if you're not, it's at markokloos.com), you may remember that I've mentioned plans to revisit the Ink & Blood world in a full-length novel. I've been planning that novel for a while, as a possible jump-off point for an alternate history fantasy series. If I get my contracted obligations turned in on time this year, I may have the time and bandwidth to start that project in the second half of 2023.

Ink and Blood

It's a slow morning in the shop. Wilhelm leans on the counter and watches the dust motes dance in the morning sun when the little brass bell on the door jingles, and the prettiest girl he has ever seen walks across the threshold.

Papa has been selling pens and ink to strangers for twenty years. Papa claims that he can smell a Wealdling from a hundred paces. Right now, however, Papa is on a train to Hannover, to buy new pens at the big factory, and Wilhelm is alone in the shop.

There's nothing obviously wrong with the girl, but somehow Wilhelm knows she is not a local. Her clothes have been assembled a bit strangely, as if she only knows the proper way of dressing from vague descriptions. She's wearing trousers, and none of the local girls would wear those in public. Still, Wilhelm can't be sure, and he doesn't want to call the police on her without cause.

"Good day, madam," he greets her, formal as his father demands, even though the girl looks to be close to his own age of fifteen years.

"Good day," she returns and looks around in the store, where the shelves present his father's merchandise in regimented order.

"I am looking for some good ink and paper," she says, and smiles at him. He isn't the kind of boy who draws smiles from girls like her. He is a touch too awkward and a bit too pudgy, and the girls here in the merchant quarter only overlook such obvious defects when they manifest along with wealth. Papa is well to do, but he is still just a paper trader, and there is no great wealth in inks and pens and sealing wax.

Now that she has spoken, he is almost certain she's a Wealdling. Her inflections have an unusual melody to them.

He knows the law, of course. Even though magic only works within the Weald, the Crown has ordered that none shall sell the people of the Weald things that can be used to write spells: no ink, no paper, no pens. Wilhelm knows that he should refuse to serve her even if he doesn't have the fortitude to go outside and call for a policeman. But she is here in this little shop, and the authorities are not, and she is smiling and flashing her brown eyes at him, so he returns her smile and gets out the ink bottles.

She samples them like his father would sample fine wines. Wilhelm shows her everything--the peacock-blue school inks, the iron gall ink, the perfumed correspondence inks used by the highborn and those pretending to be. She takes the dip pen he offers and tries out half a dozen inks on as many different varieties of paper: cotton rag, linen, French vellum, onionskin. She draws lines, geometric shapes, and little sketches of apples and horseshoes.

Then her attention is drawn to the pens underneath the glass countertop. She looks at the phalanx of cigar shapes in fascination, and Wilhelm moves the papers to give her a clear view of the display.

"What are those?" she asks.

Wilhelm opens the pen case and removes one of the pens. He presents it to her, and she takes it carefully.

"Those are fountain pens," he says. "They carry their own supply of ink in their bellies."

He shows her the lever on the side of the pen and demonstrates the mechanism.

"There is a sac of arabicum within, and this lever squeezes it. You let go, and it draws in the ink and fills the sac."

She turns the pen in her hand with longing in her eyes. She tries out the filling lever, works it carefully a few times. With her attention on the object, Wilhelm sneaks a few glances at her face. There is a dusting of freckles on her cheeks and the bridge of her nose.

"You could write a page without having to dip," she muses.

"You could write many pages without dipping," he replies. "And carry the pen for the day's writing without having to carry an ink-pot as well."

Her gaze darts from the pen to his face, and he can see sudden excitement flaring up in those brown eyes.

"I would like to buy two," she says firmly.

He wraps her purchases in coarse packing paper. When he ties the parcel up with a ribbon, he chooses a purple one, because she fancied the purple ink, and he thinks it might please her.

He rings everything up, and she eyes the noisy register warily. Once again, he gets the feeling that she is unfamiliar with the whole process, that she is merely following instructions from a book.

"That will be eleven marks and fifty pfennigs, please," he tells her.

She produces a leather satchel, dark and shiny with age, and rummages around in it. Then she puts a few aged Prussian coins on the counter next to her wrapped purchases. He picks up the money and counts it.

"This is eight marks," he tells her. "I'm afraid you're short three marks and fifty."

She looks at the money in his hand, and he can see just a trace of color creep into her cheeks. She reaches into the old leather satchel again, searches for a moment, and then puts a small handful of coins onto the wrapped package on the counter.

Wilhelm picks up one of the new coins and examines it. A coin of such weight can only be solid gold. It isn't Prussian or Bavarian. Wilhelm has never seen a coin like this. On one side, it shows a creature that looks like a cross between a lion and an eagle. On the other side, there's an unfamiliar coat of arms: a sword crossed with an axe, and a two-headed snake entwined in both blades. Wilhelm has no idea who minted this peculiar coin, but he knows how much paper money he can get in exchange for a weight of gold like this, and the handful of gold coins on the counter before him is enough to buy every pen in Papa's showcase, and all the ink in the store besides.

"Will that be enough?" the girl asks, trepidation in her voice.

For just a moment, Wilhelm is tempted to take all the gold she is offering. If he puts one of those coins toward her purchase, she has paid for all her merchandise twice over, and he could keep the rest of the gold for himself. He knows for sure now that she is a Wealdling, and that she would not object--that she would consider the overpayment a fee of sorts, for selling her outlawed goods. But he does not want this girl to think ill of him, so he takes the Prussian money and just one of the gold coins, and pushes the rest of them back toward her.

"This will do," he tells her.

Even with the single gold coin, she has still overpaid, so Wilhelm rummages around on the ink shelf behind the counter, and produces a bottle of scented purple ink, the same kind she had fancied earlier. He adds it to her purchases, and smiles at her.

"A pretty color," he says. "It suits you."

Before he can chide himself for the clumsy compliment, she rewards him with a smile of her own.

"Thank you," she says. "You are very kind."

"Not at all," he murmurs, and hands her the goods. If she is a Wealdling, he has just given her the tools to write hundreds, maybe thousands of spells, but he finds that he does not care. Why should he care what the Wealdlings do with ink and paper in their own world?

She takes the package, and their hands touch briefly. When she walks out of the store, she looks back over her shoulder and gives him one last smile, and the sudden sense of loss he feels when she steps back into the sun-lit street almost makes him stagger.

Wilhelm comes out from behind the counter and quickly walks over to the door, to keep her in his sight just a few more moments, but by the time he has reached it, she has turned a corner and disappeared.

He spends the rest of the morning dusting shelves and restocking paper without much enthusiasm. Occasionally, he pauses and pulls the odd gold coin out of his pocket to look at it. He had planned to exchange it for paper money at the Royal Bank, but the more he looks at it, the more he is inclined to keep it, to forego its monetary worth so he can hold on to this token.

Without Papa around to chide him for wasting money, Wilhelm closes the store for lunch, and walks to the bakery on the corner of the market square nearby.

He buys a dough-wrapped sausage from the corner bakery, but before he has taken a bite of it, he catches a glimpse of the girl from his shop, and the lunch is suddenly forgotten. She is walking along the row of farmers' stands on the far side of the square. Wilhelm only sees her from behind, but he recognizes the tan-colored coat she wears, and the long horse-tail of her brown hair.

He doesn't know what he will say to her if he catches up. He isn't even sure that he will try to speak to her again. All he knows as he makes his way across the busy market square is that he wants to keep her in his sight just a little while longer, because her smile had made him feel like someone other than pudgy Wilhelm from the paper store. He knows that once the dark-haired girl slips away, life will become boring and ordinary once more.

As he closes the distance, Wilhelm realizes that the girl is not alone. Someone is walking with her, a gray-haired old man who keeps pace just a few steps behind her. He is walking with a cane, but when Wilhelm gets close, he sees that it is really a staff, a gnarled old thing that looks like it grew out of the ground somewhere. His garments are even more unusual than hers. The old men here in the city wear knee-length coats and hats and cloaks, not leather breeches and linen shirts without collars.

Then the girl stops at a candy stand to purchase something, and the old man adjusts his gear as he pauses next to her. A leather satchel hangs by his side, and Wilhelm draws in a breath when he recognizes it as the satchel the girl was carrying earlier—the one that now holds half a thousand sheets of fine paper, two new fountain pens, and half a dozen bottles of ink.

Wilhelm knows that he should fetch a policeman. He knows that if someone wonders about their strange appearance and calls the authorities, he will be in big trouble for selling them the ink and paper they carry. But he does no such thing, even though the nearest police station is just around the corner from the far end of the market square. He follows them as they make their way along the fringes of the market. Then they walk down one of the side alleys, the one that leads down to the ancient warren of shops that has grown in the cracks of the city since the days of knights and castles, and Wilhelm does not follow. There are fewer people walking the alley, and he will not be able to stay unnoticed. Besides, down there is where the city's thieves and tricksters ply their trades, and not even the memory of the girl's perfect face can entice Wilhelm to venture among them. Instead, he gives the girl and her companion one last glance, and then turns around reluctantly, to return to Papa's shop and his ordinary life.

Wilhelm is getting ready to close the shop for the night when he hears a commotion in the street outside: angry shouts of arguing men, and the shrill whistles of police officers. At first, he pays it no mind. It is Friday evening, the end of a market day, and the square has a public-house every hundred steps. There are beer-fueled fights here every weekend. So he puts away the money from the till and locks the iron grates in front of the window.

He has just finished wiping all the glass countertops when a thunderclap shakes the floor beneath him and makes all the bottles on the shelves chime in dissonance. Another crash follows, this one even louder, and the gas lamp on the ceiling starts swaying. Outside, the shouts of anger have given way to yells of fear and alarm.

Wilhelm hurries out into the street. To his left, over by the market square, blue-tinted fires are lighting up the evening sky. People are rushing away from the square, flowing past him like a current.

At first, the blue fires in the market square make Wilhelm think of a natural calamity, an accident that set the gaslights and their lines ablaze. As he gets closer to the square, however, he sees that he is only half correct. The gaslight lanterns are ablaze, vivid blue fire bursting from shattered light fixtures all around the square, but this was no accident. In the middle of the square, standing on the old granite fountain, Wilhelm spots the old Wealdling. He has a stack of parchment sheets in one hand, and he is reading a spell off the topmost sheet in a booming voice. Wilhelm does not understand the words, but he can see their effect.

When the old man has finished his incantation, he thrusts out his hand and points it at a group of Prussian soldiers who have just arrived in the square. They try to bring their needle-guns to bear, but they are too slow. Another blast shakes the ground beneath Wilhelm's feet, and the soldiers scream as they are blown off their feet and flung back down the side street like ragdolls. Wilhelm watches in horrified fascination as the parchment with the spell on it crumbles in the old man's hand as if it had turned to ash, and the Wealdling scatters the fragments with a wave of his hand.

The market square is in ruins. Vendor carts and tables are overturned everywhere, burning fiercely with blue fire, a circle of perfect destruction surrounding the old man on the fountain. The old Wealdling pulls another piece of paper from the stack he carries in his hand and starts reading the spell written upon it in a loud and angry voice. Behind Wilhelm, another group of stern-faced policemen come running into the square, blocking his way back, so he ducks and rushes over to the nearest doorway to keep himself out of the line of fire. He is now in front of Ketterer's bakery, where he had bought his lunch earlier, and he tries the door to find that Herr Ketterer has locked it.

The old man flings another spell across the square, but this one doesn't seem to do what it is supposed to do. Instead of knocking over the policemen fixed by the Wealdling's index finger, the spell shatters a pair of nearby windows. They burst with loud cracks, raining shattered glass onto the cobblestones below. The policemen, unscathed, aim their big revolvers at the Wealdling and open fire, a discordant cacophony of cracks and pops that sounds feeble after the thunderous spell. But if the magic spell did not quite work the way it ought to have, the guns of the policemen do not function as they should, either. Their reports sound weak, and none of the bullets seem to go where they are aimed. They bounce off walls and careen across the square, buzzing like irritated hornets.

Wilhelm cannot conceive what madness could have driven the Wealdling to pick a fight with all the protectors of the city. More soldiers are streaming into the market square from many side streets. These men are armed with needle-guns and used to the carnage of the battlefield. The old man is reading off spells, one after another, but they take time to recite, and the fire from the soldiers' rifles grows more withering with every moment. Despite their arms' sudden lack of reliability, they hold fast and close ranks.

A group of soldiers advances along the side of the square, behind the old man. They use the doorways and awnings of the shops for cover, and the Wealdling never sees them as they draw ever closer and take aim.

The old man is in the middle of an incantation when half a dozen rifles thunder. He falls to the cobblestones without making another sound. Wilhelm feels his heart thudding in his chest. The soldiers rush forward and take aim to fire another volley. Wilhelm can see the bullets plucking at the old man's clothing as they tear into him, but he never even twitches again. In the fading light of the evening, the pool of blood spreading underneath the body looks black as ink.

Someone addresses him with an angry shout. He tears his gaze from the lifeless form of the Wealdling and turns to see a soldier aiming his rifle at him. Wilhelm freezes on the spot, the fear lancing through him like a sharp blade. Then the soldier has assessed the pudgy, white-faced boy before him, and decided that he isn't a threat. The rifle's muzzle moves away from Wilhelm.

"Get out of here, boy," the soldier shouts, his face contorted with fear and anger. Wilhelm does not need to be told again. He turns around and runs back the way he came without looking back.

Wilhelm sits down at the steps in front of his father's store with shaky knees and watches the flocks of people rushing toward the market square. What he just saw seems impossible—everyone knows the Weald's magic doesn't reach this far outside of it. But then he recalls his teacher saying that the Weald grows by a league or two every year. Even though the nearest outstretched finger of it is still over fifty kilometers to the south, it seems that the Borderlands now touch this city. Now Wilhelm knows why the gaslights have been unreliable lately, and why the factory workers complain about broken-down steam engines all the time.

Down at the bottom of the hill, a line of Prussian soldiers comes up the street, bayonets fixed atop their needle-guns. They halt in front of the bookstore, where the street is at its most narrow, and plant their rifle-pikes before them like a hedge of steel. Then a bunch of policemen pass through the soldiers' ranks and start rounding up the people in the street with shouts and the harsh trilling of whistles. They check papers and inspect clothing, and Wilhelm realizes they're looking for more Wealdlings.

Then he catches a glimpse of the girl in the crowd, and his heart skips a beat.

He gets up, and hurries over to where he has seen her long horse-tail and brown overcoat.

She is halfway down a side alley when he catches up and grabs her by the arm. She wheels around with a fearful little shout. To Wilhelm, she looks as frantic as an animal in a trap, sensing the dogs closing in.

"Not that way," he tells her. This side alley curves around to come out on the same street she has just left, only much closer to the bookstore where the soldiers now block the path. Further down the alley, beyond the bend, Wilhelm can hear the tromping of hobnailed boots. He points back up the alley with urgency. She regards him for a moment, panic flickering in her eyes, and turns to follow him.

He takes her to the store. When he pushes open the door, the policemen have moved up half the distance from the bookstore already. Wilhelm pulls the girl into the darkened store with him. He fumbles for the key in his pocket and locks the door behind him. Then he pulls down the blinds to cover the window.

The girl sits down in front of the pen counter, clutching her satchel. Wilhelm motions for her to follow him into the back of the store, and she obeys. When they are in Papa's cramped little office, she sits down on the floor and hugs the satchel again, like a talisman.

"Is he dead?" she asks in a thin voice. The expression on her face tells him that she knows the answer to her question already.

"Yes," he says. "The soldiers shot him, up by the fountain on the square."

She shakes her head slowly, and Wilhelm can see the tears rolling down her face.

"Stubborn old man," she says, the sadness in her voice blended with affection. "I told him not to fight them. I could have talked our way out."

"What happened?" Wilhelm asks.

"Two policemen came over," she says. "They asked for our papers. Then one of them tried to take the satchel from Lothar. He is good with that staff. Even better with spells." More tears stream down her cheeks. "Foolish old man, always stubborn as a cart-ox."

"Your father?" he asks, not wanting to compound her misery by using the past tense.

She shakes her head.

"Teacher," she replies. "Friend."

She rests her head on her knees and sobs. Wilhelm sits down next to her and gently puts his hand on her back.

Outside, the commotion passes the store. Someone tries the door, jerking the handle roughly a few times, and the girl looks up in fear as the doorbell jingles discordantly. Wilhelm swallows—surely, any moment a hobnailed boot will kick in the door—but whoever was testing the lock moves on after a few moments.

He knows that hiding the girl is a crime, after what her guardian has done up on the market square. Wilhelm remembers the soldiers being flung through the air as if a giant's hand had tossed them. Surely, some died before the old Wealdling fell. At the least, all the market carts are smashed to kindling—hundreds of farmers, butchers, and bakers left without their livelihoods. Still, Wilhelm knows—saw—that the two Wealdlings were no danger to anyone before the police stopped them. The two of them were just going about their business, without any unkindness.

They were shopping for candy, he thinks. Could they not have let them be?

The girl lowers her head onto her knees again. They sit on the office floor for a long time, listening to the noises outside.

It is nighttime when all is finally quiet. Wilhelm has been sitting on the floor next to the girl for hours, and she fell asleep in her awkward position a while ago. He quietly gets up on aching legs, and walks upstairs, to the apartment above the store where he lives with Papa. There are blankets in the linen closet by the bathroom, and he takes out a few and walks back down the dark staircase. He does not dare to start a gas lamp for fear it might draw attention, so he leaves the place in darkness as he makes his way back to the office.

He folds up one blanket to serve as a pillow and puts it on the floor behind the girl. He gently nudges her awake and shows her the blanket and the makeshift pillow, and she takes both without protest.

Wilhelm feels pleasingly chivalrous as he watches her go back to sleep wrapped in the blankets he gave her. Lying down next to her would be an intrusion, and improper besides, but he also doesn't want to go to his bedroom, which is as far away from the office as a room in this house can be. So he fetches two more blankets from upstairs, and makes himself a makeshift bed behind the pen counter in the store.

In the morning, the girl is gone.

When Wilhelm wakes up, still dressed in the clothes he wore the day before, he walks over to Papa's office to find it empty, save for the two blankets. They are in the middle of the floor, neatly folded.

He checks the front door of the store to find it locked. All the windows are latched, the shutters still fastened from the outside. However the girl got out of the shop, she did so without breaking a lock or window.

He realizes that he never asked her name.

Wilhelm gathers the blankets she left and carries them upstairs. Before he places them in the linen closet again, he sticks his nose into the soft wool. The scent of her hair is faint, but he recognizes it instantly.

It is close to seven o'clock, and he should be hungry for breakfast right now, but Wilhelm finds that he has no appetite. He trudges downstairs to get Papa's store ready for the day's business.

She left him something on the pen counter: a folded sheet of paper and a small leather pouch. He picks up the pouch with trembling fingers to find that it is quite heavy. When he opens the drawstring and peers inside, he almost drops the pouch in surprise. There are gold coins inside, just like the one he took in payment from the girl yesterday. He takes them out and stacks them on the counter. Twenty-one of the peculiar coins come out of the pouch, a small fortune in gold.

Wilhelm slowly unfolds the paper. She has done a little drawing with the purple ink he gave her—a large wooden bridge, covered with a roof decked with shingles shaped like fish scales.

He knows this bridge, even though he has never seen it with his own eyes. There are lithographs of it in the books about the Weald he has been reading in the bookshop down the street. It is the bridge that spans the river in the Borderlands south of here--the bridge beyond which civilization ends, and the Weald begins.

Underneath the drawing, she has written in narrow, loopy script: *Je m'appelle Venadis.*

Wilhelm sits down on the floor behind the counter and looks at the drawing and the single word beneath for a long time. When the chime of the clock reminds him that it is time to open the shop for customers, he ignores it. Instead, he runs his fingers over the lines she drew, the neat loops and hooks of her name underneath. He says it in a low voice, letting the unfamiliar combination of sounds roll off his tongue: *Venadis.*

Then he sits and thinks, with the drawing in his hands.

They will find the paper, he realizes, and the renewed fear makes his heart leap in his chest. And if he carried one of the pens I sold, they will find that one as well.

There are lots of paper stores in the city, but only one that carries the new fountain pens. Papa ordered them from the overseas trader, and when they arrived at the shop two weeks past, he had boasted that no other shop in the province carried them yet.

Wilhelm knows that he could probably talk his way out of it. He should hide the gold, burn the note, and tell the police someone stole the pens and paper yesterday. But *probably* is not a good word when the other possibility is a five-year sentence in one of the Crown's prisons.

When Wilhelm gets to his feet, he does not walk over to the door to unlock the store. Instead, he goes to fetch his leather book-bag. Then he goes back downstairs, where the regiments of ink bottles stand guard between stacks of notebooks and sheet paper. He fills the bag with inks—the expensive water-proof ones that will stay on paper even in a downpour. Finally, he walks over to the pen counter, and takes all the new fountain pens as well.

He leaves ten of the gold coins in the secret compartment his father keeps behind a lithograph on the wall of his office. Papa will not be pleased, but Papa has good business sense, and he will have the gold melted down, or hold on to it until it is safe to exchange. That much gold is enough to pay for the missing merchandise and make up for the twenty Prussian marks Wilhelm takes out of the register's drawer. He will need safe money for the journey south. If he hurries and takes the late-morning train, he can be in the Borderlands this afternoon. From there, it is only twenty kilometers to the bridge Venadis has drawn, and even a pudgy fellow can walk that distance in four hours. He can be at the Weald Bridge by nightfall.

Wilhelm walks out of the store, locks the door, and drops the key into the mail-slot.

Outside, there's a new scent in the air. The wind carries the smell of charcoal and ashes from the market square, flakes of burnt paper floating on the wind like premature snowflakes.

Wilhelm takes a deep breath and sets out for the train station with a smile.

Putting The Roar Into The Roaring Twenties: Stripes

We don't do time travel with Wild Cards, except for that one time when we did.

The theme of the Wild Cards mosaic novel LOW CHICAGO is, unsurprisingly, Chicago. The premise of the interstitial is that a bunch of high rollers sit down together in a suite in the historic Palmer Hotel for a game of high-stakes poker. Things go awry, tempers flare, and someone in the room unleashes a Wild Card ability that sends every person in the room back into time and into a different era of Chicago history.

When we got the parameters for the story and GRRM asked us for story pitches, I immediately thought of 1920s gangland Chicago, but I was also sure that everybody would jump on that era first, and that half a dozen writers would pitch Roaring Twenties novellas to the boss. Luck would have it that nobody else did, so I got the nod, and the result was "Stripes".

To set the scene: my half-tiger joker-ace Khan is the bodyguard for a sleazy mob boss, Giovanni Galante. When the temporal blast goes off, Khan is in the middle of fighting one of the other bodyguards in the room as the whole room descends into violent chaos, with abilities getting flung left and right, and furniture reduced to splinters. And then...

Stripes

ONE: PALMER

One moment, some hulked-out meathead was trying to pull Khan's head off his shoulders and, from the feel of it, almost succeeding. The next moment, Khan pushed back into empty air with all his might. Not even his reflexes were fast enough for him to catch his momentum, and he stumbled forward and plowed face-first into the carpet.

Teleporter, he thought at once. *The guy's strong as a freak, and he can teleport? Some guys get all the good skills.*

The suite around him, which a moment ago had been noisy with the sounds of no-holds-barred tussling, had turned quiet as quickly as if someone had turned off the sound with a switch. Khan gathered himself, rolled over on his back, and jumped back to his feet, claws out and ready to cut. The suite had been plunged into darkness too, but to his left eye, that made almost no difference at all. But there was nobody in here with him. Ten seconds ago, he had been wrestling with whoever had made an attempt on his client, that little prick Giovanni Galante, and the room had been full of people. All the high rollers, their bodyguards, the girls who were serving the drinks. And now it was completely empty. Khan had walked in wearing an expensive suit, a Colt .45 automatic in a python skin holster, and a thousand-dollar pair of shoes, and now he looked down at himself and saw that he was naked, without a scrap of clothing on his body. No suit, no shoes, no socks. No gun. No underwear.

"What the fuck," he said out loud. "What. The. *Fuck.*"

Nothing in the room looked right. Khan was a bodyguard, and when he had walked into this suite earlier tonight, he had memorized the layout before Galante had even made it to his chair at the end of the table. You had to be able to read a place and predict threat directions in his line of work. Never seat the principal near a window. Always make sure you have your back to a wall. Sit in a place where you can see the door, so you can spot trouble coming as soon as possible. Khan had mapped the suite in his head thoroughly--every piece of furniture, every corner, every bar or counter solid enough to hide behind. And the room he was standing in looked nothing like the one he had walked into with Giovanni Galante earlier.

Oh, it was the same room, no doubt. The geometry was the same--door ahead and to the left, two bedrooms on the far side, two over on his left, a bathroom by the little entrance hallway. But aside from the lack of people, the furniture was all wrong. The huge card table that had been in the middle of the room--the one he had flipped over while fighting off the ace who had attacked Galante-- was no longer there. In its place stood a coffee table and a couch, and two matching armchairs on the short ends of the table. They looked red in the darkness, and there were little tassels on the bottom fringes of the chair covers. The bar at the other end of the room was gone, and there was a fireplace where there had been a liquor cabinet and a sink before.

The room smelled different, too. In fact, the whole place did. It stank like tobacco smoke, the sort of smell that permeates walls and carpets in a place where smokers live for years. It made Khan wrinkle his nose in disgust. He had never liked the smell of that shit even before his card turned. Now, with the super-acute sense of smell of his tiger half, it was almost like a physical assault on his olfactory nerve. When he thought about it, the place didn't sound right either. The Palmer House was inside the Loop, and even though it was the middle of the night, it shouldn't have been this quiet out there. This was downtown Chicago, after all.

Khan checked himself for injuries. There weren't any to speak of--a bunch of bruises from where the ace who had attacked Galante had pummeled him a few times, but there were no broken bones, and he knew the bruises would stop aching and disappear in an hour at the most. He padded over to one of the windows, which now had heavy red brocade curtains in front of them. Then he reached out and moved the curtains aside to get a look at the outside.

"What the fuck," he said again. It seemed to have become the theme of the evening.

Outside, it was dark, and it was snowing. And while Khan knew that he was looking at the corner of State and Monroe--he knew the topography inside the Loop like the stripes on the left side of his face--it wasn't the State and Monroe he knew. The streetlights, the power lines, the signs on the stores, everything was off. There was snow piled up on the edges of the sidewalks, which was unusual enough considering that Galante had been bitching about the August heat and the shitty air conditioning in the Palmer when they had walked in. A car puttered along Monroe, and it looked like something straight out of a museum. There were more cars parked by the curbs on Monroe and State, and they all looked old, yet new at the same time, like someone was holding a street meet of perfectly restored vintage cars out there.

I know where I am, he thought. *The question is, when am I?*

There had been other aces in the suite with him and Cyn when the fight started. Cyn, Golden Boy, Meathooks, and a few others that Khan knew by reputation, powerful and dangerous people. The Arab prince's companion had worried Khan—not because she looked like a huge physical threat, but because none of the guys in the room could keep their eyes off her for longer than ten seconds. None of the high rollers would have been careless enough to just bring regular muscle along, not with the stakes on the table. The aces in the room had been the most impressive concentration of fearsome abilities he had ever seen in one place together. Shit, everyone knew Giovanni Galante's temper. The guy who attacked him hadn't been in the suite when the game started, though. He had been dressed as a waiter, brought Galante his steak, and then it had all gone full rodeo within a second or two. But Khan didn't think the false waiter was responsible for this. First the fists and claws had come out, Cyn had started tossing flames, then someone had whipped out a gun and started shooting...but someone else had unleashed a big can of temporal whoop-ass right in the middle of the fight. Khan didn't know if he was the only one in the suite who had been ripped from the time stream and unceremoniously dumped somewhen else, but he supposed it didn't much matter right now.

That false waiter—he knew he hadn't seen the guy before, but now his brain told him otherwise. It was like there were two sets of memories battling for dominance in his tired brain. One memory said he'd never met that freakishly strong guy swearing in Polish. Another said that he had fought him before, years ago, on a construction side somewhere on the South Side. Khan vaguely remembered fists and steel girders, and a massive headache when it was all over. And he couldn't quite figure out which memory was true. Maybe they both were.

The living room part of the suite was empty, but there were four bedrooms in the place, and all the doors were closed. Khan stepped next to each door in turn, smelling and listening, hoping the place wasn't rented out to some rich family or a bunch of foreigners on a leisure trip. But the bedrooms all smelled like nothing but laundered linen and cigarette smoke.

He opened all the doors and started going through the closets for something to wear. If he stepped out looking the way he did, he suspected that the negative attention would be much worse than usual. Whenever this was, it looked like it was well before the first Wild Card Day, and nobody out there would know shit about jokers or aces. With luck, they'd just flip out and consider him a circus freak. With a little less luck, they'd call the cops and try to pump him full of buckshot. Khan wasn't in the mood for either right now.

The closets in the bedrooms were empty. There was a walk-in coat closet by the door, but that one was empty as well except for a laundry bag on a coat hanger. Khan checked the bathroom and found two bathrobes hanging on hooks. He tried one on and promptly tore it in half along the seam in the back when he tried to slip his arms into the sleeves. He tossed the robes aside and went back to the walk-in closet. The laundry bag was a big piece of canvas that looked like a sleeping bag. He popped out his claws and tore holes into it for his head and arms. Then he slipped the whole thing on. It was tight, but it did at least make him feel like he was wearing something.

There was a mechanical clock ticking on the mantelpiece of the fireplace. It showed ten past two. Even at this hour, leaving the suite through the door and wandering the Palmer House hallways didn't seem like a good idea. Khan was good at sneaking, and he was sure that security cameras were not yet an issue whenever this was, but there was no way to make it through that huge lobby and out the door without being spotted.

He walked over to the windows on the far side of the room, which looked out over an alley and toward the next building on State. They had simple latches, and he popped them and opened both. They weren't worried about people falling out and liability lawsuits, whatever the year was right now. Khan looked to make sure nobody was out on the sidewalk right below him and leaned out of the window. There was a fire escape, but it was three floors below the windows of this suite. Outside, the wind blowing through the alley was bitingly cold.

Khan muttered a curse and swung his legs over the windowsill. Then he let himself drop down to the fire escape three floors below. He landed with a muffled crash and the alarming sound of creaking and popping steel as his three hundred pounds of mass landed on the grating. For a moment, he expected the welds of the steel to give way under him and kicking off a pancaking collapse, but the structure merely groaned under his weight. A few minutes later, his hands and feet were numb with cold, but he was safely down in the alley.

State Street to my right, he thought. *The park is to my left. Two blocks across Wabash and Michigan Avenue. Find a place to hole up, get warm, figure out what to do next.*

He set out down the snow-covered alley, as quietly and swiftly as he could on numb feet. Two blocks to cover and safety, and maybe some warmth.

TWO: LAKESIDE

There was no park yet, of course. Not the one Khan knew from his own time, the one they had just finished in the late 1990s. In what was still the present time in his own mind, you were in Millennium Park as soon as you got across Michigan Avenue. But this Michigan Avenue, in whatever year this was, didn't border a park. It was a rail yard, rows and rows of tracks, some with freight cars parked on them. It didn't look very inviting at all. But he had gotten too cold on his dash through the alleys, and his mind was still coming to terms with the fact that this now wasn't his now, so Khan leapt the fence and went into the yard to look for shelter anyway. At least he wasn't likely to run into anyone out here at two thirty in the morning.

The wind was blowing stronger out here near the lake. The rows of rail cars were tempting, but Khan didn't try to open any. He would have been able to get even into the locked ones, of course, but he was tired and didn't want to be halfway to Indianapolis when he woke up. Moreover, some of the rail cars had people in them. He could smell them, hear them moving around even in their sleep, and dealing with freaked-out bums was low on his short list of things he wanted to manage tonight.

There was a maintenance shed a quarter mile down the tracks, and he didn't sense anyone in it. The door was locked with a heavy padlock, which he grabbed with his tiger hand and tore off. Inside, the place smelled of grease and oil and mildew, but it was a shelter from the wind, and there were some tarps stacked in a corner he could use to cover up for the night. There was a metal advertising calendar on one of the walls that said CENTRAL CHEMICAL CO., MANUFACTURING CHEMISTS, and on it was a dirtied sheet of paper that said 1929 -- JANUARY -- 1929 across the top, with the days and weeks of the month in the rows underneath.

1929, he thought with amazement.

Whatever that ace in the hotel room had unleashed, it had knocked Khan eighty-eight years into the past. He wondered what had happened to the other people in the suite when it happened. Were they here--or would they be here soon--in 1929, freezing their asses off in the streets of Chicago? He almost had to chuckle at the thought of that little shit Giovanni Galante, buck-naked, without his shiny track suit and his gaudy hundred-thousand-dollar jewelry, or his cash or credit cards, trying to figure out what the fuck was going on. The kid was practically helpless without his cell phone and a responsible adult to watch his ass.

Khan scratched together his knowledge about 1929 while he was making himself a sleeping nest in a corner of the shack. His sister Naya had brought him all sorts of books from the library during those agonizing months after his card had turned and the Wild Card virus had slowly changed him into what he was now. Mostly fiction, but lots of other stuff too. He had always liked reading about history.

Prohibition, he recalled. *Speakeasies. Booze smuggling. Gang warfare.* Not a lot unlike the shit that went down in the present--his present--with crack and coke and amphetamines. It was sort of his world, they just used a different commodity.

Nothing about this made any sense, and he wasn't about to try and unravel it tonight. Khan decided to sleep on it and then figure things out tomorrow. Maybe he'd be back in the suite up in the Palmer in 2017 when he woke up, with a drunk Galante sleeping off his booze coma next to a trio of high-dollar hookers. Not exactly something Khan would wish for under ordinary circumstances, but at this point it would improve the situation massively.

He wrapped himself in the musty-smelling canvas tarps and closed his eyes. Sleep came surprisingly easy, considering what a weird-ass night it had been so far.

Khan woke up with the first daylight from the ruckus of a freight train slowly rumbling across the train yard on a nearby track. A fucking steam train, chuffing past the shack slowly like something from an old movie. It smelled like burning coal and hot grease. He checked the wall of the shed, where the same calendar still hung. 1929 -- January --1929. Outside, a way off still but coming closer, were voices, undoubtedly rail yard workers showing up for the morning shift.

Looking the way he did, he figured it wasn't wise to show himself in broad daylight. He got up, gathered the canvas tarps he had found, and looked around for other useful stuff. There were grease buckets and tools, nothing he wanted to burden himself with at the moment. He found a length of rope and took that as well, and a knife he found in a drawer underneath the workbench. Then he opened the door a crack to peek outside, and took off across the rail yard toward the lake. The snowfall had picked up in the night, and the shed was out of sight in the snow squall when he was a hundred yards away.

Down by the lake, there were plenty of spots that were just unkempt slope covered in shrubs and small trees. Khan found a spot at the base of a tree that was sheltered from the wind on three sides and spent the next half hour making the ugliest tent in the world out of the tarps and the stolen rope. Then he huddled down in it and waited for nightfall.

He had been dozing lightly when he heard someone coming down the slope where he had set up camp. It was still dawn outside, but the snow had slacked off. He could smell the two guys who were headed straight for his little tent--body odor, mostly, with some booze and cigarette smell thrown in. They stopped in front of his tent and started talking quietly among themselves, probably thinking he was asleep. Then one of them bent down and grabbed one of the side of his tent tarp.

Khan let out a low growl.

The guy who had grabbed the trap let it go as if he had burned himself.

"What the hell, Eddie. Some fucking animal."

"Piss off, the both of you," Khan said. "Find another spot and let me sleep. I don't have anything to steal, trust me."

"If you got a dog in there, asshole, it ain't gonna help ya much," the other guy said from outside. "Why don't you come on out."

"Don't make me," Khan grumbled.

"Oh, I insist," the other guy said. Khan could smell the gun oil and the powder in the cartridges before he heard the cocking of the hammer of the gun the guy had in his hand now.

"You may wish you hadn't," Khan said and stood up, flipping the tarp back and over his head has as he did.

There were two of them--his nose hadn't lied--and they both looked a little rough, winter coats that were on the ratty side, worn-out shoes, unshaven faces. One of them was maybe five nine and wearing a driving cap on his head. The other guy, the one holding the gun, was considerably larger, probably six one to Khan's six three. Khan grinned, knowing full well that even in the low light of dawn, they couldn't miss the three-inch canines on the left side of his mouth. Both guys stepped back quickly, and he could smell the sudden, sharp stench of fear on them.

"What the hell are you," the smaller guy said.

The bigger guy--presumably named Eddie--didn't bother trying to find an answer to that. Instead, he raised the revolver in his hand and aimed it at Khan's chest. Then he pulled the trigger. His finger made it halfway through the trigger's arc before Khan lashed out with his left hand, the tiger one, extending his claws along the short way to Eddie's wrist. Eddie's hand, now separated from the rest of him, was still holding the gun when it flew past the shorter guy and thumped down into the underbrush on the slope somewhere.

"Didn't I say you may wish you hadn't insisted?" Khan said. "Now look what you've done. Idiot."

The shorter guy didn't have a gun, that much Khan could smell. But he did have a knife, a fixed blade that looked like it had started life as a butcher's knife. To his credit, the short guy had balls. He pulled the knife from his coat pocket and thrust it at Khan's side. Khan leaned back and avoided the blade easily. With his feline reflexes, he could have lit a smoke while waiting for the blade to arrive at the spot where his chest had been just a few tenths of a second ago. Then he grabbed the smaller guy with his right hand, pulled him close, and threw him down the slope and into the underbrush, the same way Eddie's hand and gun had gone. The small guy yelped as he crashed into the thicket and rolled down the slope in the darkness.

Eddie didn't seem to be in the mood for a fight anymore. He stood doubled over, his left hand around his right wrist, which now ended in a stump that squirted blood onto the snow rather messily. He groaned and looked up at Khan with an expression of utter disbelief.

"What the hell are you?" he echoed the earlier words of his shorter pal.

"I could explain, but you don't have the time," Khan said. "You need to get your ass to a hospital and get that sewn up before you bleed out."

"You're not gonna kill me." Eddie's face was contorted with pain, but Khan saw the concern, and the quick glance toward the claws still sticking out of his left hand. Khan wiped them on the laundry bag he was wearing for a tunic, then retracted them.

"I should. Probably do the world a favor before you jack someone else and try to shoot them in the gut for nothing. But I'm not going to. Now get the fuck out of here."

The big guy turned around, still half-crouched and holding his bleeding wrist.

"Wait a second," Khan said. "Leave your coat. I'm freezing my ass off."

Eddie peeled himself out of his coat without complaint, probably more than happy to only lose that worn-out garment instead of his head.

"You're not worried about me ratting you out?"

Khan laughed. With the vocal cords from his feline side, it sounded like a cross between a cat purring and a motorcycle idling.

"Go ahead, if you think they'll believe you. Now drop the coat and beat it."

With the two transients knowing where he had camped out, Khan pulled his pathetic little tent up and looked for a new place to wait out the day, which was a pain in the ass. On the plus side, Eddie's coat was warm and almost fit him properly, even if it did smell like someone had dragged it through a piss-filled ashtray repeatedly. And he would have had to lie if he'd claimed that roughing up those two idiots hadn't been the first fun he'd had since right before he'd walked into that fucking Palmer House, one night ago and eighty-eight years in the future.

THREE: DOWNTOWN

After three nights in the underbrush by the railway yards, Khan was starting to get convinced that this was not a temporary thing. Every morning, he woke up hoping to see the familiar walls of his apartment's bedroom, or even the suite at the Palmer Galante had booked for the night. Khan had worked for many clients he didn't like personally, but Giovanni Galante was now the first one he officially hated. Not only was the guy a punk and a shitbag, he had also triggered whatever had bounced Khan back in time the better part of a century. The worst thing was that he couldn't even look the little prick up and cut him to ribbons because Galante wouldn't be born for another sixty years.

If he was going to be here for good, he figured that he'd have to find a way to get around and do something constructive, because huddling in a tent by Lake Michigan in the freezing January weather was getting tedious. On the fourth night, Khan decided to make a few supply runs into downtown.

There were plenty of stores nearby, in and around the Loop, and neither of them had an alarm system worth a shit compared to 2017 standards. Khan hadn't even known they had burglar alarms all the way back in the 1920s, but a lot of the bigger stores had them installed, primitive things working with copper contacts on the door frames and windowsills. They were easy enough to bypass or destroy outright by pulling the alarm boxes off the walls, where they were usually mounted high up near the gutters.

Clothing proved to be a bit of a problem. There were lots of clothing stores and tailors, but none of them had anything on the racks for a physique like Khan's. He got lucky in a place where they sold working clothes, overalls and heavy winter work jackets for longshoremen or rail yard workers. That made him look more like a regular person except for the fact that half his face and one hand sticking out of the sleeves of his new heavy jacket looked decidedly inhuman.

He found a temporary solution in a pharmacy down by Randolph and Lake, which had medical supplies stashed in the back: bandages, Plaster of Paris for casts, crutches, and all kinds of stuff that looked like quackery to Khan. He loaded up a bag with stuff that looked useful for what he had in mind. Two hours and a side trip for food to a corner grocery on Lake later, Khan was back in his hideout for the night. He had found another service shack at the southern end of the trainyard, and that one had a proper bathroom in it. At least he had gotten knocked back to a time when indoor plumbing was already a thing.

It took a bit of time and practice, but a little while later, he had used a bunch of bandages and a plaster half-mask to turn himself into a fairly convincing recovering burn victim. The plaster mask covered the tiger part of his face completely, and the bandages helped tie everything into place and cover his furry left paw. He could still rip everything off quickly, but now he could pass casual muster on the street as just some poor longshoreman who had gotten himself torched in a warehouse fire or something. People in 2017 weren't very aware of their surroundings most of the time; he suspected that things weren't all that different in 1929.

There was no cooking setup in the shack, but Khan had taken stuff from the grocery store that didn't require preparation--bread, sandwich meats, cake, candy, a bunch of other high-calorie junk. He ate all of it while sitting at the small table in the service shack and reading the newspapers he had grabbed on an impulse on the way out of the store. If the date on the masthead was right, it was Wednesday, January 30, 1929. The prices on the grocery store ads in the back of the paper were ludicrously low--Campbell's soups for ten cents a can, peanut butter for 29 cents a pound, six cents for a 16-ounce can of pork & beans. He had hauled back a shitload of groceries from that store, and all in all, he had probably stolen five bucks worth of food. Of course, the average weekly paycheck right now was fifty or sixty bucks, he reminded himself.

1929, he thought in wonder, reading newspaper articles with local names he didn't know, reporting on events that had happened almost ninety years ago in Khan's head.

I won't be born for another 56 years, he thought. *Naya won't be born for another 57. Shit, by the time the old man is born over in Punjab, I'll be three years from collecting Social Security.*

Naya. Thinking of his little sister stung much more than the biting cold outside, more than the hunger he had felt the last three days before the grocery store break-in.

I'll never see her again, he thought. *I'll be 89 by the time she's born. If I make it that long.*

He knew his history, and he knew that the time between now and 1987 was anything but peaceful. The Great Depression. World War Two. The Wild Card virus. He'd have to live for another eighteen years disguised as a burn victim or somewhere out in a shack in the wilderness before he could even be himself again without people trying to kill him or stick him into a circus.

I can't live in a shack and steal bread and canned pork and beans from the grocery store for eighteen years, he thought. *If I'm stuck in this, I have to make the best of it. I have to go back to doing what I know.*

He wasn't much into sports, so he had no idea what to bet on to become rich in the past. He didn't know anything about the stock market other than the fact that it would crash hard later this year and usher in the Great Depression, and he had no money or contacts to mess with stocks even if he did. But he did have his strong arms, the claws at the end of his left hand, and the ability to see and smell trouble coming. Khan was a bodyguard for shady people with money, and if he wasn't certain of much else right now, he knew that the city of Chicago was lousy with those in 1929.

Every place has a feel to it, especially big cities. New York felt like New York, L.A. like L.A., and you were never in doubt which one you were in even if you were to lose your eyesight. Smell, sound, weather, even the din of the bustle around you were different in every city. And Chicago still felt like Chicago, even though the sensory details were muffled and filtered somehow, like he was looking at everything while wearing tinted glasses and noise-altering headphones. But after walking the nighttime streets inside the Loop for a few days, even the old cars didn't seem out of place anymore, and he had gotten used to the smell of cigarettes and 1920s personal care products. There was the familiar rattle of the L cars overhead, the cold wind coming in from the lake, everything he remembered from 2017, so familiar that he could imagine himself back in his time when he closed his eyes.

The criminal scene, however--there was nobody he knew. No contacts, no family, no reputation. The Galante family wasn't even on the map yet. None of his old principals were. Khan knew about Capone, of course, and his rival Bugs Moran. But there was no easy in for him, nobody he could ask for an introduction or a favor. He briefly thought about getting some attention by walking into a speakeasy or two and stirring up trouble, but he dismissed the idea almost as soon as it popped into his head. He knew he could scare the shit out of the locals, but that wasn't the kind of attention he wanted, not yet anyway.

Can't work my way up the way I did after my card turned, he thought. *I need something big, something that will put me on the map instantly.*

The answer came to him somewhere on Wabash, at one in the morning. He was out for one of his nighttime walks, when few people were out in the freezing cold. A poster in one of the grocery store windows--a six-pack of soda bottles, with a frilly heart next to them and a Cupid in one corner.

VALENTINE'S DAY! YOUR PARTY GUESTS WILL WELCOME COKE -- TAKE HOME SEVERAL CARTONS TODAY!

He felt like slapping himself on the side of the head. All those history books he read, born and raised in Chicago, and the date and year hadn't popped into his head earlier. The St. Valentine's Day Massacre--February 14, 1929. That was less than two weeks away. Khan knew it was going to be a bunch of Bugs Moran's guys getting shot to ribbons by a Capone hit squad. He knew it was going to happen. He even remembered some of the names. Hard-ass John Gusenberg, one of Moran's enforcers, who would briefly survive the shooting and tell the cops that "nobody shot him" even though he'd have fourteen bullet wounds in him. Fred "Killer" Burke, a nasty piece of work pulling triggers for Capone. Khan didn't remember all the players, but he knew when and where it would go down, and that was all he needed.

He didn't remember the address, but he knew the name of the warehouse--SMC Cartage. Two minutes in a phone booth were all he needed to get the address of the place, 2122 North Clark Street. The travel map of Chicago Khan had swiped a few nights earlier-- *God, how did people ever live before GPS and cell phones?*--told him that 2122 North Clark was up in the Lincoln Park neighborhood. And blessedly, he saw that Lincoln Park, all 1,200 acres of it, already existed in 1929. Best of all, 2122 North Clark was only a block from the park.

Khan felt more energized than he had been since that fucked-up poker game. It felt damn good to have a plan again. He didn't bother going back to the rail yard to collect his stuff. It was a bit of a hike to Lincoln Park from downtown, he could hit a shop or two along the way for more food and supplies, and he wanted to beat the sunrise.

FOUR: CLARK

The two-block area around the SMC Cartage warehouse was much smaller than the Loop. Khan scouted it every night, and by the time Valentine's Day came around, he knew every last detail about this little stretch of 1929 Chicago--every store, every alley, every streetlight, and he had even started to memorize the license plate numbers of the cars in their regular nighttime parking spots.

For a little while, Khan had been worried that the time stream may have been thrown off by his arrival, that history had started to take a different flow around him somehow. Maybe the massacre wouldn't happen. Maybe everything he thought he knew about the events to come was already wrong. But it eased his fears when he noticed that he wasn't the only one staking out the warehouse. This part of North Clark was lined with residential buildings, and one of them was almost right across the street from the warehouse. Khan had a nose for danger spots--it was his job, after all--and he knew that three our four guys were holed up in one of those apartments and kept a steady watch on the garage every day for three days running. He knew which car they drove. One night, he even ventured into the apartment building from the rooftop and stood in front of their door for a while, listening to them talking in low voices. They carried guns, all of them. Khan could smell the gun oil and the powder in the cartridges. He could have popped the door off the hinges and cut all three of them up before they could draw their guns, of course. But there would just be three dead mobsters in a rented apartment, with nobody to carry word back to the guys they were trying to kill. Khan had to let them go through with their plan until the last moment, until the triggermen had Moran's men lined up.

On the plus side, February 14, 1929 started just like Khan's old history books said it did, but it didn't end precisely how he had planned to rewrite it.

The dawn had brought light snowfall, and the streets were covered in dirty slush. Khan was out in the daytime for the first time in a week. A guy his size with half his face in a mask would have drawn attention no matter how much he tried to blend in, so he was crouched on the flat rooftop of the brownstone building next to the warehouse, huddled underneath a ratty and dirty piece of tarp. He roughly knew how the whole thing was going to go down, and once Capone's gunmen showed up, timing would be critical.

The sun had been up since seven, but neither Capone nor Moran's men were early risers. It was well past eight before Khan saw the first of Moran's men arrive at the warehouse. They were all dressed much more nicely than Khan--suits, ties, long winter coats, snazzy hats. It looked like the movies hadn't lied, and that the mobsters of this day liked to be dressed their best when out and about on business. He had to admit that these guys looked much sharper than Giovanni Galante in his track suit.

I'm going up against Capone, Khan thought, and the idea put a grin on his face, cold and uncomfortable as he was on that snowy rooftop. Al motherfucking Capone. This was stuff right out of the history books.

A bit past mid-morning, two cars puttered down the alley toward the garage. The one in the lead was a marked police car. It was followed by shiny black sedan. Khan slipped off the tarp that had kept him covered and stretched his arms and shoulders a little to get the blood flowing again. He extended the claws on his tiger hand and took off the oversized boot that covered his left foot so he could extend his toe-claws as well.

In the alley below, the two cars came to a halt. Khan saw movement out of the corner of his left eye and looked down the alley to see two men in suits and winter coats stop cold at the sight of the police car. Then they turned and walked back around the corner toward North Clark. Moran's men, Khan figured, or maybe even Moran himself. They think the place is getting raided.

The doors of the cars opened. Two cops got out of the police car. Khan knew they were Capone's triggermen, merely dressed like cops, but Moran's men had no way of knowing that, and they'd all line up for them in front of the wall without a fuss in about thirty seconds. Phase Two of Capone's plan undoubtedly involved the two men in civilian clothes who stepped out of the second car. They were dressed smartly as well, long woolen winter coats and fedoras, and each of them carried a Thompson submachine gun. Khan watched with a little thrill as they took magazines out of their coat pockets and loaded their guns. Tommy guns, he thought. Just like in the fucking movies. He knew his way around guns after ten years on the job. Nobody used Thompsons anymore because they were heavy as fuck and about as ergonomic as railroad ties, but he had fired one a few times before, and they made a lot of .45-caliber holes in things very quickly.

The guys dressed as policemen took shotguns out of the back seat of their police car and opened the back door of the garage. Then they walked in while the two guys with the Thompsons waited silently, one on either side of the door. A few moments later, Khan heard shouting from the inside of the warehouse, someone shouting commands, a dog barking. The two guys with the Tommy guns waited a few beats, then followed the fake cops inside.

The roof of the SMC Cartage building was two floors below that of the brownstone, so Khan swung himself over the edge of the roof and climbed down, using his claws for traction and the vertical gutter tube on the corner of the building for a handhold. He dropped onto the garage roof as quietly as he could. Then he jumped from the edge of the garage roof to the alley, an easy twenty-foot drop. Both cars in the alley had their engines running, and the black sedan behind the police car had a driver behind the wheel who gave Khan a wide-eyed stare. Khan decided that he didn't have the time to deal with the driver. He just shot the guy a hard look and went inside through the back door.

There was a truck parked in the garage. It stood between the back doors and the main part of the warehouse, where the two fake cops had finished lining up Moran's men against the wall. They were busy disarming them, pulling weapons out of waistbands and pockets and tossing them toward the middle of the garage. There was a dog tied to the bumper of the truck, a German Shepherd, and it was barking at the fake cops, who went about their business undeterred. The two smartly dressed hoodlums with the Tommy guns stood by the front of the truck, just out of sight of the men who were lined up against the wall, and with their backs turned to Khan.

This is going to be a piece of cake, Khan thought. He covered the distance swiftly and quietly. Maybe he could pull this off and save Moran's men without any shots alerting the neighborhood.

Then a car horn blared outside in the alley. The driver had found his nerve after all.

Khan was almost within arm's reach of the two suits with the submachine guns when they turned around at the sudden noise. One of them was a little faster than the other, and obviously not new to the killing business. He brought up his Tommy gun just as Khan reached him. Khan swiped at the gun with all the force he could muster, which was a lot. The ten-pound submachine gun went flying across the garage and crashed into the brick wall to Khan's right, hard enough to make the stock shatter and the drum magazine fall out. Gun, stock, and magazine clattered to the cement floor of the garage. The back of the drum magazine popped off when it hit the floor. The .45-caliber cartridges inside, propelled by the wound-up mainspring of the magazine, spewed out of the drum with a strangled-sounding sproing. With the gun out of the way, Khan grabbed the gunner by the coat and threw him roughly along the same trajectory the gun had taken. He hit the wall hard, bounced off with considerably less resilience than the Tommy gun, and fell to the floor.

The second Tommy gunner managed to get a burst off just as Khan grabbed the muzzle of his gun and pushed it away from him. The hot gases from the compensator at the end of the barrel burned Khan's hand, and he let out an inadvertent roar. He doubled his grip on the barrel of the Tommy gun, yanked it away from the shooter, and flung it backwards and out of sight. Then he grabbed the goon by the lapels of his coat and head-butted him. The move had the desired effect--the Tommy gunner went slack-- but the plaster mask on the tiger part of Khan's face took half the hit and crumbled like an eggshell. A good chunk of it fell off and disintegrated on the cement floor.

In the garage in front of Khan, things had gotten a little more restless at his appearance. Moran's men, who had been lined up along the wall in grudgingly docile fashion, were now turning their heads to see just what the hell was going on behind them. The two fake cops, both holding their double-barreled shotguns, clearly didn't know what to make of this unplanned turn of events. Khan could smell sudden and sharp fear on both.

"Guns down," he half-roared. "Don't do anything stupid."

When you tell someone to not do anything stupid, they'll go ahead and do something stupid nine out of ten times. One of the fake cops couldn't quite make up his mind whether to keep aiming his shotgun at Moran's men or swing it around at Khan, so he did neither, kind of waving the barrel around halfway. The other cop wasn't plagued with indecision. He brought his own shotgun up to his shoulder and aimed it right at Khan.

Khan was still holding the unconscious Tommy gunner by his coat lapels. He picked him up and threw him toward the cop with all the force he could muster, which was a lot. The unconscious guy probably weighed two hundred pounds, and when he hit the fake cop, both went to the floor hard. The shotgun in the cop's hand barked and spewed a load of buckshot into the wall above the back door.

The other fake cop had finally made up his mind about which threat to prioritize and swung his shotgun toward Khan. Now unencumbered, Khan dodged to his right and crossed the distance with a single leap just as the shotgun roared. Then Khan had the gun barrels in both hands, wrenched the shotgun from its owner, and snapped it in half. The fake cop scrambled backwards and pawed at the holster on his belt to get out his revolver. Khan swiped his tiger hand down the front of the fake cop's uniform, and his claws sliced neatly through leather harness, pistol belt, uniform fabric, and skin. The leather harness gave way, and the gun thumped to the floor, still in its leather holster. Khan made a fist with his right hand, the human one, and pounded the fake cop in the temple. He was a big guy, six one at least, but he went down like a dropped sack of cement.

If Khan had intended to keep his intervention low-key, the plan was a total failure. Two shotgun blasts, a burst from a Tommy gun, one very loud and angry tiger roar, and now lots of yelling and screaming as Moran's men finally realized that the cops weren't genuine, and that the guy roughing up the hitmen was half Bengal tiger. Nobody even tried to go for the guns piled up in the middle of the garage floor. They all just started running for the back door. Outside, in the alley behind the garage, the getaway driver must have heard enough to convince him that things had very much not gone according to plan, because Khan got a brief glimpse of his face as the car drove past the back door and up the alley at what passed for full throttle in 1929. A few moments later, the garage was empty except for Khan, the four unconscious would-be killers, and a dog who was barking himself hoarse.

"Oh, for fuck's sake," Khan said.

He went over to where the dog was tied up and severed the leash with a swipe of his claws. The dog shot off toward the back door without so much as a look back.

"You're welcome," Khan shouted after him.

FIVE: MORAN

Moran's men had split up in the alley. Most of them were running to the left, toward Dickens Avenue. Two had picked the other way and turned right to run north. One of them--Khan couldn't decide if he was the smartest or the dumbest of the bunch--had climbed into the fake cop car to make a motor-assisted getaway, but he was either not familiar with the car model or not a very skilled driver. By the time Khan reached the back door, the cop car was just barely in gear and moving. Khan caught up to it easily. He jumped onto the passenger side running board, opened the door, and plopped himself down on the passenger seat. The driver yelped and tried to open his own door to jump out on the move, but Khan yanked him back by the collar of his shirt.

"Whoa there, sport. You sit tight."

"What do you want?" The driver sounded like he was about half a degree away from blowing his mental circuits. Khan reached over with his right hand and straightened out the steering wheel before the car continued its momentarily rudderless course and plowed into the side of the brownstone next to the garage.

"I want you to calm the fuck down. Take the wheel and drive this fucking car before you kill us both. Now look forward. Don't look at me."

"All right, all right," the driver said.

"You try to jump out again, I'll haul you back and twist your head off, do you understand me?"

"Yeah, okay. Okay. Jeez. Okay."

Khan tried to file the face of the driver in his brain's database of historical knowledge but came up short. He knew what Capone and Moran looked like, but he hadn't known the names of most of the people at the garage, would-be killers or would-be victims.

"Keep it straight. Get out of the alley and take a right on Dickens, go toward the park. Got it?"

"Yeah, I got it."

"What's your name?"

The driver looked at him sideways and swallowed hard. Khan supposed it didn't help that the side of him the driver could see was his tiger half, not the human one.

"May," the guy said. "Johnny May. Look, I'm not even with those guys. I'm just a mechanic. I fix cars."

"Johnny May," Khan repeated. "Turn right here on Dickens."

"Yes, sir."

They took the turn, and Khan looked around for the rest of the Moran gang, but they were all out of sight already. Fear can make a man pretty fast, Khan thought.

"Do you have any idea how lucky you are, Johnny May? You and the other Moran boys?"

"Look, I told you I'm not really..."

"Yeah, you're just the mechanic. Those guys that lined you up right before I got there? What do you think they were going to do?"

"I don't--I don't know. The two cops came in and told us to get up against the wall. They frisked us. Took all the guns. Those other two? I didn't even see them."

"They came in after the cops," Khan said. "With loaded Tommy guns. Did they look like cops to you?"

"Aw, jeez."

"Yeah," Khan said. "Capone's guys. They were after Moran. They were going to shoot everyone in there. And they wouldn't have given a shit that you're just the mechanic, trust me."

"My dog," May said. "We gotta go back. I left the dog tied up."

"I cut him loose. Does he know where home is?"

"It's too far. I live on North May. We gotta go back for him."

"Forget it. Unless you want to talk to the cops. They're probably on their way right now. That was some noise we made back there. What's his name?"

"Huh?"

"The dog. What's his name?"

"Highball."

"Highball," Khan repeated. "Shepherd?"

"Huh? Yeah. I've had him since he was a puppy."

"He'll be fine."

They drove in silence for a little while, Khan pointing whenever he wanted Johnny May to make a turn. He noticed that May tried to avoid looking at the tiger half of Khan's face, but that he wasn't quite successful, glancing at Khan quickly whenever he thought his passenger wasn't looking.

"Where are we going, Mister?" May finally asked after they had gone five or six blocks.

"You're going to go home," Khan said. "To your wife or girlfriend or mother, or whatever. After you ditch this car somewhere. It's got cop markings all over it. But first, you have to do me a favor."

"And what's that?"

"You take me to wherever Bugs Moran hangs out these days. I need to talk to him."

May blanched visibly.

"I can't do that, Mister."

"Sure you can. You think I want to kill the guy? If it wasn't for me, he'd be seven guys short tonight. Do I look like I'm with Capone? Huh?"

"No, Mister, you do not."

May swallowed hard and focused on the road again. Khan hoped that nobody had called in a suspicious police car leaving the scene, because he really didn't want to duke it out with the Chicago cops out in the middle of Lincoln Avenue.

"So help a guy out. Drop me off and point me in the right direction. And then you can go home. Look for your dog. Have a damn drink. Be happy that you're not bleeding out on the floor of that garage right now with a bullet in your brain."

May was badly shaken, and Khan didn't have to pry much. They turned west, then north again, until Khan was pretty sure they were back in the general area just west of Lincoln Park. The snow had started to fall again, fat flakes drifting from the sky and reducing visibility. Somewhere north of Armitage Avenue, May pulled the car over and pointed ahead.

"I don't want to drive up there in this thing, but it's the Parkway Hotel. Mister Moran's apartment is up on the fifth floor, in the place that overlooks the corner. Look, just don't tell 'em I showed you, okay?"

"Relax," Khan said. "But do remember that I have a really good memory, Johnny May who lives on North May Street and has a German Shepherd named Highball. You lead me on a wild goose chase, have me knocking on some Italian grandma's apartment door while you high-tail it back to town, I'm gonna come look you up. Are we clear?"

He let out a rasping little growl for emphasis, just enough to make May squirm in his seat and lean over to get as far away from him as he physically could without opening his car door.

"Yes, we're clear, Mister."

"Good. Now get out of here. Go home to your sweetheart. And start checking the paper for a new job tomorrow. Fix cars for people who don't have enemies with machine guns."

"The money's good," May said. "I got a family to feed. I got seven kids at home."

"You won't be feeding nobody when you're on a slab at the city morgue," Khan said. "Ditch the car. Go home."

It was snowing harder now, so it didn't look too odd for Khan to cover his head with the top part of his coat. He got out of the car and watched as May drove off and turned right at the next intersection. Then he started walking in the direction May had pointed him.

The Parkway Hotel building was right across the street from Lincoln Park. Khan had been sleeping a few hundred yards from Moran's apartment, almost in his line of sight, for a week without knowing it. He went back to his hideout in Lincoln Park and made himself another burn mask disguise with the supplies from the drugstore. Then he waited out nightfall, reading the newspaper and eating cold baloney sandwiches. Well after dark, he went to the Parkway Hotel and ducked into a side alley. Fire escapes were easy to reach when your vertical leap was fifteen feet on a lazy day. He climbed up to the fifth floor and let himself into the corridor through a window. The corner apartment was directly to his left, and the locks in 1929 were shit compared to the modern high-tech stuff in his time.

The apartment didn't exactly scream "gangster boss", but it was also clear that there was no little old Italian grandma living here. There was a booze cabinet, all the furniture was nice, and it took Khan only five minutes of snooping around to find a stash of cash and three guns hidden in various locations around the apartment, out of view but ready to access in a hurry if you knew where to look. He put the guns on the kitchen counter, picked up the nicest one--a lovely blued Colt 1911, the bare-bones ancestor of the gun he had carried in 2017--and unloaded the others. The Colt had a full magazine, and Khan chambered a round and flicked the safety on. Then he went over to the liquor cabinet, which was artfully concealed behind a bookshelf, and helped himself to some whiskey. It was rotgut compared to the stuff he usually bought back home, but it was his first drink in a week, and he sure as hell needed one after the last few days. He sat down in a comfortable armchair in the corner of the living room, put the gun in his lap and the whiskey on the side table, and killed some time counting the money from the stash.

Moran and his lieutenants must have been thoroughly spooked by the shooting at their main headquarters, because they didn't show up at the apartment until just before midnight. Khan could hear and smell them long before he heard the key turning in the lock he had picked earlier. He counted four different voices and smells, and three of them were familiar to him from the warehouse tussle earlier.

The first one into the living room was one of the guys from the garage. Khan guessed he was one of Moran's enforcers, because he smelled like violence and didn't seem like the accountant type. Moran came in second--Khan recognized him from the pictures in the history books. He didn't know the third guy, but the fourth looked a lot like Mook Number One, so Khan guessed they were brothers. The living room was dark, and he waited until everyone was in the room before he turned on the little standing lamp next to the armchair.

"What the f--"

The brothers both went for their guns. Khan raised the cocked pistol and shook his head.

"*Nuh-uh,* boys. Let's not make any undue ruckus."

They hesitated, which wasn't a hard thing to do when you stared down the barrel of a .45 automatic. Moran, to his credit, seemed more concerned than outright afraid. The guy behind him gasped when he saw Khan.

"It's the guy, Bugs. The same guy. From the warehouse."

"Tell your boys to keep their heaters in their waistbands, Mister Moran," Khan said amicably. "I have really, really good reflexes. But I'm not here to harm you."

Moran looked at the two bodyguards, then back to Khan. He bit his lower lip and shrugged.

"Pete, Frank. You heard the gentleman."

The two brothers relaxed their stances. Khan wasn't worried about the third guy with Moran. He had kind of a bookish look to him, and he didn't radiate the same sort of attitude the two enforcers did. Khan couldn't even smell a gun on the guy despite the events earlier today.

"You came pretty close to getting your tickets punched today," Khan said. "All of you."

"You would know. You were there," Moran said. "Or so Adam says."

"He was there," one of the brothers confirmed, and the other one nodded. "Took out all four of them. He's not lying about those reflexes."

"So you're not here to kill me," Moran said. "And you're not here to kill my guys, or you could have done it back at the warehouse earlier. So why are you here?"

"For a job interview," Khan said. One of the brothers chuckled, and Moran joined him.

"For a job interview," Moran repeated, and looked at the guy next to him, the one he called Adam. "Can you believe this guy?"

Khan lowered the gun, but left the hammer cocked. Then he nodded at the couch and the other two armchairs that were set up around the coffee table in front of him.

"Why don't you have a seat, and we'll talk things over. But please don't try to make a run for it, any of you. I'm not here to hurt you, but if you run off to bring back trouble, I'll put two rounds into each of you before you can make the door."

Moran looked at his enforcers and nodded. Then he walked over to the armchair directly across the coffee table from Khan and sat down.

"He's got a cat face under that mask," one of the brothers said. "Looks like a damn tiger. Like some sideshow trick."

"I'd like to see that," Moran said.

Khan lifted his left hand and held it out for them to see, covered in orange and white fur as it was. He extended his claws slowly, and all four of the men in front of him flinched or gasped. Then he hooked one claw underneath the plaster of his mask and pulled it off carefully.

"I'll be damned," Moran said. "What on Earth are you, exactly?"

"I can't really explain that in a way that would make sense to you," Khan said. "At least not yet. For now, let's say I have an affliction."

"An *affliction*," Moran repeated. "I see. Do you have a name?"

"They call me Khan."

"That's it. Just Khan?" Moran smiled. "I can work with that. Nice to meet you, Mr. Khan. Now, you want to tell me what went down at my warehouse this morning?"

"You should have a rough idea by now. That wasn't a police raid. The cops weren't cops. They were a hit squad. Looking for you. I don't think I need to tell you who hired them."

"I knew it," Moran snarled, and looked at Adam, who was still standing and regarding Khan warily. "That fucking low-life beast."

"Jesus, Bugs. He damn near got all of us. You, me, everyone," Adam said. Khan's brain finally supplied a last name for the guy: Adam Heyer, the gang's bookkeeper, Moran's business manager.

"I saw the cop car pull up in the alley," Moran said. "Figured it was a shake-down raid. So Ted and I turned around and went for a coffee. Warned off Henry, too. If I'd gotten up a little earlier..."

"If it wasn't for him, we'd be dead now," Heyer said. "Them guys were locked and loaded. They weren't there to collect. You should have seen it, Bugs. He just tossed 'em like they were nothing. Snapped one guy's shotgun right in half."

"How did you know this was going to go down?" Moran asked Khan. "You didn't just happen to stroll through the alley, did you?"

"No," Khan said. "I knew they were going to hit someone because they were staking you out, so I decided to stake them out in return."

"They were staking the place? From where?"

"They had a room in the apartment building across the street. The one with the double entrances. I didn't know who they were after," Khan lied. "So I had to wait it out and figure something out on the fly."

"I'll be damned," Moran said. "Right under our noses." He looked back at the two brothers standing on either side of Heyer. "We gotta get out of town for a bit. Let things cool down. Figure out what we're going to do about that greasy little prick."

Khan noticed that Moran had not called Capone by name so far, as if the name was distasteful to him.

Moran turned around and looked at Khan again. He let his eyes wander to Khan's clawed hand, then to the pistol on his lap.

"Mr. Khan," he said.

"Just Khan, please."

"*Khan.* Okay. We are going to go out to a little place in the country. I was wondering if you'd care to join us. We can discuss your proposal on the way. Whatever it is you're proposing."

"Bugs," one of the enforcer brothers said. "You sure that's a good idea? I mean, look at the guy. You want to take *him* out to the place? If he's with Capone, he can do whatever he wants with us out there."

"If he's with Capone, we'd all be dead by now," Moran said. "And I think that this gentleman could do whatever he wants with us anytime, anywhere."

He smiled curtly at Khan.

"You don't like Capone, do you?"

"I don't like bullies," Khan said. The answer seemed to please Moran.

"Sure," Khan said, and lowered the hammer of the gun in his lap. "I'll come along. Let's go for a drive."

"Great." Moran slapped his thigh and stood up. "Call the rest of the boys, Frank. We're going to go out for some fresh air."

SIX: INDIANA

The gang left Chicago in a small convoy of three cars just before sunrise. Khan sat in the back of the first car, with Moran next to him and one of the enforcer brothers--Frank Gusenberg--in the front passenger seat. Khan had reapplied his plaster mask, and his tiger hand was gloved. He had Moran's .45 tucked away underneath his coat, but he wasn't worried about having to use it. In the tight confines of the car, his claws were quicker and better than any gun. He wasn't even encumbered by a seatbelt, because there weren't any. It felt weird being in a car without basic safety features. Khan wondered what they would think if he started telling them about head rests, satellite navigation, and anti-lock brakes, or the 500-horsepower Benz with the 2,000-watt sound system he drove back in his own time. Gusenberg was nervous, the driver even more so, and both of them smoked like chimneys, flicking the glowing butts out of the windows and letting in a cold burst of winter air every time. Khan watched the wind-blown, snowy February landscape of central Michigan roll by outside as the Cadillac sedan purred its way south.

"So what do you do when you're not knocking Capone's guys around?" Moran asked.

"I'm in the personal protection business," Khan replied. "I'm a bodyguard."

"And you've been doing that for a while now?"

"Twelve years," Khan said.

"So you're pretty good at what you do."

"I'm the best at what I do."

In the front seat, Frank Gusenberg let out a little derisive snort, but Khan ignored him.

"I've never lost a principal," he said. Until a few weeks ago at the Palmer House, he thought. But as far as he was concerned, his sheet was still clean. He had only lost Giovanni Galante-- physically, temporally lost him. Khan didn't know which year Galante had found himself in, but he knew that the little shit had still been alive when the event happened, and only thanks to Khan.

Chicago was smaller back in 1929, and they were in the countryside soon, crossing from Illinois into northern Indiana. The farmlands south of Gary were the boring ass end of the world as far as Khan was concerned, and he found that they had already been the boring ass end of the world back in 1929.

"As long as that vicious little greaseball is out there, I guess I'll always have a need for bodyguards," Moran said. "And you've certainly given one hell of a job interview at the warehouse already." He pointed to the cars behind them with his thumb. "Without Adam and Jimmy May and the Gusenberg boys here, I'd have to close up shop on the Northside. You did me a big favor back there. You stick with us for a bit, I'll see what I can do for you."

An hour south of Gary, they left the main roads and turned onto a series of ever-narrowing side roads, crossing train tracks, passing isolated farms and driving through small two-stoplight towns: Kersey, Stoutsburg, Wheatfield. The snow had picked up steadily on their drive, and Khan was starting to get worried about the winter handling qualities of 1920s tire technology.

Ten miles out of Wheatfield, they took a left onto a dirt road. A few miles further down, the driver took a right turn onto a narrower dirt road that hadn't been cleared of snow yet, and Khan thought they'd get stuck for sure and freeze to death here in Ass Bend, Indiana. But the Cadillac puttered on, and the two other cars followed slowly in its wake.

There was a farm at the end of the dirt road, set back from the road a quarter mile. Khan saw a large barn and a grain silo, and the farmhouse was a big one, two floors and a wraparound porch. The three cars chugged up the driveway and parked by the side of the farmhouse. Khan got out of the car and stretched his limbs. It was freezing cold out here in the middle of nowhere, but the place was isolated, and they'd notice anyone coming up that quarter-mile dirt driveway well before they got to the farmhouse.

Inside, the place was warm and cozy. They all walked into the side door, which led into a big kitchen with a cast iron stove in the center of the room that was radiating heat. Moran and his guys took off their coats and hung them from hooks by the door, and Khan followed suit. A few moments later, a woman came down the stairs nearby and walked into the kitchen, and the men acknowledged her with respectful nods and murmured greetings.

"Very sorry to drop in on you on short notice, ma'am," Moran said.

"You know it's not a bother, Mister Moran," she replied. "I've got the back bedrooms ready upstairs, but some of your boys may have to bunk on the floor. I wasn't expecting all of you."

She looked at Khan, who felt a little out of place in this kitchen, dressed in longshoreman weather gear when everyone else was wearing suits.

"Who is your tall friend?"

"This is Khan," Moran said. "Just Khan. He helped us out back in the city. Khan, this is Mrs. Sobieski. She owns this farm. We stop by from time to time when we need to get out of the city for a while."

"Izabela," she said. There was just the faintest familiar Polish lilt in her voice, and Khan figured that if she hadn't come right off the boat, her parents had.

"Dzień dobry," he said on a hunch. *"Jak się Pani miewa?"*

"Bardzo dobrze, dziękuję," she replied, almost reflexively. Then she turned to Moran and smiled a little.

"Your friend speaks very good Polish."

"My mother is Polish," Khan said. "Her parents came from Łódź."

"Mine are from Katowice," Izabela said. She reminded him a bit of his mother, back when he was a teenager, right before his card turned. She had the same dark hair, the same understated beauty that a hard life hadn't quite managed to paint over yet.

Moran's men obviously knew the place. They made themselves right at home, pulling up chairs to the big kitchen table and getting out their cigarettes. Khan tried to map the place in his head discreetly--entries, exits, corners, approaches to the kitchen door from outside. For a bunch of guys who had almost gotten machine-gunned by their rivals the day before, Moran's guys were not nearly paranoid enough about their safety, but Khan wasn't about to change his habits. Letting your guard down could get you killed, whether it was 2017 or 1929.

Later in the afternoon, when the gang was dispersed all over the house, Khan sat at the now-empty kitchen table and awkwardly sipped a cup of coffee around the plaster bandage with the right side of his mouth. Behind him, Izabela took a big pot of hot water off the wood stove and filled two tin buckets with it. He gave her a curious look.

"For the chickens," she said. "It warms them up."

She took a bucket handle in each hand and lifted the buckets. Then she walked toward the kitchen door, with the hot water in the buckets trailing wisps of steam behind her.

"Let me help you," he said and stood up. He opened the door for her, then deftly took the buckets out of her hands as she passed him. She looked amused.

"I can take care of this," she said.

"I'm sure you can. Lead the way," he said.

They walked over to the barn, through snow that was knee-deep. Izabela opened the sliding door wide enough for them to step through, then flicked a light switch on the inside wall. There were a few cows, not even half a dozen, some goats and sheep, and maybe two dozen chickens that were huddled in an enclosed coop at the other end of the barn. Khan put the buckets down, and Izabela filed up the water pan in the coop, which had a layer of ice on top of it. The hot water dissolved the ice and steamed in the cold barn air. The chickens hopped off their roost one by one and came to get their free warm-up.

"That's not a lot of animals for a farm this size," Khan said.

"We had more," Izabela replied. "When my husband was still alive. Ten horses, thirty cows. A hundred chickens. But there's only so much I can do by myself."

"Sorry to hear about your husband."

Izabela stepped into the back of the coop and stooped down to collect eggs from the laying boxes. She put them into the pockets of her apron. To Khan, they didn't look like a lot of eggs for so many birds, and he said so.

"They slow down in the winter. When it's warm, it's one egg per day from each of them. And when they stop laying, they go in the soup."

"What do you have to do with these guys?" he asked. "Moran and his gang. You know what they do, right?"

"They are bootleggers," she said. "My husband ran a still. Two hundred gallons a month. One day, they stopped his truck while he was delivering to Mister Moran's warehouse. Capone's men. And they shot him."

"Sorry," Khan said again.

"Mister Moran helps me out. I don't run the still, but they come and stay here sometimes, and he pays me for it."

She looked at his face and reached up to touch the plaster mask.

"What happened there? This doesn't look like you really need it."

Khan was intrigued by her total lack of fear. He was three times her weight and a foot taller, and they were alone in a semi-dark barn in the middle of rural Indiana, but she wasn't afraid of him at all.

"I'm hiding my face with it," he said. "Half of it, anyway."

"Why?"

"So I don't scare people."

"Let me see," she said in Polish. He sighed and pulled the mask off the left half of his face. He had expected her to scream and run for the door, but instead she put her hands in front of her mouth. Then she reached out to touch the fur fringe hanging down from his jawline.

"How did this happen?"

"A virus," he said. "A sickness. When I was fifteen."

"Did it hurt?"

"Oh, yeah. Worst pain I ever felt. It took months. When it was done with me, I looked like this."

"How long ago was that?"

Khan didn't quite know whether to answer sixteen years ago or in seventy-two years. The week was already complicated enough. So he shrugged and said, "A while ago."

He picked up the buckets and stepped around the chickens that were filling their beaks from the warm water pan.

They trudged back to the house through the snow. The farm looked nothing like his own place, or even the house he grew up in, but Khan felt a swell of homesickness when they walked back into the warm kitchen. Not the kind you feel for a place, but for people. For some reason, it hadn't fully hit him until now that he'd never see Naya or his mother again, that he was stuck here for good out of his own time, among people who regarded him as a sideshow curiosity. The Wild Card virus wouldn't hit New York City for another seventeen years. They would be long and lonely years, and whatever fun he'd had finding himself at the tail end of the Roaring Twenties was dissipating quickly. There was no way home, because home was Naya and Mom, and they didn't exist yet.

Galante, he thought. *I hope you got bounced back to 1929 too. Or 1931, or 1935. Just as long as there's a chance I'll bump into you, and I get to strangle you with your own fucking guts.*

SEVEN: FARMVILLE

The next day, Moran sent one of the guys into town for sundries and newspapers. When he came back a few hours later, he brought several different papers with him, which Moran and his lieutenants read over breakfast. Several of the papers mentioned the incident at the warehouse. The cops had arrived not too long after the gunfire, but the warehouse had been empty, with just some shell casings and two broken guns on the floor. Without suspects or victims, the cops had nothing to do, nobody to arrest or question.

"He's gonna try again," Moran said, slurping his coffee. "Son of a bitch knows I'm gonna come after him for this."

He turned to one of the Gusenberg brothers.

"Remember when we went to his place a few years back? In Cicero? A thousand rounds into that inn, and the bastard walks away."

"Yeah, but there wasn't a clean set of drawers left in that place," Gusenberg said, and Moran chuckled. Then his expression turned serious again.

"He guns for us, we gun for him. One of these days he's gonna run out of luck. He can't stay holed up in that hotel forever."

Or yours is going to run out, Khan thought. He was standing across the room by the kitchen window, sipping his own coffee and looking out of the kitchen window. The history books said that the cops really started cracking down on Capone after the St. Valentine's Day massacre, and that the whole thing spelled the beginning of the end for both Capone and Moran. Four more years of prohibition, and Capone would be in prison for tax evasion before the end. That was the old history, of course, before Khan had stuck his claws into the time stream. Without the massacre at the warehouse, both Capone and Moran would ratchet up the conflict. Moran certainly seemed like the type. Khan could smell the anger radiating off the man.

Well, at least I'll have secure employment for a while, he thought.

Khan spent the day checking the farmhouse from all angles.

The snow out beyond the farmyard was knee-high, but he slogged through it to circle the place. To see how to protect a location, you first need to think like someone who's trying to get into it. Some of Moran's men were watching him from the windows as he did so, talking among themselves as they did. He knew that they still didn't trust him fully, especially not the Gusenbergs, whose main contributions to Moran's organization wasn't intellectual wattage.

He helped Izabela with the water and the animal feed again, grateful to have something to do that let him use his muscles. Physical labor made him feel useful, like he hadn't just gotten all that strength to hurt people. The hay bales for the cows weighed eighty pounds at least, but he took one in each hand and carried them over to the cattle enclosure over the gentle protestations of Izabela. Then he brought in half a cord of firewood and restocked all the wood stacks the house, which gave him a good opportunity to see more of the interior layout.

Moran and his guys had booze and playing cards out after dinner. Khan was a fair poker player himself, but he didn't feel like socializing with the gang or blunting his senses with bootlegged hooch. Instead, he got some more coffee and took a chair by the kitchen door, in sight of the others but far enough away to remain out of their tobacco smoke cloud. They stayed up until well past midnight, strategizing and talking about people Khan didn't know, and by the time they all turned in, it was blissfully silent in the kitchen again except for the popping log in the wood stove that kept the place cozy.

When he startled awake, he had no idea how long he had been asleep by the wood stove in the still-warm kitchen. The house was quiet except for the occasional creaking of settling wood beams and the soft tick-tock from the clock on the mantelpiece in the living room next door. Moran's men were asleep in their bedrooms on the other side of the house. Izabela must have turned off the lights and covered him up, because the kitchen was dark, and there was a wool blanket loosely laid over him. The drowsy human part of Khan's brain told him to go back to sleep, but the tiger part was awake and restless. Something wasn't right. And when something set Khan's fur on edge, he knew that it was wise to listen to the tiger.

He swept the blanket aside and kicked off his shoes quietly. Then he stood up and tuned into his senses.

There was movement on the driveway outside. It was a dark, moonless light, and there were no outside lights on either farmhouse or barn, but his tiger eye didn't need the light to see the trouble coming. Five, six, seven, eight guys, all in winter coats, coming up the driveway from the dirt road, where Khan saw the two cars they had parked a quarter mile away to keep the noise down. Everyone was armed. Khan saw the distinctive drum magazines of Tommy guns, and one of the guys coming up the driveway carried an honest-to-goodness BAR, a Browning Automatic Rifle that could pop out twenty .30-06 shells in three or four seconds. A broadside from that thing would do even him in for good. By the time Khan had startled from his sleep, the armed group had already covered half the distance between road and farmhouse.

Khan considered shouting down the house to warn Moran's guys, but that would just end badly. They had as many guys inside as the crew outside did, but Moran's men were asleep. By the time they were awake and ready to fight, the prepared group coming up the driveway would be pouring fire into the farmhouse already. He hoped that Izabela's bedroom was toward the back of the house as well. The Ought-six from that BAR would pierce through wood and drywall like an icepick through a loaf of bread.

Darkness worked in his favor much more than in theirs. Khan opened the kitchen door as quietly as he could, and then dashed across the farmyard and into the barn.

He had almost reached the door on the other side of the barn when it opened, and one of the armed visitors stuck his head in and looked around in the darkness. The chickens were in their usual nighttime stupor, but the cows shuffled around a bit, and one of the sheep made a muffled noise. The guy in the doorway made a face at the smell. Not a country boy, Khan thought.

There was no time, no opportunity for going light on these guys. The man in front of Khan had a Tommy gun in the crook of his arm, and if he managed to fire off a burst, the cat would be out of the bag, so to speak. So Khan leapt the rest of the distance, yanked the Tommy gun out of the guy's grip, and then slashed his throat with one forceful swipe of his claws. The guy fell forward with a gurgle, twitched a few times, and let out a last wet breath from his ruined throat. Khan picked up the submachine gun. It had a hundred-round drum in it, a heavy thing the size of a dinner plate. The bolt of the gun wasn't cocked yet, and Khan worked the charging handle quietly. Then he stepped out of the door and stealthily made his way to the corner of the barn.

The other seven hitmen were almost past the barn, and only fifty yards from the front of the farmhouse. Once they were in the farmyard, they started fanning out in a semicircle. Khan raised the Tommy gun, but immediately realized that any missed rounds from this angle would hit the house instead.

Well, shit. But it's not like they are paying attention to what's behind them, he thought. Khan put the Tommy gun down into the snow beside the barn, flexed his muscles, and let the tiger take over.

Even after all these years, it was still a little frightening to Khan just how easily the fighting and killing business came to his tiger half when he put it fully in control. He moved so quickly that the world seemed to shift into slow motion. He was on the first two hitmen half a second after his leap. Both men went down hard, clotheslined by a 300-pound half tiger at the end of a thirty-foot leap. Their guns skidded into the snow. The next man down the line was missing an arm and the shotgun he was holding before he had even turned toward the new disturbance. Khan slashed him twice across the throat and chest for good measure.

Four left.

One got a shotgun blast off that clipped Khan in the side with a few buckshot pellets. It took his breath away for just a moment, and the tiger brain went into full autopilot mode. Khan yanked away the shotgun with his human hand, grabbed the hitman's head with his tiger hand--it fit easily--and wrenched it sideways. There was a sharp snap, and the hitman dropped on the spot with the lack of coordination particular to the freshly and suddenly deceased.

Three.

The first machine gun fire of the night broke out. The farmyard was dark, and the remaining hitmen didn't know what or who was ripping them to shreds from the rear, and Khan could smell their sudden fear and panic. He dodged and rolled to avoid the burst of fire from the BAR. Then he kicked out with his clawed foot and took the shooter's right leg off just below the knee. The hitman screamed as he went down. Khan yanked the heavy BAR from his grip and swung the gun around. The last three attackers were running up to the farmhouse, where a light had just come on in the kitchen, outlining the door. There was nothing but dark Indiana landscape behind the trailing hitman from Khan's angle, so he brought the gun up and squeezed off a quick burst. The guy dropped and skidded through the fresh snow face-first for a yard or two, then lay motionless. Then the last two hitmen were inside the farmhouse.

Khan cursed and ripped the magazine from the gun, then tossed it aside. Then he sprinted back toward the kitchen door.

Inside, there was shouting in the living room to Khan's left, and then three gunshots in quick succession. A moment later, another shot rang out that had a ring of finality to it. But in front of him, in the middle of the kitchen, one of the hitmen had Izabela in a chokehold, and the muzzle of a shotgun pressed against her chin from below. He looked at Khan with unconcealed terror in his eyes.

"I'll fucking blow her head off! I'll fucking shoot her! I'll fucking..."

Khan had been to the firing range several times a week for the last twelve years. The 1911 in his waistband was not very different from the one he carried back in his own time, and it functioned the same. With his tiger reflexes, he could have made the shot three times, but only one was necessary here. Khan drew the .45, flicked off the safety, brought the pistol up in a two-handed grip firmly enough to make the grip panels creak, and pulled the trigger. The bullet hit the middle of the guy's forehead. Khan knew that the man was dead already before he was halfway to the floor. He would have pulled Izabela to the ground with him, but she flinched with a shout and shrugged him off, then went to her knees.

Moran's men streamed into the kitchen, all of them armed and in various states of dress. Khan flicked the safety of his gun back on and stuck the .45 into his waistband.

"Any more?" Frank Gusenberg wanted to know. He seemed out of breath, and Khan could smell he was so high-wound with stress that his nerves were practically humming with tension.

"Other than this dope here? I got five more in the yard," Khan replied. "One inside the barn. You get the one in the living room?"

"Yeah," Gusenberg said. "The fuck did they come from?"

"They parked out by the road," Khan said. Walked the rest of the way. They were halfway to the house before I heard them."

"Some fucking bodyguard you are."

"He did just fine," Moran said. He had walked into the kitchen last, a snub nose revolver in his hand. "If he laid out seven guys. Go check, Frank. Take Peter. And go see if they left someone with those cars."

Peter and Frank Gusenberg came back into the farmhouse ten minutes later, their coasts frosted with snow.

"Like he said, Bugs. Five guys out in the yard. He ripped the arm off of one."

"You know any of them?"

"Yeah. One's Fred Burke. The one in the barn."

"Fred Burke," Moran said. "Egan's Rats. That ape." He looked at Khan. "You did the world a favor, my friend. That was Capone's number one clean-up crew you just took out."

Moran's face contorted with anger. He snatched a coffee mug from the kitchen table and threw it against the wall, where it shattered and made a dent in the plaster.

"That bastard. That filthy *swine*."

"We've been using this place for years," Frank Gusenberg said and looked at Khan. "Then this guy shows up, and the first night we're back here, they know exactly where we went. I wonder why that is."

"Somebody ratted us out," Moran said. "Or we had a tail all the way from Chicago. Who gives a shit. You think Capone would let this guy kill his best wrecking crew? Use your fucking brain, Frank."

Next to Khan, one of Moran's men--Weinshank?--had finished frisking the dead guy on the kitchen floor. He'd had that shotgun of his, a Colt pocket pistol, and a wallet with a small stack of bills in it. Weinshank took out the money, counted it, and put it in his own pocket.

"Get that piece of shit out of here before he gets his blood all over Mrs. Sobieski's floor," Moran ordered. "Get rid of the other bodies too."

"Ground's frozen, Bugs," Frank Gusenberg said. "What do you want us to do with them?"

"Put 'em in their fucking cars, drive 'em out into a field somewhere, and set them on fire," Moran snapped. "Do I have to all the thinking around here?"

He looked at Khan.

"Go help these guys, will ya? And when you're done, we're heading back into town, first thing in the morning. You're riding with me, 'case we got stuff to talk about."

He jammed his hands into the pockets of his trousers and looked out into the dark farmyard.

"Two hits in three fucking days. We're gonna go back downtown and show that greaseball how it's done right."

They carried the bodies back to the cars parked by the road a quarter mile away. The Gusenbergs each drove one of the cars, and Khan rode with Frank Gusenberg in the second car while four of the dead hitmen were stacked up on the backseat like bloody cordwood. They drove around in the dark Indiana countryside for twenty miles until they found an old abandoned homestead. They drove the cars behind a half-collapsed barn, and the Moran boys got out gasoline cans and splashed their contents all over the vehicles. Then Frank Gusenberg lit a cigarette with his Zippo and lit the trail of gasoline. It took a little while for the cars to catch, but after a few minutes, the tires and ragtops caught fire, and then the upholstery in the interiors. Khan had smelled burning bodies before. People who claimed it smelled like barbecue never had to smell a human body burn up. While they watched the cars go up in flames, the Gusenbergs and the other Moran man, a jumpy guy named Schwimmer, went through the wallets from the bodies and removed the cash before tossing them into the burning cars. Frank Gusenberg counted out the money from the two wallets he had emptied, then turned to Khan and held out a stack of bills.

"Your share," Gusenberg said.

"Keep it," Khan replied. "I don't need it."

Gusenberg shook his head and smirked at Khan.

"You did these guys, you should claim your share. One hell of a thing you did. You barely left any for us to finish."

One of the other guys, the accountant named Heyer, had followed them with one of the gang's Cadillacs, and Khan and the other three returned to the farm in the Caddy. Khan had the scent of gasoline and burning hair in his nostrils all the way back.

They rode back to Chicago not too long after sunrise. Khan rode in the back of the lead car with Moran again, who was still seething.

"You asked for a job, I'll give you a job," Moran said. "I can't keep looking over my shoulder every time I walk down the street on the North Side. Kill Capone. Take the bastard out for me. I'll pay you fifty thousand."

Khan tried to calculate how much fifty grand were in 2017 money. Moran took the silence as hesitation.

"Seventy if you get Frankie Rio too. That's his bodyguard. And if you kill Frank Nitti--a hundred thousand. I'm dead serious. A hundred thousand, cash. You'll never have to work a day in your life again."

"I'm a bodyguard, Mr. Moran," Khan said. "I'm not a contract killer. I don't do that kind of stuff."

"What are you talking about? You just killed seven of Capone's best guys like someone swattin' flies on a windowsill."

"They were coming to kill us. That's different."

"Ain't no difference there," Moran said. "Any of his guys will do us in if they get the chance."

"And if they come for us, I'll kill them too," Khan replied. "But I'm not in the business of striking first."

"Don't matter who strikes first. Only who strikes last. You get rid of my problem for me, I'll be running the whole market in Chicago. I can make you rich. Think about it."

Khan had no problem taking a life. His ledger had a lot of names on it. But every last entry on his list was someone who had swung the knife, aimed the gun, struck the blow first.

"I'll think about it," Khan said, even though he already knew that his answer wouldn't change, not for any amount of money.

Moran leaned back in his seat and rubbed his hands together.

"Oh, and you're hired," he said. "You're my chief bodyguard now. How's five hundred a week sound?"

"Five hundred a week sounds good to me," Khan said, but his mind was already somewhere else. This would have to do until he had his legs under him, but he had decided that he didn't care much for Moran. The man reminded him too much of Galante, throwing money around to make others clean up his shit for him. The Roaring Twenties had seemed so wild and romantic in his history books when he was a kid, but it turned out that the game was the same it was in his time, and it didn't matter whether its name was bootlegging or crack hustling. It was all just little minds in expensive clothes climbing over piles of bodies to get power, dogs pissing on lampposts and snapping at each other.

EIGHT: RESET

They were back in Chicago in the early afternoon. Moran didn't want to use the warehouse at 2122 North Clark just yet, in case the cops were still going through it or Capone's men were staking it out for a second attempt. Instead, they went back to the Parkway Hotel, two blocks from the warehouse and a much more public setting. Moran had Khan walk ahead and scout the lobby and the elevator, and the two Gusenberg boys were bringing up the rear, guns ready under their winter coats. But Khan smelled no trouble. He didn't doubt Capone would go after Moran again--the two seemed to have a massive anger hard-on for each other--but it wouldn't be today.

"We need to get you a place to stay," Moran said a little while later when they were sitting in his living room. Moran had a drink in his hand even though it was just two in the afternoon. "I want you close by. I've got some of my boys here in the Parkway. How do you feel about that? I'll call downstairs and have them set you up here on the fifth floor."

Khan shrugged.

"Sure. Beats a tent out in the park."

"That's where you've been living? Jeez. You can afford better now. And we need to get you to a tailor and get you something nice to wear. So you don't stick out as much."

"He's gonna stick out no matter what," one of the Gusenbergs said.

"We can fix him up with something better than that plaster. Don't worry. By the time we're done with you, ain't none of Capone's guys want to come close to you, my friend."

Peter Gusenberg and Moran took him to a place downtown

where a very old and slow tailor measured Khan for the better part of an hour with his tape measure. Khan had to take his overcoat and shirt off for the measurements, and he didn't miss the veiled looks of fascination and repulsion from Gusenberg when they saw his unconcealed muscular frame, with the demarcation line between fur and skin running exactly down the center of his body. Even though he must have been the strangest and most unusual person the tailor had ever measured, the old man never lost a word over his appearance or anything else, limiting his utterances to directions for Khan to lift an arm, turn halfway, let his arms hang by his side, and so on.

By the time they got back to the Parkway, there was an apartment ready for Khan, a three-room unit two doors over from Moran's place. His tailored suits wouldn't be ready for another two weeks, but they had bought him some off-the-rack clothes that were a lot nicer than the workman's overalls and weather coat he had been wearing.

"Put your stuff away and settle in," Moran told him. "Make yourself at home. We're going out to dinner at Ralphie's in an hour. I'll need you to keep an eye out while we're there."

"Not a problem, boss," Khan said.

They left him to square his things away. The apartment was pretty nice, even if Khan didn't care much for 1920s decor. At least it wasn't the Seventies, he told himself. He stashed the new clothes in the bedroom closet and put on a pinstripe suit. They hadn't found a dress shirt with a collar wide enough for him to button it and wear a tie, but even without that accoutrement, he looked much better than he had since he arrived in this decade. There was some money in his pocket, a loaded .45 on his hip, and he didn't feel like a tent-dwelling bum anymore.

One day at a time, he told himself while he checked the fit of his suit jacket in the mirror. In seventeen years, the Wild Card virus would hit New York City, and then he could be himself again. He planned to be long out of the bodyguard business by then. Prohibition would end in another four years, and then people like Capone and Moran would have to go back to robbing banks or holding up racetracks again. That gave Khan four years to pile up enough mob cash to ride out the Great Depression and World War Two, preferably in a neutral country where the dollar went far.

They went out to dinner. Well, Moran and his accountant had dinner, while Khan sat in a booth close by and sipped club soda, keeping an eye on the place while Moran and Heyer ate steak and asparagus tips. After dinner and drinks, one of the Gusenbergs picked them up in front of the restaurant, and Khan walked ahead and made sure the neighborhood was clear before Moran and Heyer got into the car. They drove back to the Parkway Hotel, talking business, Khan mostly ignoring them while he kept an eye on the surroundings.

Back at the hotel, Moran dismissed Khan at the door of his apartment.

"I'm going to talk some more shop with Adam. Why don't you tap out for the night. But keep your eyes and ears open. You smell any funny business, you come and tell me. Ain't nobody got any business on this side of the fifth floor except our guys."

"Will do, Mister Moran," Khan said.

"Peter says the cops are done with the warehouse. We're going back in the morning to get the trucks running again. Show that greaseball guinea he can't run us off our turf. Make sure you're ready to go by eight. I'll send Frank over to fetch you."

"I'll be ready," Khan said. "Have a good night, sir."

He went into his own apartment, locked the door and the security chain, stripped off his suit, and took a long, hot shower. Then he checked his .45, put it under the pillow, and climbed into bed while still damp from the shower. Stretching out and sleeping in a proper bed after weeks of camping out felt decadent--not quite as great as making love to a beautiful woman or eating a perfect two-hundred-dollar filet mignon, but pretty damn close.

The radio woke him up in the morning. It popped into life in the living room at low volume with a commercial for laundry soap.

He knew the radio hadn't been on when he went to sleep, and he was pretty sure they didn't have timed outlet switches back in the 1920s. Khan reached under his pillow for the .45, flicked the safety off, and quietly climbed out of bed.

He sensed his visitors even before he opened the bedroom door. They were sitting on the living room couch, side by side, looking like they were waiting for room service or the morning paper. Khan recognized them both immediately. They had been attending one of the players back at the Palmer House in 2017, the guy with the skull face--Charles Dutton. One of them was a small black man with wrinkles in the corners of his eyes. He was sitting with his hands on his lap, looking around in the room with a mildly interested expression. His companion looked considerably more ragged. Khan had run across plenty of tweakers, and this guy was pumped to the gills with amphetamines. He too looked around the room, but he was fidgeting and tapping his feet on the carpet. He looked like he hadn't slept in days.

Khan pushed the door open all the way and leveled the .45 at the two visitors.

"Good morning," the black man said, unperturbed.

"So it happened to you too. Whatever that was. I was starting to think I was the only one."

"Oh, no." The black man started to pull off the glove he was wearing on his left hand. "You were not the only one. Khan, was it? You were with Mister Galante."

"Please tell me he's around too. I'd love to have a word with him in private."

"We have not, uh, bumped into him yet. But he's not in 1929, if that's what you mean. You're the only one who ended up in this year."

"So it happened to everyone? Whatever it was."

"I'm afraid we don't really have the time to get into the details, but my companion here, Mr. Meek, accidentally blasted everyone in that suite all over time. We have tracked down a few of you, but we still have a lot of pick-ups to make, and my companion is getting tired."

"He looks a little rough."

"He feels a little rough, too," Mr. Meek said. "Cut the palaver and get to the point, Nighthawk."

"The point," Nighthawk said. "The point is that you, Khan, have a choice right now. You can't stay in 1929. Your presence has mucked up the time stream. Just our being here with you is altering reality in 2017 as we speak. Are you familiar with the Butterfly Effect?" He exchanged a look with Mr.Meek, who frowned.

"What you did two days ago at the mob warehouse is having downstream effects you can't even begin to predict. You prevented the St. Valentine's Day Massacre."

"So I kept a few mobsters alive," Khan said. "It was just seven guys, you know. And two of them weren't even with the gang."

"The public outrage after the massacre got the Feds motivated to bring Capone down. It was the beginning of the end for him. Without that event, you've probably extended the gangland wars by five years," Nighthawk said.

"Who really gives a shit who controls the bootlegging in Chicago?" Mr. Meek growled. "Capone, Moran, whatever. You know someone's gonna rise to the occasion. Prohibition's over in four years anyhow. Let's just grab this guy and go back."

Nighthawk shook his head and held up a hand to interrupt Mr. Meek. Then he looked at Khan intently.

"Even worse--those seven Moran boys are alive when they should be dead, Khan. They will kill people who would have lived full lives without your intervention. They will have children that should not be born, that will mess up the time stream in ways nobody will be able to fix. What if one of them has a son who turns out a street thug, and that kid kills your grandfather before your mother is born?"

"You can undo what you did in the hotel suite?" Khan asked.

"My associate can," Nighthawk said. "He can bring you back to 2017...or the version of it that exists after you've thrown a big boulder into the time stream."

"And if I say no?"

Nighthawk looked around in the hotel room.

"Then we would have...conflict. But you really want to remain here? In this year? A joker-ace like you? How long do you think you'll be able to fool people with disguises?"

Khan's first thought was of Naya and his mother. He had already resigned himself to the fact that he'd never see them again. How could he not go back home? His presence here mucked up the timeline, Nighthawk had said. What if he stayed, and changed history to the point where Naya wouldn't even be born? The thought gave him nausea.

"No," he said firmly. "You can get me back, you get me the hell back. I only did what I did because I figured I'd be stuck here for good."

"I completely understand," Nighthawk said. "I can't say I wouldn't have done the same thing." He smiled, and there was a twinkle in his eyes. "And changing the outcome of the St. Valentine's Day Massacre. Who gets a chance to rewrite history like that?"

"So let's go," Khan said. "Get me back to our own time. You'll get no argument from me."

Nighthawk and Mr. Meek exchanged a glance.

"There's only one problem. You have to fix what you changed. Get the time stream back on track. So we get back to our own reality, not one we won't recognize."

"And how do you propose I do that?" Khan asked.

Nighthawk looked at his companion again and shook his head with what seemed like genuine sorrow on his face.

"The people that should have died two days ago need to take their predestined place in history. And that's against the wall of that warehouse. The public needs the outrage. The Feds need the catalyst to go after Capone."

"Oh, you have got to be kidding me." Khan lowered the .45 and leaned against the frame of the bedroom door. "You want me to go over there and machine-gun the whole lot?"

"They were already machine-gunned," Nighthawk said. "They died two days ago. You're just making sure they stay dead. For history's sake. That is the price you'll have to pay to go home."

"Hell of a price," Khan growled. "I'm a bodyguard. I'm not a murderer."

"I wish I had a more palatable alternative, trust me. I don't relish the idea either. But you need to decide, and you need to decide *now*. My companion is getting more tired by the minute, and we have more people to track down and get back in time before he goes to sleep again. We can't do it because it has to look like Capone's guys did it."

"Give me just a minute," Khan said, even though he knew that he had made the decision the second his sister's memory had popped into his head again.

"Let's just get him back right now," Mr. Meek said. "I'm fucking tired, and I have my limits. If he takes off, we'll spend too much time tracking him down again. And then we'll lose all the rest of them, if you want to talk about fucking up the timeline completely."

"No," Nighthawk said firmly. "Khan will undo what he did. And we will give him an hour to get it done." He gave Mr. Meek a sharp look, and there was a tense moment of silence between them.

"Fine," Mr. Meek said. "One hour. But you best keep me busy. Because if I nod off, we are all fucked. You, me, Tiger Boy here, and all of known history."

Frank Gusenberg came to fetch Khan twenty minutes later. Nighthawk and Mr. Meek were in his bedroom, out of sight, waiting for him to return--or getting ready to hunt him down again if he didn't.

"Where's the boss?" Khan asked when they stepped outside.

"The boss likes to sleep in a little," Gusenberg said. "He'll be along after he's had his coffee. We don't need him to get the trucks ready anyway."

They walked down Dickens Avenue and took a right onto North Clark. Khan could see the front of the warehouse just a block ahead. The sidewalk edges were lined with knee-high walls of dirty snow, pushed up by the city plows.

"Hey, just so you know, I wanna say sorry for what I said back at the farm," Gusenberg said. "About you being in cahoots with Capone's guys. You're all right. No hard feelings, right?"

"No hard feelings," Khan said, feeling like the world's biggest asshole.

They walked into the front entrance of the garage. Everyone was there, milling around and smoking cigarettes--Peter and Frank Gusenberg, Heyer the bookkeeper, the other four guys who had been there two days ago. In the back of the garage, Khan saw the familiar face of Johnny May, looking up from under the hood of one of the trucks.

You dumb bastard, Khan thought. *Jesus. Seven kids. Shoulda read the Wanted ads in the paper.*

There were seven men in the garage, the .45 in his coat pocket held seven rounds, and Khan's hand-eye coordination was out of this world. He cocked the hammer of his pistol quietly and let out a sigh.

For Naya.

"Just so you know, fellas," he said to the room in general as he brought out the Colt. "This ain't personal."

A Europe With Magic: Steel and Paper

"Steel and Paper" is a sequel of sorts for "Ink and Blood". It takes place in the same world, an alternate 19th century Europe to which magic has returned, but a decade or two after the (unrelated) events in the first story.

The Weald is an impenetrable magical forest that splits Europe in half. It pops up sometime after the Napoleonic Wars and grows over the course of a few decades. By the time it stops growing, it forms a barrier between old foes and completely reshuffles the balance of power on the continent as countries, trade routes, and alliances are split in half from the mouth of the Rhine on the North Sea all the way to the Danube delta on the Black Sea.

My mind has been busy with this for quite a few years now. The elevator pitch is "Harry Potter meets Game of Thrones." (Publishers and producers, please form orderly lines for the novel deal offers and adaptation rights.)

Steel and Paper

The City of Kings is burning from end to end.

To the Duke on the balcony, the scene has beauty to it, like the stage pieces of the dramatic operas he loves. The fires are turning the night sky a bloody crimson, and flakes of ash are floating in the summer night's breeze like aimless moths.

The servants brought up the ancient French red wine from the cellar—no use saving it for the Wealdlings and the Bohemians, he told them—and he is taking deep sips from his glass as he watches the fires and the flashes of rifle fire and bursting cannon shells. The fighting is not yet close to the palace, but it will reach them long before sunrise.

Below the Duke on the balcony, everything worth ruling is going up in flames. What the Wealdlings cannot loot, they smash and set ablaze. They are burning every scrap of high culture in his city—the opera, the art galleries, the teahouses, everything that cannot be carried off or consumed on the spot. He knows that only the libraries will escape destruction. At least they love books.

He hates them for it, of course, but he cannot begrudge them the violation. *It is after all what we did to them whenever we could,* he thinks.

When his glass is empty, he hurls it into the darkness. The irreplaceable crystal goblet tumbles out of sight and bursts on the cobblestones of the courtyard below.

Behind the Duke, the balcony door opens, and a servant steps out.

"I fear the fight isn't necessarily developing to our advantage," the Duke tells him.

"No, sire," the servant says with a wry smile.

"Fetch my dress uniform. And then go and see to your family."

"Very well, sire," the servant says and departs, perhaps a little more hasty than usual.

The palace is in disarray for the first time in the Duke's memory. Servants and officials are running around like panicked poultry, clutching pieces of art or stacks of papers. Most still remember to bow or salute when he passes them. He goes up one of the back staircases, away from all the noise and disorder. At the top of the stairs, four uniformed guards stand watch. They render crisp salutes and open the door for him. He returns the honors and briskly walks into his private quarters.

The baby is sleeping in her crib, unbothered by the world falling to pieces all around her. He picks her up and puts his nose to the soft warm skin of her cheek. She smells clean, and he could look at her and breathe in her scent all night, but there is no time for a drawn-out good-bye.

He swaddles the sleeping girl in a quilted blanket. She stirs and twitches in her sleep, but she does not wake. The nurse packed a bag for her as ordered, cloth diapers and some clothes from one of the servants' daughters, nothing that will look out of the ordinary.

He leaves the room with the tiny bundle in his arms and the bag slung over his shoulder.

The woman Nadine is waiting in the library when he walks in. She turns when she hears the door, and he waves off her salute.

"No more formalities, my dear. Is everything prepared?"

She nods. "The Guard still holds the river gate. With luck we will make it to the harbor before morning."

"Luck won't play into it," he says. "You've never needed it before."

"I've never tried to break out of a siege with an infant before," she says.

"It is the last thing I ask of you. Do not fail me."

He hands her the child. As she takes the bundle gently, he lets his hand rest on his daughter's cheek for one brief instant.

"Did the spy master give you all you need?"

She nods. "He was thorough. Six sets of papers, and enough money to buy a ship."

"You have your blades, I trust."

Nadine looks at him like a mother would look at a son who just said something charmingly bone-headed.

"I always have those, my lord."

Outside, there are rifle shots, much closer to the palace now than before. A cannon out on the parade ground fires, and the concussion rattles the windows of the library.

"Go then," he says.

She nods and leaves the room without looking back, the child safely cradled in her arms. He feels as if his will to live has left with her.

Outside on the parade ground, the Guard is marshaling for a last defense. With so many men gone, there is no lack of arms. Quartermasters are handing out needle-guns and satchels of paper cartridges to anyone who can hold them. Soldiers stand at attention when the Duke makes his way across the grounds. He speaks encouraging words and shakes hands, and the Guardsmen crowd around him, eager for someone to lift their spirits.

There is a roar overhead, a strange and horrible shrieking, and the flapping of giant wings that sound like a ship's sails unfurling in a stiff breeze. Nearby, pottery tiles rain down from the roof of the palace and smash on the cobblestone with dull cracks.

Then a dragon lands in the middle of the parade ground.

Even the battle-hardened men of the Guard shy away from the beast. This far from the Weald, it is no longer a creature of magic, but it is still a monster, fifty paces long, with teeth the length of a man's arm. It folds its wings against its flanks and lets out another shriek. The Wealdlings have clad the beast in crude plate armor, sheets of steel that still show the marks of the heavy hammers used to force the metal into shape. The Guardsmen on the parade ground retreat from the dragon like a fast ebb pulling away from a shore.

On the battlefield, the Guard would deploy in ordered ranks, fusilier lines of needle-gunners protected by lancers, firing volleys in turn. There is no such order on the parade ground now as soldiers fire at the dragon as they can bring their guns to bear. The

Duke pushes through the crowd, back toward the palace. He carries no weapon that can harm the monster, and he has an important task left to do, one that will require more fortitude than battling a dragon.

The streets are full of people, citizens who waited until now to flee the city. The river gate is the only one of the city's gates still under Prussian control, but the Wealdlings and their Bohemian allies are close now. The Duke knows that the gate will fall within the hour. He knows that Nadine and his daughter have made it through the gate and out past the siege lines. Nadine has been in more dangerous places than this one, fought against worse odds, and he knows that the girl is as safe with her as she can be.

It does not take him long to find what he is looking for on the streets. There are many women with children in the crowd fleeing toward the river, and he picks one with a child that looks suitable.

She recoils when he wades through the current of people and grabs her by the arm. She has the wide and fearful eyes of a hunted doe. He throws back his cloak to let her see his uniform.

"This way," he says. "There is a passage by the armory. We have boats waiting."

She hesitates for a moment. Then her gaze flicks to the golden braid on his shoulder boards and the rack of medals on his chest, and she clutches her child tightly and nods.

"Come, then. We must hurry."

He leads her out of the bustling street and into the side alley that leads back toward the palace. The gunfire and the sounds of clashing steel blades are close now, and she needs no encouragement to follow him swiftly.

There is a tunnel by the armory, but it does not lead to the river. She does not know this, however, and rushes into it willingly when he shows her the way. He follows behind her and unsheathes the knife he always wears in his high uniform boot. She never sees the blade that slips into her back. He wraps his arms around her to keep the child from falling as she sinks to the ground.

He takes the child out of her arms. It is a dreadful thing to do, but he has so many despicable deeds on his conscience already that this one barely adds to the weight. This woman's death will buy his daughter life, and if he had to kill a dozen more mothers to let his own child survive this day, he would do it without blinking.

When he returns to the palace, the fighting is just a few streets away. Overhead, in the dark sky above the palace, there is the rushing of huge wings again. The guards have set up barricades inside, and he casts off his cloak to let them see his uniform. He rushes past the Guardsmen setting up the kingdom's last line of defense and goes upstairs.

His personal guards are still at the door to his private rooms, steadfast as ever. The child in his arms is wailing, confused and frightened by the battle noises outside, and he pulls her blanket down to shield her face from the guards.

"Lock the doors behind me and let none pass," he tells them. "Friend or foe."

They all click the heels of their boots in unison. He smiles with pride and sadness.

"Good men. The world shall never see men like you again."

He walks into his quarters and the guardsmen close the heavy oaken door behind him.

The child calms down when he puts her into his daughter's crib. She looks at him, and he is glad for the fortunate resemblance, blue eyes almost the shade of his own.

He sits down in the high-backed chair in the corner of the room. There is a crystal decanter on the table next to him, and he takes out the stopper and pours himself a glass. Then he leans back, savors the wine on his tongue, and listens to the sounds of battle outside.

When the time comes, he is ready.

He can follow the progress of the fighting in the palace by the sounds coming through the walls and floors. The Wealdlings and the Bohemians come in through the main portico first, the most obvious and tempting entrance. Three times, the Guard beats them back, but each time there are fewer guns in the defenders' volleys. Then the rear entrance falls, and the Wealdings and their allies swarm into the palace unchecked. There are the sounds of hand-to-hand clashes, the ringing of steel on steel and the shouting of men locked in mortal struggle. Then the defenders fall silent.

The Duke knows that the savages will be at the door in just a few moments, and he knows that his last few guards will not hold them for long. He puts the wineglass aside, walks over to the crib, and unsheathes his knife.

The blade is small, no longer than the width of his palm, but against the child's neck it looks enormous, excessive for the task at hand.

Now that the moment has arrived, he finds that he almost doesn't have the heart for it. But in a few moments, they will break down the door. There is no more time for reflection or regret.

He always keeps the blade sharp enough to split a fleeting thought. The cut is effortless, and the child never wakes as she passes from life into death in an instant.

He turns away and walks back to the armchair in the corner, unwilling to look at the result of his last atrocity in this life. Soon he will find out whether there is another.

There is a small glass capsule in a tiny silver pillbox in his breast pocket. He takes it out and looks at it under the light of the lamp on the table beside him. The physician called it cyanide, but the man prefers the common name for it: Prussic acid. It seems proper for the thing that will kill him to be named after the kingdom he has served all his life.

When the Wealdlings smash the door and flood into his private rooms, the Duke puts the capsule between his teeth. He looks out of the window as he bites down. He wants his last sight to be of his beloved city, not some angry unwashed rabble from the lawless forest that is dividing Europe like a festering scar.

His last thought is of his daughter, and the last thing he feels is profound gladness.

At first, Nadine lets herself drift along in the current of people streaming out of the river gate. The cobblestone road leads along the west bank of the river, and the harbor is only a kilometer away. Out here, past the gaslights of the city, the world is dark, and the sounds of fighting are not far off.

Nadine does not fear the darkness. She has moved in its embrace many times before. As soon as the throng of people around her is clear of the city and out among the orchards and pastures of the countryside, she drifts away and takes to the cover of the trees and hedges. There are other ways to the harbor than moving along the river road with a frightened herd of city folk likely to be fleeced by the first Wealdlings they come across. Alone, she can move faster and attract less attention.

She does not have to go far before she finds the first group of Wealdlings. They are less than a good arrow shot away from the road, and there are no defenders left between them and the city walls.

Alone, she could have avoided them easily, but the child gives her away. The sounds and sights are unfamiliar, and the little girl starts wailing when Nadine moves through the thicket to sneak past the Wealdlings that are scouring the forest. There are five of them nearby, all dressed in the old-fashioned garb of the Weald, where spinning looms don't work properly. Two of them have bows; all carry blades.

She looks harmless, dressed the way she is, and with a small child in a sling on her chest. They take her bag and rifle through the child's clothes and the little bit of food the nurse has sent along. The Wealdlings do not take any of it. Instead, they stuff her things back into the bag and hand it back to her. But when she gathers her things and makes to leave, one of them bars her way with the blade of his sword.

"Wait," he says. "Check the child, and under her coat."

She knows they are merely looking for rich people trying to flee the city with gold or valuable trinkets, not members of the royal house disguised as servant children. But the words are their death sentence nonetheless. She cannot let them find the gold and the travel papers she keeps on her body.

Instead, she lets them have her blades.

The first two men are dying on the ground before any of them realize their peril. The third one, the older man who barred her way, manages to raise his sword before she opens his throat and drives a foot into the side of his knee. He crashes to the forest floor, his sword clattering to the ground. The fourth man makes the mistake of trying to draw his bow. She is on him just as he completes the draw. When she plunges both knives into him, he launches the arrow into the darkness with a shout. Then he is on the ground as well.

The last Wealdling is wise enough to drop his bow and run. She flips one blade in her hand. It is a far throw, even for her, but she cannot allow him to get away and carry word back to his people.

She hurls the blade. The Wealdling stumbles with a cough, then falls on his face. By the time she has reached him, there is no need for her to use the second blade.

She doesn't take the time to search the bodies. She likely carries a hundred times what they have managed to loot, and there are voices and the sounds of leaves underfoot heralding more of their number nearby. The next group may be too large for her to take by surprise.

The child is still wailing. She is safe in her sling, strapped as she is to Nadine's chest. There was no time to put her down before the brief fight, and the sudden movement and noise have frightened her anew.

Nadine puts away the knives, wipes her blood-flecked hand on the coat of the dead Wealdling before her, and touches the girl's cheek gently. Then she hums softly to calm the child.

When the crying has diffused into mere unhappy sniffles and coughs, the woman moves on. Under her feet, the leaves and twigs on the forest floor do not crunch.

At the harbor, the remaining soldiers have stopped their attempts to keep order. Most of the docks are empty, and the few ships still tied up at their piers have crowds of people before them.

Nadine does not join the crowds trying to secure passage. Instead, she follows a well-worn footpath down to the waterside at the fringe of the harbor, where the ancient grain-houses and taverns are growing out of the shoreline.

There is a hidden berth behind one of the taverns, but instead of a ship, Nadine finds a small skiff. On the dock beside it, a man is waiting for her. She asks him a question, and he gives the right answer. Her blades disappear in their sheaths again.

"I was expecting someone else," the man says.

"And I was expecting a ship, not a nutshell with a sail."

"Zephyr is out in the bay, away from the shore a bit. Things got lively around here. Dragons and all." He has a pipe in his mouth, and he puffs on it, calm as if the notion of dragons in these parts isn't particularly remarkable to him.

"We are your passengers," Nadine says. "The arrangement still stands."

He looks at the child in her arms.

"There was no talk of a child. The captain will not care to have an infant on board for the crossing."

"It is what it is," she says. "I will compensate the captain for the trouble. But we have little choice now."

The sharp cracks of needle-guns roll across the water from the main part of the harbor, as if to give credence to the woman's assessment. The man sucks on his pipe as he looks at the child again. Then he nods and points a thumb over his shoulder.

"Best get underway, then. The captain will want to leave before daylight."

He turns and walks across the gangplank without looking back or offering help, and she follows.

When Nadine steps off the stone pier and onto the weathered teakwood of the plank, she knows that her feet are leaving the soil of this kingdom forever. But there is no time to dwell on this, and she steps onto the skiff.

It is what it is, she thinks as the sailor unties the skiff and pushes it out into the dark and smelly harbor.

Nadine has been on enough profiteer ships to know a good one when she sees it, and Zephyr looks like she has no peer in that profession. The sleek hull is painted the hue of a moonless midnight sky, and she does not even spot the ship until the sailor has steered them close enough to throw rocks at it. When the skiff comes alongside, the woman hears the soft hum of electric motors.

She pays the captain the gold for the passage, and half again the arranged fare for the child. It is far too much gold for the journey, almost enough to buy a vessel of lesser stature outright. With a handshake, they have become the ship's most valuable cargo. But she has done business with these American profiteers many times before, and she knows that the money is well spent. It is after all the kind of task for which this vessel was built—to speed precious cargo into and out of well-guarded places. They will get her past the blockades and across the ocean, no matter how many warships will be looking for them along the way.

The sky in the east is fringed with dark crimson when they get underway. Zephyr's bow swings to the west, and the electric motors push the hull through the water faster than Nadine has ever seen a ship move. She stands at the portside railing near the bow and watches the coastline of her fatherland recede in the darkness. The child is asleep again, oblivious to the finality of their departure.

Nadine takes out the travel papers the spy service has prepared. She has documents from a dozen nations: Austro-Bavaria, England, the Kingdom of Scotland and Ireland, Bohemia, all the kingdoms of Scandinavia. She speaks all the proper tongues, and she will use whatever papers suit her best once they get to America.

The document pouch also holds a few documents that aren't forgeries. She unfolds one to find that it is the birth record of the child sleeping against her chest. Another is the girl's letter of nobility, and this one has a lithograph of her parents tucked into the fold.

Nadine looks at the documents for a long time. Then she folds them again and slowly tears the stack into little pieces.

When the time comes, I will tell you who you are, she thinks. Until then, you are my daughter, and these papers belong to a dead girl.

She holds out her hand and lets the ocean breeze take the paper scraps from her hand and blow them out over the sea. They scatter in the wind like a small swarm of frightened butterflies.

The ship picks up speed and races into the west wind toward the Americas, outrunning the sunrise.

Wild Cards Goes British: Probationary

With the mosaic novel "Knaves Over Queens", Wild Cards went British for the first time. There was no overarching theme for the compendium other than the location: we had never set any stories in the United Kingdom, so every contribution to this book had to feature a British character doing British things in a British setting.

My main trade is military science fiction, so I tend to gravitate to wartime settings. With "Knaves Over Queens", the war that immediately came to mind was the Falklands War in 1982, when Great Britain reclaimed the Falkland Islands from the Argentine military, which had invaded and seized them a few months earlier. (Argentina calls the island group the Islas del Malvinas and claims it as its own territory, which has been a bone of contention between Argentina and the UK for a very long time.)

Once I had my war, I needed someone to fight in it, of course. It would have to be a military man, but with an ace power that made them an asset in battle. I didn't want to create another brawler like Khan, someone good at physical conflict, so I came up with Rory Campbell, a.k.a. Archimedes. I wanted him to be the polar opposite of a 300-pound half-tiger who does dangerous stuff for a living. Rory is mild-mannered and a little soft, the kind of guy who joins the Royal Navy to get out of his hometown and becomes an electrician on a warship. His ace talent is the ability to create and direct electromagnetic energy. He can shut down all kinds of electronics or even destroy them by overloading their circuits. It's a very useful talent for military applications, so the Royal Navy assigns him a very important job at the beginning of the war. Because he's new to the Silver Helix (the British organization of Wild Card aces) and because he's not really a warfighter, he gets a minder in the form of Major Rangit Singh, the Lion, an experienced ace.

The novella starts on the first day of the Falklands War. It begins how it began in our timeline, but Rory's participation changes the ending a little bit.

(A note on the formatting: Because the story is featured in a novel released in the United Kingdom, the formatting and vocabulary are British English. I left that intact on purpose.)

Probationary

A Wild Cards Novella

Phase I: Hermes
South Atlantic, 30th April 1982

The sea was as grey as battleship steel, and it looked angry, white foam caps topping ten-foot swells. Sub-Lieutenant Rory Campbell knew that the large American aircraft carriers were so immense that you couldn't feel you were at sea unless you drove through the middle of a hurricane. But HMS Hermes, the largest carrier of the Royal Navy, was only a third the size of one of those Yank monstrosities, and she bobbed up and down in the wave troughs as she made her way south into ever more atrocious weather. But to Rory, the frigid air and the salt spray out here on the weather passageway were preferable to the smells of jet fuel and engine exhaust on the busy flight deck above.

'What dreadful weather to go to war in,' he grumbled and flicked his cigarette over the steel cables of the safety railing.

'On the contrary,' said the man standing next to him. He was a full foot taller than Rory, and the turban he wore made him even more imposing. Major Rangit Singh, the Lion, would have looked out of place on a Royal Navy ship even without the camouflage-pattern Army uniform he was wearing, or the large curved kirpan knife on his web belt.

'It's perfect weather to go to war in,' Major Singh continued. His voice was deep and sonorous, and Rory suspected that his Silver Helix minder could probably sing very well. Not that this environment or the occasion called for any singing.

'This? Glasgow in December is a tropical paradise compared to this shite.'

'It keeps the enemy sentries under their ponchos and close to their warm gear,' Major Singh said. 'In the Army, we call that "recon weather".'

Rory had been with the Lion for three weeks now, and the man never had anything but a calm and mildly pleased expression on his face. There were droplets of seawater spray in his bushy, chest-length beard, and his turban looked damp, but he looked out over the churning waters in Hermes' wake with unperturbed serenity, taller than Rory even as he stood bent over a little, with his wrists resting on the safety rail and his palms pressed together. An iron bangle hung from one of his wrists and swayed softly with the movements of the ship.

'Well, I hope it clears up by the time we get to where we're going,' Rory said.

'I hope it doesn't.' Singh looked up at the gloomy sky. 'I hope it gets worse. It will keep the Argentinian air force on the ground.'

Rory gazed back at the dirty-looking silvery wake of the carrier. In that direction was England, seven or eight thousand miles away. And they were steadily steaming on toward the Falkland Islands, now only a few hundred miles to their south, and whatever the Argentinian military had waiting for them there. It had taken the task force most of a month to sail this far from Portsmouth, and that was a long time for the Argies to prepare their positions.

'We're really going to do this, aren't we?'

'Go to war?' Singh flexed his hands and looked at the bangle on his wrist. 'They know we are on the way. If diplomacy hasn't got them off those islands yet, I don't think it will end without bloodshed. A foolish thing, this whole affair. All over a load of wind-blown rocks in the cold sea.'

'I talked to a lad who served in garrison there once. Says it's a lot like the Highlands. In parts, anyway. I suppose we've fought over less before, we Scots.'

Rory and Major Singh didn't have much in common physically, but they shared a Scottish background. Rory had been pleased to find out that his mentor was also from Glasgow. Rangit Singh was almost ten years older, but they had frequented some of the same stamping grounds back home in their youth, and it was always an easy bond when your histories shared landmarks and geography.

Rory was from East Kilbride, Singh from Hillhead, and while these neighbourhoods were on opposite sides of the river, both men were Partick Thistle fans, and favouring the same football team was practically as good as sharing a religion. Rory liked the big, muscular Sikh, and he felt safer and calmer in his presence. He still didn't really think of himself as an ace – he couldn't fly, or bend steel bars, or shoot lightning from his hands – but the Lion was one without a doubt, and being teamed up with him made Rory feel legitimate.

'That's just my bloody luck,' he said. 'My first time out for the Silver Helix, and it has to turn into a shooting war.'

The Lion chuckled softly. 'That is what we do. They don't call on us unless things get ugly, my friend. But you are an officer in the Royal Navy. You would be here anyway, I think.'

'Yeah.' Rory tried not to sound defeated. When you sign up for military service, you have to expect the risk of having to go to war, but it's all very abstract when you are just out of secondary school and looking for a way out of East Kilbride. The recruiters emphasized travel, adventure, and pay-cheques. They didn't talk about month-long journeys into frigid waters and enemy air forces looking to put anti-ship missiles into your conveyance. When you are seventeen, you think yourself immortal anyway. But the Lion was right, of course – if Rory's card hadn't turned a year and a half ago he would probably be on a ship in this task force anyway, sitting in front of a radar console on one of the frigates or destroyers steaming along with Hermes in the distance.

There were other sailors taking fag-breaks on the weather passageway, but they all kept a respectful distance from Rory and Major Singh. They were both aces and Silver Helix agents, but Singh was also an Army major, and to a professional sailor, staff officers were just a rank or two below the Almighty, even the ones from a different service. Rory appreciated the privacy perks his probationary Silver Helix status afforded him, because even on a warship as large as Hermes, space was a precious commodity.

The speakers up on the flight deck blared their announcement tone.

'Now hear this: we are now entering the Total Exclusion Zone around the Falkland Islands declared by Her Majesty's government. From this point on, there will be no drills. If you hear the Action Stations alert, it will be the real thing. Stand fast and do your duty. Announcement ends.'

Rory and Major Singh exchanged glances. Singh sighed again and put his hand on the hilt of his kirpan.

Above, a pair of Harrier jump jets took off from the flight deck with their engines at ear-splitting full throttle. They came into view when they cleared the front of the flight deck ramp and turned west, then started the ascent to begin their combat air patrol, position lights blinking. Rory saw that both jets had missiles under their wings, white-painted war shots instead of the blue exercise missiles he usually saw on the Royal Navy's Harriers. The sight of the live missiles increased the feeling of dread he had been nursing for a while. They were a wartime navy now.

'So it begins,' Major Singh said. 'Let us hope it ends quickly. For their sake and ours.'

As the flagship of the task force, Hermes had a flag bridge. This was where the task force commander and his staff had their duty stations as they directed the dozens of Royal Navy and auxiliary vessels in the fleet headed for the Falklands, and Rory was the most junior officer in the room by age as well as rank. There were consoles and plotting tables and lots of ratings busy at all of them. Rory felt like the fifth wheel on a milk wagon in this room, and only the fact that he and Major Singh had been ordered here specifically by the task force commander put him at ease. He still wasn't used to being a command asset instead of a simple console jockey, and he doubted he would ever think of himself that way.

'Hermes is on station, and we shall remain at spear length from the islands,' Admiral Woodward told the assembled officers. The plot table in the centre of the flag bridge had a map of the theatre under a sheet of Plexiglas, and the admiral tapped a spot to the northeast of the Falklands with a grease pencil. 'It is my intent to send on the frigates and destroyers to provide an anti-aircraft and

ASW screen for Hermes and the invasion transports, and prepare the landings as we make progress against the opposition. Winter weather is coming, and our timetable is accordingly strict. If we do not have air superiority by mid-May or troops on the ground by the end of the month, conditions will not favour any further military operations.'

Rory looked out of the porthole on the hatch behind him. Outside, the rain had slacked off a little, but it still looked like the worst weather Scotland had to offer. If this wasn't winter weather yet, they were in for trouble. He couldn't quite understand how anyone would live in a climate like this, much less fight over it.

'At no point will Hermes conduct operations closer than two hundred miles from the Falklands. I realize that this greatly limits the combat range of our Harriers, but this ship is too valuable to risk. There's not a pilot in the Argentinian air force who wouldn't love to put a few Exocets into her and win the war with the press of a button.'

There were murmurs of agreement, but clearly not every officer in the room seemed to concur with the admiral's assessment. The naval airmen in particular looked less than happy. 'The Harriers have short legs as it is, sir,' one of the squadron commanders said. 'The lads will have very little loitering time over the battlefield.'

'Then we had best hurry and take the runway at Port Stanley. But this ship will be kept well away from the islands. If the Argentine air force sinks her they win the war, and we lose half of the Royal Navy's force projection capabilities.' Admiral Woodward turned and looked at Rory. 'And that's where you come in, sub-lieutenant.'

'Sir?' Rory felt intensely uncomfortable with the sudden undivided attention of so many staff officers.

'Your job on this deployment is to do whatever you have to do to make sure that no enemy airplane or missile gets close to Hermes.' The admiral looked at Major Singh and back at Rory. Then he sighed and shook his head. 'Admiral Fieldhouse asked the Silver Helix for force multipliers,' he said. 'He emphasized the critical nature of this operation for our national interest and prestige. I believe he even badgered the Prime Minister. Repeatedly. And they send two men. One of them an acting sub-lieutenant on probationary status with the Silver Helix. Hardly the war-changing arsenal of special abilities I had hoped for.'

Rory had only met the admiral in person once, at the end of a briefing back in Northwood naval headquarters before the task force sailed. He had decided on the spot that he didn't like the man. He was abrasive and didn't seem to care one bit whether he gave offence, and emphasizing the acting in Rory's rank meant he was patronizing both Rory's Silver Helix membership status and his military rank in one sentence.

'Well, it is what it is, I suppose,' Admiral Woodward continued before Rory or Major Singh could reply. 'Major Singh will be going with the Royal Marines once the landings begin. We will be needing your abilities sooner, sub-lieutenant. Where do you need to be when action stations sound?'

'I need to see the target, sir,' Rory replied. 'Line of sight, the longer the better. A line to the radar room so they can point me towards incoming threats. And a few sailors with binoculars to share the watch with me. In case I miss something.'

'If we're under attack, they will come in low and fast to avoid our radar. Intelligence says they mainly have Skyhawks armed with iron bombs, so they will have to do a terminal climb before they drop. Those we can handle with the Harriers and the Seacats. But they also have a few French Super Etendards with those blasted sea-skimming Exocet missiles. If the frigates and the destroyer picket don't get those, you'll be the last line of defence other than our SeaCat launchers.'

'Yes, sir.'

'Let me make one thing clear about your rules of engagement, Sub-Lieutenant.' Admiral Woodward tapped his fingers on the hard surface of the plotting table. 'Disable or destroy whatever comes our way, whether the SeaCats launch at it or not. Bloody things are too slow for Exocets anyway. If it comes down to it, you are to use area-of-effect EMP. I don't care if all the lights and radios on this ship go out as long as we don't have a few hundred pounds of high explosive warhead going through our hull and lighting up thousands of gallons of aviation fuel. Is that understood?'

'Yes, sir,' Rory replied. He knew that if he let loose an unfocused electromagnetic pulse burst with all his might, he would disrupt more than just lights and radios. Part of him almost wanted to have an excuse to do that, just to see what it would do to the superior expression of the admiral to find himself on an aircraft carrier with every single electronics circuit shut down.

'Very well,' Admiral Woodward said. 'I'll see to it that you get all the personnel and binoculars you need. Place yourself wherever you see fit. But don't get in the way on the flight deck.' He rapped the plotting table with his knuckles. 'Five days ago, we took South Georgia back from the enemy. The Royal Marines got off to a good start on this one. Now we will do our part. Let's get on with it, gentlemen.'

Rory's first day at war was far less exciting and eventful than he had anticipated. They were two hundred miles from the Falklands and far out of reach of the Argentinian air force bases on the mainland, so the odds of an air raid were low. The Harriers flew regular combat patrols toward the islands, and the destroyers and frigates in the task force had started their screening deployment, interposing themselves between the valuable carriers and the likely directions of attack. Rory took up his post on top of Hermes' island superstructure, high above the flight deck, to get a feel for his new action station. He could move from one side of the island to the other in short order to get a full 360-degree view of the ocean surrounding Hermes, but the top of the island was also the highest point of the carrier other than her radar masts and funnel tops, and the South Atlantic wind up here was like an ice-cold hand pushing him around. The sailors assigned to the watch with him had been excited at first, but two hours of scanning the austere grey seascape with binoculars in the cold wind had dampened their excitement somewhat. Rory didn't know what Major Singh was doing right now, but he knew that the major would go with the marines of the invasion force when the time came. Whatever he was up to right now, he was down in the dry, warm ship somewhere instead of wiping freezing spray off binocular lenses.

The flight deck was packed from bow to stern with aircraft and equipment. Hermes had taken on more helicopters than she was designed to carry in her regular complement, in anticipation of Argentine submarines. With all the men and equipment on the deck below him, Rory didn't think they'd be able to conduct any offensive operations before unloading some of the extra stuff. But around noon of their first full day in the exclusion zone, the ship's Harriers started taking off one by one. They were laden heavily with bombs and missiles under their wings, so they had to use the ski ramp at the bow of the carrier to get airborne instead of taking off vertically. He watched them roaring down the deck and leaping into the sky, engines bellowing, their wing tips clearing the noses and folded rotor blades of the parked helicopters lined up alongside the take-off strip by what looked like just a few feet. The ground crews smartly saluted every Harrier pilot before each take-off run. Rory had been an enlisted radar technician before he became an ace and a minor Royal Navy celebrity, so tactical flight operations were out of his realm of expertise, but it didn't take a master strategist to know that the Harriers were setting out for Port Stanley, the capital of the Falklands, currently under Argentinian management. The sailors on the carrier's command island with him watched the small squadron struggle into the sky with their heavy ordnance loads and head southwest, disappearing in the low cloud cover after a few minutes.

'I don't really want to go to war, sir,' the sailor next to Rory said without taking his eyes off the leaden sky.

'I don't either,' Rory replied. 'But the public have been paying our salaries. I suppose we can't take the money and then complain when our number finally comes up.'

'Yes, sir. I was just hoping mine wouldn't come up while I was in.'

'Everyone was hoping that,' Rory said.

The Harriers returned a few hours later. Free of their bomb loads, they descended onto the flight deck vertically, hovering over their designated landing spots gracefully before settling down. Rory counted them and was relieved to find they were still the same number of planes that had taken off earlier. There was no cheer or jubilation among the deck hands as they chocked the Harriers' wheels and helped the pilots out of their cockpits. It was just an efficient business-like atmosphere, professionals at work, just like any other day in the service. Rory wondered what the bombs from those planes had hit, and whether it had made a dent in the Argie defences. Part of him still hoped that the Argentinians would back down after the first show of force from the Royal Navy, that they would see reason once they saw modern warplanes with live bombs overhead. They were the Royal Navy, not some third-rate corvette navy from a backwater nation. But after the return of the Harriers, an hour passed, then two, and by the time he ended his watch and went down to the officer wardroom for dinner, there had been no announcement from the commander that everything was over, that Argentina had decided they had lost the game of chicken. But it looked as if both sides had decided they weren't bluffing after all.

Rory was in the middle of his meal when the commander finally did make an announcement, and everyone paused their conversations at once.

'This is the commander. I am glad to announce we had a very good day today. We have started to soften up the defences at Stanley with no losses of our own. And earlier today, the Argentine cruiser General Belgrano was torpedoed by one of our submarines on station south of the Total Exclusion Zone. That removes the threat posed by the Argentinian navy to our southern flank. That is all. Commander out.'

This time there was some cheering going on in the wardroom, and the conversations that picked up again had a decidedly more excited note to them.

'The Belgrano,' the lieutenant across the table from Rory said.

'That's their biggest surface ship. She's an ex-Yank cruiser. USS Phoenix, I think. Served in World War Two. Shame, really.'

'Wonder if they sank her,' Rory replied.

'As long as she's out of the picture and not pointing her guns at us. So what exactly is it you can do?' the lieutenant asked. 'I mean, if that's not a state secret.'

'It's not,' Rory said. He was a recent addition to the crew, a newcomer in a group of officers who had been working together for many months or even years, and he was glad whenever he had a chance to socialize with someone other than his Silver Helix minder. His story was well-known in the Royal Navy – he was one of only a handful of aces who were on active military duty – but he also knew there were a lot of embellished versions of that tale out there, and he rarely had an opportunity to correct the rumour mill.

'I make directional EMPs,' he said. 'I can turn off any electric system. Slag it, too, if I want.'

'Anything? So, could you shut down this ship?'

'Most of it, I suppose,' Rory said. 'Whatever I can see, anyway.'

'That is bloody brilliant,' the lieutenant said.

'Small bits too,' Rory continued. He pointed at the lieutenant's wristwatch with his fork. It was one of the new digital quartz models, the ones that showed the time on a little display window. 'I could focus and just pop the circuit board in that watch of yours.'

'Please don't,' the lieutenant smiled. He put a protective hand over the face of his watch. 'My wife gave that to me before we left Portsmouth. When did you find out you could do that EMP thing?'

'I was on HMS Juno year before last. I was a radar tech. One day, we were working up on the dish for the anti-aircraft system. It was supposed to be de-energized, but it turned on while we had three lads in front of it. I could feel it somehow. Can't explain it, but I knew how to shut it down, and I did. Just by thinking hard about it.'

'Bloody brilliant,' the other lieutenant repeated.

There were other officers at the table with them, and one of them looked rather sceptical at this pronouncement. 'So when the Argie ships come into sight, you can turn their lights off. That will be useful. Right after they fire their Exocets at us.'

'If I can see the missile, I can blow its guidance systems up,' Rory replied.

'Right,' the other man said. He wore the flight suit of a Fleet Air Arm officer, which meant that he flew a Harrier or a helicopter. 'I suppose we don't have anything to worry about, then.'

'I'll do what I can,' Rory said.

'As will we all. It's just some of us are going to go out to drop iron bombs on the Argies instead of sitting on a carrier two hundred miles away. Different risk factor. And my lads don't get special perks for doing their jobs.'

'Knock it off,' the lieutenant across the table said. 'The aces get their own berth because they're bloody aces, mate. They hadn't come along, you'd be whinging about them not sending any with us.'

'The other guy's all right. The Army major. He'll be handy on the ground. I've seen him bench press five hundred pounds in the gym with the marines.' The pilot turned his attention back to Rory. 'But you're going to be bored. With the Harriers, there's no Argie plane getting close enough to this ship to launch anything. We'll be getting it done the old-fashioned way. Guns and missiles.'

'I do hope you're right about that,' Rory replied. The other man's eyes narrowed, and Rory could tell he was looking for signs that Rory was being clever with him.

'You'll see,' the flight officer said. 'The Royal Navy hasn't lost a ship in combat since World War Two. And that was before we had anti-air missiles and fighter jets.'

Their side has those too, Rory thought. But instead of voicing it, he just nodded and focused on his dinner again. He loathed conflict, whether it was a shooting war with Argentina or an argument over fish and chips in the wardroom.

'Don't mind that tosser,' the other lieutenant said after the flight officer had left the table a little while later. 'Those fighter pilots all think they're special. Jealousy's a terrible thing.'

'I still hope he's right,' Rory replied. ' And if we do lose a ship, I hope it won't be my fault, he didn't add.

Phase II: Sheffield
Inside the Total Exclusion Zone, 3rd May, 1982

The crew mess and wardrooms had television sets mounted on the bulkheads, and they all watched the news during the next few days whenever they could. It was odd to catch up on events that had happened just a little over a hundred miles away, sent to the ships of the task force via satellite relay from BBC stations seven thousand miles to their north with a day-long delay.

ARA General Belgrano, the Argentinian cruiser, had been severely damaged by the torpedo attack, with substantial loss of life. Even as the BBC report was finishing, some of the officers in the room said they heard that Belgrano had been sunk, not just damaged. In the military, there was no communications system faster than the wardroom rumour mill, but Rory knew that some of the officers had their posts in Hermes' Action Information Centre or on the bridge, and were privy to information the rest of the crew didn't have. He didn't know the exact complement of a cruiser like the Belgrano, but his lads in the wardroom had mentioned she had served in World War Two, and old ships like that needed a lot of manpower, many hundreds of sailors. Even if most of them got out of the ship and onto life rafts, the South Atlantic was freezing right now. If someone had to get sunk, he'd rather it be the Belgrano than Hermes or one of the other Royal Navy ships, but it was still not pleasant to think about sailors drowning or freezing to death, even if they were the enemy right now.

At the end of the news, the BBC reporter used the phrase 'Falklands crisis', and the lieutenant commander in the chair next to Rory's huffed a little.

'"Crisis",' he repeated. 'We've dropped bombs on a town and sunk a cruiser. They shot down two Argie planes yesterday, too. If this is a crisis, I want to know what qualifies as a war.'

War came to Hermes the next morning for the first time.

Rory was on watch again on the command island. Several radar contacts had been spotted by the picket ships the fleet commander had sent out to screen the carrier from air attack, and Rory was the last-ditch insurance. It was a precaution because the contacts were too far away from Hermes to pose an imminent threat, so when the action stations alarm sounded, Rory jumped a little at the unwelcome surprise of it.

'Action stations, action stations.' The alarm blared, and all around him things got busy as crewmembers ran up and down stairs and gangways and slammed shut watertight hatches. 'Silver Helix personnel to the flag bridge. I repeat, Silver Helix personnel to the flag bridge at once.'

Rory was already on the command island, so he didn't have far to go to reach the flag bridge, where Admiral Woodward and his support staff were already waiting along with the ship's captain. Rory's mind raced as he stepped across the threshold of the watertight door and reported in. Major Singh, the Lion, had to come from much further below decks than Rory, but only twenty or thirty seconds after Rory stepped onto the flag bridge, a door on the opposite side of the compartment opened, and the big Sikh stepped through it. He didn't even look particularly out of breath.

The admiral and several of his staff officers were still in the middle of a discussion at the plotting table, so Rory made sure he stayed out of the way of the sailors hurrying around and console operators delivering reports from the nearby Action Information Centre.

'Glasgow announced 'handbrake' at 1104 hours,' one of the officers told the admiral. 'Sheffield was in contact with Coventry at the time and signalled they were hit just two minutes later. No further details from Sheffield. Their UHF is silent.'

'Send out Arrow and Yarmouth to Sheffield's last known position,' Admiral Woodward ordered. 'And launch one of the ready helicopters to verify what the blazes is going on.' He looked across the flag bridge and only now seemed to notice Rory and Major Singh. 'Gentlemen,' he said, and waved them closer. Rory approached the plotting table, still unused to the sensation of senior officers making space for him in the confines of the small compartment. 'We dispatched our three Type 42 destroyers as anti-submarine pickets between our position and the south-eastern Falklands. A few minutes ago, we got a signal that indicates HMS Sheffield took a hit. We don't know what exactly happened or the extent of the damage. It looks like it may become a busy day for you, Sub-Lieutenant. HMS Glasgow indicated that the attack came from Argentine Super Etendards. That means they have started using their Exocet arsenal.'

'Do we know how many Exocets they have?' Major Singh asked.

'Not a terrific amount, but enough to make us lose this war by the end of the week if they use them well, Major.'

Admiral Woodward turned and looked at Rory.

'Tell me how far out you can spot a sea-skimming missile moving at seven hundred miles per hour, Sub-Lieutenant Campbell.'

'If I know the bearing from a radar fix, and if the seas aren't too choppy, two miles, maybe more, sir.'

'That's a damned thin safety margin,' Hermes' captain said with a frown. 'That gives you, what, ten seconds to bring it down? And that's if you spot it as soon as the radar does.'

'It beats relying on just the SeaCats,' the admiral replied. 'Those can only get head-on kills. If we get an air radar contact within fifty miles of this ship, you are to be on your perch, sub-lieutenant, with a live comms link to the radar operator. Of course, plan number one is to not let the buggers that close to begin with.'

'Radar contact bearing two-one-five, distance five-seven miles, sir,' the radar operator called out, as if on cue. 'IFF says it's one of our Lynx helicopters.'

'Get them on radio, then. Sub-Lieutenant Campbell, head to your action station right away.'

'Aye, sir,' Rory replied and left the compartment in a hurry.

The Lynx helicopter that had appeared on the radar screen touched down on Hermes' flight deck half an hour later. Rory had a perfect vantage point from the command island to see them unload two officers and then several obviously wounded personnel. Some had parts of their overalls cut away, other had thick bandages on their faces or hands. The medical personnel of Hermes met them almost as soon as they set foot on the carrier deck and helped them to nearby stretchers. The officers engaged in some brief but heated conversation with the Hermes personnel who had met them and then went over to the command island. Rory picked up his radio.

'Archimedes to radar ops. What's the airspace look like?' This was the first time he had used his official ace moniker. If he was to be a semi-permanent living weapons mount on this ship, he reckoned he ought to go by his ace name instead of his military rank, which didn't have much clout on a ship with an admiral and dozens of staff officers anyway.

'Airspace is clear of contacts, sir. We have a flight of Harriers out on combat air patrol eighty miles out at two-seven-zero degrees. You have a clean board for the moment.'

Rory went back down to the flag level, where the newly arrived officers were talking to the admiral and the rest of the ship's senior officers. At first, he had felt like an interloper, going wherever he wanted on the ship if he wasn't specifically ordered to be in a certain spot, but that was another perk of Silver Helix membership. If he deemed it necessary to be somewhere to accomplish his assignment, his ace status overrode even his military rank.

'Sheffield's a mission kill,' one of the new officers reported. 'We took an Exocet amidships. It knocked out our electric system and the water main. We have nothing to fight the fire. The way she's burning, she'll be gone by morning.'

'What's the casualty count?'

'At least a dozen men, probably more. The missile hit the

ratings galley and the computer room.'

'Bloody hell,' the Hermes' captain cursed. 'What about the SeaCats?'

'None were fired, sir. I think ops thought it was a false alarm again. They didn't even have the gun ready.'

'What a monumental cock-up. Get Arrow and Yarmouth out there on the flank to help put those fires out and get Sheffield under tow. I will not be the first task force commander to lose a ship in action since they signed the bloody armistice in Tokyo Bay,' Admiral Woodward said.

He focused on the plotting table and pointed a finger at the point on the map marked with the icon for HMS Sheffield. 'Shift Glasgow's patrol pattern north-east so she can close the hole and give Arrow and Yarmouth air defence support. I want two more flights of Harriers going that way as well. One from us, one from Invincible.'

Rory cleared his throat. 'Sir, I should go out there on a Lynx. Put me on Coventry or Glasgow. I can do a lot more good closer to the line than back here on Hermes.'

The admiral looked at Rory in unconcealed disbelief, then shook his head. 'Out of the question, sub-lieutenant. You are one third of this ship's air defence arsenal.'

'This ship is over a hundred miles from the action, sir. I could be a much better picket against enemy aircraft if you put me in a spot where they are likely to be. Hermes has Harriers. They can intercept what comes past the destroyer screen.'

'The destroyers are spaced out too far. If I put you on Glasgow and they engage Coventry next instead, there won't be anything you can do about it because you'll be thirty miles away. And then you'll be useless to Hermes as well.' He made a dismissive hand gesture. 'Hermes carries half the task force's air power, and she's the most essential ship we have. I will not risk the Royal Navy's biggest carrier to maybe keep an Exocet away from a Type 42. They can take care of their own air defence without you. If they're not sitting on their bloody arses while other ships are broadcasting air raid warnings. And lest you think me callous, I'll have you know that I used to be Sheffield's commanding officer. Now someone get me a strong coffee and some aspirin, please.'

There was nothing more dispiriting to Rory than having to witness the casualties from Sheffield being brought onto Hermes' deck and not being able to do anything to help. A lot of the injured Sheffield sailors had obvious burn injuries. The helicopters came in intervals, in between take-off and landing operations for the Harriers. The fighter aircraft were out for blood, now that one of the task force ships had been hit, with British sailors killed and wounded. But hour after hour, the Harriers came back, trading spaces with newly rearmed and refuelled ones leaping off the ski ramp at Hermes' bow, and Rory heard no reports of any air victories. The Argentine air force had got their bite out of them for the day, it seemed.

A few long, demoralizing days of monotonous watch-standing later, the commander made an announcement that didn't do anything to lift Rory's mood.

'This is the commander. I regret to inform you that HMS Sheffield foundered today on the way to South Georgia while under tow by HMS Yarmouth. That is all. Commander out.'

Rory let the news sink in for a few moments. As Admiral Woodward had reminded him, the Royal Navy hadn't lost a ship in action since the end of World War Two, thirty-seven years ago. Almost ten enlistment cycles had passed without one of Her Majesty's warships getting so much as fired upon, and now one was sitting at the bottom of the North Atlantic. And not just an old, outdated ship like the Belgrano, but a modern state-of-the-art Type 42 destroyer, fitted with some of the best weapon systems in the Royal Navy.

If they can sink Sheffield, they can sink any other ship in the fleet, Rory thought. And here he stood, standing watch on the command deck of Hermes, a hundred miles from where the frigates and destroyers of the task force were shelling Argentine positions in preparation of the invasion, and he hadn't seen so much as the contrail from an enemy plane this whole time.

Rory was at the end of his patience. He was still a Royal Navy officer, albeit only an acting Sub-Lieutenant and therefore at the very bottom of the commissioned pecking order, but he was an ace and a member of the Silver Helix. It was disrespectful to treat him like a stationary weapons mount out here when the real war was going on a hundred miles to their west. He hated confrontation, but nothing was worse than standing around in the cold on this carrier doing nothing.

He handed his binoculars to the sailor next to him. 'You have the watch for a few minutes, petty officer. I am going to the flag bridge.'

The admiral wasn't on the flag bridge when Rory stepped through the door, but Commodore Clapp and Major General Moore were there, discussing something in low voices while consulting a map. The Commodore was the commander of the landing fleet that would ferry the troops to the beaches when the ground invasion started, and Major General Moore was in command of the land forces, Royal Marines and Army alike.

'Something on your mind, sub-lieutenant?' Commodore Clapp asked when Rory stepped up to them.

'Yes, sir. I was looking for the admiral, actually.'

'He's out on a Sea King headed for Invincible,' the commodore replied. 'Anything of concern we need to know about?'

'No, sir,' Rory said. 'But that's just the problem, see. I've been up there for a week with binoculars glued to my eyes while the lads on the frigates get bombs chucked at them. There has got to be something else I can do. I don't think the admiral quite understands what I can bring to the field.'

'So you want to be on the line,' Major General Moore said in a tone that sounded almost appreciative to Rory. 'And what is it that you can do that I can't do with a squad of my Royal Marine commandos?'

'Your commandos have to get close to the enemy. Close enough for rifle fire or anti-tank rockets. I just need to be close enough to see a plane. Even if it's just through binoculars. And I can slag its radar and electronics in five seconds.'

The major general and the commodore exchanged a glance that looked meaningful.

'Really now,' the Major General said. 'That's from several kilometres out. In any weather.'

'As long as I can lay eyes on it,' Rory said.

The commodore and major general exchanged another look, this one more poignant than the last, and Rory could have sworn that the Royal Marine general smiled a little.

'Tell you what, sub-lieutenant. We will have a chat with the admiral and see where we can slot you in. There may be an upcoming opportunity for you to demonstrate your skill set. No promises, though.'

'Yes, sir. Thank you, sir. I really don't want the Silver Helix to think the armed forces are not using their special assets to best effect.'

Rory sketched a salute and walked back to the starboard door of the flag bridge.

'Is that cheeky little bugger blackmailing us?' Commodore Clapp asked the major general, who chuckled.

'I believe so,' Major General Moore replied. 'Enough pluck for a Royal Marine, that one.'

Outside, the driving frigid Antarctic wind doused Rory with a fresh shower of seawater, but he found that his mood had improved just a little bit.

Just a few hours later Rory found himself in an air group briefing room filled to the last chair with some of the toughest-looking troops he had ever seen. Most were wearing the Army and Royal Marines DPM-pattern camouflage uniforms instead of Navy dress, and all of them radiated a mood that felt rather like what Rory sensed in his regular hometown pub when a particularly critical Partick Thistle match was about to start on the telly. Major Singh was in the room too, but he sat on the other side when Rory came in, and there was no way to make it across the compartment full of seated troops to join his Silver Helix colleague. At the head of the room, Major General Moore stood behind a briefing lectern.

When the General spotted Rory taking his seat, he nodded grimly. 'You got your wish, sub-lieutenant. I rather hope you don't come to regret it.'

Rory took his seat, one of the last two remaining ones. Behind the general a projector screen was set up at an angle, showing the white square of a blank slide. General Moore pressed a button on his wired remote, and the first slide whirred into position with a click. It showed an overhead reconnaissance photo of a grass airfield. Several aircraft of different types were parked to either side of the airstrip.

'Our two Silver Helix guests were not present at the original mission briefing, so I will repeat the main details for their benefit.' He extended a small pointer stick and tapped the projection. 'This is a small Argentinian airbase on Pebble Island, on the northern tip of West Falkland Island. The Argentines set it up right after they moved in. It's just a short grass strip, but it's in a rather inconvenient spot for us.'

He moved the pointer to the Argentinian planes lined up on the grass above and below the runway. 'The Argentine air force have about a dozen planes there. They are mostly Pucarás. Twin-engine turboprops, used for light attack and recon duties. The light attack capabilities don't worry us too much because our Harriers can run rings around them if they try to make runs on the fleet. What's more of a concern is their reconnaissance function. We are in full preparation for the landings, and reconnaissance by these aircraft will compromise our planned manoeuvres and give the enemy advance warning of our intended landing sites. Therefore, we have tasked D Squadron, 22 SAS Regiment, with the destruction of these aircraft and their support facilities.'

The general changed slides. The projection on the screen changed to a wider shot of the airfield. Several small structures were circled in various colours. 'D Squadron will ingress by helicopter to a point five miles from the objective. The Boat Troop has scouted the target last night. Due to the strong headwinds coming from the southwest, the range of our helicopters will be reduced, so we had to cut the window for offensive operations on the ground from ninety to thirty minutes. Therefore, the aircraft on the ground are top priority targets. The fuel and ammo dumps and the support personnel are secondary concerns. Take out targets of opportunity, but your primary objective is those aircraft. HMS Glamorgan will provide artillery support from offshore once the aircraft are destroyed or disabled.' He looked over at Rory, who started feeling very out of place in a briefing room full of hardened commandos. 'The original plan had Mountain Troop infiltrating the facility to lay explosive charges on the aircraft the while the other troops provide overwatch. That is a risky endeavour because the Argies undoubtedly expect a raid and will have sentries out. Sub-Lieutenant Campbell over here will ingress with D Squadron and take up overwatch position with the covering team. If you can disable or destroy their planes from that position, infiltration won't be needed, and the risk to D Squadron will be greatly reduced. I probably need not tell you that the lads would greatly appreciate it if they could remain out of small-arms range.'

Some of the SAS men laughed. Most of them had shifted in their seats to look over at Rory. He saw the appraising glances from the commandos and wondered briefly if he should have kept his mouth shut on the flag bridge after all.

'If Sub-Lieutenant Campbell – Archimedes – cannot disable the Pucarás from the overwatch position, we will go to Plan B, and things will get considerably noisier. But keep the timing in mind, because the window of operations is a small one. Do stick to the timetable if you want to get off that rock and back to Hermes, unless you have a desire to sample the quality of the cooking in an Argentine POW camp.'

There was more laughter from the troops. Rory smiled weakly at the joke. He was Navy, not SAS, but even he understood very well that having to spend time in a POW camp was not the worst possible outcome for anyone on this mission.

Major General Moore ran them through the timeline of the raid once more-undoubtedly for the benefit of Rory and Major Singh, the last-minute additions – and concluded the briefing a few minutes later. Rory didn't feel any more prepared than before he had walked into the compartment.

'A word, sub-lieutenant,' the general said when everyone started filing out of the compartment, and Rory stayed behind. 'I got Admiral Woodward to agree to this because it's a night-time raid, and there won't be any air threat to Hermes while it's dark. But we are taking a risk sending you out like that. Major Singh will come along and make sure that you come back in one piece. And please make it worth that risk. Don't make me regret convincing the Admiral to let you come along.'

'Understood, sir,' Rory said. 'I'll do my very best.'

Outside in the passageway, Major Singh walked up behind him and patted his shoulder. The Silver Helix agent was in his camouflage Army uniform, but tonight he had web gear on top of his jacket, and he had exchanged his blue turban for a black one.

'Congratulations,' he said. 'You are a commando now. Let's get you to equipment issue and dressed for the part. The mission starts at 2200 hours.'

Phase III: Pebble Island
West Falkland Island, 14th May, 1982

After three years in the Royal Navy, Rory didn't get seasick often any more, but riding in the back of a Sea King helicopter into forty-knot headwinds charted some brand new territory for nausea in his brain. It didn't help that the cargo compartment was crowded with battle-ready commandos and their equipment. The SAS lads looked calm and collected, but Rory could tell that everyone was tense, except maybe for Major Singh. The Lion sat in the jump seat next to Rory, his backpack and rifle upright between his legs, the fingers of his left hand lightly touching the pommel of the kirpan on his web belt while the big Sikh looked at the helicopter's bulkhead absent-mindedly. Rory would have liked a calming chat before the start of the action, but the interior of the Sea King was noisy, and conversations had to be held at near-shouting volume. Whatever space inside the helicopter that wasn't taken up by a geared-up soldier was filled with ammunition and equipment. The Sea King had windows, but it was pitch dark outside, and the total lack of visual references combined with the buffeting from the winds made Rory queasy.

They flew through the darkness for what seemed like hours until the helicopter finally started a series of banking and descending manoeuvres.

'Thirty seconds,' the pilot called out towards the back.

All around Rory, the SAS troopers started readying their gear with practised movements. Rory tried to emulate them, fumbling with the straps of his assault pack and untangling the Sterling submachine gun they had issued him back on Hermes.

'Relax,' the Lion said next to him and reached down to free Rory's gun sling from the support strut of his seat. 'We are not doing a parachute drop. We are just getting off the normal way.'

'In the dark. Onto enemy territory,' Rory added, and Major Singh grinned. His teeth looked very white in the semi-darkness of the Sea King's cargo hold.

'That is how war works,' he said. 'Especially when the Special Air Service is involved.'

The helicopter settled on the ground, and the troops opened the sliding doors to either side of the Sea King. The SAS men filed out of the cargo hold quickly and smoothly, and it was evident they had done this a thousand times. Rory tried not to hold up the egress too much and followed Major Singh as fast as he could. A few dozen yards away another Sea King landed, this one carrying the other half of D Squadron.

Outside, the SAS charged their L1A1 rifles, and some of them set up a security perimeter. Rory hadn't realized just how much extra ordnance they had brought with them until the other troops and the Navy airmen had unloaded the helicopters completely.

'Everyone check their loads,' the officers announced. 'Everybody will carry at least two rounds for the mortars in addition to their combat load.'

The SAS added the green plastic containers with the mortar bombs to their rucksacks and secured them with straps. Rory did the same. When he looked over to Major Singh, he saw that the Lion had lashed three double containers to his pack.

'Mountain Troop, take point with the lads from Boat Troop. Keep your intervals. And don't get distracted admiring the scenery. Once we get there, we have thirty minutes,' the SAS major in command ordered.

They all synchronized their watches, and the SAS squadron marched off into the darkness. Rory wasn't an infantryman, and the last time he had marched with a pack and a rifle had been during basic training. But these men were the best at this particular sort of thing, so he decided to stick close to Major Singh and do everything the SAS men did.

There wasn't much scenery to admire on Pebble Island. Rory remembered the assessment of his Navy friend that the Falklands looked a lot like the remote parts of Scotland, and he had to agree. It was all rock-strewn and hilly, with very little vegetation other than grass. Doing everything the SAS men did turned out to be easier in intent than practice because even with all their heavy gear they were the fastest marchers he had ever seen. Rory puffed along behind Major Singh and the supremely fit commandos.

'It's just like Scotland,' he said to the major as they were ascending a little hill, the wind whipping into their faces, making everyone pull the cords on their parka hoods tighter. 'There's even bloody sheep. Look.' He pointed over to a herd of them, barely visible in the darkness a few hundred yards off their path on the slop of the hill.

'Ten thousand sheep on this island,' Major Singh informed him. 'Been a sheep farm for a hundred and fifty years. I doubt the sheep care whether they get shorn by Argentines or British.'

They reached the summit of the little hill a few minutes later. On the plains ahead of them, maybe a mile or so in the distance, Rory could barely make out some structures, a few low buildings rising from the sparse grass. When he checked with his binoculars, he could make out the silhouettes of airplanes backlit by the moonlight reflecting from the nearby ocean.

'Send a signal to Glamorgan and let them know we have the objective in sight,' the SAS major ordered. 'Mountain Troop, let's get to work. Air and Boat troops, move out to the blocking and reserve positions. Ten minutes until go time, gentlemen.'

Rory and Major Singh went ahead with the Mountain Troop, whose task it had been to sneak into the Argentine installation and place demolition charges on the aircraft before Rory volunteered his talents. The SAS men moved silently and professionally, using hand signals to coordinate their movements. Major Singh stayed close by Rory's side and directed him silently whenever Rory didn't see or understand a hand signal. As a Navy sailor, he had only received minimal weapons instruction years ago, and he had forgotten almost all of his knowledge about infantry formation tactics from basic training. He had never been afraid of the dark, but this place was unsettling, especially given the knowledge that hundreds of armed men were camped out in that installation just a mile and a half away, ready and willing to kill them if they made their presence known.

Mountain Troop was five hundred yards from the edge of the airfield when the captain in charge ordered everyone to spread out and take up firing positions. He made his way back to Rory and Major Singh. 'Can you do your thing from here?' the captain asked Rory. 'Any closer and we have to keep an eye out for their sentries.'

Rory checked his surroundings with the binoculars again. 'I see three I can get for sure. But that low building there – I can't see what's next to that, or behind it. Too bloody dark.'

'Try these.' The captain opened a pouch on his web gear and handed Rory a set of goggles on a head strap. Rory put them on, and the captain reached out and turned a knob on the goggles. Rory's field of view instantly turned from various shades of black to a grainy green, but everything further than fifty feet away instantly became visible as if it was merely the beginning of dusk.

'Latest generation image intensifier,' the captain said.

'You SAS boys get all the expensive toys,' Rory replied. He looked around at the men in their fighting positions, then back at the airfield. A few small lights were burning over at the installation, and even though they looked like little glowing pinpricks to his naked eye from this distance, they flared bright as stars through the night vision goggles. What had been largely a featureless expanse before now looked perfectly defined to Rory. 'There's the runway,' he said. 'And four ... five ... make that six Pucarás. There's some sort of transport as well. And four more I don't recognize.'

'Let me see for a moment.'

Rory handed the night vision gear back to the SAS captain. 'Looks like Turbo-Mentors,' he said after looking at the field for a few moments. 'Training craft. But they can still report back our positions once the invasion fleet starts moving.' He returned the night vision goggles to Rory. 'Question is, can you slag the bastards from this far away?'

'Absolutely,' Rory said. The captain grinned at the conviction in his voice.

'That's what I wanted to hear. Wait for my go. Confirm?'

'Waiting for your go, sir.'

'Good man.' The captain got out his radio and spoke into it in a low voice. 'We have positive ID on the primary assets. Our man is ready to turn them into lawn decorations. Lock and load, and prepare for a response from the garrison force.'

The troop leader radioed back their acknowledgments. For a moment, it was dead silent on their little hillock apart from the ever-present South Atlantic wind.

'Glamorgan is standing by for bombardment,' the SAS captain said. 'You are cleared to engage, sub-lieutenant.'

'Do your thing, Archimedes,' Major Singh said next to him.

Rory took a deep breath. Then he scanned the line of ground attack craft parked five hundred yards away and focused his attention on the leftmost one, the plane closest to the end of the runway and therefore the one likely to take off first in the event of an alert.

Whenever anyone asked – and plenty of people had since his card turned – he never quite knew how to explain his ability. The closest he had ever come was to liken it to secondary school, to his biology classes. They'd had a human anatomy model in the classroom, a plastic dummy that had removable parts. You could strip all the layers away – first the pectoral and abdominal muscles, then the rib cage, then the internal organs. Heart, lungs, intestines, until you had the shell of half a body with nothing but the spinal column and the strands of the nervous system. Whenever he looked at a machine with electronics in it, he felt as if he was back in that classroom looking at the anatomical mannequin with its layers peeled away and the nerves sitting out in the open. He could feel the energy in the batteries and capacitors, sense the silica and copper pathways of the electrical systems. The Pucarás were over a third of a mile away, but he could still focus on each node in their artificial nervous systems in turn. They were simple machines compared to the Royal Navy's Harriers, but they still had basic computers, gyroscopes, radios, inertial navigation devices, all sorts of things that required circuit boards and capacitors.

Rory concentrated on the plane in the centre of his night vision goggles' field of vision. As always, he got just a little dizzy when the electromagnetic energy built up between him and his target. He directed it toward the nose of the plane and swept the electronics with a sharply focused pulse. Even from five hundred yards away, he could feel the pathways of the wiring and the circuit boards start to glow as he pumped a voltage into them they were never designed to withstand. It was silent and invisible to the commandos, and he reckoned they'd want tangible evidence that he was doing what he said he'd be able to do, so Rory focused again and doubled his effort. The second sweep had rather more dramatic results than the first. The overheated circuits were already damaged beyond repair, but now the wiring in the plane burst into flames. Rory gave it a third EMP pulse just to make sure the plane was thoroughly slagged.

'Well?' the SAS captain asked.

In the distance, flames started licking out of the crack between the Pucará's avionics access panel and the fuselage. In the near-complete darkness, they were visible even without night vision goggles. Rory nodded toward the plane in response. 'That one's flown its last sortie,' he said.

The captain trained a set of binoculars on the distant aircraft. Then he grinned and slapped Rory's shoulder. 'Bloody brilliant. Now do the rest, if you wouldn't mind.'

'Not at all,' Rory said, feeling a little smug. He wished the admiral had come along for the mission, even though he knew that flag officers ordered commando raids, they didn't join them. He turned his attention to the next plane and repeated the process, focusing a tight beam of electromagnetic energy and then sweeping it over the next Pucará in line, then the one next to that. The other three were lined up on the other side of the runway, so he got up and shifted his position a little to get a better viewing angle. Major Singh and the SAS captain moved with him and took up positions on either side of him again when he settled on the grass and adjusted his night vision goggles once more.

'Movement,' someone behind them called out in a low voice. 'Sentry, single mover. Two o'clock, coming out from behind that low Quonset.'

Rory looked in the direction the other SAS trooper indicated. There was a lone Argentine soldier out there, walking from one of the few buildings on the airfield over to the fuel pumps, which blocked his view of the plane that had started to burn. In a few moments, he'd either see or smell the fire coming from underneath the Pucará's hood.

'Look lively, lads,' the SAS captain said. 'Things are about to get interesting. Do hurry up, sub-lieutenant.'

Rory swept the remaining three Pucarás. They were small, graceful aircraft, and they looked as if they would be a blast to go for a ride in. It seemed a waste to destroy them, but he remembered the burn victims from the Sheffield being offloaded on the Hermes, and what little regret he felt dissipated at once.

He had just disabled the sixth and last Pucará when the first one on the other side of the line exploded with a dull thunderclap that rolled across the dark glen. The fire he had set just moments earlier had probably spread to the fuel tank or loaded ammunition. The orange-red bloom of the explosion roiled into the night sky and lit up the airstrip. The sudden brightness washed out the display of Rory's night vision goggles. When his vision returned, the Argentine sentry was no longer in sight.

'They'll be looking for us any second now,' the SAS captain said. 'Do the rest. Corporal Park, signal Glamorgan to commence bombardment.'

Rory's heart pounded as he returned his attention to the rest of the parked aircraft. The four Turbo-Mentors were next. He swept them one by one, as hard and tightly focused as he could, and three of them caught fire almost instantly, one of them belching a tall jet of flames from its portside wing before disappearing in a bright orange fireball. The boom that followed was so loud that it felt as if it made the ground shake a little even at this distance.

Somewhere out over the ocean Rory saw what looked like lightning flashes. A few seconds later, another explosion threw up a geyser of earth and rocks near the fuel dump. This one looked a lot bigger than the one caused by the aircraft blowing up. A few seconds later, another explosion followed, then a third. That one hit something unseen but volatile. Even the disciplined SAS men couldn't hold back their astonished excitement at the fireworks display in front of them. It looked like New Year's Eve over the Thames. Glowing bits of debris flew outward from the explosion in a huge shower of sparks and smoke trails. The destroyer HMS Glamorgan, waiting several miles offshore, had started her planned bombardment with her 4.5-inch main battery guns. A second or two later, the heat from the explosion washed over them. It smelled like hot metal and gunpowder.

'They hit the ammo dump,' Major Singh said with satisfaction in his voice. 'On the fourth shot. Good show.'

'Are the planes all slagged?' the SAS captain asked Rory.

'All done for,' Rory confirmed.

Glamorgan's high-explosive shells came in with clockwork-like regularity, a round hitting the airbase every five or six seconds. It seemed extremely foolhardy to lie prone only a few hundred yards from an airfield that was being worked over by artillery from miles away, but the gunnery officer on Glamorgan knew his job. The destroyer's big guns walked their fire all over the area of the base, but none of the rounds fell close to Rory and the SAS. After a few minutes, the bombardment ceased. The silence that followed was almost total. Only the crackling sounds from the fires on the airbase reached their ears.

'Right, then,' the SAS captain said into the silence. 'Scratch one airfield. Everybody ruck up and fall back for assembly. Mountain Troop, keep overwatch. And radio the mortar crews to leave their tubes. Ditch the bombs, too. We'll go light and fast on the way back.'

Rory got up from his prone position with a little groan. Using his ace ability always tired him out. It usually felt las if he had just washed down a dose of downers with a dram of cask-strength Scotch. He pulled the night vision goggles off his head and held them out to the SAS captain.

'Here's your toy back, sir,' he said. 'I wouldn't mind a set of those myself.'

'Tell you what,' the captain said. 'I'll give you that set when we get back to Hermes and report them lost. You saved us a lot of blood and sweat just now.'

The captain reached for the goggles and started stowing them in their pouch again.

A few yards to their right, the Lion looked back at the airfield in the distance and sniffed the air. Then he held up a hand and froze. 'Something's not right.'

Rory followed his gaze. There was no movement he could make out with his naked eyes despite the illumination from the fires. 'What—' he began. Then a fusillade of gunfire from the direction of the airfield cut him off. Rory could hear the supersonic crack of bullets screaming past them in the darkness. A machine gun opened up, green tracers reaching out to them like laser beams from a science fiction film.

'Down!' Major Singh shouted. He whirled around and dove for

Rory. The SAS captain was closer to him, though, and just a little bit faster than the Lion. He grabbed Rory by his web gear and yanked him down onto the ground. Rory saw some of the tracer rounds skip on the rocky soil nearby at a shallow angle and bounce off in various directions. The SAS captain let out a strained little grunt and tumbled to the grass with Rory. Next to them, the SAS men dropped prone again and started returning fire. The reports from their rifle shots were deafeningly loud. Rory groped for his submachine gun, but found that he had dropped it, and the rounds snapping past his head made him disinclined to look around for it right now.

'I'm hit,' the SAS captain said in an almost conversational tone. Rory looked over to the man to see the expression on his face. He didn't looked panicked or in pain, but surprised.

Major Singh appeared next to them. He grabbed Rory by the belt with one hand and the SAS captain's web gear with the other. Then he hauled them both off the ground and dashed away from the incoming fire. Rory didn't even have time to yelp in surprise. Even with four hundred pounds to carry, Major Singh was twenty-five yards behind the line of SAS men in a matter of seconds. There was a little depression in the terrain, and the Lion deposited Rory and the SAS captain in it carefully. 'Medic to my position,' he shouted, a deep and sonorous roar that momentarily cut through the cacophony of the gunfire.

Two SAS soldiers came out of the darkness and dropped next to Rory and the captain. 'You hurt, sir?'

'I don't think so.' Rory patted himself down to check for bullet holes, but came up clean. 'But the captain's hit.'

'The enemy has a concealed trench line parallel to the northern runway edge,' Major Singh said. 'A very well concealed trench. I didn't see it until they moved their GPMG up into position, right before they opened fire. Contact Glamorgan and have them send a barrage. Tell them to shift their fire a hundred yards north from the last volley.'

'Yes, sir,' the SAS soldier said and dashed off. The other SAS man had taken off his pack and was already working on the captain, whose surprised expression had at last shifted to one of extreme discomfort.

For a little while when he had rendered the Argentine aircraft inert from a distance, Rory had felt as if he had his thumb on the scale, that he was making a difference. Right now, that feeling had dissipated completely. He tried to stay as low to the ground as he could. All around him, the SAS were shooting at the Argentinian defenders. The troop with them was made up of only a dozen commandos, and one of them was wounded on the ground in front of him, but it seemed implausible that eleven rifles could produce such world-ending noise. Rory felt as if he had been dropped into the middle of World War Three. He had no idea what to do or where to be.

Major Singh didn't have any problem working out his role on the battlefield. With the captain out of commission and the major with another troop on a hill several hundred yards away, the remaining SAS men deferred to the Silver Helix agent without hesitation.

'Fall back to Boat Troop's position by squads, bounding overwatch. And what is that blasted destroyer waiting for?'

As if on cue, the first shells from Glamorgan's renewed barrage exploded at the edge of the airstrip, and this time Rory felt the tremors of the detonations traveling through the ground below him. They were like hammer blows from a very pissed-off deity – the short, sharp whistling of an incoming shell followed by the concussion of the high explosive fragmentation warhead. The small-arms fire from the Argentinian defenders instantly slackened off and then faded into silence.

'They're getting back under cover,' Major Singh said. 'All squads, disengage and rally at the exfiltration assembly point. We have forty-five minutes to reach the aircraft.'

'Come on, Archimedes.' The big Sikh walked up to Rory and pulled him to his feet. 'You made this a victory. Let's not have the enemy turn it into a defeat.'

The SAS captain in charge of Mountain Troop had been shot in the lower back. He was unable to stand or walk, and they had brought no stretchers to carry out the wounded.

'You lads get back to the helicopters and leave me here with a few flares,' the captain said, his face a grimace of suppressed agony. 'I'll make sure the Argies find me. I'll see you all in England when this bloody war is over.'

'That is a load of noble nonsense, Captain,' Major Singh said. 'Corporal, give the man his second morphine dose. I will carry him back with us. And there will be no discussion about this. Now get a move on, everyone. There isn't any time for St Crispin's Day speeches right now.'

They speed-marched across the dark landscape faster than Rory had ever marched before. The SAS squads took turns guarding the rear of the spread-out column, and every five minutes they switched places. That meant they had to cover four times the distance Rory did, but he was still close to the limits of his physical endurance. Next to him, Major Singh strode along without any signs of fatigue, even though he was carrying the wounded SAS captain. They had left their mortar and all its heavy ammunition behind, and every other man just carried a weapon and a light assault pack. Nobody knew exactly how large the Argentine garrison was, or whether they had the fortitude to chase a squadron of elite SAS commandos across the island in the dark, but the SAS men all went by the book as though they had a thousand angry enemy marines on their heels.

They reached the helicopters with just ten minutes left in their exfiltration window. The major in charge held brief tactical counsel with the troop leaders and Major Singh, but everyone decided to proceed with the exfiltration rather than return to the airstrip to attack the defenders again and attempt to claim the field entirely. Rory had never been so relieved in his life as when they boarded the Sea Kings and took off for the relative safety of HMS Hermes.

The mood on the flight back to the carrier was very different from the ingress. The men were laughing and joking as if they hadn't just exchanged live fire with the enemy in actual battle. The wounded SAS captain was doped up on morphine, but conscious, and he gave Rory a weak thumbs-up when he saw him looking.

'You're a bloody hero, sir,' one of the SAS sergeants sitting across the troop compartment shouted to Rory. 'You won't have to buy a pint for yourself again until we're back in Portsmouth. The Special Air Service will make sure of that.'

Rory smiled and returned the commando's grin. He was glad to have played the role he had. It had felt good and right, exactly the sort of thing he had hoped to do when he had joined the Silver Helix. He had saved lives and used his ace power without hurting or killing anyone. But when he looked at the SAS captain who had taken a round to the back to keep him safe, his satisfaction was considerably tempered.

Phase IV: Bomb Alley
North Falkland Sound, 21st May, 1982

During the days after the Pebble Beach raid, Rory was treated like a celebrity in the fleet, and for a little while he came close to believing that he deserved at least some of the applause.

The Pebble Beach mission had been a resounding success. Rory had destroyed all six light attack aircraft and four reconnaissance planes. The shelling from HMS Glamorgan had taken out the ammo and fuel dumps. There were still Argentine troops on the ground at the airfield, but those were of little concern to Admiral Woodward and his staff, now that the Argentinian air threat from that part of the islands was completely neutralized. And thanks to Rory – Archimedes, as everyone now called him without hesitation – the operation had gone down with no British casualties except the wounded SAS captain, who had been flown out to the hospital ship to be airlifted back to the UK.

'The Black Buck raids tore up the runway at Stanley, and our lads are flying combat air patrol around the clock between us and there,' the admiral told the assembled staff officers at the invasion briefing. 'Thanks to Archimedes, the enemy will have no use of landing strips on the islands any more. Whatever airpower they bring to bear will have to come from the mainland, and they will be at the very limits of their operational range. Therefore, we are accelerating the invasion schedule to beat the winter weather. Operation Sutton begins tomorrow at 2300 hours. We will land 3 Commando Brigade as planned at San Carlos and work our way south from there once we have established a beachhead.'

He turned his attention to Rory, who was starting to get used to being the centre of attention. 'Archimedes is going to land with the Royal Marine commandos on Fanning Head at San Carlos and take a position on the high ground overlooking Falkland Sound and the inlet of Port San Carlos,' he said and indicated the places on the projected wall map. 'They expect us to land at Stanley, on the other side of the island. It will take them until daybreak to realize that we're coming from the opposite side. But once they do, they'll send the rest of their planes from the mainland bases to bomb the landing craft. They will throw everything they have left at that beachhead. Your job is to make sure they don't succeed. Our ships will have little space to manoeuvre in that narrow sound. You have demonstrated that you can disable those aircraft faster and more reliably than the Sea Cat missiles from the surface ships. Drop their planes out of the sky before they can release their bombs.'

This was on a different scale from Pebble Beach. That raid had been a squadron of SAS, only forty-five men and two helicopters. This was a full-scale amphibious landing, five thousand men plus equipment, ferried onto the landing beaches by dozens of ships. It would be a target-rich environment for the Argentines. But the admiral's esteem of Rory had risen immensely since Pebble Beach, and the rest of the officer corps on Hermes had treated him with far more respect and deference than before. Nobody had addressed him merely as 'Sub-Lieutenant' since that night, and Rory didn't want to give them a reason to doubt his abilities. Besides, the frigates and destroyers supporting the landing craft would have their own air defence missiles and guns, and the marines would bring shoulder-fired ones to shore when they landed, so he took comfort in the knowledge that he was far from being the only anti-air asset for the landing.

'We'll keep the lads safe,' Rory replied. 'Whatever it takes.'

'You are an asset now. I will send you out with D Squadron again. They'll be tasked with clearing your observation post and keeping you safe.'

'What about Major Singh, sir?'

'Major Singh will be needed to augment and assist 2 Para when they land at San Carlos. Have no fear, the SAS lads will take good care of you. Just make sure you make it worth the investment. We are scrapping one of the recon missions at Darwin to free up D Squadron for your use.'

'Yes, sir.' The thought of going into battle this time without the reassuring presence of the Lion nearby made Rory anxious. But Silver Helix or not, he was still a junior officer, and when the admiral told you to jump, it was best to be in the air before asking for an altitude parameter.

'This is it. If we do this right, we'll have the Union Jack flying over Stanley again within a week or two. I don't know about you gentlemen, but I'd rather prefer to be on the way home once the bad weather sets in down here. See to your units and prepare for executing Operation Sutton in twenty-eight hours. Dismissed.'

D Squadron, 22 SAS Regiment, seemed to have adopted Rory as their personal ace and good-luck charm. They kitted him out in the same gear they were wearing, which was considerably better than what the Paras or even the Royal Marines were issued with. The submachine gun he received was integrally suppressed, they fitted him for splinter protection armour, and – as promised – he got his own set of night vision goggles. When they boarded their helicopters for the main assault after nightfall the next day, Rory felt a little better knowing that he was protected by the best the British Armed Forces had to offer, but the memory of the brief but violent engagement at Pebble Beach kept the fear simmering in the back of his brain. The raid had been a prelude. This was full-out war, everything they could put on the board against everything the enemy had. Rory spent the last few hours before the start of the operation writing the letters he had been holding off on since they left Portsmouth. Before, he thought they'd bring bad luck and maybe cause the event for which they were contingencies. After Pebble Island, he had changed his mind. One letter to his parents, one each to his siblings, all crafted as well as he could to soften the blow of his death, should it happen, and give them something to remember him by. It was much harder than he had expected, harder even than gearing up for the battle itself, and when he had finished, he felt emotionally drained.

They took off from the darkened deck of Hermes an hour after local sunset. Before Rory stepped through the door of the Sea King, he looked out over the ocean to starboard, which was full of ships, all running with dimmed position lights. So many ships, so many lives at stake.

The weather was better on this flight. The Sea King didn't get buffeted as it had in the raid a few days earlier, and Rory kept most of his dinner in this time. He knew most of the men of D Squadron by name and sight now, but he still missed seeing Major Singh. This would be the first time out on his own as a Silver Helix operative, and naturally it would be in support of the biggest amphibious invasion the Royal Navy and Marines had staged in almost forty years.

Their target zone was a hilltop called Fanning Head. It overlooked the San Carlos estuary, where the amphibious landing ships would soon be making their way to shore, slow and vulnerable and loaded with hundreds of Royal Marines and Army paratroopers. As they approached the hilltop, their escorts, smaller and more nimble Gazelle helicopters, rushed ahead to scout the landing zone. Rory sat near the front of the Sea King's cargo bay, close to the cockpit, so he could see outside through the front canopy. Out of the darkness, tracer rounds reached up, streams of glowing fireflies, and connected with one of the Gazelles just as it crested the hill. The Gazelle banked hard to the left and dropped out of sight.

'Incoming fire!' the pilot shouted. 'Going evasive. Hang on to something, lads.'

The second Gazelle, somewhere out of sight on the port side of their Sea King, opened fire with its rocket pods. The unguided rockets streaked toward the hilltop, but Rory didn't see the results of the impacts because their pilot had initiated a sharp banking turn to starboard. The helicopter raced down the slope of the hill, away from the incoming fire.

'We'll have to abort!' the pilot shouted. 'There's Argie infantry on the hilltop.'

'You put this son of a bitch down right now!' the SAS major in charge shouted back from his jump seat just behind the cockpit bulkhead. 'We'll take care of the infantry.'

'Ten seconds,' the pilot replied without argument.

'Lock and load,' the major shouted. All over the cargo hold, SAS soldiers cycled the bolts on their submachine guns.

'You stay between me and Corporal Park,' the burly sergeant sitting next to Rory shouted. 'Do what I say when I say it.'

The helicopter touched down hard. The corporal sitting next to the nearest sliding door was out of the craft even before all the wheels had fully settled, and the rest of the section piled out of the Sea King after him. Outside, there was immediate small arms fire.

'Come along now, right behind me.' The burly sergeant pulled Rory along, and they left the cargo hold. As soon as they were outside, the sergeant pushed Rory into the prone position.

'Don't get up unless someone tells you to,' the sergeant said as he took up a firing position close to Rory. 'And you bloody well better hope they tell you in English and not Spanish.'

The fire fight was brief. There was only a small Argentinian team on this hilltop, and they only put up token resistance in the face of opposition from a full SAS squadron. Some fell, most of the rest ran, and a few surrendered when they saw they were outnumbered and outgunned. The SAS men secured the hilltop and stripped the Argentinian soldiers of weapons. These were the first enemy troops Rory had seen face-to-face. They looked tired and haggard in the light from the SAS field torches.

'Left us some gear,' one of the SAS troopers said. The Argentines had set up an observation post – three tents, a few trenches, a mortar pit, recoilless rifle positions, and a number of radios connected to a twenty-foot antenna that was whipping in the stiff breeze.

'Signal the naval gunfire support that we have control of Fanning Head,' the major ordered. Everything the SAS did was efficient and businesslike, right down to collecting and stacking the discarded rifles from the surrendering Argentinians.

'Two and a half hours until daylight,' the major continued. 'Time for you to set up your stuff, Archimedes. I guarantee you that these skies will be thick with aircraft as soon as the Argies work out where the landings are.'

They had brought three different sets of observation binoculars and tripods in the Sea King. The SAS unloaded the gear and helped Rory set everything up. This was equipment usually built for artillery observation, but today Rory had a different use for it. He lined one of the high-powered binocular tripods up so he could see down a large part of the length of Falkland Sound, the most likely approach route for enemy aircraft. The other two went to face to the west and northwest respectively. This way, Rory had two hundred degrees of magnified vision from this spot. The SAS manned a security perimeter, and three of them set up their own radio sets. They were ready for action just as the sky in the east started getting light. Overnight, dozens of amphibious ships had moved to the shoreline of the inlet below them, and almost as many frigates and destroyers were out in the Sound, screening the vulnerable troop carriers. The retaking of the Falklands had begun in earnest.

The sunrise was almost beautiful. Rory watched the scene in the sound below from the hilltop observation post. Most of the troops had landed by the time the sun peered over the mountaintops to the east, and now the landing ships unloaded the heavy equipment, vehicles and light armour. Out in Falkland

Sound, the frigates had taken up station in a rough line that extended for several miles. Any enemy plane coming up the Sound would have to run the gauntlet of their air defences before they got to the transports, but the frigates would also have to bear the brunt of the bombing runs.

'Tea, sir,' one of the SAS men said behind him. Rory turned to see that the commandos had set up their personal folding stoves to heat water. The soldier handed him a mess tin that had steam rising from it.

'Thank you, sergeant.' Rory took the hot tin, grateful to have something to warm himself up. The wind up here bit even through the many layers he was wearing. It was bearable if you moved around, but standing still and watching the horizon was freezing business.

It was just after ten in the morning when the first Argentine plane appeared in the sky over Falkland Sound. A single jet popped over a mountain ridge to the southwest, changed course sharply, and dropped low over the water. The roar from its jet engines reverberated from the hillsides.

'Light attack plane, bearing two-twenty, coming in right above the water,' one of the SAS observers said, already tracking the target with the super-powered binoculars mounted on one of the tripods. 'He's got underwing ordnance.'

Rory got behind the eyepiece of his own stationary binoculars. It took maddeningly long to find the plane through the high-power optics. The Argentine plane was a light jet, slender and graceful, with a pointy nose and bulbous tanks on the wingtips. It roared up the Sound at what had to be full throttle. There were cylindrical objects under the wings, but Rory couldn't tell whether they were fuel tanks, bombs, or rocket pods. He focused his attention and felt the familiar light dizziness as the electromagnetic energy between him and the distant plane built up. Just as he was about to direct an EMP blast at the nose of the aircraft, the pilot pulled up from his suicidally low approach run, and Rory lost him with the binoculars as the plane rapidly gained altitude in the middle of the Sound.

'Fuck!' Rory shouted. He didn't bother trying to reacquire the plane with the optics. Instead, he shielded the left side of his face with his hand against the morning sun and looked out over the Sound with just his eyes. By now, the Argentine plane was within half a mile of the southernmost ship in the screen.

'He's making a run on Argonaut,' someone said behind him. 'Take him down, take him down!'

The Argentine plane levelled out and dipped its nose towards the water once more to line up whatever weapon he was about to release. There was a distant pop and a whooshing sound coming from the frigate, and an anti-air missile left the launcher mounted on the side of the ship. At the same time, Rory let loose a strong blast of EMP energy in the direction of the plane. It must not have been quite as focused as he had intended, because both the plane and the missile racing to meet it went haywire at the same time. The plane spun around its longitudinal axis until it flew inverted. The missile corkscrewed wildly and splashed harmlessly into the water five hundred yards from the frigate and its intended target. Rory knew that the pilot had just lost everything in his cockpit that had an electric wire connected to it – every screen, instrument, radio. He still had his flight controls, though, and he managed to roll the plane upright just a second or two before it hit the water. At this distance, Rory didn't see the canopy blow off the plane's fuselage just before the splash of the impact, but the orange and olive-green parachute canopy that bloomed in the sky a moment later was hard to miss. The pilot had managed to eject at the last second.

'Splash one!' an SAS lad shouted, and the rest of them cheered as if someone had scored at a football match. Except that Rory was trying for the opposite – he was there to stop anyone scoring. He was the goalkeeper right now.

'Argonaut says they've lost their radar,' the SAS radioman reported. 'They are swapping positions with Antelope.'

Whoops, Rory thought. The Argentine pilot hadn't gotten any ordnance off before Rory shut him down, but part of Argonaut must have been caught in the slightly unfocused blast he had panic-fired at the attacking plane.

The sounds of anti-aircraft gunfire and jet engines ebbed. Far out in the middle of Falkland Sound, Argonaut halted her forward motion, then started steaming backwards. Another frigate, presumably Antelope, had changed course and was heading towards Argonaut. The Argentine pilot's parachute was in the water now, but the hull of Argonaut blocked Rory's view of it. He hoped they were fishing the pilot out of the water before he drowned.

The respite did not last very long. Maybe ten minutes later, the next Argentine plane appeared, and this one had brought company. The two-plane flight came over the ridge that bordered the Falklands Sound and banked and dived at the task force at a much closer distance than the light recon plane that had come before them. These were much more lethal-looking, with triangular delta wings that had big bombs slung underneath, fighter planes obviously built for speed. This time, Rory didn't bother waiting for someone to call out a bearing or a type designation. He focused on the first plane and pushed all the energy he could muster into the pointed nose cone of the fighter jet. There was a bright flash and a muffled explosion. The sound only reached Rory a few seconds later, and by then the enemy pilot had pulled his jet into a steep climb. Presented with such an easy target, the frigates and destroyers of the screening force didn't need a special invitation. Heavy gunfire thundered across the Sound, half a dozen warships opening up with their gun mounts. Two of the frigates launched their SeaCat missiles, which homed in on the stricken jet from two different directions. One shot past the plane and flew down Falkland Sound, where it splashed into the water far in the distance. The white smoke trail of the other SeaCat converged with the plume of black smoke in the wake of the Argentine jet, which was still heavy with the bombs the pilot had failed to jettison. This time, Rory saw the canopy fly away from the sleek fuselage, and the pilot ejected just before the SeaCat struck home and blew the plane apart in a brilliant plume of sparks and smoking parts.

The second Argentine jet had barrelled on undeterred, and it was fast, so much faster than the little plane that had made the first attack run on the Argonaut. It banked to the right, fired flares, then banked to the left and past Argonaut, which was still going in reverse. Then the pilot pulled up the nose of his plane and pointed it at the next ship in the screening line on the Sound, a destroyer. Rory focused and blasted the jet like he had the first one, but he was a fraction of a second too late. Two bombs detached from the triangular wings of the Argentine jet and tumbled through the air toward the British destroyer. One bomb skipped off the water and bounced past the destroyer's stern. The other one hit the hull in the aft quarter of the ship. Rory held his breath, expecting the huge explosion that was sure to follow. He could see the stern of the destroyer rocking from the impact of the heavy bomb, but it didn't blow up. The Argentine jet, its nose section now on fire, made a valiant attempt to line up on another British ship, maybe to fire its cannon or ram it, but the plane was too low and the pilot had too little control of his craft left. One wingtip clipped the surface of the water, and the plane cartwheeled into the sea with an enormous splash. As quickly as this latest duo of attackers had appeared, silence descended over the Sound again.

'Bomb didn't go off,' the SAS man next to Rory said in amazement. 'They released too low. Didn't give the fuse time to arm itself. Lucky buggers on that ship.'

'Antrim confirms they got hit by a dud,' the radioman called out. 'No word on damage yet, but it holed the hull.'

Rory sat down hard on the sandbags next to him. He felt as if he had the world's worst case of vertigo.

'Splash three,' the SAS sergeant said. 'Good job, mate. You okay?'

'I can't hold them off if they keep coming in like that,' Rory replied.

'Can't you blast them all at once?'

'Focus is too wide,' Rory replied. 'It's like a flashlight, see. The wider you make the beam, the more gets caught in it. I try to do two or three planes at once, I'll catch one of our ships in it too. They're coming in too bloody low.'

'They've got some guts, all right. Didn't think they had it in them.'

The battle had been on for fifteen minutes, and already Rory felt drained. Between him and the anti-air systems on the Navy ships, they had downed all three attacking aircraft, but two of the screening force ships were already damaged. Antrim had a hole in its hull, and Argonaut's radar was out, probably because of his failure.

Overhead, two Royal Navy Harriers thundered past and headed down Falkland Sound. Rory and the SAS sergeant watched them climb as they flew over the formation of warships assembled on the Sound, then peel off to the southwest in search of targets.

'About time they turned up,' the SAS sergeant said.

The land battle around San Carlos was still being fought by the Royal Marines and the Army paratroopers. They could hear regular exchanges of small arms fire from the hills on the far side of the inlet. The settlement of San Carlos wasn't even big enough to be called a town. It was just a handful of buildings that looked like a very spread-out farm. Armoured vehicles in British camouflage were advancing past the houses and into the hills beyond, and the beach was bustling with activity.

In the distance, Rory heard jet engines again. He hoped they belonged to the Harriers that had overflown them on their way south just a few minutes ago, but when the planes came over the hills to the southwest, their wings had triangle shapes, loaded with bombs. Rory saw the puffs from the cannons of the frigates on the south end of the formation as they started pumping shells towards the new attackers.

'Incoming air!' the SAS sergeant shouted. 'Two Daggers, bearing two-three-zero. Here we go again.'

Below them, Falkland Sound came alive once more with gunfire and the sound of anti-air missiles launching. Rory focused on the lead plane descending into the Sound and went back to work.

For the next two hours, the Argentines came in like clockwork, a new pair of planes every ten minutes, then flights of four. Rory had never expended so much mental energy. Focusing his EMP blasts at targets several miles away took an enormous amount of concentration. He knocked down plane after plane, frying their electronics to slag and setting their wiring harnesses on fire. Most pilots ejected, but some went into the sea with their planes. And despite his best efforts, some of the Argentine jets still got close enough to strafe British ships with their guns or drop bombs. Most of the drops were misses, and almost all the rest didn't go off because the Argentinians came in low to avoid the curtain of gunfire and SeaCat missiles the fleet threw at them. Rory dropped two planes from a four-plane flight into the ocean with one forceful EMP blast, but watched in horror as the other two Argentine jets lined up on a frigate and peppered her superstructure with cannon fire. Rory blasted one of the jets out of the sky just as it pulled out of its attack run and started to climb away. Then two missiles streaked in out of nowhere and connected with the remaining Argentine attack jet. It disintegrated in a thunderous explosion that echoed across the Sound. The remains of the wreck, carried by the momentum of the jet, ploughed into the hillside at the other end of the inlet. A moment later two Harriers streaked across Rory's field of vision. They split up and banked away, one west and one east.

'Antelope is hit!' the radio operator in the tent behind them shouted.

'We can bloody well see that!' the SAS sergeant next to Rory shouted back. Out on the water, smoke came from the superstructure of the damaged frigate. The cannon shells had managed to set something on the ship on fire. But she was still in the fight, radar antenna spinning and gun turrets turning to point back toward the southwest end of the Sound.

Rory sat down on the sandbags with a groan. The SAS sergeant handed him a canteen, and he drank half of the water in one greedy gulp.

'You're doing brilliant,' the sergeant said. He picked up a stick and pointed at a row of marks he had scratched into the earth next to his binocular tripod. 'That was number thirteen through fifteen.'

'We downed fifteen planes this morning?'

'You did. The SeaCats and the Harriers got seven more. That's twenty-two down. They really want us off this beach, don't they?'

'How many bloody aircraft do they have in their air force?'

'I don't know for sure, sir. But I think we'll see most of them today at some point or another.'

By the early afternoon, the Argentine planes had stopped coming. When an hour had passed without any attack runs, Rory allowed himself a little flash of optimism. Maybe they did run out of planes.

The SAS captain in charge of the troop came up to Rory's position.

'The ships are offloaded. The Marines are advancing south toward Goose Green. There's a command post set up two klicks past the settlement,' he said. 'I suppose we can get off this hill now. Good work all around. You saved a lot of lives today.'

Rory thought about all the planes that had splashed into the waters of the Sound below them before the pilots had had a chance to eject. But their planes had been carrying bombs, and the British warships, for all their martial looks and intimidating weapons-bristling presence, were fragile and staffed by a lot of sailors. A few lives traded for many, but it was still a grim trade when you were the one whose thumb tipped that scale.

End Phase: Blood and Coffee
Goose Green, East Falkland Island, 25th May, 1982

Back home in Scotland, Goose Green would barely register on a map. On the Falklands it was a town – its third-biggest settlement, in fact – but it consisted of only about two dozen buildings, clustered on a little peninsula jutting into Falkland Sound. It reminded Rory of the remote towns in the Highlands, the ones with one shop and one pub supporting populations of a hundred people and a thousand sheep. But after a whole week of camping out on wind-blown hilltops all along the shoreline as the British troops made their way south, the place looked like civilization to Rory.

While he was keeping away the Argentinian planes trying to make attacks on British ships and ground forces on their way south, the troops had pried Goose Green away from the Argentine troops that had dug in all around the town, and it had taken two bloody days and nights of hard fighting. But now the Union Jack was flying over the town hall again, there was a pile of surrendered Argentine rifles and machine guns sitting by the dock, and Rory stepped into a heated room for the first time since they had left Hermes to assault San Carlos.

'There's the walking weapons system,' Major General Moore greeted him when he walked into the command post set up in the town hall. 'You have done fantastic work, sub-lieutenant.' Instead of returning Rory's salute, the general held out his hand. Rory accepted the handshake.

'Thank you, sir. I think I could sleep for a month straight now.'

The other officers and senior sergeants in the room, Army paratroopers and Royal Marines alike, looked just as tired as he felt. They were all in battle fatigues and still decked out in combat gear, and most of them were dirty and still had camouflage paint on their faces. He didn't dare ask how many they had lost in the fight, but he knew that medical evacuation flights had been leaving from the hills around Goose Green constantly since the end of the battle.

'If you are looking for your Silver Helix colleague, he's in the kitchen. You should get yourself some hot coffee while you're here. You bloody well earned it, I'd say,' the general said, but his smile looked hollow.

'How is your war going?' Major Singh asked when Rory walked in. The Lion sat on a kitchen chair that looked far too rickety for the weight of the big Sikh. He looked exhausted as well. The major's boots and the hilt of his big knife were flecked with mud, and there were dark stains on the major's uniform that didn't look as if sweat or spilled coffee. He looked like he'd had a very busy week with the Royal Marines.

Rory looked around for the promised coffee. There was a pot sitting on an electric heating plate on the counter nearby. The Lion pointed to a cupboard wordlessly. There were cups inside, and Rory took one out and filled it from the pot, trying hard to control himself and not just guzzle the stuff straight from the spout.

'To be honest, it has been the most boring and most terrifying week of my life. Both at the same time, somehow, if that makes sense.'

'Yes, it does. Long periods of boredom interspersed with moments of sheer terror. That's what it's like to go to war.'

Rory took a sip of his coffee and promptly burned the roof of his mouth, but the taste was so decadently delicious after a week of lousy campfire tea that he didn't care.

'Thirty-nine planes,' he told the Lion. 'They just kept coming. And I kept sending them into the water. Why did they keep coming? They had to notice that none were coming back.'

'They did their duty,' the Lion said.

'They fished out the ones that ejected. Some didn't. I saw a few of them go in, and no chute. Pilot and all.'

'And you find it bothers you.'

'Yes,' Rory said. 'It does. I killed those men. Of course it bothers me. I used my powers to kill people.'

'And it should,' Major Singh said. 'It will always bother you. Killing isn't a natural act. We do it because we must, not because we like it.'

Rory's gaze flickered to the kirpan on the Lion's belt. He knew that the weapon wasn't merely ceremonial, that Major Singh kept it honed to a shaving-sharp edge, and suddenly he found himself pitying the Argentine defenders who had stood in his way to Goose Green. 'You've been to war before,' Rory said. 'You're used to it.'

'You never get used to it.' Major Singh stretched his legs with a sigh and took another sip of his own coffee. 'I was in 1 Para ten years ago,' the Lion continued. 'I was just twenty years old. It was during the Troubles, right after Bloody Sunday.'

A shiver ran down Rory's spine. Northern Ireland was still dangerous ground for British soldiers. Ten years ago it had been a free-fire war zone, car bombs and snipers and night-time assassinations.

'I went out on patrol with a few lads in a Land Rover, and we got lost in a very bad neighbourhood. Ended up in the middle of a crowd. They turned the car over and set it on fire. That's when my card turned. I don't remember how I got out of the upturned car. I don't remember pulling everyone else out of the burning car. I don't remember how long it took me to fight my way through the crowd, or how long it took for reinforcements to find us. But I do remember the faces on the bodies of those I killed that day to save my comrades. All nine of them. I pity them, and the families that must have mourned for them. But I do not regret it.'

Major Singh turned his cup in his hands and held Rory's gaze with tired-looking but unwavering dark eyes. 'The men in those planes were brave beyond measure, and they meant to kill you. You and the people you were charged to protect. You did what you had to do. That's why you wanted to join the Silver Helix. To protect. To defend. And sometimes that means having to kill. That is something you must accept.'

The Lion got up and walked over to the counter to refill his cup. The top of his turban brushed the ceiling of the kitchen in the old farmhouse. 'Most people hear "Silver Helix", and they think of the flashy business they see on the telly. Aces flying or lifting girders off people. But most of what we do isn't flashy. It's going to ground with the lads and helping the cause. Think of all the men on those ships who didn't die because you were there. I know the thought doesn't help much right now, but it will. Later, after all of this is over. When you've had time to remember.'

He walked back to his chair and patted Rory on the shoulder on the way past. 'It's a good thing that you're bothered. I wouldn't like it much if you weren't. It tells me that you are right for the Silver Helix. When we get back to to England, I'll tell Sir Kenneth that I endorse the removal of your probationary status.'

The news of his impending full acceptance into the Order, the professional validation he had sought ever since his card turned, would have made Rory feel proud and grateful at any other time than now, and anywhere else but this godforsaken, wind-beaten little patch of rocky ground in the North Atlantic. But after this week, his ability to feel anything but bone-deep tiredness seemed to have gone on extended leave.

'Thank you, sir,' he said to Major Singh. 'I will not disappoint you or the Order.'

Major Singh sat down again and nodded. 'You're welcome. You've earned it. But make sure that this sort of thing is what you want to do with the rest of your life. Because what you have seen here is not the worst you'll ever see. Not even close.'

Outside, the newly hoisted Union Jack on the flagpole in front of the town hall whipped fiercely in the wind. In the brief time Rory had spent in the town hall's kitchen with the Lion, the number of Royal Marines and paratroopers in the town seemed to have tripled. Overhead, Navy Harriers roared past towards the hills in the east, where the Argentinians were still holding on to Port Stanley, even though Rory knew their chances of winning this war had gone in the sea with all the planes he had splashed.

In the distance, Rory heard the distinctive whop-whop-whop rotor noise from Chinook transport helicopters, and the sound made Major Singh smile.

'It seems we will not have to walk all the way across this blasted island after all,' he said to Rory. 'Those are the transports from Atlantic Conveyor.'

A Royal Marine lieutenant came trotting up to them, one hand on his green beret to keep it from flying away in the wind.

'If you don't mind, sirs, General Moore is asking for you. Looks as if we're accelerating the schedule and going for Port Stanley early now that the choppers are off the boat safely.'

'We'll be right in,' Major Singh told the lieutenant, who nodded and trotted off without a salute. They were in the field, Rory reminded himself, in a shooting war. You don't salute on the battlefield because you don't want to tell the enemy marksmen who's important.

'Well then,' Major Singh said. 'Let's get this unpleasant

business over with. I'm ready to go home. Until the next war.'

They walked up the muddy path to the town hall, the Union Jack on its pole flapping an urgent beat, like a tied-up animal frantically trying to shake itself free.

Until the next war, Rory thought. *Hope that one breaks out long after I'm retired.*

Rehabilitating Zombies: Rottertown

"Rottertown" is the first time I've taken on the zombie sub-genre. Contrary to what readers may think, I did not write it during the pandemic. I started it years ago, then finished it just *before* the pandemic when a good ending came to mind. Then COVID-19 happened, and I didn't want to submit it anywhere because I knew from conversations with editors that all the short fiction publishers of science fiction and fantasy stories got inundated with pandemic stories of some kind.

Zombie apocalypse stories are extremely well-trodden ground in science fiction. I didn't want to walk down that path because it's been done so many times. Instead, I tried to think about what would happen if the zombie infestation had come and gone, that humanity had developed a vaccine and brought the virus under control. What would the aftermath of a months-long global outbreak look like after everything was calm again and people tried to resume their old lives? And if there were survivors, people saved from the end stage of infection by the vaccine, what would life be like for them?

Rottertown

"It's our money," Kendra says. "I don't understand why you won't let me take it out."

The bank manager exhales in a not-quite-sighing sort of way.

"As I have told you already, we have no way of knowing that you are who you say you are. And it's a joint account, so it would be against our regulations."

The manager is well-dressed and good-looking. Kendra is neither. She closes her eyes briefly and enjoys the air conditioning in the office. There are sweat stains on her clothes, but she knows he's not looking at those. He's looking at the spiderweb of tell-tale lines on her face and neck, veins turned a sickly green and blue by the anti-viral serum.

"I've been coming in here for years. We got our mortgage here. You have seen my face a hundred times," she says.

He puts his hands down on his desk blotter, fingers spread out slightly, and Kendra can tell that he considers this conversation over, that nothing she can say will change his mind.

"I need to find my husband and my daughter," she says. "I need to get the money out of our account to do that. *Please*," she makes one last attempt.

"I'm sorry, but I can't help you," he replies. "I simply can't. Not without seeing some official proof that your husband is deceased. A death certificate. A police report. Something of that nature."

He's not even bothering with the courtesy of a fake apologetic smile. There's a pistol on his belt, something small and Italian in an expensive-looking holster that matches the suit. Kendra wonders if he has a closet full of holsters to coordinate his appearance every morning. Ever since the Outbreak, uninfected America has embraced the right to bear arms with newly unanimous enthusiasm.

Our house burned to the ground with everything in it, you dumb motherfucker, Kendra thinks, but she doesn't voice it out loud. Arguing with him will do no good at all. At best, he'll call the police. At worst, he'll shoot her between the eyes and tell the cops he thought she was a relapse.

"Sorry for wasting your time," she says even though she isn't.

He doesn't reply, but he doesn't take his eyes off her either. Kendra turns around and walks back into the lobby, then out into the afternoon heat. Her clothes, bought when she was thirty pounds heavier, are flopping around on her frame. They smell like sickness, a faint sweet-and-sour whiff that follows her wherever she goes. She can't stand her own smell, but no deodorant has a chance of covering it up for long, not in the Southern summer.

When she gets back to the car, the alarm on her wrist chirps. Injection time.

The prick of the needle hurts, but it's almost pleasant compared to what follows. The serum burns in her veins like battery acid. When it reaches the brain, a wave of nausea makes her retch. She knows that for the next hour, she will feel sick enough to want to die. But as unpleasant as the injection is, the serum will keep her from rotting, keep her from losing her mind again. The disease isn't gone, just arrested, and the serum in her blood keeps it at bay.

Kendra pushes the plunger all the way in and rides out the nausea with her eyes closed. She sits and feels the sweat running down her face and back, permeating the worn seat covers with the stench of her condition.

There's a knock on the window. Kendra opens her eyes and sees one of the bank's security guards. This one carries a shotgun and forty pounds of flab. The guard motions for her to move along, and Kendra starts the engine and drives off without arguing. Trigger fingers are twitchier now than they used to be.

Home is a worn-out government trailer in a mobile home park, set up in the parking lot of a long-vacant industrial site by the

Interstate overpass. There's a fence all around the lot, but the barbed wire at the top is angled inward, not out.

Out in front of the lot stands a huge granite block that used to hold a corporate logo. The old letters are long gone, and someone has spray-painted an updated location marker onto it: ROTTERTOWN.

They've broken into her trailer again. The front door is ajar, and the screen door slowly bangs against the frame in the stifling almost-breeze of the evening. This is the third time in three weeks, but it doesn't matter. The trailer is just a place to sleep, marginally safer and a little less filthy than a highway bridge overpass. Kendra keeps all her remaining money—what little there is left—in a lockbox somewhere else. Nothing here has any value.

The mattress is still in the bedroom, but someone has sliced it open. Fuzzy polyester guts are poking out of the untidy cut. It doesn't matter. Kendra takes off her clothes, puts the sheet back on the wounded mattress, and lies down.

She does not sleep well anymore, not since the serum hauled her back out of the fever-dream of the infection. She has no memories of that month, but the dreams that sometimes seep into her consciousness give her glimpses of it: blood and hot asphalt, rage and hunger, and always fear.

In the morning, Kendra goes back to her old neighborhood. This time the roadblocks are unmanned, for the first time in days. The recovery teams have done their work, and there's nothing left to loot.

The subdivision was a quiet nest of cul-de-sacs before the Outbreak. Now it's a deserted row of burned-out shells, like ruined teeth in a diseased jaw. They have closed the access street with concrete barriers, so she parks the car and walks a quarter mile in the brutal heat of the afternoon. Every house is scorched and broken here. What the Infected didn't destroy, the military finished off when they started containing the Outbreak. For the first few weeks, before the serum, they turned to fire for purification.

They had a house here: green-and-white cloth awnings, a small fence around a tiny front yard, a swing set for their daughter in the backyard, flowers in little planters underneath the kitchen window. Only the outside brick walls survived. They stand blackened and roofless, bereft of Josh's crafty little touches. In the backyard, Abby's swing set looms, the plastic seats melted away to leave only the chains dangling from the metal tubing.

This was her whole life, everything she owned and everyone she cared about, right up until the day she left for work and arrived at the office with a pounding headache that wouldn't quit. Her husband and child would have been at home when it happened. Did they die here? Or did they try to flee the city, away from the epicenters of infection that suddenly started blooming all over?

He would have taken Abby and gone to his parents, she decides. The phone systems are still only working intermittently, and she hasn't been able to get through to her in-laws. The parking spot in front of the house is empty, her husband's Jeep gone from its usual spot. With the Jeep, he would have been able to get around clogged highway interchanges and roadblocks.

She hurries back to the spot where she left her car, and for the first time since they woke her up in the hospital, she feels hope. It twists her guts, bids her aching legs to run faster, makes her forget the nausea and the constant whiff of sour decay coming from her in waves on this summer day. She had given up on the feeling, but it's the first evidence that she may still be more than just biologically alive.

Her in-laws live in the next state, out in the country on a hundred acres of farmland. They probably weathered the Outbreak, with their chickens and pigs and his mother-in-law's cellar full of canned and pickled goods.

Kendra fills up her car on the outskirts of town and drives north, as fast as her old shit-box will go.

Before the Outbreak, the drive to the in-laws took three hours. In this new world of power outages, unlit streets, random roadblocks, and whole stretches of devastated Interstate highways, it takes much longer. By the time Kendra crosses the state line, it's dark outside, and the gas tank is half empty.

Out here in the country, things look the way they did before the Outbreak. There is electricity, and none of the farmhouses are scarred by flamethrowers or machine gun fire. Kendra drives down the familiar back roads with the windows down, and the smell of the grass and the songs of the nocturnal bugs make her feel almost human again for a while, as if the last few weeks have merely been a particularly unpleasant nightmare. But she is driving this road by herself for the first time, without Josh and Abby, and the empty seats in the car are a reminder that none of this was a dream.

The farm of her in-laws sits on a hill away from the road. Kendra steers up the driveway slowly, lest they think her unfamiliar car is a threat, even though the possibility of her husband and child being just a hundred yards away from her makes the impatience burn painfully in her chest.

The front door opens even before she has put the car in park. Her mother-in-law steps out, a shotgun cradled in the nook of her arm. When she sees Kendra, she drops the gun and covers her mouth with both hands. The shotgun clatters onto the welcome mat.

Even at night, she can't hide her condition. Kendra sees her mother-in-law's gaze flit to the road map pattern of discolored veins on her face and neck, the tattoo of the reclaimed rotter.

"My God, Kendra," she says. She does not come to hug her the way she usually does. "You too?"

"Yeah," she says. "Me too. Are Josh and Abby here?"

Her mother-in-law's hands go back in front of her mouth, and Kendra sees her eyes glistening with a sudden rush of tears. They run down her cheeks and onto her hands, but she makes no attempt to wipe them away.

"We hoped they were with you," her mother-in-law says. "One way or another. Not a word since it all happened."

The hope Kendra had held in her chest for two hundred miles dissipates with a swell of nausea that makes the pain from the injections seem like banality. She sits down on the side of her car's hood.

Her father-in-law appears in the door behind his wife. He too carries a shotgun. His hands clench around the wood of the gun's stock and forearm, and his mouth becomes an unsmiling sharp line. For a long moment, Kendra looks at the father of her husband, convinced that the old man will bring up the gun and shoot her dead on the spot. Part of her wishes he would.

Then the old man turns abruptly and goes back into the house. A few moments later, Kendra hears a door slam shut inside, and then the door of the nearby garage rattles open on squeaking tracks. A car engine starts, and Kendra's father-in-law drives his truck out of the garage and down the driveway without sparing another look.

He never really cared much for me anyway, Kendra thinks. Now he finally has a reason to hate me outright.

"I'll leave," she tells her mother-in-law.

"He'll come around," she says. "Just stay in town somewhere. I'll talk to him."

"I have to go. I have to keep looking."

Her mother-in-law nods. She does not protest. She does not ask Kendra inside, does not offer at least a bed for the night in the house where she has been a welcome guest a hundred times. She realizes that the older woman too will be glad to see her gone. Whatever their ties before the Outbreak, they broke when she showed up tonight a reclaimed Rotter, without their only son and grandchild.

She gets back behind the wheel of her car, but when she turns the key, nothing happens. She tries a few more times, but there's not even a click from the starter, even though the instrument lights are all on. Kendra is too drained to even curse. She puts her forehead against the steering wheel and closes her eyes.

"Take my old truck," her mother-in-law says. "It's been sitting in the garage for weeks now anyway. I'll get the keys."

The truck is almost as dilapidated as the car that brought her here, but it starts on the first try, and the tank is full. Kendra knows that her mother-in-law is purchasing her departure with the old pickup, but she finds that she doesn't mind the deal.

"Good luck," her mother-in-law says to her as Kendra drives off. She just nods. The hurt of the rejection is raw, but it's nothing compared to the disappointment of not finding Josh and Abby here.

Kendra doesn't look back as she leaves the driveway. Instead, she checks the air conditioning. The air coming out of the vent stays warm and humid. There are no comforts for her tonight.

There's a nation-wide curfew now, midnight to sunrise. Kendra parks the truck by the side of the road when the clock on the dash reads 11:55. She lies down across the backseat to sleep.

In her dreams, she is back at the old house in the 'burbs, burned down to nothing but stumps of charred brick walls. She walks through the ruin and kneels to sift through the ashes with her bare hands.

When she hears shuffling footsteps from the driveway behind her, she knows what she will see even before she turns around. She tries to will herself to wake up before she can see what's coming up the driveway, but the dream won't let her go. She stands up and turns her head to see Josh and Abby staggering toward her, both Rotters too far gone for the serum. There's no hint of recognition in their decomposing faces, just the dull, furious hunger of the Infected.

There's a gun in her waistband, the little thirty-eight she made Josh sell when Abby got old enough to walk. She takes it out and aims it at her husband and child, now just a little more than an arm's length away. Then she shoots them both between the eyes. They fall like clumsy toddlers as the sharp cracks of the shots roll across the ruined suburb.

She puts the gun to her own head, but before she can pull the trigger, the dream lets her go and she wakes up.

The seat covers are soaked with her sweat. Kendra sits up and rolls down the window to let the cool morning air in. She has slept for six hours, but she does not feel rested at all.

She's still shaking off the sleep when the alarm on her wrist starts screaming. She turns it off and fishes one of the disposable serum injectors out of her shirt pocket. There are only two left—she will have to return to Rottertown today to get a new stash. They dole it out in three-day supplies, just enough to keep the Reclaimed tied to their home areas.

She fumbles the injector, and it falls from her fingers and bounces onto the floor of the truck. She leans forward and searches for the injector amid the mess of discarded food wrappers and other travel debris that covers the floor of the car.

Her fingers find not one, but two injectors.

She pulls them up one by one. The first is her own injector, still full. The other one is empty, judging by the weight. The plastic safety cover over the needle end has been put back into place, but the seal is broken. She looks at the label. It says Z-STOFF(r) BAYER AG — 15mg

The sticker on her own, full injector has the same label, but the dosing information says "30mg". Fifteen milligrams is a half-dose, a child's dose.

There's only one reason why her mother-in-law's truck would have a discarded half-dose injector of serum on the floor mat. The realization makes her sick enough to double over. She sits for a while with her eyes closed and her forehead pressed against the steering wheel. When the alarm chirps again to remind her of her injection, she is briefly tempted to rip the device off her wrist and throw it out of the open window along with the full injector, to let things take their course.

Then she recalls Abby's face. She has seen it every day since her daughter was born. She knows every line in its perfect topography, and she can't picture it with the merciless tattoo of serum-tinted rotter veins.

She rips the safety cover from her injector with her teeth and rolls up the sleeve of her shirt to find a vein. When she sticks the needle into her arm, the rush of nausea is an almost welcome distraction this time.

When Kendra pulls up in front of her in-laws' house again, she throws the truck into park and leaves it idling in the middle of the driveway. The front door is locked, and she pounds against it with her fist, channeling the grief and anger she feels into the blows, yelling out her in-laws' names with each one.

"Where is she?" she shouts when the door finally opens, and her mother-in-law looks at her with wide and fearful eyes.

"I told you, we haven't—"

"No," Kendra interrupts, her voice just short of a scream. She fishes the vial she found earlier out of her shirt pocket and throws it toward her mother-in-law, who recoils from the object flying at her face.

"I know what you told me. And I know you're lying to me. Where is Abby?"

The older woman opens her mouth and starts stammering a response, but Kendra is out of patience. She pushes her way into the house, and when her mother-in-law tries to block her way, she shoves her aside. Then she strides into the hallway, toward the kitchen and living room, and starts calling her daughter's name.

She makes it all the way through the living room and to the threshold of the kitchen when her father-in-law pumps a round into the chamber of his shotgun behind her. Kendra turns to find him aiming the weapon at her with trembling hands. The muzzle of the twelve-gauge looks like a highway tunnel from only three feet away.

"Get out," he barks, and his voice cracks on the second syllable. *"Get. Out."*

Yesterday, with fatigue and uncertainty dragging on every muscle and bone in her body, she would have complied. But the hope kindled by the knowledge of her daughter's survival has pushed everything else in her brain aside, even the fear.

"No," she says. "Abby's here. Shoot me if you're going to, but don't lie to me. Not about her."

Her father-in-law wavers a little. She can see the anguish in his eyes, but he doesn't lower the gun.

"Shoot me, then," she says again.

Seeing him standing there and trying to decide whether to pull the trigger kindles a sudden and all-encompassing fury in Kendra. He shouldn't have to decide. She has been in this house for birthdays and holidays, eaten meals in the dining room and laughed with the rest of the family, swum in the pool set up in the backyard every summer, grilled hot dogs and drank cold beer on the lawn on the Fourth of July. The father of her husband shouldn't have to think about whether to shoot the woman that married his son and gave him his beloved grandchild.

Kendra lets the lid blow off that boiling rage. She takes a step forward and grabs the barrel of the shotgun to wrench it aside, away from her face. As she does, the gun goes off with a bang that is deafening in the confines of the living room. She feels the hot gases from the muzzle blast slapping the side of her face like a physical punch. Her father-in-law cries out in surprise and fear, and she yanks the shotgun out of his hands by the barrel. He did decide to pull the trigger, to end her after all.

He retreats to the doorway as she grabs the shotgun like a club and comes after him. As she swings it at his head, he slumps down against the door frame, and the butt of the gun hits the wall above his head, punching a crater into the drywall and dusting him with debris. He curls up into a cower and covers his head with his hands.

Kendra takes out her fury on the living room instead. She screams out her anger as she swings the weapon in wide arcs and starts smashing things, using the buttstock like an axe. The glass of the showcase holding her mother-in-law's porcelain collectibles bursts into a thousand pieces that spray onto the hardwood floor. She smashes the porcelain too, sweeping everything out of the case. She sweeps the artwork off the walls, the books from the shelves, the candy bowl off the coffee table, then smashes the table for good measure, blow after blow with the butt of the shotgun until it splinters and comes loose from the rest of the weapon. There are family pictures on a shelf, photos of her and Josh and Abby in various stages of their lives, always smiling and happy, relics from another lifetime. Kendra smashes them all to pieces. If her mind can't hold on to the memories of that life, they don't deserve them either.

Her rage only starts to ebb from her when every breakable thing in the living room is bashed into shards and splinters. She drops the broken shotgun into the rubble of the ruined coffee table. Over by the door, her mother-in-law is hunched down next to her husband, protectively cradling him in her arms. When Kendra walks up to them, she looks up with fear in her eyes.

"Abby," Kendra says, a question and command rolled into one word. The older woman lowers her eyes, and when she looks at Kendra again, the fear has given way to resignation.

Her daughter is in the old playroom down in the basement, in the quietest corner of the house. She's asleep, and the smell of rotter sickness and medications permeates the air down here. Kendra wants to rush over to the bed and gather her in her arms, but Abby looks so exhausted and insubstantial that she can't bring herself to wake her child up even though the desire is boring a hole through her chest from the inside. Kendra walks over to the bed on light feet and bends over her daughter's sleeping form. Abby's sweaty forehead has hair plastered to it, and Kendra brushes it out of her face gently and carefully. The rotter tattoo on her child's face is weak, but undeniable, faded green and blue veins beneath her pale and otherwise flawless skin. But Abby is alive, and the sight of her daughter makes Kendra feel like the part of herself that was broken into pieces when the Outbreak began is coming back together. It's the first time since the start of the nightmare that she is feeling an emotion other than anger or fear, and she's profoundly glad to find out that the virus didn't excise her ability to love.

She stays that way for a while, watching her daughter sleep, taking in the sight and smell of her, wiping the sweat beads off her forehead with a feather-light hand. When she finally gets up and leaves the room, she finds that her mother-in-law has been waiting for her in the hallway the entire time. She suspects that she knows the answer to the question she is about to ask, but she asks it anyway because it's the missing third of her life from before, and whatever closure the answer holds is better than a question mark.

"What about Josh?"

His grave is at the far end of the backyard, by the line of dogwoods that ring the property. It's a nice spot, shady and cool, even if the grass is now standing knee-high all around it. Nobody wastes fuel on landscaping anymore. Her mother-in-law started crying when they stepped out of the front door, and when they both step up to the grave, Kendra's eyes are burning as well, but the tears refuse to come, as if releasing them will mean that she's acknowledging the reality that Josh is dead.

"What happened?" she asks, and her own voice sounds to her like it's coming from the bottom of a well.

"They got here a week after it started," her mother-in-law says. "But he was too far gone. Nobody knew about the serum yet. We took them both to the hospital over in town, but there was a roadblock." She sobs.

"He wasn't himself anymore, Kendra. He went for one of the soldiers, and they shot him. Right there in the middle of the street. Like a rabid dog."

The older woman kneels in front of the grave and buries her face in her hands.

"They let us take him back to bury. The doctors said Abby would have been beyond saving too if we had gotten her there six hours later."

She breaks down into sobs. Before all of this, Kendra would have felt the urge to kneel beside her and offer comfort, but after what happened today, she can't bring herself to feel empathy. Half of her future is buried in the ground by her feet, but the other half is sleeping back at the house, and Josh's parents tried to steal it from her, send her away into the wilderness without anything to live for.

"Give me some time with him, please," she says.

Alone, Kendra sits at the grave in silence, running her fingers through the dark soil. There's nothing about this mound of dirt that reminds her of Josh in any way, his soft hands or his easy laugh, his casual but razor-sharp wit. Whatever is in the ground here is not him. She knows that he didn't leave her behind on purpose, that when things went apocalyptic, his main objective was to get Abby to safety. Once, before the world as they knew it had ended, they talked about dying in their old age, and they had both concluded they'd want to go together. But that was before they had Abby. And as much as Kendra wants to make good on their resolution and join her husband here underneath the dogwoods, she has to pick up the thread he laid down for her at the cost of his life, because even though she is still broken, she is no longer alone in the world.

"I'm taking her with me," Kendra says to her mother-in-law back at the house, in a tone that leaves no room for an argument. They forfeited their right to a discussion when they tried to keep her daughter from her, and from the pained look her mother-in-law gives her, Kendra can tell that she knows it. Her father-in-law still tries because that's the sort of man he is.

"To where?" he says from the kitchen table where he is sitting, hunched over and looking twice his age right now. "What kind of future does she have out there? You leave her here with us, she'll be safe. We have food. Pigs. Chickens. Nobody bothers us out here."

"I'm her mother," Kendra says. "And whatever you think I am now, she is that too."

"She's all we have left now," her mother-in-law says in a pleading voice. "All that's left of Josh. After all we've been through..."

"After all you've been through," Kendra repeats. She sees the look her in-laws exchange, and then she begins to understand. She looks at her hands. The soil from Josh's grave is still under her fingernails.

They didn't bury the rotters, she thinks. *The army incinerated them, in mass graves. They'd never let anyone take their dead home.*

"Which one of you had to do it?" she asks slowly.

They don't respond. They don't even meet her gaze. Her mother-in-law lets out a long, drawn-out sob and buries her face in her hands again. Her father-in-law just stares at the table in front of him, and Kendra can see that he's kneading his shaking hands. For the first time since she arrived, she feels sorrow for them. But it's not enough to let her forgive what they tried to do to her. Abby is all she has left, too, and she does not owe them the rest of their lives with her child just so they can have their absolution.

Behind her, Kendra hears the patter of bare feet on the hardwood floor. She turns around and sees Abby walking down the hallway, tousle-haired, clutching the stuffed squirrel they got her at the museum in D.C. last year. She blinks when she sees Kendra standing in the kitchen.

"Mommy?" she asks, in a small and halting voice.

Kendra rushes to embrace her daughter, and for the first time in months, she feels tears rolling down her cheeks. It's good to know that she can still cry, to feel enough for tears to come. Whatever she was during that month of feral insanity, and whatever else she may be now, she's a mother again, and she will give up her life before she loses that.

They drive south in the lingering heat of the late afternoon, but Kendra doesn't mind the temperature right now. She is driving with the windows rolled down, and she keeps glancing at Abby, whose long hair is fluttering in the wind as she holds her squirrel out of the window to make it surf the air currents rushing past the car. In Kendra's lap, there's a toiletries bag with ten thousand in cash and all their remaining serum doses, Abby's and hers. She figures they can make Rottertown well before the curfew. Tomorrow morning, she will get more serum for them both, enough to last them for a long drive away from this state. In the north, the weather is cooler. Maybe up in the rural areas of the snow belt, there are still places willing to rent to the Reclaimed instead of making them live in trailers out on fenced-in parking lots. Down here, the summers are too stifling, and the memories of their old lives are everywhere.

"Where are we going, mommy?" Abby asks. Kendra finds that she already barely notices the serum tattoo under her daughter's skin.

"Home," she replies.

Outside, there's a thunderstorm brewing above the horizon, and the air carries the scent of distant rain sweeping across the hills, washing away the smells of dust and gasoline as it rolls over the land.

Accidental Ace: How To Move Spheres And Influence People

As I have mentioned in the introductions to some of the other stories in this volume, the stories that turn out best for me are almost always the ones that just popped into my head and demanded to be written down.

The idea for this novella, a teenage girl with a disability suddenly becoming a powerful ace, had its genesis in another Wild Cards story, "The Thing About Growing Up In Jokertown" by the insanely talented Carrie Vaughn. It's the origin story of one of her aces, and what grabbed me about it was the tone—a third-person, present-tense narrative that conveyed intimacy and immediacy, a perfect match for the mind of a teenage protagonist. When I finished reading it, I wanted to capture that same tone in a story of my own, and Tilly "T.K." Kendall stepped into my head, a shy red-headed teenage girl with a disability whose card turns in gym class at her private school.

Don't tell Khan, but I think this novella is my favorite Wild Cards contribution. I wrote it quickly because it bounced its way to the top of my writing priorities right away and sent it to GRRM completely out of the blue and out of turn. Luckily, he liked it as well, and it was published on tor.com as part of Tor's Wild Cards rotation.

How To Move Spheres And Influence People

A Wild Cards Story

1 -- Card, Turning

The first time it happens, she's in P.E. class, because of course it has to be P.E.

It's fashionable to hate P.E., and most of the other girls at Mapletree Academy claim they do, but T.K. really doesn't mind it. It's only twice a week, and they mostly stick to sports she can do with her one working arm. She knows she could easily get out of P.E. by pulling the Cripple Card (although she never calls it that; her parents and teachers would flinch in horror at her own insensitivity toward *herself*, go figure), but she doesn't because she likes to run around even if she's not very good at it. She also doesn't want to give her stuck-up classmates the satisfaction of being able to shoot her pitying glances as she sits on the sidelines and eats Goldfish crackers while doing her math homework. Truth be told: it's the only time during the week when T.K. doesn't feel like everyone's pussyfooting around her disability.

They're playing dodgeball that day, at the end of the class. T.K. is pretty good at it considering she can only use one arm, even if she gets nailed by the ball a little more than the other girls. But this session is a shooting gallery, with her as the target. Again. It's just two girls who are targeting her specifically—and her left side, too, where she can't block—but they're stealthy about it so Mrs. Williams, the P.E. teacher, doesn't come down on them. For some reason, Brooke MacAllister has decided that if T.K. wants to play with the varsity, she can take the hits too. And for this week, she seems to have recruited Alison Keller to be her wingman, because T.K. is getting targeted fire from two angles. Mapletree has a special version of dodgeball where you have to crank out five push-ups on the spot if you get hit. Mrs. Williams wanted to give her a waiver on the push-ups, but T.K. refused the special treatment. She's not strong enough for one-armed pushups, but she can do crunches just fine, so she does those instead. And today, she's doing a lot of crunches courtesy of Brooke and Alison. In the middle of her fifth set, a ball comes in and beans her on the left side of the head just as she is coming up from a crunch.

"Ow!"

T.K. glares in the direction of the ball's origin and spots Brooke, who gives her a curt and jock-like *"Sorry!"* without even the slightest tone of apology in her voice. T.K. doesn't want to make anything of it, so she doesn't even look for Mrs. Williams, but she has her limits, and Brooke's attention is starting to poke at the edges of them. She finishes her crunches and gets back up to rejoin the ranks. Another ball shoots past her face, so close that she can practically smell the rubber, and she ducks and flinches. This one came from the other side of the court, from Alison's direction, but Alison pretends not to notice T.K.'s glare as she conspicuously picks another target. T.K. grabs a ricochet off the gym floor and chucks it at Alison, but it misses her by a foot and smacks into the mats lining the wall behind her. Alison looks over to T.K. and smirks, which only serves to crank up the dial of T.K.'s Pissed-Off-O-Meter another notch. She can't really complain about them throwing balls at her, because that's what the game is about. But getting singled out for no good reason takes the fun out of it.

"One minute," Mrs. Williams shouts from the sideline. "Wrap it up, ladies!" Then she turns around and checks her cell phone. T.K. groans.

"Don't you—" she calls over to Brooke, but Brooke does, and so does Alison. Of course they were waiting for the opportunity for one last cheap shot. Alison's shot hits T.K.'s right thigh and bounces off. Brooke's ball comes in a flat arc, and T.K. knows that she'll take the stupid thing right on the bridge of her nose.

That's when the thing happens.

Later, she'll puzzle about what triggered it. She's hot and

sweaty, angry at Brooke and Alison, hurting from the shot to the bare skin of her leg, and the muscles on her left side, the one with the paralysis, are taut enough to snap, which is what happens when she overexerts herself. But she knows that she feels a swell of fresh anger, and something goes snap in her brain. There's a hot, trickling sensation, like someone just opened the top of her skull and poured a cup of coffee directly on the back side of her brain and down her spinal column. T.K. raises her hand to keep the ball from hitting her in the face, even though she knows it's too late for that. But then the strangest sensation follows the hot trickle. She can feel the ball not three feet in front of her face—its roundness, the way it displaces the air around it—and she gives it a tiny little shunt with her mind, and it's the best feeling she's ever had, like finally scratching an itch you couldn't get to for an hour, only a hundred times better. The ball—the one that was about to give her a nosebleed—hooks ever so slightly to the left and whizzes past her left side, close enough to her ear that she can hear it whistling through the air.

Nobody notices. T.K. isn't even sure that Brooke saw the ball didn't fly true, that it made a little skip at the end of its arc. There are still half a dozen other balls in the air, and there's a lot of movement and yelling, kids paying attention to throwing or not getting hit. But she is dead sure that she caused that little skip, because she knows that for just that half second, the ball was in her control, and that it went precisely where she had wanted it to go.

They hit the showers and get dressed, and T.K. is too amazed and shaken to seek out Brooke and Alison to bitch at them. Now that P.E. is over, nobody pays attention to her anymore. In the first few weeks after she joined the class, her awkward-looking one-handed maneuver to get back into her bra and shirt got some interest from the other girls in the locker room, but that's old hat now, and she finishes up and leaves as quickly as she can.

P.E. was the last class of the day, and now they have an hour of library time before dinner. But T.K. doesn't feel much like going to the library. Instead, she unloads her backpack at the dorm and then goes back to the gym.

She had figured the place to be empty by now, because Mrs. Williams usually leaves on time. But when she walks back in, Mrs. Williams is still there, walking toward the door with a bag on each shoulder.

"Tilly," Mrs. Williams says, and T.K. tries not to frown. Most of the teachers address her by her chosen name instead of Tilly, which she hates almost as much as its proper long form, Lintilla. She knows she's named for a great-grandmother she never even knew, but "Lintilla" sounds like a species of exotic rodent to her. So she was Tilly until she was thirteen, at which point she decided that "T.K." was edgier than "Tilly Kendall." Like she's a New York City spray tagger or a skateboarder instead of a skinny fifteen-year-old redhead from rural Vermont with freckles and left-side hemiparesis. But Mrs. Williams insists on using her actual name, which strikes T.K. as slightly disrespectful.

"Mrs. W," she replies. "I, uh, forgot something in the locker room."

It's a quick and shoddy lie, but Mrs. Williams, loaded down with bags as she is and clearly in a hurry, buys it without trouble. Besides, the gym is always open for the students anyway—there's a keypad at the door and everyone knows the code, and what kind of trouble can you get into in a school gym?

"Well, go get it. But make sure the door is latched when you leave, okay? The latch sticks sometimes if you don't push it shut all the way."

"Will do, Mrs. W," T.K. says. "Have a good evening."

"See you tomorrow, Tilly."

T.K. heads toward the girls' locker room and pauses in the doorway to wait for the "click" of the sticky door latch. Then she turns and goes to the door that leads into the gym. That feeling she had just a little while ago, when she moved that ball away from her face, had been the most wicked rush of her life, and she wants to see if she can repeat it.

The balls in the gym are neatly stashed away in nets hanging from the wall on the back of the gym, right next to the equipment lockers. T.K. walks over to one of the nets and pulls it open. She fishes out a ball and tosses it into the middle of the gym, where it bounces a few times and rolls to a stop.

"Here goes nothing," T.K. says to herself. Her voice echoes a little in the empty gym.

She's afraid that the moment of total control during the game was a fluke, a one-time thing, some momentary and non-recurring phenomenon, maybe a glitch in her brain. That she'll stand here in the gym and stare at that ball like an idiot for a bit while nothing happens. But when she concentrates, that control comes back with absurd ease. It's like looking at the curve of the sphere throws a switch in her mind, one that wasn't there before. It's not as strong as it was the first time around, but when she feels the curvature of the ball with whatever new sense her brain has flipped on with that switch, that feeling of deep satisfaction comes back, and she knows that it wasn't a momentary thing. It feels like she's holding that sphere in the palm of an invisible hand, one that's much more strong and limber and precise than her own.

T.K. laughs with relief. Then she picks up the ball with her mind and flicks it halfway across the court to the basketball rim on the far end. The ball hits the rim and bounces off. Before it can hit the gym floor, she picks it up again without effort, raises it slowly, and dumps it straight through the hoop.

"Holy shit," she says and laughs again.

She has superpowers. She's a damn *ace*.

For the next hour, well into dinnertime, T.K. practices in the empty gym. She pitches the ball all over the place, and every time she does, she gets more accurate with it. It's like her new talent is a muscle that can be made stronger with practice. When she tries to manipulate other things, other shapes, that feeling of control evaporates, almost like the angles on the thing poke through whatever force she uses on the spheres and pops the bubble. But if it's round, she is in full control of it. She tries one of the heavy medicine balls out of the equipment locker, the ones she can't even lift with her own physical strength, but with the new power she just turned on, it's just as easy to throw those as it is to pitch a basketball. She throws the medicine ball around until she gets a little too giddy and tries to slam-dunk it onto the hoop rim. It smacks against the backboard hard enough to make the nearby windows shake, and the crash from the heavy ball on the board is so loud that she's sure they'll hear it all the way up in the library. She quickly picks up the medicine ball and moves it back to the equipment shack, before someone can come in and wonder how the partially paralyzed girl managed to move a twenty-five-pound ball ten feet up in the air by herself. Then T.K. tidies up and leaves the gym to head back up the hill to the dorm, with some reluctance.

2 -- Soda Cans and Brick Walls

The next day, T.K. can barely muster the patience to sit through her classes. She was up until three in the morning, playing with tennis balls and marbles in her room, experimenting and chasing that euphoric feeling of control. The tiredness makes the day even longer and more unbearable. She has an idea for the afternoon, and she can't wait for the clock to hit 3 p.m.

When classes are finally over for the day, she rushes back to the dorm to dump her backpack and her books. Then she leaves the school property to go to the mixed-use building that sits just a quarter mile away from campus on the rural road. There's a country store here and a pizza joint, and the back of the building houses a little post office and a hardware store that's much bigger than it looks from the outside. T.K. usually comes here to get snacks, just like lots of other Mapletree students, but today the stuff she wants is in the hardware store.

The store has quarter-inch ball bearings at seventy cents apiece, individually bagged. She cleans off the whole peg, a dozen bags, and carries them to the register. T.K. has an alibi handy if they want to know why she needs a dozen ball bearings—school science experiments—but she must not look particularly shady, because the clerk rings her up without comment. Then she spots little plastic containers of BBs on the shelf behind the clerk and asks for one of those too, fully expecting to be treated like an aspiring terrorist any second. But the clerk just adds the total to the bill—eight bucks—and bags her stuff for her. She reads the label on the pellet container right before he bags it: 2,400 BBs.

Well, I wanted to know if I can do multiple spheres at once, she thinks. *Guess I'll find out.*

There's an old, abandoned factory half a mile away from Mapletree Academy, dilapidating on the bank of the Connecticut River. A few of the juniors and seniors sometimes go there to drink, but the place isn't much of a hangout, littered as it is with old factory debris and broken glass. But it's away from people, and there's nothing T.K. can break here that's not already broken.

She brought a twelve-pack of soda from the country store, and for her first experiment, she lines up three cans on a crumbling brick wall in the central yard between the buildings. Then she walks back fifty yards and unbags her ball bearings. They feel weighty and serious, both in her hand and in her mind, when she lifts them one at a time with her power. T.K. expects the first one to drop to the ground when she lifts the second one, but it doesn't. She grins as she repeats the process, and three quarter-inch ball bearings are floating in the air in front of her.

She gives the first one a push, about as much as she pushed the basketball yesterday. It shoots off and knocks the first can off its perch. It lands on the pock-marked concrete with a huge dent in the center. T.K. finds that even at fifty yards, aiming the spheres isn't difficult at all. She pushes the second ball bearing a little harder than the first. This one streaks across the yard in a blur and punches into the second can dead-center, sending soda spraying everywhere.

T.K. concentrates on the last floating ball bearing and pushes it as hard as she can.

The third can disintegrates in a spray of soda and aluminum

shrapnel. She knows the ball bearing went through the can and into the brick wall of the building twenty yards behind because she can see the puff of brick dust and hear the shattering brick as the bearing cracks it.

"Whoa," she murmurs, awed by the power she just unleashed with nothing more than half a second of concentration. She could seriously hurt somebody with this ability, even kill them.

T.K. steps up to the brick wall of the building she just shot with her ball bearing. Several of the bricks are cracked from the impact, and one of them is almost completely gone. She can see the hole the bearing made as it passed through. It went right through four inches of brick, and she suspects it also went through the back wall of that building, because that quarter-inch ball of steel was moving fast.

She spends half an hour experimenting with the rest of the ball bearings. She target-shoots the rest of the soda cans and finds that she can modulate her power very precisely, right down to the point where she can send a sphere right into a can with just enough power to knock it down without even denting it. Used like this, she can retrieve her ammunition and reuse it instead of having to dig it out of holes in broken bricks.

Then T.K. opens the container of BBs. They're so much tinier and lighter than the ball bearings that it hardly seems she'll be able to do much with them, no matter how fast she pushes them. So she pours them out on the ground in a pile and then tries to lift as many as she can at once.

They all rise like a little silver cloud in front of her—all 2,400 of them.

"No way!" T.K. laughs.

Then she starts playing with them like they're a flock of birds, moving them in one direction, then another, sideways, up, down. It's weird—she can feel each individual BB in her mind, but she can move them all as a mass, and it feels almost like she's manipulating a liquid made of thousands of perfectly spherical little drops. A hundred of those BBs don't weigh what one of the ball bearings did, but with so many of them in front of her at the same time, she realizes that not much can get through to her if she keeps them moving quickly. She directs the BB cloud into a stream around herself, around and up, then down and up again until it looks like she's the vortex of a metallic tornado. The BBs move so fast that she can't make them out individually anymore. They're just a blur of flashing silver.

It's like armor, she thinks. *Like a suit of armor you can carry around in your pocket.*

And then, on a whim, she wants to see if her power is divided among all those BBs evenly, or if each of them pushes off with the same speed as the ball bearing before, regardless of the number of spheres. And these BBs are tiny and lightweight, and how much damage can they possibly do? So she focuses on the cloud of spheres swirling all around her and pushes out with all her might, shoves them in all directions. They explode out from around her in a flashing ring of polished steel.

The result is instant and terrifying. T.K. hears glass breaking and brick cracking all around her, and for a moment she thinks she killed herself with her new powers, like a complete idiot. There's brick dust in the air, and as she stands there, cowering with her right arm over her head, it settles on her clothing and the ground in front of her.

She looks up and takes a sharp breath. All the way around the yard, the walls look like someone just blasted them with the world's largest shotgun, thousands of little holes bored into the brickwork, whatever glass was remaining in the window frames blown out and pulverized.

"Let's not try that again," she murmurs to herself.

It's kind of sobering to know that she can turn herself into a living shrapnel grenade with nothing but an eight-dollar container of BBs. That's more easy destructive power than she—than anyone—should be allowed to control.

But still, even as cowed as she is by her own display of sphere mayhem, she takes two of the quarter-inch ball bearings and sticks them into the pocket of her jeans as she packs up to go back to Mapletree. After all, you never know when you might need a sphere-shaped object handy in an emergency, and she won't always have a hardware store nearby when she needs one.

3 -- P.E., Reloaded

The next day is a Thursday, which means P.E. again.

T.K. goes into the inevitable round of dodgeball at the end with a live-and-let-live attitude. If it hadn't been for Brooke trying to cream her with a ball two days ago, she wouldn't have discovered what she can do. Or maybe it would have come out of her at some other time. But she's willing to forgive and forget, if Brooke and Alison don't pick her for target practice again.

But whatever chip Brooke has on her shoulder this week, it's still there today. T.K. makes it three minutes until Mrs. W has to take a call on her cell. And sure enough—five seconds after Mrs. W turns her back, a ball comes zooming at T.K. from where Brooke and Alison are playing side by side today. Brooke isn't even hiding that she took that shot. She grins at T.K., who gets smacked on her bare thigh again, in almost exactly the spot the other ball landed two days ago.

T.K. doesn't shout at them to cut it the hell out. She just drops for her five crunches. But even as she does, she keeps an eye on Alison, because she knows that Alison isn't the sharpest crayon in the box and probably thinks she can plant another one while T.K. is crunching away.

Alison takes her shot right as T.K. finishes the last crunch. T.K. knows that both girls are watching her, and that she can't pull the same sort of last-ditch save she performed on Tuesday. So she takes the ball to the side of her head on purpose. It's just a glancing blow, but it clips her ear and hurts, and she yelps involuntarily. Alison and Brooke, satisfied with their strafing run, turn their attention away again.

"All right then," T.K. says. She picks up the ball that bounced off her head. Then she chucks it at the spot where Alison and

Brooke are standing and gives it more push and a more precise direction with her new power.

The gym is noisy, and there's lots of crossfire, so nobody notices the utterly perfect path the ball takes. It flies a foot or more past Brooke's head, who whips her head around and smirks at her as if to congratulate her for the missed shot. But as soon as the ball has passed Brooke's peripheral vision, T.K. accelerates it and makes it bounce off the wall right behind her head. The deflection is implausible for the angle of the throw, but not impossible, and nobody notices anyway. The ball smacks into the back of Brooke's head, and it's just the right angle and momentum to bounce off her skull and hit Alison in the side of the head as well.

Brooke takes the brunt of that hit. T.K. swears she can hear her teeth slam together from the impact even across the noisy gym. Brooke goes to her knees. Next to her, Alison just lets out an indignant *"Ooowww!"* and then looks at Brooke, pissed off, as if her friend had chucked that ball from half a foot away.

T.K. almost laughs. She can do this over and over until they're tired of the game and leave her alone. But she can't help but feel a little bit concerned for Brooke, who's still on her knees and looking dazed, even though T.K. knows that she calibrated the pitch enough to not rattle that girl's cage too hard.

I could have knocked her unconscious, T.K. thinks and looks away.

And then a small voice in her head chimes in.

You could have knocked her head into the next zip code, it says, and it chills her to the bone.

And right then and there she resolves to only use that power on people when she absolutely needs to. It's too much, and it's not right to use it for frivolities like a high school tiff with a stuck-up rich girl who will have forgotten T.K.'s name two days after graduation. And then, despite it all or maybe because of it, she walks over to Brooke to make sure she's all right.

4 -- Edinburgh

Here's the thing about Mapletree: everyone who goes there is pretty much by definition a rich kid. The tuition is fifty grand a year, and there are no scholarships. But T.K. doesn't consider herself one of the rich girls because her allowance is small, and her parents didn't send her to boarding school with a wallet full of credit cards. At the beginning of the holiday break, however, there's no denying that she's from a loaded family. The parking lot in front of the gym looks like an exotic car dealership on pick-up day as all the parents are trying to out-Porsche and out-Benz each other.

Her mom and dad come by precisely twice a year—when they come to pick T.K. up for the summer break, and when they take her home for the holidays. That's when the big ceremonies for the parents take place. It's graduation in June, and the holiday concert in December, everyone dressed up and watching all the grades perform. T.K. supposes that when you shell out that much tuition money, you want to see caps and gowns and hear some uplifting display of liberal arts education at least twice a year. Mapletree doesn't teach any one-handed instruments, so T.K. sings in the choir, which is much more fun than she had expected. The grades do their performances to lightning storms of camera flashlights, a darkened gym full of middle-aged parents all holding up phones like they're at a concert. Then there's the milling and hand-shaking at the end, and then they are released for the holiday break, a whole week sandwiched between two long weekends.

"How was your trimester, sweetie?" her mom asks from the front seat as they are driving the fifty miles back home to Casa Kendall.

For a moment, T.K. thinks about answering truthfully. Oh, it was awesome, Mom. I learned how to move round objects with my mind, and now I could wreck our house with a bowling ball just by thinking hard. She tries to suppress a grin when she imagines that scenario and mostly fails, which her mother takes entirely the wrong way.

"That well, huh?" her mom says and winks knowingly. "Is he a junior or senior?"

T.K. only catches on after a second. Her mom thinks she's

smiling about a boy. As if the whole school didn't have only two hundred students, less than half of them boys, none of whom are exactly falling over themselves to romance the only girl on campus with an obvious handicap. Not when all the other girls are well-bred, pretty, and with left arms that don't hang by their sides like recently broken wings.

"Neither, Mom," T.K. answers. It's not exactly a lie, after all, and her mom takes the evasiveness as cute embarrassment.

"Playing your cards close, I see. Well, I'm glad the trimester was fun for you."

"Where are we going for the holidays?" T.K. asks, mostly to change the subject. Dad always takes them out of the country for the holiday week as a treat. Last year it was Montreal, and the year before they went on a cruise and then stayed in Puerto Rico for three days.

"Edinburgh," her father says from the driver's seat. "Do some Christmas shopping in the old town, see the lights, have some good food. What do you think?"

"Sounds awesome," she says and gives her dad a thumbs-up. Then she sits back in her seat and thinks about the upcoming holidays. If she does the job while her parents aren't watching, hanging all the ornaments on the tree should be super easy this year.

They head to Edinburgh for their usual holiday week fun rituals: shopping, restaurant meals, and enough sightseeing to fill the memory card on her dad's camera even though they've been here half a dozen times at least already. Edinburgh is pretty, especially the old town, which is aglow with Christmas lights everywhere, and it takes T.K. no time at all to get into the holiday spirit when snow starts falling on the evening of their first stay.

On the morning of their second day in Edinburgh, T.K. is out by herself to get Christmas presents for her mom and dad, who are off doing their own thing. Dad's having brunch with an old medical school buddy of his, and mom is getting a massage back at the hotel spa. There's a huge Christmas market set up on George

Street, a rustic village of hundreds of booths and vendor stalls. T.K. spends the morning browsing the rows of merchants and taking in the sights and sounds. By lunchtime, she has converted most of her pocket money into gifts and trinkets for her friends. It's not bitingly cold, but the two hot chocolates from the beverage stalls have worn off, and T.K. is ready to head back to the hotel to stash her purchases and get some lunch.

At the end of George Street, there's a big, park-like square. It's a wide expanse of grass surrounded by a perimeter of trees and a high wrought-iron fence. T.K. is about to cross the street and walk through the park to get to the hotel when she hears a commotion on the other side of the square, screeching tires and then a loud metallic crash. The pigeons on that end of the park take to the sky seemingly all at once. T.K.'s first thought is that someone just had a bad traffic accident. Around her, heads are turning toward the noise. Then there's a second crash, louder than the first one, and then she spots the source of the commotion. A delivery truck has knocked down a section of the iron fence on that side of the park. As T.K. watches, the truck drags part of the fence with it into the park square. There are people walking on the garden pathways of the park, and they are dashing out of the way of the truck now, shouting in alarm.

Everything happened so quickly that T.K. hasn't even had time to get scared yet. After a morning of Christmas lights and warm drinks and cheery holiday mood, the scene unfolding just a hundred yards in front of her seems surreal and out of place. T.K. stands rooted to the sidewalk at the end of George Street, transfixed by the sight of the delivery truck bulling its way across the neatly manicured park, while people around her gape or shout or rush to get out of the street. The truck swerves to avoid the huge statue standing right in the center of the park. As it does, the piece of fencing it was dragging comes loose and clatters against the statue's plinth with a thunderous racket that reverberates across the park.

Three police officers come dashing down George Street and past T.K., shouting at people to get out of the way. They run toward the edge of the park and the approaching truck. Now the crowd really starts moving, as if the appearance of the police makes the danger official and concrete. T.K. glances back down George Street, which is still packed with holiday shoppers. The end of the street is blocked off to traffic, but the barriers are just orange-and-white plastic blocks with hip-high metal fencing at the top.

Two of the police officers try to block the truck as it approaches the gap in the park's perimeter fence where the walkway lets out onto the street where T.K. is standing. They wave their arms and shout at the driver, who pays them no mind. The officers jump out of the way when the truck reaches the gap, which isn't quite wide enough. The front of the truck, already dented and scraped from the previous collision, smashes into the iron fencing and knocks it aside. The truck's forward momentum is slowed down briefly by the barrier, but the truck's driver revs the engine and starts to push through.

Up until now, T.K. thought it may have been an accident, or maybe a medical emergency. But then she sees the face of the driver through the windshield of the truck. He doesn't look like he's scared or in distress. His face is all wide-eyed focus, so devoid of obvious emotion that it almost looks like there's a department store mannequin behind the wheel. He steers the truck slightly to the right, then to the left again, to shunt the sections of fencing aside that are scraping along the side of the truck's cabin. One of the policemen jumps up onto the running board on the driver's side and hammers a baton against the window. The driver opens the door abruptly and forcefully, and the police officer goes flying and lands on the sidewalk.

T.K. doesn't consciously decide to act. She just looks at the people crowding the street behind her and the truck that's about to drive right into them in a few moments, and there's no way for her to get all those people out of the way, no way to stop that truck in its tracks. But there are hundreds of decorated Christmas trees all the way down George Street, and almost every stall and vendor booth is festooned with decorations as well. And so many of them are globe-shaped ornaments.

Without thinking about it, T.K. drops her shopping bags, reaches out with her good hand, and lets that newly awakened part of her mind pull every round holiday ornament in sight toward her.

It sounds like a thousand birds taking off all at once. All the way down the street, people shout and yell as trees rustle and sway, and a multicolored swarm of glass and plastic spheres rises into the cold winter air and speeds toward the truck just as the driver has managed to break all the way through the fence. The ornaments are bigger and much lighter than the ball bearings she has been using for practice. T.K. tries to keep control of them all, but they are so light, and there are so many of them, that the light breeze blowing over George Street is enough to make her lose her grip on many of them. It's like trying to hold on to a handful of powdery sand. Dozens of the ornaments fall out of the swarm and bounce or shatter on the street, careen off vendor stall roofs, or bop people in the head. But she manages to hold on to most of them, and there are a lot, many hundreds, maybe thousands. T.K. hurls the stream of colored orbs against the front of the truck, where they start to shatter in little silver-bright explosions.

The ornaments have almost no mass, and they burst against the front of the truck and its windshield without doing damage, spraying glittering fragments of glass and plastic. But the cloud of ornaments T.K. has yanked loose from their trees and light chains has so much volume that dozens of them smash into the windshield every second, a flurry of green and red and silver shards that envelops the front of the truck like a cloud and obscures the driver's vision completely. The truck starts swerving. For a heart-stopping moment, it heads right for T.K., who redoubles her mental efforts. Then the driver swerves back to the right, over-corrects, and clips one of the traffic control barriers. The left front wheel of the delivery truck hits the corner of the barrier, and the truck jolts with the shock of the impact. It careens further to the right, bounces onto the sidewalk, and crashes into the front of the house on the other side of the street.

T.K. releases her hold on all the spheres that are still in the air. They fall to the ground, once again beholden only to gravity, and for a few moments, it's raining Christmas ornaments all over George Street. Maybe five seconds have passed since she started pulling the spheres with her mind and steering them toward the truck, but she feels like she has just run a track relay all by herself.

The policemen run up to the truck's cabin. One of them jumps up on the sideboard again and yanks on the door handle. The door flies open with a bang, so forcefully that one of the hinges pops off. The policeman jumps out of the way at the last instant, and the weight of the door bends the other hinge as well and makes the door flip forward and hit the ground with a shriek of tortured metal. The driver jumps out of the cab and onto the sidewalk, and T.K. lets out a shocked gasp. He's a joker—or whatever they call those in this country. Taller than the biggest of the policemen by at least a head, he is bare-chested, and a set of leathery wings is protruding from his back. But that's not even the most joker-like thing about him. Out of his chest, T.K. sees two extra vestigial arms protruding, each with three long fingers that end in sharp-looking claws. He grabs the nearest policeman by the front of his bulletproof vest, lifts him off his feet, and throws him backwards. The second policeman swings his baton and hits the joker on the side of the head. The joker almost goes to his knees. Then he whips his arm around and returns the blow with a backhand from his left arm. He's much stronger than the policeman, who takes the hit to the side of his head and bounces off the delivery truck's cabin only to crumple to the pavement.

The joker looks around, fury in his face. He yells something, but his Scottish accent is so thick that T.K. can't make out what he's saying. Then his gaze locks on her, and the fury turns to naked hatred in his expression. He gets up from the half-crouch the cop had beaten him into with his baton, and strides toward her. The wings on his back unfold with a little shudder and then pop out to their full extension. They are leathery like a bat's, and they make him look like a gargoyle or a demon from a comic book. She freezes in wide-eyed fear.

Then it's the joker's turn to get wide-eyed. He bellows a strangled scream and falls to his knees. Behind him, the last standing police officer is aiming a small black gun-looking thing at the back of the joker. She can see two little wires coming from the device and reaching all the way to the joker's back, to a spot right between his wings. Whatever the policeman is doing to him must hurt, but it doesn't seem to hurt enough to keep him down. He twitches a bit and rolls around, and his big leathery wings make an awful soft scraping sound on the pavement of the sidewalk. Then he reaches back and yanks the little wires right out of his back. The policeman fumbles with his little black taser thingie, but the joker is getting to his feet again, and T.K. can see that whatever the cop is doing won't be done in time.

She only realizes that she took her two ball bearings out of her pocket when they are floating above her palm and in front of her eyes already. The joker has his back turned to her as he is advancing on the remaining police officer, who is retreating and yelling into his radio.

T.K. doesn't want to kill the guy. She doesn't even want to hurt him. But she does want to keep him from hurting anyone else, and this is the only thing she has right now that will make a difference in time. She focuses on the ball bearings above her palm.

Easy, she reminds herself, remembering the holes she bored clean through bricks with these things not too long ago. *Pretend you want to bop Brooke with a basketball.*

She lets the first one go, but even as it flies toward the joker, she knows that she went a little too light on this shot. The ball bearing hits the joker square in the back of the head. He stumbles and goes to one knee, but catches himself and gets up just as the police officer tries to take advantage of the situation. The policeman tries to use his baton again, but the joker snatches it away from him and throws it aside. Then he grabs the policeman and flings him backwards. The officer crashes into the wall of the house behind him and slumps to the ground.

The joker turns around and glares at T.K. He bares his teeth and tenses his body like someone about to launch into a fifty-yard dash. She doesn't take the time to think about how to calibrate her next shot. She only has one ball bearing left, and there's no time to look around to see where the other one bounced. So she gives it a harder push than before and lets it fly.

The little silver steel orb hits the joker right in the middle of his forehead. This time, she can hear the dull thud of the impact from twenty yards away. And this time, the joker doesn't just go to his knees. He collapses to the pavement like T.K. has just turned off his main power switch. His wings splay out on the sidewalk, and then he lies still.

Sounds come rushing back to her brain like an aural flood. There are sirens everywhere now, and people are shouting and talking all around her. Three more police cars come screaming around the corner, sirens blaring and lights flashing. T.K.'s knees are shaking. She feels like all her energy has drained from her in the last few minutes.

There are police converging on this intersection from all directions now. Someone grabs her shoulder and shouts something at her, but it's like her brain has temporarily lost the ability to understand English. She can't take her eyes off the joker who's lying motionless on the pavement twenty yards in front of her, his wings draped over his body like a shroud.

Then one of the wings twitches a little. She sees a hand rising, then an arm. The joker tries to push himself up or roll on his side, but he doesn't get far because at least half a dozen police officers descend on him and pin him down. But he's alive. She knocked him out, maybe cracked his skull, but she didn't kill him.

T.K.'s legs give out, and she sits down hard on the cold pavement. Then she bursts into tears.

5 -- Aftermath

What was supposed to be a three-day trip to Scotland ends up turning into a week-long event. After Edinburgh, it seems like everyone in the country with a badge or a government ID wants to talk to T.K. Everyone is super nice to her, but she's still having to go to various places guarded by men in uniform who are carrying guns, and she never once has the feeling that all these talks are optional.

Her parents are dumbfounded to find out that their handicapped daughter is basically a superhero now. At first, T.K. is worried that her dad is going to ground her until college. But when he sees that everyone seems grateful for T.K.'s intervention and amazed at her ability, T.K. can tell that he enjoys basking in the positive attention by proxy a little.

After a few days of interviews and unceasing attention, T.K. is kind of over the whole thing. She's tired, both in body and mind. Whatever she did in Edinburgh took as much out of her as finals week in school. And when they spend the last day before their return home in London, she gets nervous every time she hears a car horn or the squealing of tires. The cops tell her that she just knocked the joker terrorist out—only they call him a "knave" instead of a joker here—and she is glad to know that she didn't hurt him permanently or end his life because then she knows she'd never use her ability again. But when she falls asleep in her hotel bed in the evening before the return flight, she sees the angry grimace of the truck's driver in her dreams, that twisted expression of fury directed at her, and she wakes up with her heart pounding in her chest and doesn't close her eyes again for the rest of the night.

Her first inkling that life at home isn't going to be normal again comes when they arrive back in Boston. Before they even get to the immigrations check, three uniformed police officers and two men in dark suits wait for T.K. and her parents on the jetway right outside the plane's door. There's some hushed commotion behind them because the flight attendants are making everyone wait until

T.K. and her folks have deplaned first. She feels uncomfortable with this unexpected attention, and when they grab their carry-on bags and leave the plane, she feels like she has done something wrong. But everyone is cordial and professional. They lead the Kendalls into a quiet room away from all the bustle, and all they want is to have a chat with her about what happened in Scotland, and for her to show them her ability again. They have donuts and coffee, and they're just as friendly as the cops in Scotland, but once again T.K. has the distinct impression that this isn't optional, that she wouldn't be able to just say "no, thank you" and walk out of the room. So she spends two hours with her parents and the cops in yet another boring conference room and retells the same story for the fiftieth time this week. Finally, the men in the dark suits thank her and let them go through immigrations and customs, and T.K. is relieved right up until the point where they walk into the international arrivals hall and see about two hundred camera lenses aimed at them. A crowd of reporters is waiting in ambush, and the flashes that go off when T.K. and her parents walk through the sliding doors leave no doubt about who they're here to see.

"Can we go back to check-in and fly somewhere else?" she says to her dad, even though she's bone-tired and wants nothing more than to go home and crash in her own room and on her own bed. "Like, Antarctica maybe?"

Her father replies with a chuckle, but from the expression on his face, she can see that he's tempted to at least consider the idea.

6 -- Ace, Outed

"Absolutely *not*," her dad barks into the phone downstairs for what seems like the tenth time today. "She's fifteen years old, and she has to go to school on Monday."

At first, the constant barrage of calls and stream of people at the door were amusing to T.K., but the novelty has worn off very quickly. She has been holed up in her room since they got back from Scotland while her parents have been fielding reporter questions and interview requests. Every morning newscast in the country suddenly wants to talk to T.K., and so far her dad has shot down every request. But the phone hasn't stopped ringing even though Casa Kendall has an unlisted number, and T.K. has no idea how she is supposed to make it to school while there are news crews camped out on their street.

"So you basically suck for not telling me about this earlier," Ellie says over the phone. Ellie has been T.K.'s best friend since kindergarten—their families have been friends since T.K. and Ellie were toddlers—and Ellie is one of the few callers who makes it through the mom-and-dad screening vanguard today.

"I didn't know until, like, two months ago, I swear," T.K. says.

"You found out at school?"

"Yeah. In the middle of gym class."

T.K. gives Ellie the condensed version of the week her card turned, leaving out the part where she accidentally found out that she's basically a walking weapon of mass destruction now.

"That's insane," Ellie says. "I saw the news story. The stuff you did in Europe. You're gonna be a rock star at school. You saved people."

"I don't know about rock star. More like freak show, probably. Like I wasn't sticking out enough already."

The thought of returning to Mapletree with her new abilities known to everyone makes T.K. feel queasy. But the cat is out of the bag, and there's no stuffing it back in, not after cell phone camera footage of her from eight different angles showed up on television screens all over the world a few days ago.

"Can you come over?" T.K. asks. "I'd say let's go out to the Creamery and get some monster sundaes, but my folks won't let me within twenty feet of the front door."

"Tell you what," Ellie replies. "You show me your new superpower thing, and I'll come over with a half-gallon of Moose Tracks and two spoons."

T.K. laughs, relieved that at least some things are still the way they were last week, back when she was just a high school girl with a busted wing to everyone.

Thirty minutes later, Ellie walks into T.K.'s room and plops herself down on the bed. She has a grocery bag in her hand, which she puts on T.K.'s nightstand.

"There are six news vans out in the street right in front of your house. This has gotta be the most exciting thing that has ever happened here. They practically peed themselves with excitement when my dad pulled into your driveway."

T.K. groans and drops onto the bed face-first next to Ellie.

"I'll never be able to leave the house again," she says into her pillow.

"They'll go away sooner or later. Or you could just go and talk to them, you know. It's not like you did something terrible."

T.K. sits up again and eyes the plastic bag on her nightstand.

"You saw the whole thing on TV?"

"Who didn't. It's been on the local news for days now. They kept replaying the footage."

Ellie opens the bag and takes out a half-gallon container of ice cream. She pops off the lid, fishes around in the bag for two spoons, and tosses one onto the bed in front of T.K.

"You should have seen my mom and dad when I showed them the newscast. It was the best. Like they just found out that their daughter's best friend is secretly moonlighting as a rock star."

T.K. wants to keep up the indignation, but she has to admit that Ellie's report pleases her. She was worried how her friends and family would react, but so far everyone is interested and even excited about her new ability. She feels like she just won the multi-state lottery jackpot. Even her parents, put out as they were by the sudden media siege and the disruption of their regular lives, had reacted with wide-eyed amazement when she demonstrated her powers to them. She wonders if everyone's reactions would have been the same if her card turned joker instead, but she knows the anthropological interest and slightly repulsed fascination with which her father reads the occasional features on New York City's Jokertown in National Geographic. No, she concludes almost instantly. Things wouldn't have felt like a lotto win if she had started sprouting tentacles or horns or something.

They make it through half the container before Ellie puts down her spoon and looks at T.K. expectantly.

"Well? I held up my end of the bargain. Now let's see what you can do."

"I thought you saw that on the news already."

"That's different," Ellie says. "Come on, don't back out now. I ran the camera gauntlet for you with that ice cream."

"Fair enough," T.K. demurs, secretly excited about having an excuse to pull the ball bearings out of the pocket of her jeans.

Ellie flinches a little when T.K. opens her hand and lets the ball bearings float above her palm. Then her friend leans in closer to look at the glossy orbs circling each other slowly, making orbits around a common center of gravity like a miniature binary star. T.K. has been practicing plenty since Edinburgh, and she has honed her fine control over the last few days. Turns out it's harder to move the balls in a slow and tightly controlled path than it is to fling them somewhere quickly or with a lot of force. Moving heavy stuff or shooting bricks require effort, but fine control takes concentration, and the more precise she wants to be, the more she has to focus.

Ellie watches as T.K. makes the ball bearings in her hand spin around each other, first slow and then faster, until they're just a chrome blur. Then she slows them down again and sends them zooming around the room. She makes a low pass of her desk with one of the bearings, but misjudges the flight path a little. The ball bearing taps against the edge of her desk lamp's metal arm and knocks it over with a clatter.

"Whoops," T.K. says. Ellie just watches, mouth agape, as T.K. brings the errant ball bearing under control again and lets the orbs resume their formation-flying.

"You're doing that with your mind?"

"Yeah," T.K. replies. "Pretty awesome, huh?"

Ellie holds out a hand, and T.K. steers one of the ball bearings over and drops it gently into the center of Ellie's palm.

"Heavy," Ellie says. She bounces the ball bearing on her palm and turns it with her fingertips. "How fast can you make those things go?"

"Pretty fast," T.K. says, intentionally vague because she doesn't want to give Ellie the idea that she's dangerous now. "I still have to be able to see what I'm moving, though, so not that fast."

She's fibbing a little, of course—while she needs to be able to see the sphere to get its movement started, she can push it so fast and so hard that it instantly goes out of her control, like a bullet fired from a gun. But that's something that she will keep to herself for the moment.

"So what are you going to do now?" Ellie asks. "I mean, you're an ace. Everyone knows about it. You're going to go back to school like nothing happened?"

"Yeah. I mean, what else am I supposed to do? Put on a spandex leotard and go fight crime?"

"You're going to get your diplomaChanged to "diploma".. And then you're off to college. When the whole country knows your face. And what you can do." Ellie looks at her with a skeptical little smirk.

"Yeah," T.K. repeats. "And famous people go to college all the time. Actors and stuff. If they can do it, I should be fine." She scoops out a big spoon of ice cream from the now half-empty tub.

"Besides," she says around a mouthful of Norwich Creamery Moose Tracks. "It's not like they'll mob me for autographs before gym class. I'm nobody."

"Right." Ellie waves her own spoon vaguely in the direction of T.K.'s bedroom window. "And nobody has camera crews from all the major networks laying siege to her house."

Then Ellie uses her spoon like she's holding a ruler and sizing T.K.'s measurements up.

"Speaking of spandex leotards—we need to design a costume for you. And you'll need a catchy ace name. Like Sphero. Or Ballistica."

"Absolutely not," T.K. says and flicks a small spoonful of ice cream at her friend, who retreats with a little squeal. "Not in a million years."

7 -- Ripples in the Pond

With the rest of her life so off the hinges right now, T.K. looks forward to going back to school after the holiday break, to see things return to normal. Mapletree is a private school, with controlled access to the campus and electronic keypads on every exterior door. There are kids at Mapletree whose parents have a lot of money and influence, so reporters aren't welcome there without a good reason, ace students or not.

But the day before school is about to begin again, her parents get a call from the school asking them to see the headmaster at drop-off in the morning, and the dread T.K. feels in her stomach tells her that normal may not be happening for her this school year.

"You're *expelling* her?" T.K's dad says. He's using the same tone and facial expression he adopts whenever someone pitches an unwanted solicitation over the phone. They're sitting in the headmaster's office, and it's a cold and gloomy January morning outside, to match T.K.'s current mood.

"It's not an expulsion," the headmaster replies. He looks a little uncomfortable. "The board got together last week and decided that the school is not equipped to deal with the media fallout. And some parents have voiced concerns about safety. We don't allow students to bring weapons to school. And your daughter's, uh, abilities can certainly be used in an offensive manner. As we've all seen on TV."

T.K. doesn't like that the headmaster is speaking about her in the third person as if she wasn't sitting right in front of him.

"I've had these powers for months now," she says. "I've gone to class every day, just as always. And nobody got hurt."

"Of course we don't think you're out to hurt anyone, Tilly," the headmaster says.

"But you are kicking her out of school," her dad interjects. He still sounds like he's telling someone on the phone that no, he doesn't want or need any supplemental life insurance, thank you very much. Like he's haggling over an annoyance, not discussing whether to yank half of T.K.'s life out from under her feet.

"The board has decided to not renew the enrollment contract for this year. We feel that Tilly would be better off at a school that can take her abilities into account. But it's not an expulsion. We will send her on with a recommendation that reflects her flawless academic and disciplinary record."

It sure feels like an expulsion, T.K. thinks. *Whatever you want to call it.*

Her dad tries to argue because that's what he does. But T.K. can tell that the headmaster is done with them, and that her dad's protests and attempts at negotiation are going to extend this unpleasant business, and she is relieved when her father finally gives up and takes himself and his checkbook out of the room in a huff. T.K. trails him out of the school office and into the parking lot. Her schoolmates are going to classes, alone and in small groups, catching up with each other after the holiday break, and she has never felt so shut out in her life. She skipped right from disabled to too-abled, without getting to spend any time in between at just abled.

"We were thinking about a different school anyway," T.K.'s dad tells her on the way home. "There are lots of great places in the area. Your mom really likes that boarding school in Quebec, the one with the houses and the school ties."

T.K. is sad and angry, and her father's forced cheerfulness doesn't help. She has no interest in thinking about a new school right now, with the sudden and complete separation from Mapletree still hurting like a razor cut. She didn't even have time to say goodbye to anyone. But she doesn't talk to her dad about her feelings. He's well-meaning, but he'd misdiagnose the problem and try to apply the wrong solution. In his world, everything can be fixed by writing a big enough check, and this isn't something money can mend. It's easy to make him think he's helping, though.

"I'll think about it," she tells him. "Do you think you could take me over to the Powerhouse and let me hang out there for an hour or two? I don't want to deal with the cameras at the house right now."

"Oh, sure, honey." From his expression, she can tell he's relieved that she is speaking in a language he understands. "I can drop you off and go see the accountant for a bit. Tax time is coming up, after all."

He gets his wallet out of the inside pocket of his sport coat and fishes out a credit card without taking his eyes off the road.

"Here. Use this one if you want to get a few things. Just don't buy a new car or anything."

"Not likely," she replies and returns his smile. But when she thinks about it, buying a little convertible and pointing it west isn't the worst plan of action she can think of right now, and if she had her license already, she knows she'd be tempted.

Their rich little town has an expensive little mall. It's a converted old powerhouse, renovated at great expense to look like something out of Victorian England, two levels of cute little shops along an indoor concourse lined with hardwood and decorated with lots of wrought iron. This early, most of the shops aren't open yet, but there's a cozy little cafe on the ground floor where T.K. can wait for ten o'clock to roll around.

She's halfway through her vanilla chai latte and picking at her blueberry scone when a magenta-haired girl walks into the cafe. The girl looks around, spots T.K., and heads straight for her table. At this time of day, most of the patrons in the cafe are blue-hairs from the nearby retirement village, so the girl walking T.K's way sticks out even more than she usually would. She stops in front of T.K.'s table, pulls out a chair, and sits down without asking. She's definitely past high school age, but that brightly colored pixie cut and her goth outfit make her look like she doesn't want to be a grown-up just yet. As she sits down and scoots the chair closer to the table, T.K. spots a golden nose stud.

"Hi," the girl says. "You are Lintilla Kendall."

T.K. makes a face.

"It's T.K. Or Tilly, if you don't do the initials thing. I haven't been Lintilla since preschool."

"T.K. I'm Simone. Simone Duplaix." The girl holds out her hand. She's wearing a bunch of bracelets on her wrist, and they jingle softly as T.K. accepts the handshake almost automatically.

"Nice to meet you," Simone says. Her English has a charming French accent that somehow matches her inoffensively cute appearance perfectly.

"Vous êtes Québécois," T.K. guesses, and Simone nods.

"Oui, c'est vrai. I see you took French in school. Very good."

"Wait, I think I've heard of you. You're one of the Canadian aces." T.K. looks around in the cafe to see if anyone's head has turned their way, but the mostly old folks are sipping their coffees and talking to each other without paying any attention to them.

"They call me Snowblind," Simone says, with dramatic effect in her voice on the last word. "I can blind people for a while. Like they are caught in a, how do you say, nor'easter? It is a good talent, but it is not quite as good as yours, I think. I watched the news footage. What you did, it was very impressive."

T.K. squirms a little in her seat, but she doesn't try to protest the compliment. It's the first time someone has said something unequivocally positive about her new talent. In truth, it pleases her a great deal, even if the memories of that day still twist her stomach.

"How did you know where to find me?" she asks.

"Oh, the place where I work, we have ways of tracking people. And you have been in the news lately quite a bit, no? It was not hard to find you."

Simone glances around the room poignantly, leans across the table, and lowers her voice.

"You need to keep that in mind, after what you did in Europe,

T.K. Now that everyone knows what you can do. You don't know yet what things are like for people like us in the world. There are jokers who already resent you for what you did. And there are many people who will want what you have."

T.K. looks at the café patrons again. The people sitting at their tables and drinking their coffees are still the same ones that were here before Simone walked in, but now T.K. feels anxious and a little afraid. The ball bearings in her pocket are a comforting weight, but she's still only a fifteen-year-old girl with a physical handicap and no talent or stomach for fighting. Aces and jokers, government agencies and terrorism. When did her life turn into a bad international mystery thriller?

"I got kicked out of school today," she says glumly. "They think I am dangerous."

"Well, of course you are," Simone says.

"But I'm not," T.K. protests. "I'm still the same person. I don't want to hurt anyone. I just want to go back to the way things were."

Simone looks at her with unconcealed pity and shakes her head with a little sigh.

"Oh, cherie. Your old life? That is over. From now on, when you meet new people and they know what you are, they will either want something from you, or they will be afraid of you."

"Really? And which kind are you?"

It comes out a little snippier than T.K. had intended, but Simone just smiles.

"Well, I am not afraid of you," she says.

"So what do you want from me?"

Simone reaches into the pocket of the leather jacket she's wearing and takes out a business card, which she puts facedown on the table right next to the plate that has the rest of T.K.'s blueberry scone on it.

"I want you to think about your future. About what you will do with this talent of yours. You will find that it opens a lot of doors for you. But you will have to decide which of those doors you want to step through."

T.K. picks up the business card and flips it over to read it.

"I work for the Committee," Simone says. "The Committee on Extraordinary Interventions. You may have heard of it."

"You work for the government?"

"Not for a government. We work for the United Nations, for all governments. People like you and me. Aces and joker-aces, keeping the peace. Helping out where we can with our talents."

"I'm fifteen," T.K. says. "I can't work for the United Nations yet. My parents won't even let me get a summer job at the gelato place."

"But you will be eighteen before too long, no?"

Simone nods at the business card T.K. is still holding.

"Maybe in a few years, if you decide you want to use your talent for a good cause, we can show you the sort of things we do. Until then, we just want you to know that we are around. So call me or send me a message if you need help. Or if you just want to talk. You know, with someone who knows what it's like."

"I'll think about it," T.K. says. She would laugh at the ludicrousness of the situation if she wasn't so overwhelmed by it all. If she hadn't gotten kicked out of school this morning, she'd be back in P.E. right now, and she's reasonably sure that Brooke and Alison wouldn't throw any balls within fifty feet of her ever again. But instead of doing crunches while thinking about lunch hour and afternoon science lab, she has the United Nations and international intrigue swirling around in her head, and that's not a leap her brain is willing to make right now. Her face must show some of the stress she's feeling, because Simone reaches across the table and squeezes her hand lightly.

"When you did what you did in Europe, it was like you threw a rock into a pond, T.K. It started making ripples. You do nothing, the water will smooth out again, eventually. But you know what you can also do?"

"What's that?"

"Start throwing in bigger rocks," Simone says. "Turn the ripples into waves."

When T.K. leaves the cafe half an hour later, she's in a better mood. Getting expelled from school still hurts because it makes her feel like she's done something wrong, that she's being punished. But when she thinks about her future now, it's no longer indistinct and scary.

On the drive home with her dad, she imagines herself like Simone: dyed hair, nose stud, running around in some exciting foreign city like Tokyo or London, using her new ace powers in the service of the Committee. *Brooke and Alison would absolutely lose their shit,* she thinks.

That evening, T.K. sits down with her parents in the living room to talk about school stuff. The way they are accommodating her right now, they must think she's devastated about getting kicked out of Mapletree. T.K. chooses to reaffirm their parental instincts by telling them how unfair she thinks the whole thing is, which is true. She doesn't tell them about her meeting with Simone today, or about the fact that unlike them, she was never fully in love with that school anyway. But when your parents have dropped fifty grand a year in tuition for two years running, that kind of information would probably be unwelcome, and she feels like she should keep it on a need-to-know basis for now.

While they are looking through high-gloss brochures for half a dozen other private high schools, her dad is sort of half-watching the hockey game that's playing on low volume on the living room TV. T.K. has her back to the screen, so she doesn't see what's going on in the game. She's reading through the list of offered sports at one of the interchangeable prep schools her parents have picked out—most of which require two functioning arms, naturally—when her dad lets out a suppressed cheer and pumps his fist.

"Really, honey? Now?" T.K.'s mom scolds him. "We're looking at schools now, dear. Can't you turn that off?"

T.K. turns to see what spiked her dad's excitement. They're showing the replay of the goal now. One of the players stops the puck with his stick and then does a sort of vertical roundhouse swing with all his force. Even at the low volume of the TV speakers, the puck shot sounds like a thunderclap, and she can barely follow its course as it rockets into the goal and makes the net twitch violently with the impact. T.K. sits up straight and follows the next replay closely with excited amusement. It looks exactly the way it did when she launched a ball bearing or a cue ball in that old factory down by the river near Mapletree: the puck, sitting at rest, then shooting off so fast that it's just a blur in the air.

"What do they call that swing?" she asks her father.

"Huh? What do you mean, sweetie?"

"When they swing the stick like that, with force. You know, smack." She mimics the motion with her good arm.

"Oh, that. It's called a slap shot."

"Slap shot," she repeats with a little smile.

"Yeah. It's the hardest shot to pull off in hockey. Powerful, but not very accurate. Unless you have a lot of control." Her dad seems pleased that she's drawing on his knowledge of his favorite sport.

She returns her attention to the brochure in front of her, but her attention isn't with the nationally renowned equestrian program at St. Whatsit Academy, which she wouldn't be able to participate in anyway because she can't hold the reins of a horse with both hands. Instead, her mind is on the events of the day—the hurt and shame she felt this morning when she got kicked out of school, and then the weird excitement when she met Simone and got treated like an equal by a genuine grown-up, internationally famous ace. And right then and there she knows that her future probably won't be determined by whatever new rich-kid high school her mom and dad pick for her tonight.

Later, when she's in bed and scrolling through the messages on her phone half-asleep, she shoots off a text to Ellie.

Forget Sphero or Ballistica. How about Slapshot?

The reply comes only a minute later.

OMG THAT IS PERFECT. It's so freaking regional.

Slapshot it is, then, T.K. sends back. Then she puts the phone on her nightstand and pulls up her covers.

I'm still not doing a costume, though, she thinks before the day catches up with her and she falls asleep.

Printed in Great Britain
by Amazon

26712182R00198